P9-EAO-029

CHASING THE NIGHT

Chasing the Night

Iris Johansen

An Eve Duncan Forensics Thriller.

Thorndike Press, a part of Gale, Cengage Learning.

Thorndike Press® Large Print Basic.
The text of this Large Print edition is unabridged.
Other aspects of the book may vary from the original edition.
Set in 16 pt. Plantin.

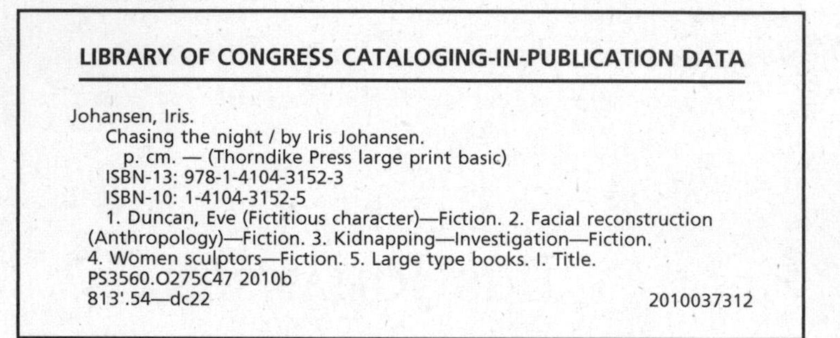
LIBRARY OF CONGRESS CATALOGING-IN-PUBLICATION DATA

Johansen, Iris.
Chasing the night / by Iris Johansen.
p. cm. — (Thorndike Press large print basic)
ISBN-13: 978-1-4104-3152-3
ISBN-10: 1-4104-3152-5
1. Duncan, Eve (Fictitious character)—Fiction. 2. Facial reconstruction (Anthropology)—Fiction. 3. Kidnapping—Investigation—Fiction. 4. Women sculptors—Fiction. 5. Large type books. I. Title.
PS3560.O275C47 2010b
813'.54—dc22 2010037312

BRITISH LIBRARY CATALOGUING-IN-PUBLICATION DATA AVAILABLE
Published in the U.S. in 2010 by arrangement with St. Martin's Press, LLC.
Published in the U.K. in 2011 by arrangement with the author.
U.K. Hardcover: 978 1 408 49359 5 (Chivers Large Print)
U.K. Softcover: 978 1 408 49360 1 (Camden Large Print)

Printed in the United States of America
1 2 3 4 5 6 7 14 13 12 11 10

For my wonderful Tamara,
who juggles golden balls
and carries heavy burdens
with equal grace and style

CHAPTER 1

Broken Bones.

Eve Duncan shuddered as she looked down at the pitiful remains of the little girl's skull that she'd carefully spread on the special tarp on her desk.

The child's skull was shattered, and the cheekbones and nasal and orbital bones were only unidentifiable splinters. The Detroit Police Department thought that the child had been beaten to death with a hammer. How the hell was she going to put that little girl's face together again?

"You're angry."

Eve glanced at Joe Quinn sitting on the couch across the room. "You're damn right I am." She reached out and gently touched one of the little girl's remaining facial bones still left intact. "Whoever killed this child had to be insane. Who would think it necessary to do this . . . this monstrosity? She couldn't have been more than eight years old."

"And after hundreds of these reconstructions, it still makes you furious." His lips tightened. "Me, too. You'd think we'd get used to it. But that never happens, does it?"

Yes, Joe might be a tough, experienced police detective, but he could be as emotional as Eve when the victims were helpless children. "Sometimes I can block it. But this savagery . . . A hammer, Joe. He used a hammer . . ."

"Son of a bitch." Joe got up and moved across the room to stand behind her. "Have you given her a name yet?"

Eve always gave her reconstructions names while she worked on them. It made her feel a connection while she strove desperately to give a name and identity to those poor, murdered children who had been thrown away. She shook her head. "Not yet. I just got the skull by FedEx this afternoon. Detroit forensics warned me to expect this, but it still came as a shock."

"It looks like a lost cause." Joe was gazing down at the splintered bones. "It's going to be a nightmare putting her back together. How do you know you've got all the pieces?"

"I don't. But there's a good chance. Forensics thinks that she was already completely wrapped in the yellow plastic raincoat in which he buried her when her murderer started this carnage. Maybe he just wanted to make sure that she was dead or that no one would ever recognize her."

"This one is going to tear you up." Joe reached out and began to massage her neck. "You're already tense, and you haven't even started."

"I've started." She closed her eyes as his thumbs dug gently into exactly the right spot on the center of her neck. After all of these years of living together, he knew every muscle, every pleasure point of her body. He was right, she was tense. She would take this brief moment before she began to work. Joe's touch, Joe's support. It was a soothing song that helped to drown out the ugliness of the world. Once she actually began the reconstruction, there would be only her and this child, who had lost her life over ten years ago. They would be bound together in darkness until Eve could finish working and shine a light that would bring the little girl home. And she would bring her home. She'd give her back her face, then let the media publish a photo and surely someone would recognize her. "I started the moment I saw what that bastard had done to her."

"You haven't given her a name yet," Joe said. "Tell Detroit to give her to Josephson to do the reconstruction. You may be the best, but you're not the only forensic sculptor in the country. You've got a backlog of requests that will keep you slaving for the next six months. You don't need this kind of pressure."

"She didn't need for some creep to do this to her." She opened her eyes and gazed down at the broken skull. "She's my job, Joe." She thought for a moment. "And her name is Cindy." She straightened in her chair. "Now let me get to work."

"Dammit." He stepped back, and his hands dropped away from her. "I knew it was a long shot, but I thought I'd give it a try. You've been working yourself to exhaustion for the last few months." He wheeled and went back to the couch. "Go ahead. Break your heart trying to put that kid back together again. Why should I care?"

"I don't know, Joe." She smiled. "But I thank God you do." She looked down at the bone splinters that might belong to the nasal cavity . . . or might not. "And Cindy will forgive you for trying to push her off on Josephson."

"I'm relieved," he said dryly. "But I'll take my chances on being in her bad graces. After all, she's been dead ten years. At the moment, you're the only one I care about. I don't want —"

Eve's cell phone rang.

She glanced at the ID.

She tensed.

"Who is it?" Joe asked.

"Venable."

He frowned. "Not good."

That was Eve's reaction. They had dealt with Venable and the CIA on several occasions, and it usually ended with her being pulled away from her work and into deep trouble. Not this time.

She punched the button on her cell. "What do you want, Venable?"

"Why are you on the defensive?" Venable asked. "Maybe I only want to check in and see if you're okay. You were in a hospital in Damascus recovering from a gunshot wound the last time I saw you."

"That was six months ago, and I'm sure that you know I'm fully recovered. You make it your business to know everything."

"I'm not the NSA. I'm only interested in specific subjects . . . and people. I feel a certain attachment for you and Joe."

"What do you want, Venable?"

He hesitated. "A favor."

"What kind of favor?"

"Nothing that's dangerous or out of your realm of expertise. I'd like you to do a computer age progression."

"No."

"It wouldn't take you that long, and I'd appreciate it."

"I'm swamped, and even if I weren't, you know I won't work for the CIA. Get one of your own experts to do the job. You have qualified people. Some of them are far more experienced than I am with computer age progression. I don't even know why you're bothering to ask me."

"Because I *have* to ask you, dammit," he said sourly. "It has to be you."

"Why?"

"Because like everything else in my life, it's a question of bargaining and balancing. I need you to do this, Eve."

"Then you're going to be disappointed. I just started a new reconstruction, and I won't drop it for one of your twisted little jobs. I'm not going to help you identify someone so that you can track him down. I'm never sure whether the prey you're stalking is a saint or a slimeball. Or if he's a saint, that you're not using him in ways that I'd never go along with. You're capable of manipulating anyone to shape a deal."

"Yes, I am," he said wearily. "And some of those deals keep you and your friends from being blown to kingdom come by the bad guys. Someone has to stand guard, and I do a damn good job of it. Dirty sometimes, but effective."

She supposed he did, but she didn't want to be involved in that morass even on a purely scientific level. "Let your own agents do it, Venable."

"What can I offer you to do the job?"

"Nothing that I can't refuse," she said softly but emphatically. "Take no for an answer. It's all you're going to get from me."

"I'll try, but I may have to come back. You're a prime bargaining chip in this one, Eve."

"Listen, you're beginning to annoy me. I'm not a chip, and I'm not a chess piece for you to manipulate."

"We can all be manipulated. It depends on the determination factor." He paused. "You'd be safer if I'm the one who does it. I'm trying to avoid throwing you to the wolf."

"Are you threatening me?"

She put up her hand as she saw Joe straighten at her words.

"I wouldn't be that stupid. I'm just trying to keep you from making a mistake. I've always liked you."

He probably believed he was telling the truth, but it wouldn't keep him from using her. She was tired of arguing with him. "I'm hanging up now, Venable."

"Change your mind, Eve."

She pressed the disconnect button.

"The bastard threatened you?" Joe was frowning, his tone grim. "I believe I need to pay a visit to Venable."

"He said it wasn't a threat. More like a warning."

"That's a fine line where Venable is concerned. I take it he wanted you to do a reconstruction?"

"No, that would make more sense." Her brow knitted. "I won't deny I'm one of the best forensic sculptors around." After her own little girl, Bonnie, had been kidnapped and murdered all those years ago, she had gone back to school and made sure that she had the skill to help bring final resolution and solace to other parents. Out of that nightmare of torment, when she had come close to madness and death, had emerged at least one decent thing from the agony. She could re-create the faces of those lost, murdered children. But not her little Bonnie. Search as she would, she had not found her child. What good was all her fine skill if she couldn't use it to bring her daughter home to rest, she thought bitterly. Her Bonnie was still lost, and so was her killer.

"Eve?"

She jerked her attention back to the subject at hand. "But Venable doesn't want me to sculpt a reconstruction, he wants a computer age progression. I'm good at that, but I don't do enough to be called an expert. He could find someone faster and possibly more accurate just by making a few phone calls. I know the CIA has good technicians."

"But maybe he doesn't want to go through the agency," Joe said slowly. "He's paranoid about leaks, and he could trust you. Venable doesn't trust many people."

"Too bad. I'm not volunteering."

"You'd be crazy if you did." His lips tightened. "You're better off working yourself to the bone than playing in his ballpark. Who's the subject of this age progression?"

"I didn't ask. Maybe some war criminal they're trying to trace? For all I know, it could be Bin Laden. I don't want to know. It's not my job." She gazed down at the bones in front of her. "This is my job."

"Then do it." He flipped open his computer. "Let Venable pull his own chestnuts out of the fire."

At least the call from Venable had made Joe more reconciled to her accepting the reconstruction on Cindy, Eve thought. He was willing to admit that the long, painstaking hours she'd have to spend on piecing the little girl back together was the lesser of two evils.

You'd be safer if I'm the one who does it. I'm trying to avoid throwing you to the wolf.

Wolf. Singular. Not wolves.

Who was the wolf Venable was trying to save her from?

And she was still thinking about Venable's words, she realized impatiently. Forget him. Forget everything but the little girl who must become something more than this pitiful heap of bones. She had been someone's child. Long ago, someone had heard her prayers and tucked her into bed for the night. She deserved to go home to her parents and have them tuck her into her resting place one last time.

She reached out and gently touched the cranial bone. It will take a little while, but we'll get there, Cindy. We'll bring you home and find the bastard who did this to you.

She felt a wave of sickness wash over her. No matter how many times that she was brought face-to-face with this savagery, she never became calloused. But the sight of these shattered bones was particularly painful.

She couldn't imagine the barbaric mind-sct that would allow someone to smash the bones of another human being. . . .

Salmeta, Colombia

She'd have to break the sentry's neck.

Catherine Ling moved silently down the path of the rain forest.

She couldn't risk using even a knife. He mustn't cry out.

No sound. Every movement had to have purpose and deadly intent.

The phone in her pocket vibrated.

Ignore it.

The other outer sentries had to be eliminated to clear the way back to the helicopter.

She was a yard from the sentry. Now she could see that he was bearded and close to middle age. Good. She hated to kill those fresh-faced kids even though they could sometimes be more lethal. Anyone who worked for Munoz was dirty, but she always had to work to get past that element of youth. Stupid. She should know better. As a teenager, she had made sure that no one performed with more deadly precision than she did.

He was tensing. He was sensing danger.

Move fast.

He was a good six inches taller. Bring him down to her level. Her booted foot sliced between his legs and hit the side of his right kneecap. He lost his balance. Before he could regain it, her arm encircled his neck.

She jerked back and twisted. His neck snapped.

He went limp.

Dead.

She let him fall to the ground, then dragged him deep into the shrubs. She'd already disposed of the other sentry guarding the path along the brook. Her way should be clear the three miles to Munoz's encampment.

Maybe. She had learned there was nothing certain where Munoz was concerned. She had been assigned to this hellhole for the last three years and made a study of the drug dealer. He was sadistic, volatile, and unpredictable. The stories that circulated about his brutality were sickening. His vicious profile was the major contributor to the storm of anxiety surrounding his kidnapping of coffee executive Ned Winters and his fourteen-year-old daughter Kelly. He was holding them hostage until the Colombian government released his brother Manuel from prison and every day a new and bloody threat was issued.

Her phone was vibrating again.

She glanced at the ID. Venable.

She punched the button, and whispered, "I've nothing to report. I'm on my way, but I won't be at the Munoz camp for another fifteen minutes."

"Call it off. Now that you've located him, we'll send in the Special Forces to get Winters and his daughter out."

"And get them killed. They don't have my contacts and they don't know this terrain and, by the time they do, it may be too late. Munoz has promised he'll kill Winters and his daughter unless his brother's released. Those idiots in the Colombian government are stalling. I think they want Winters killed so they can get U.S. help to stage a full-scale attack on Munoz and the rebels."

"I don't give a damn what you think. Back off."

"No, we made a deal. You agreed to give me what I wanted if I managed to locate and free the Winterses. I can do this. I've been watching the Munoz camp since yesterday, and I know exactly how I can pull it off."

"It's too dangerous."

She stiffened. She caught a note in his voice that made her uneasy. "You didn't give a damn about that when I called you and told you that I'd find a way of getting Winters and his daughter away from Munoz. All you cared about was that it was going to get the heat off the director."

"No, that's not all I cared about. Two American citizens are at risk. That matters to me."

"Then you back off. Let me get them out."

"Alone?"

"No, Ron Timbers is going to be on watch outside the camp. There's only one guard at the tent where they're keeping the hostages. I can slice through the back of the tent and get them out that way. Ron will warn me if there's any move from the guard. Bill Neely is bringing in the helicopter at a glade four miles from the camp. Why are you questioning me? I'm good. You know I can do this."

"I know you have a decent chance." He paused. "But I thought I should tell you that I may not be able to give you everything you want in exchange. I'll give you access to the Rakovac file. I can't promise you Eve Duncan. She turned me down."

Catherine muttered a curse. "Then go back and find a way to make her do it. I have to have her."

"I can get you someone better. Technically, this isn't Eve Duncan's area of expertise."

"I want Eve Duncan. Persuade her."

"You can have the file, but I can't promise

Duncan. She walks her own path. Like you, Catherine."

"Bullshit. I stopped walking my own path when you pulled me into working for the Company when I was seventeen. Since then, I've worked every dirty assignment you chose to toss me."

"True. But how could I resist? You were a natural. Clever, lethal, and with a survival instinct that made you almost unstoppable. I considered it a recruiting masterpiece. After twelve years, I still do, Catherine."

"I'm not complaining. I knew what I was getting into. I never expected anything else." She'd grown up on the streets of Hong Kong and barely managed to exist without starving for her first six years. All her life she'd had to fight for what she wanted, and Venable was no worse than other men who had tried to use her. Sometimes, she even liked him. He was totally dedicated to his work with the CIA and would let nothing stand in his way. It was surprising that she'd managed to work a deal with him about releasing that top secret restricted file. If the director hadn't been getting so much heat from the media about the Winters kidnapping, she might not have fared so well. But the file wasn't enough. She had to have more. "Eve Duncan. You know where the bodies are buried on every continent in the world. Bribe her, blackmail her, make her an offer she can't refuse. I don't care how you do it. Just get her for me."

"I'm not promising you anything. I don't have to. You're obviously going to go in after Winters anyway."

He was right. Even if she could only get the file, she would risk anything to have it handed over. "But if you don't get Eve Duncan for me, I'll get her myself. Do you want me to go after her?"

Silence. "No. I know you too well. You'd cause an incident that would cause me big trouble." He paused. "I'll do the best I can, but I don't know where Eve Duncan's bodies are buried. She's clean, Catherine. If you've researched her as well as I think you have, then you know I can't blackmail her."

"That's what I have to find out. Where her bodies are buried. Try. Do everything you can." She started down the path toward the Munoz camp. "And I'll do everything I can. I can't talk any longer. I have to get moving. Has Munoz been in touch with anyone lately?"

"No, he's not answered any of our messages." He was silent a moment. "And I should tell you that late last night the Colombian government refused to release

Munoz's brother until the Winterses are free. They say they think he's bluffing."

"He's not bluffing. If they don't back down, Munoz will cut those hostages' throats."

"I agree. And that may mean whether I get you Eve Duncan or not may be a moot point. You may have nothing with which to bargain." He hung up.

Catherine shoved her phone into the pocket of her jacket. Venable was right. Thanks to those politicians in Bogotá playing their little games, she'd be lucky to whisk Winters and his daughter away before Munoz decided to butcher them.

She wasn't going to let that happen.

There was something wrong. Catherine's gaze wandered over Munoz's encampment. It was after three in the morning, and she hadn't expected activity, but there was no — tension.

The man guarding the hostage tent was a good ten feet from the entrance flap, and he was the only one of Munoz's men who appeared to be awake.

It made her uneasy.

She hesitated. It could be nothing.

She had passed Ron Timbers on the edge of the forest and knew that he'd had the camp under surveillance for most of the evening. He would have called her if there was a problem.

If he knew about the problem.

At any rate, she couldn't stop now unless she had good reason.

She circled around in the trees until she was behind the hostage tent.

Catherine slit the canvas of the tent. Carefully. Silently. It was a small tent and the guard at the front entrance was only a scant ten feet from where she was working. But that lack of tension she'd sensed in the camp might be a positive. The guard had appeared both sleepy and bored.

Let him stay that way, she prayed, as she lifted the torn flap. And let Winters and his daughter realize that there was no threat from someone trying to break *into* the tent. But then hostages weren't guaranteed to be thinking straight after two weeks of terror and incarceration. She started wriggling into the tent.

Darkness.

She couldn't make out anything for the first moment.

She froze.

Good Lord, the *stench.*

She was too late. She knew that smell.

Rotting corpse.

They were dead, and the tropic heat had already begun the decomposing process.

She had to be sure.

Her eyes had grown accustomed to the dark now, but she didn't need to see to find her way to the dead. The overpowering smell led her unerringly across the tent.

A man, hands tied, shot execution style in the center of his forehead. Catherine Ling swore beneath her breath as she sat back on her heels beside the body. She had known that it was a strong possibility Munoz would keep his word and kill Ned Winters when the Colombian government refused to give up Munoz's brother. Stupid bastards. What difference did it make if they had to go back and catch one more scumbag drug dealer? No, they'd rather risk an international incident and the death of an innocent American businessman.

"He's dead. You should have come sooner."

Catherine whirled to the corner of the tent at the whisper. Even in the half darkness she could see the glint of fair hair of the girl huddled against the fabric of the tent. Kelly Winters, fourteen years old, taken in Caracas two weeks ago at the same time as her father. Catherine felt a rush of relief. At least she had a chance of getting the girl out.

"Shh." She crawled toward the girl. "I'm Catherine Ling. I work with the CIA. Don't talk. They'll hear you."

Kelly gazed numbly at her. "You should have come sooner."

"I'm here now." She nodded at the slit in the tent. "Come with me."

The girl didn't move.

Catherine glanced at the flap. The guard was a good ten feet on the other side of that thin canvas, but she couldn't afford to argue and have him hear her. Choose her words and hope that they strike a chord. "Stay and we'll die and they'll win. They killed your father. Do you want them to win?"

The girl looked at her for a moment. Then she shook her head and began to crawl toward the slit.

Relief flooded through Catherine. She quickly crawled after her. "Now listen," she whispered, as they emerged from the tent. "Run into the forest, try to be as quiet as you can. I have a friend, Ron Timbers, who will keep an eye on the camp for the next few minutes and make sure that your escape isn't noticed. Then he'll take off and meet us at the helicopter. When you come to a stream, you stop and wait for me, and I'll take you the rest of the way. The helicopter will be landing about three miles from the stream, and we'll board it and fly away from here. You'll be safe."

Kelly shook her head. "No, I won't," she said dully. "No one is safe."

How could Catherine argue when she knew that was true? "As safe as you can be. Wait at the stream no more than about five minutes, then take off running north. Don't wait for me."

Kelly glanced back over her shoulder, her blue eyes wide. "You think Munoz may catch you."

"No, but if he does, you don't want him to get his hands on you again. Then he'd win, wouldn't he? If you're smart, he won't be able to catch you." She put her finger on her lips. "No more talk. Run!"

Kelly didn't hesitate. She was already on her feet and streaking into the shrubbery.

Good.

Now to make sure any pursuit was disrupted and thrown off track when they heard the sound of the helicopter.

And the best way to do that would be to remove Munoz himself from the mix.

No guards at his tent. From the reports she'd read, Munoz was too macho-arrogant to think he would need help in any situation.

Let's see if you do, Munoz.
She started crawling toward his tent.

Chapter 2

Munoz went limp against Catherine's body as her dagger entered his heart.

She pushed at him and struggled to free herself from his bulk.

It had been close. He had been almost as good as he thought he was. Her side was bleeding, but she had no time to deal with it now.

Get out of Munoz's tent. Their struggle had been brief and almost silent, but she couldn't be sure that someone didn't hear.

Move!

The stream was just ahead.

She saw the glint of moonlight on Kelly's fair hair.

"Run!" Catherine broke through the shrubbery that bordered the stream and grabbed the girl's hand. "We don't have much time before the helicopter gets here."

"I thought you weren't coming."

For a moment back in Munoz's tent she had thought the same thing. Munoz had been awake and lethal. "I had something I had to do." Did she hear the sound of rotors to the north? "Don't talk. Run!"

Running.

Pushing through the bushes.

The earth soft beneath their feet.

Two miles to go.

It *was* the helicopter. Catherine could hear it plainly now.

And if she could hear it, Munoz's men would be hearing it.

Kelly glanced up at her in panic. "Are they coming after us?"

"Not yet." But it wouldn't be long. Munoz was dead, but his men wouldn't chance there being anyone left alive to bear witness. "We're almost there."

But five minutes later Catherine heard crashing in the bushes behind them. How close?

The glade was just ahead. She could see the blue lights of the helicopter as it started to land.

But Kelly was faltering, slowing.

"No!"

Catherine grabbed her hand and half pulled her, streaking toward the helicopter. "Only a few yards more."

Ron Timbers stepped out of the shadows and was opening the door of the Apache helicopter for her. "You cut it close, Catherine. Her father?"

"Dead." She pushed Kelly into the copter and climbed in after her. "Tell that pilot, Neely, to get out of here. They're only a step behind us."

Timbers glanced at her shirt as he jumped in after her and headed for the cockpit. "There's blood all over you. The kid?"

"No. Kelly is fine. Tell that pilot to move!"

He was already moving. Seconds later they were lifting off.

But not soon enough.

A bullet buried itself in the fuselage of the copter.

Another shattered the windshield.

Kelly froze. "Are we going to die now?"

"No." Catherine's arms closed fiercely around her. She hoped she was telling the truth. They'd be okay if they didn't get the gas tank. "I've got you. We're out of here."

Another bullet struck a rotor with a loud ping.

"Just a minute more, and we'll be out of range," Timbers called back to them.

If they made it through that minute.

"Your heart's beating so hard," Kelly whispered. "Are you scared?"

"Yes, it's stupid not to be scared if someone's trying to hurt you. You just have to hold on and either wait or fight back." She smiled down at her. "But you have to realize that they can't really hurt you. Maybe your body, but not what you are inside. That's what's important. None of the rest matters."

"All clear," Timbers called back to them.

Catherine gave a sigh of relief. "But it seems we don't have to worry about anything right now. We're on our way. In a few minutes, I'll call Agent Venable and tell him to meet us at the airport in Bogotá. He'll be very relieved. Everyone has been worried about you."

Kelly was silent a moment. "But Daddy is dead."

It was natural that after the first explosion of danger was over, the girl's hideous memories would surface. Distract her. Keep her busy. "I need your help." She sat up and reached for the first-aid kit fastened to the wall. "I'm hurt and bleeding a little. Will you bandage it for me?"

"I'm not sure I know how." Kelly's eyes widened as she watched Catherine take off her black shirt and saw the deep cut in her side. Her lips tightened. "But I'll try. Tell me what to do."

"First the antiseptic. Take a pad and clean the wound. The bleeding seems to have almost stopped." But it had bled enough to make her feel woozy, she realized. "I'm a little tired. Don't be afraid if I fall asleep."

"You mean pass out," she said bluntly.

"I guess that is what I mean." She leaned back against the wall. "But if I do pass out, it won't be for long, and the pilot knows how to take you home to your mother."

"My mother doesn't want me." Kelly was dabbing at the wound. "That's why I live — lived with my daddy."

Great. After a nightmare like this, the kid didn't even have someone to hold on to until she healed. If she healed. No, Catherine wouldn't accept that possibility. Kelly would heal. She was strong, or she wouldn't have been able to survive what had happened to her. Just that time in that tent with the remains of her father should have made her catatonic. "Your mother may want you more than you think. Sometimes when parents quarrel, things are said that aren't really true."

"No," she whispered. "Daddy said she feels uncomfortable around me." She put the pad aside and sat back on her heels. "It's okay. Daddy said it wasn't my fault. I'm just not like her. She thinks I'm weird. I think your cut is clean. What else should I do?"

"Just put a couple gauze pads and tape across the wound. That will be fine until I get to a doctor." She paused. "You did that very well, Kelly. Thank you."

"I studied first aid at camp last year. Most of the other stuff was pretty dumb, but that was kind of neat. But this was different. Real blood." She took the gauze from the package. "You could have done this yourself. You thought it would help me to do it."

Smart girl. It was amazing that she had been able to see through Catherine's subterfuge considering the shock she was suffering. And there was no doubt that she was hurting. The girl's hands were shaking, and her blue eyes were wide and haunted. Everything about her seemed terribly fragile and childlike. She was delicately boned and appeared younger than her fourteen years. "Yes, I could have done it. But it was easier for me to have you do it. And if it helped you, too, that was a plus." Her lips twisted. "And there's not much that can be considered a plus in what happened tonight."

"Or yesterday." Kelly turned away and quickly snapped the first-aid kit shut. Her voice was muffled. "It was because of me he died, you know. He tried to keep Munoz from hurting me. Munoz came into the tent angry and shouting and he was saying that he'd been screwed and he was going to get his own back. He tore my clothes and —" Her voice broke.

"Hush." Catherine's arms closed around her. "You don't have to describe it. Just tell me one thing. He hurt you?"

"He raped me," Kelly said baldly. "Why don't you say it? Do you think I'm a kid? He kept telling Daddy he'd do it if they didn't let his brother go."

She *was* a kid, Catherine thought, but she'd been jerked out of any semblance of childhood. Smother the anger. It wasn't going to help Kelly. But damn she was glad she'd taken Munoz out. She wished she had him here so that she could do it again. "No, I don't think you're a kid."

"Daddy shouldn't have fought him." Her voice was almost inaudible against Catherine's shoulder. "It didn't matter if he —"

"It matters. I know what you're saying, and I would probably think the same as you. He didn't take anything from you that was worth losing your father." Catherine's arms tightened around her. "Don't talk about it now. You'll have to do that later, but not now, when the wound is raw."

"Daddy shouldn't have tried to stop him." Her hands were clutching Catherine. "It didn't do any good, and maybe Munoz wouldn't have killed him. He hurt me, but it wasn't worth that."

"No, it wasn't worth that." Her hand brushed Kelly's hair back from her face. "But your father wouldn't have understood. Rape is something that most people have a problem with."

"But not you?"

"No, it happened to me, too." She was silent a moment. "Only I was a little younger than you, and I didn't have a father to try to protect me. I guess that could have been a good thing. I was the only one hurt." She added softly, "Later, when you get past the sorrow, you'll be angry, and you'll feel dirty. That will go away, too. But what you must never feel is shame. What happened to you is no more reason for shame than this wound of mine you just bandaged. We may have scars, but we'll heal. It will only make us stronger."

"I don't feel . . . strong."

"You will. Just don't let anyone pity you because of what Munoz did to you. They won't understand that you don't need it, and you might begin to think that they're right." Unconventional advice to a wounded child, but it was all she could offer. It came from the depths of her heart and personal experience. "You can't expect them to understand since they didn't go through it."

"But *you* understand." Kelly nestled closer. "If you let me stay with you, I wouldn't need anyone else . . ."

Need? Dependence. Even as her arm tightened protectively around the girl, she felt a rush of dismay. Lord, she couldn't afford to be responsible for anyone. Not now. That wasn't what she had bargained for when she had taken on this job. The minute she dropped Kelly off in Bogotá, she had to pressure Venable and get the Rakovac file.

"You don't want me either," Kelly said in a low voice. "Why should you? I'll just get in your way."

That was exactly what Catherine feared. "You might," she said with blunt honesty. "And I might get in yours. You can't judge me from the little time we've had together. You have a mother, you probably have other relations. You'd be better off with them."

"I understand," Kelly said dully. "Whatever you say."

Dammit. "We'll have to see what happens. As soon as we land in Bogotá, I'll turn you over to Agent Venable. He's my superior, and he'll have to make a decision about what's best for you."

"You're best for me." Kelly pushed her

away and sat up. "Even if you don't want me. I wouldn't have to pretend that I —" She leaned back against the wall of the helicopter and closed her eyes. "I'd try not to get in your way."

"Kelly, I have something to do." She paused. "I have something I *have* to do."

"I could help you."

Catherine shook her head. "No."

"I could, you know," she said. "You said I was strong. I have to be strong, or I'll break apart. I won't let Munoz do that to me. I'll have to think about it . . ."

Bogotá, Colombia

"You have my phone number." Catherine leaned into the limousine where Kelly was sitting with the social worker. "I told you what to expect at the hospital. Just do what they tell you, and the exam will be over soon. Remember that everything bad eventually passes. Go blank, and it's over."

Kelly nodded without speaking.

"Call me if you need someone to talk to."

"I will." Kelly leaned back in the seat and gave her a pale smile. "And I'll do what you said. I'll let them pity me about losing Daddy, but never about Munoz."

"Good." She stepped back and slammed the door.

"Poor kid." Venable watched the limousine with the social worker and Kelly Winters drive slowly from the private airport. "She looks shell-shocked."

"Considering what she's gone through, I think she looks damn good," Catherine said. "She's got guts. She'll be okay if they let her heal and come to terms with what happened." Kelly had turned and was looking back at her. Catherine nodded and waved her hand. The girl didn't smile, didn't wave. "Look, she doesn't get along with her mother. Make sure those social worker Goody Two-shoeses don't toss her back to her without supervision."

"I can see why her mother might have difficulty. Lisa Winters is a Denver socialite who likes everything smooth and commonplace. Kelly is too brilliant to be commonplace and too inquisitive not to be disturbing."

"You seem very familiar with Kelly."

"You might say I had an occasion to study her once. I found her exceedingly . . . promising."

"Promising? Interesting word. I believe you once found me promising. But she's just a kid, Venable. And, I don't give a damn if her mother doesn't like having a smart daughter. She should step up to the plate.

Kelly needs help."

"You obviously gave it to her." Venable smiled faintly. "And I'll follow through."

"You'd better. Or I'll come looking for you." She turned to face him. "Payoff time. You owe me, Venable."

"You'll have the Rakovac file on your e-mail by day after tomorrow."

"Good." She paused. "You're not mentioning Eve Duncan. I regard that as a serious omission."

"You rescued the girl, not Winters himself. I figure that's only fifty percent of the deal. I only owe you for Kelly Winters." He tilted his head, considering. "And you killed Munoz. I'm not sure of the ramifications of that. We used him occasionally, and we'll have to find another information source."

"You're quibbling. You know anyone who went into that camp would have had to deal with Munoz. You couldn't have used him again with all this media attention focused on him. You said you were having trouble getting me Eve Duncan."

"Maybe." He turned and headed for his car parked by the hangar. "At any rate, I'm washing my hands of the problem. Deal with Eve Duncan yourself. I've thought it over and decided that I don't have to protect Eve from you. You're different as night and day, but she's strong enough to handle you." He glanced over his shoulder. "I only hope that you don't get her killed."

Atlanta, Georgia
Lake Cottage
Two days later

"Joe?" Eve opened her eyes to see Joe coming out of the bathroom, shrugging into his jacket. It was still dark, she realized drowsily. Where was he . . .

"Shh." Joe's lips brushed Eve's forehead. "Go back to sleep. I got a call from the precinct. Something nasty on the south side."

"What kind of —"

"I don't know. No details. Go back to sleep," he repeated. "You need it. It's only five. You didn't stop working on Cindy until two this morning." He gave her another kiss and headed for the door. "I'll call you."

"Do that." It must have been something urgent for them to call Joe from his bed. Urgent sometimes meant dangerous. "As soon as you know. Bye . . ."

A few minutes later, she heard his car start outside and tried to settle down and go back to sleep. She didn't think it was going to happen. She usually worked late, but her eyes were strained and stinging from trying to put together the shattered puzzle that was Cindy. She should rest her eyes even if she couldn't doze off again.

Fifteen minutes later she gave it up and sat up in bed. The longer she stayed in bed, the more tense she became. She'd get up, grab a cup of coffee, and go back to work on Cindy. She slipped on her robe and left the bedroom.

Joe had evidently grabbed a cup of coffee to go because there was a light burning in the kitchen. She chose a coffee pod and punched the button on the Keurig.

"That's interesting. I've never seen a coffeemaker like that. But then I haven't been in a civilized part of the world for a long time. Does it make good coffee?"

A woman's voice.

Eve whirled toward the shadows of her lab across the room. "What the hell —"

"Don't be afraid. I'm not here to hurt you." The woman who spoke was sitting on Eve's stool in front of the reconstruction of Cindy. "I just have to talk to you."

"The hell you do." Her gaze raked the woman from head to toe. Thin, dressed in dark jeans and sweater. No apparent weapons. That was good. Joe had taught Eve how to defend herself in any hand-to-hand battle. "Get out and call me on the phone.

How did you get in here anyway? Joe always sets the alarm."

"He did this time, too. It's a good alarm. It took me a little while to get past it after he left." She was gazing wonderingly down at the shards of bone on the tarp. "Are you really going to be able to put this face back together?"

"Yes. Get out."

"I'm not handling this right." She looked away from the bones to Eve's face. "It's just that when I saw those bones, it blew me away. My name is Catherine Ling. Venable might have mentioned me. I work with him."

"Venable?" Eve relaxed a little. The invasion was still totally unacceptable, but if she was associated with Venable, there was no physical threat. "No, he didn't mention you."

Catherine Ling grimaced. "He didn't even get that far? The age progression. He did call you about it?"

"Yes, I told him to get someone else. I'm too busy."

"I want you. I need you."

"Too bad." She picked up her cup of coffee. "You and your CIA can go take a flying leap. I don't work on Venable's orders." She went to the front door and opened it. "Now get out."

Catherine didn't move. "I don't want you to work for Venable. I don't want you to work for the CIA. This has nothing to do with them. It's my job. I knew you had a relationship with Venable, and I thought if I could get him to offer it to you, that it would be easier to get you to do it."

"Wrong." She jerked her head at the open door. "Don't come back. Next time, I'll call the police."

Catherine slowly rose to her feet. "Will you listen to me?"

"I might have listened to you if you hadn't invaded my home like a cat burglar. Now you don't have a chance in hell."

"I was in a hurry. I didn't want to have to argue with you. I thought if I hit the ground running, the shock would get us down to basics early."

"Don't come back."

Catherine moved toward the door. "I will come back. It's something I have to do. I'll come back time and time again until you listen to me." She passed Eve and went out onto the porch. "And until you do, I'll sit out here and wait."

"Not in my house, not on my porch, not on my property."

"Here. You'll have to stumble over me."

Catherine sank gracefully down on the floor and crossed her legs tailor fashion. "Until you listen."

Eve gazed at her in frustration. Early dawn light was now filtering onto the porch and dimly illuminating the woman. Catherine Ling looked to be in her late twenties. She was tall, thin, with small breasts and long legs. Straight, shoulder-length dark hair framed a face that was an interesting mixture of Western and Asian characteristics. High cheekbones and faintly tilted dark eyes contrasted with full lips and a square chin. Her brows were as dark as her hair and slightly winged over those large, intense eyes.

Everything about Catherine spoke of intensity, Eve thought. She was surrounded by it, burning with it. "I'm not about to stumble over you. I'll either throw you out myself or call the police."

"Then I'd have to fight. I'm very good at fighting. Someone would get hurt. Wouldn't it be better just to listen to me?"

Eve slammed the door shut and locked it.

She hadn't handled the situation well, Catherine thought.

She had been caught off guard. When Eve had come into the room, everything else had flown from her mind. She had waited so long . . .

Then Eve had been there before her, angry, wary. Her shoulder-length red-brown hair slightly mussed from sleep, her hazel eyes glaring at her in the lamplight. Catherine had seen photos of Eve in magazines, but she was more than she'd expected. Her thin face wasn't pretty, but it was fascinating and full of character. Everything about her spoke of alertness, vitality, and intelligence.

And there had been no fear. Eve should have been at least a little afraid.

Was it because she dealt with the results of death every day?

Oh, for heaven's sake, this was no time to try to analyze Eve Duncan's reactions.

She would just sit here and wait. No matter how long it took.

She would wait until Eve came back to her.

She'd just ignore the woman, Eve thought, after she'd locked the door. Maybe she'd go away.

No, she wouldn't. Catherine Ling would stay out there until hell froze over. Eve had seen that passionate intensity before.

In her own mirror.

She took a swallow of her coffee and turned and walked toward her worktable, where Catherine had been sitting when Eve had walked into the room. If the woman had disturbed any of her carefully placed bone fragments, she'd murder her.

Somehow, she didn't believe she would be that slipshod. Catherine Ling didn't impress her as someone who would be careless about anything.

No, everything was exactly as Eve had left it.

She reached out and gently touched a splinter of bone. "Sorry, Cindy, I'll get back to you as soon as I can. I have to take care of this idiotic problem now."

And how to do that?

Call the police as she'd threatened?

No, she believed Catherine Ling when she'd told her that she'd fight. This was Eve's home, and she didn't want violence to enter it. The outside world was too violent, and this was her haven.

But she *would* get rid of the woman.

She took out her cell phone, checked the number, then dialed.

"Venable, what the hell are you doing?"

"Nothing. I'm out of it. I take it that Catherine has paid you a visit?"

"Right now she's sitting on my porch

looking like a patient Buddha. She won't go away."

"Did you talk to her?"

"No, I threw her out. For heaven's sake, she invaded my house like a thief in the night."

"She can be impatient. It might be better if you let her talk to you. She won't go away. You can starve her, you can beat her, and she'll still be there."

Her hand clenched on the phone. "Then you tell her to get out. You're CIA, she's CIA, there has to be something you can do."

"She's obsessed. You can't deal with obsession in any normal manner."

"Are you saying she's nuts?"

"I'm saying that obsession can sometimes make people unbalanced."

"Unbalanced," she repeated. "That's a polite way of saying nuts. And you expect me to deal with her? Oh no, she's one of your people. You take care of it. My schedule is jam-packed. I have no *time* for this."

"I told you, I'm out of it. It's between the two of you now."

"You said you didn't want to turn me over to the wolf. You were talking about her, weren't you?"

"Yes, I should have said she-wolf, shouldn't I? I was hoping to persuade you to do the job and not have any contact with her. It would have been better for you."

"I'm not going to have any contact with that woman. As soon as I can, I'm going to send her on her way."

"I hope you do turn her down. I made a bargain with her, but I'm backpedaling as fast as I can. If she gets what she wants, she's going to cause me a lot of headaches."

"I don't care about your bargains. If you're not going to help, tell me how to make her leave."

"Listen to her. Say no. Make her believe it. She's no real threat. Not to you."

"Easy words. She's not easy. I can tell."

"Oh, you recognized a kindred spirit? I admit I noticed a few similarities myself."

She ignored those words. "Tell me how to get through to her. I have to know about her if I'm going to find a way to handle her. Tell me about Catherine Ling."

"How much?"

"Everything."

"I don't know everything. I had to depend on Catherine to tell me about her early years. There weren't any records. She's illegitimate. Her father was an American soldier based in Saigon. Her mother was a half-Korean, half-Russian prostitute and took Catherine to Hong Kong when she was four. She died two years later, and Catherine was left alone to try to survive on the streets. She survived very well. She was smart, and her instincts were excellent. Some of the things she learned during those years were amazing, and completely illegal and immoral."

"Considering how she broke into my house that doesn't surprise me."

"Anyway, she managed to sort it all out and avoided the worst pitfalls of prostitution and drugs. Probably because she came to realize that the most valuable commodity in Hong Kong was information. She taught herself to be fluent in eight languages and made herself an expert on selling and buying. From the criminal underbelly to high-end political secrets, she became the person to go to. That's where she first came onto our radar."

"I can see how she would come to your attention," Eve said dryly.

"Oh, she did. She was only seventeen and a complete tigress. She did a few contract jobs for us, and I was very impressed. I recruited her. I had her trained by one of our best agents. In the last twelve years I've sent her all over the world, and she's been a remarkable asset. I couldn't ask for a more competent operative."

"Until she became 'unbalanced'?"

"Everyone has a few problems to overcome. Once she works through this patch, she'll be as valuable to me as ever."

"You're incredible."

"No, I just do my job in the best way I can." He paused. "Tell her no. Don't get involved, Eve." He hung up the phone.

She didn't understand that last command. She had no intention of getting involved. Considering the circumstances, she didn't see how Venable could think she was in any danger of giving in to anything that Catherine Ling asked of her.

She jammed her phone back in her pocket. What to do? Venable had been of no real help. He had given her a little insight into the woman's character, but revealed no vulnerabilities. She had obviously developed scar tissue over all the pain of her childhood if she'd become the powerhouse Venable described.

Listen to her.

She hesitated, thinking.

Oh, what the hell. It was either violence or persuasion.

It might end up either, or both.

She strode toward the door and threw it open.

Catherine Ling didn't move, but Eve

could sense a subtle change, an increased alertness. She was ready to spring or defend herself from attack.

Good Lord, the woman was beautiful. Eve had been in such emotional turmoil, she had only been vaguely aware of Catherine's appearance.

The sun was shining, surrounding her with light. Her straight dark hair, enormous eyes, and smooth golden complexion seemed to glow.

But it was her vibrant intensity that held and fascinated. Eve had never seen anyone more alive.

"I just talked to Venable," Eve said curtly. "He's being a complete ass. He won't come and get you, and he says you won't do anything he asks."

She nodded. "He's right. He doesn't really want you to help me. He's glad that he found an excuse to put a roadblock in my way."

"I can't help you. Not as well as some of your CIA computer gurus."

She shook her head. "It has to be you."

"Dammit, why?"

She was silent. "Because of your Bonnie. Do you think I haven't studied and researched you? I know all about you. I know that you have a lover, Joe Quinn. I know you have an adopted daughter, Jane MacGuire, who is an artist and is in London right now." She paused. "And, most important of all, I know you lost your little girl, Bonnie, when she was seven to a serial killer, and it's given you a passion and dedication that none of those tech guys will ever have. I need that passion. I have to have that dedication."

"Then you'll have to do without. I have another job I have to do."

"Put it off."

"No, that little girl's parents have waited too long already. And why should I? To find out how age has changed some low-life criminal on whom you have some kind of twisted vendetta?"

"No." She reached into her jacket pocket and pulled out a photo carefully protected in clear plastic. "So I can find *him*." Her hand was trembling as she held out the photo to Eve. "Help me. I'll give you anything, do anything for you. I have to find him."

Eve slowly took the photo.

It was a picture of a little boy of not more than two years of age wearing a red sweater. Dark hair, enormous dark eyes that were alight with joy and mischief. He was smiling, and Eve had never seen a sweeter expression. It was a smile to melt the heart. "Who is he?"

"Luke. My son."

CHAPTER 3

Eve's gaze flew back to Catherine's face. "What?"

"Luke. That picture was taken on his second birthday. He was taken from me a week later."

"Taken? By whom?"

"Sergei Rakovac. Major criminal who was involved with the Russian mafia and manipulating various politicians in Moscow. My husband, Terry, and I were sent in to break up his organization. He was interfering with the current American administration's attempt at peacekeeping over the Republic of Georgia's conflict with Russia."

"What conflict? If there was a conflict, it sure didn't get much press."

"Enough. There was a particularly nasty conflict in 2008 between the Republic of Georgia and Russia that killed over a thousand people, but the ethnic infighting has been going on for decades. It involved South

Ossetia, a territory belonging to the Republic of Georgia. South Ossetia declared its independence from Georgia, and Russia supported them." She made a face. "While trying to gently pull them under Russian domination. It would probably have been the first move toward annexing Georgia itself. At any rate, the tempers have been flaring on both sides ever since, and it's still a hot spot. When Russia weighed in on the side of the Ossetians and sent in a 'peacekeeping' force is when it became a bloodbath. Guerilla fighting, massacres. Even after the supposed truce, there was spotty guerilla warfare on both sides. The attacks are still going on today. The hatred never stops."

"And Rakovac was involved?"

"Very much involved. But his involvement started much earlier than the outbursts that occurred later with Russia. As I said, there was hatred and fighting for decades. Rakovac actually was born in the Republic of Georgia and fought with them as a teenager in a guerilla group against the Ossetians. But after he went to Moscow he was supplying arms to both sides and when Russia joined in the conflict he was causing the situation to escalate even more. Our orders were to take him down." Her lips tightened.

"We did it. It took over a year of bribery and undermining of his contacts, but Rakovac was on his way out. He was furious. He dug and dug until he found out who had been behind all his problems. He got our names and he wanted revenge."

Eve felt sick as she looked down at the photograph of the child. So beautiful. So innocent. "Your Luke?"

"I found out I was pregnant just before we left Russia. I left the Company and settled in Boston. Terry still worked for the CIA, but I thought I could have a normal life. But Rakovac was just biding his time. He worked and schemed and gained back all the power we'd taken from him. Then he was ready to go after us." She moistened her lips. "One night, I put Luke to bed and went to my room. I received a call in the middle of the night. Rakovac. He had Terry. He shot him to death while I was on the phone. Then he told me to go to my son's room."

"And he was gone?"

Catherine Ling nodded jerkily. "I went crazy. Rakovac called back and said the minute I involved the police, he'd kill my son . . . slowly." She closed her eyes. "And I knew he'd do it. I'd studied him. I knew what a sadistic bastard he could be." Her eyes opened, and they were glittering with tears. "I felt so damn helpless. I called Venable and told him he had to help me get my son back. He was very sympathetic but cautious. Very cautious. It seems there had been a wind change in Moscow-Washington relations. Rakovac had made himself invaluable to the CIA and the White House. Washington didn't want any change in the status quo."

"Even at the expense of a child's life?"

Her lips twisted. "You don't understand it either. You're a mother. Nothing is as important as keeping a son or daughter alive. I suppose I should have realized that it could happen. I know how things work. But I couldn't connect any of that knowledge with Luke." Her voice dropped to a whisper. "Not with my son."

"So what did you do?"

"I started after Rakovac on my own. Until I got another phone call. Luke was crying so I knew that he was still alive. I recognized his voice. Rakovac said that the CIA would cause him too much trouble if he killed him, but he wasn't going to give him up. He wanted me to suffer. I was never going to see him again, and he'd remain alive if I didn't make waves." Her voice broke. "But he was crying, and I couldn't do anything about it. He was *crying.*"

"Dear God."

"Venable said he'd do everything possible, but it would be safer for Luke if I didn't disturb Rakovac until he could manage to negotiate a release." Her voice hoarsened. "Disturb? I wanted to kill him. My baby . . ."

"And they haven't negotiated a release yet? How long has it been?"

"Nine years," she said dully. "It's been nine years."

Eve's eyes widened. "How could that be?"

"Rakovac made sure that he was invaluable enough to keep Venable and the CIA at bay. He kept stalling and offering one more favor if they'd forget about Luke's release for a little while longer. It stretched on and on."

"Couldn't you go in and find him yourself?"

"I tried. I went to Russia at every opportunity and tried to locate him. But Rakovac had hidden him away somewhere, and I couldn't locate him. He'd been planning Luke's kidnapping since Terry and I had left Russia." She shook her head. "And I couldn't let Rakovac know I was on his own turf searching. He'd warned me that he'd kill Luke if I came after him." She added bitterly, "And I was making Venable nervous. He had me assigned to the other side of the world, lately in the jungles of Colombia. After that, I was only able to break free every now and then and go back to Moscow."

"I would have told Venable and his buddies to go to hell. I don't see how you could keep on working with them."

"He was my only connection. He might have been the one element that was keeping Luke alive. Rakovac was hesitating to take that final step that might cause the CIA and Washington to have to contend with a public-opinion issue. Just having Venable making occasional inquires about Luke was a reminder that his position wasn't totally invulnerable." She took a shaky breath. "But things may be changing. I've been noticing that there seems to be a shifting . . . I can't put my finger on it. Rakovac's power may be increasing. It's scaring me."

Eve could see that fear. It was reflected in the woman's face and the slight trembling of her lips. She sensed it as a living force. Who could blame her? How would she have felt if she had gone through those years of searching, never knowing if her Bonnie was alive or dead? But at least there had been hope for Catherine Ling. From the beginning, Eve had known in her heart that Bonnie had been killed.

"You're thinking about your daughter." Catherine was studying her face. "You're making comparisons. I made comparisons, too. That's why I'm here."

"Bonnie's death has nothing to do with your son's kidnapping. I'm sorry for you, but I can't help you. Talk to Venable."

"You *can* help me." Catherine's voice breathed intensity. "You're the only one who can. Why do you think I'm here? I'm not stupid. Do you think I haven't gone over every way, every person who could bring Luke back to me? I've been trying to find a way for over a year to get Venable to persuade you to help. Why do you think I was willing to camp out on your doorstep to make you listen to me?"

Desperation, pain, hope. Eve knew the emotions that were motivating Catherine all too well, and her heart ached for her. "I've listened to you." She turned. "And I want you off my porch. Come into the house, and I'll give you a cup of coffee. Then we'll discuss how we can get Venable to help you. I know several qualified professionals at Langley who can do the job."

Catherine stared at her a moment, then rose to her feet in one graceful, fluid movement. "Coffee would be good."

But she wasn't committing to any of Eve's other suggestions, Eve noticed ruefully as she preceded Catherine into the kitchen. She probably should have closed the door and not invited the woman back into the cottage. But that wasn't an option, not since she had seen that photo of Luke. She would just have to use persuasion and firmness to ease Catherine Ling out of her life.

"You're letting me get one foot back in the door. It's not going to be easy to get rid of me," Catherine said quietly. "If I were you, I'd have slammed the door and barricaded myself in the house."

"You're not me." Eve pressed the button on the coffeemaker and watched the liquid pour into the cup. "And I don't need to barricade myself against you. I'm not afraid of you, Catherine Ling. Cream?"

"No. Black. And call me Catherine." She took the cup Eve handed her. "No, I can see you're not afraid. You weren't even afraid when you first saw me and didn't know whether or not I was a threat." She sipped the coffee. "And, no, we're not alike. Venable keeps seeing resemblances, but he's wrong. We only have one thing in common, and I intend to exploit that to the fullest extent."

"Go ahead. It won't get you anywhere." She gestured for her to sit down on the couch. "I have a job I have to do. Cindy has been lost too long, and I have to bring her home."

"She's dead. Bring my son home instead. He's alive, and there's no telling how long he'll stay that way if I don't get him away from Rakovac. I can't wait any longer. I have to go after him. But he's eleven years old, and I don't even know what he looks like. I haven't seen him since he was two." She whispered, "So many years . . ."

"Age progression isn't my area of expertise. Even if I wanted to give up work on my reconstruction of Cindy, I couldn't do as good a job as someone who does it day in, day out."

"That's not true. I've studied your reconstructions, and they come amazingly close." She looked down into the coffee in her cup. "You have all that scientific stuff down pat, but that isn't what happens in the final step, is it? You make a connection."

"Do I?" she asked warily.

"Oh, I'm not saying that there's anything weird going on. I'm too practical to think anything like that. But Michelangelo once said something about the figure coming out of the stone. Certain artists have the passion that makes their work come alive." She raised her gaze to look at Eve. "You have that passion. I can see it. I could feel it when I looked at your reconstructions. I have to have that passion. I'll do anything you say if you'll show me a photo of my Luke as he is today."

"Working on a computer isn't like doing a sculpting reconstruction," she said gently. "Perhaps there is a kind of connection when I feel the clay beneath my fingers, but this is different."

"Try." Her gaze went to the bones on the dais. "I know you want to finish what you started. I don't like to leave anything undone either. But can't you see this is more important?"

"I can see it's more important to you. I can see that it might be more important to me if I thought I was the best person to do the progression." She raised her cup to her lips. "So I'd better continue with what I do best and let you go your own way."

"I don't care what you think." Her eyes were suddenly blazing. "I know you're the best one to find my son. Time's running out. I'm not going to let him die. You *have* to do it." She stopped. "I'm doing this all wrong, aren't I?" She raised her shaking hand to her head. "I'm usually not this clumsy. It means too much to me."

"I can understand that, Catherine."

"I know you can." Her gaze returned to the bones on Eve's worktable. "I think you want to help me. I just have to give you a reason to do it. And a way to remove any roadblocks in your path."

Eve raised her brows. "And how are you going to do that?"

"Guilt."

"I beg your pardon?"

"You saw the photo of my son. He touched you. You want to help him." She stared Eve in the eye. "What if I'm right, and you're the best one to identify him? What if I went to one of Venable's techs, and they steered me wrong? Venable doesn't want me to stir up any trouble. It's a delicate situation in Moscow, and he knows I won't give a damn about diplomatic relations if it means rescuing Luke." She took a deep breath. "What if Rakovac kills him before I can find him? How would that make you feel?"

"Sad. Not guilty, Catherine. I won't play into your hands that way."

"Not even a little? Oh, I think you will. You'll remember that my every instinct was shouting that you were the one who could help me save Luke. I think you'd feel a little guilty. There is always a reaction to an action." She paused. "Or the lack of an action."

Eve muttered an oath beneath her breath. "I believe you may be something of a calculating bitch, Catherine Ling."

"Oh, I am. When I have to be." Her voice became crisp. "Now for the roadblock. You don't want to leave your reconstruction of that little girl to do a job that you feel can be done by someone else. Correct?"

Eve slowly nodded. "Yes."

"Then I won't ask you to delay your work on her. It shouldn't take you too long to complete the age progression. It's going to take a while to put that little girl's face back together. You can start on Luke's age progression while the prep work on the little girl is being done."

"What?" Eve was frowning. "You're not making sense. I can't do both at once."

"No. You'll need help. I can help you with the little girl."

"The hell you can."

"Look, I'm not saying I could do any of the reconstruction. That would be insane. But what you have is a puzzle. I'm good at puzzles." She made a face. "Though those bones are going to be a nightmare."

"And I'm supposed to trust you with them? Cindy is my responsibility."

"Try me. Oh, I know that there's probably all kinds of training you go through for this kind of thing. But in the end, isn't it basically just a puzzle you have to solve?"

"Yes," she said slowly.

"I'll access the Internet and study bone structure. I'll consult with you. You can look over my shoulder every minute of the way. I can do it. I can put her back together." She paused. "And I'll do it with respect. The same respect you would show her, Eve."

"No."

"Please. You're not losing anything, not even time. Just do this for me, and I'll owe you for the rest of my life."

"I don't want you to owe me."

"Do you think I'm lying? I'm not lying."

"Catherine, I don't think you're lying." The woman's pain was too agonizingly obvious. "I believe you're going down the wrong road with me. But you've got me so dizzy, I have to straighten my head." She got to her feet. "I think I'll go for a walk and do a little thinking."

"May I stay here and wait for you?"

"Politeness?" Eve smiled faintly as she headed for the front door. "That's the first hint I've had of that quality from you. How refreshing. Yes, you may stay. Have some more coffee."

"I will." She moistened her lips. "I know you don't like to be pushed. But I did it for Luke. It's all for Luke."

Eve nodded. "I know, Catherine."

"Eve."

She looked back over her shoulder.

"I thought I should tell you. Joe Quinn may phone you. I set up the call that took him away this morning. There was no emergency call on the south side."

"I suspected that might be the case," she said dryly.

"I had to see you alone."

"Then you've accomplished your aim." She shut the screen door behind her and drew a deep breath. She could still feel the waves of emotion Catherine was emitting. She'd had to escape before she wavered and gave in to the woman's plea. She was still wavering and caught in that web of pity and empathy. That photo of Luke Ling had touched her heart.

But Catherine was clever, even calculating, and she had probably planned on that response from Eve. What did she know? That might not even be Catherine's child. Maybe Luke was just another pawn in one of the CIA's complicated agendas.

But Eve didn't believe that. Her every instinct was telling her that Catherine's story was tragically, painfully true.

Professionals didn't rely on instinct. Not when it concerned the CIA. She didn't know Catherine Ling, but she had a minimal knowledge and respect for Venable. He was at least a starting point.

She took out her phone and dialed his number.

"I was expecting to hear from you," he said with a sigh when he picked up. "You couldn't just send her on her way?"

"How much am I to believe about the kidnapping of Luke Ling?"

He was silent a moment. "Everything. Catherine can be deceptive, but not about her son."

"You bastard. Nine years."

"I was under orders not to disturb our relationship with Rakovac. He's very volatile, and he still has a deep hatred of Cathcrine."

"So you let him keep a child prisoner rather than rock the boat? How do you know that he wasn't mistreated? That would be the best way for Rakovac to get his revenge."

"I made it clear that we wouldn't tolerate that happening."

She couldn't believe her ears. "How would

you know? Did you just take his word for it?"

"Yes, with appropriate threats of repercussions."

"Dear God."

"It's all I could do. It might have been enough."

"If I were Catherine, I'd have strangled you."

"But you're not Catherine. She's CIA. She knows the dirty underbelly of the world better than you ever will. And she's aware that I was the only man standing between her son and Rakovac." He added, "If I could have run the risk, I would have sent a Special Forces team in to get Luke. But I didn't have that option. I couldn't even give Catherine reports on her son. Rakovac didn't keep him with him in Moscow. He'd sent him away and undercover almost immediately after he was kidnapped."

Eve's stomach clenched. "Then how do you know he's still alive?"

"We're not entirely sure. Rakovac calls Catherine now and then to taunt her and gives her so-called reports on her son. He hasn't let her talk to him since about a year after he was taken."

Eve felt cold and sick. Eight years with no way to know if that little boy was alive or dead. "But, of course, she still takes the calls." Eve would do the same. There was always hope, and you could bear the torture as long as the faintest chance existed that it would bring a child home. "Why didn't you tell me this when you first asked me to do the age progression?"

"I didn't want you to do it," he said bluntly. "I was only paying lip service to a bargain I made with Catherine. The current files on Rakovac are top secret, and we made sure they were kept away from Catherine. They contain surveillance as well as contacts that she had no knowledge about from her previous assignment in Moscow. She wanted those files." He paused. "And she wanted your help. To get them, she risked her neck going after Ned Winters and his daughter, who were being held hostage in Colombia. You may have heard of them. They've been all over the TV."

"Who hasn't? The father was murdered, you saved the girl."

"Catherine saved the girl."

"And you gave her the file?"

"I kept my word. The director was more concerned with getting the Winters father and daughter free. The Rakovac connection has been disintegrating lately." He paused. "He's becoming unstable."

"And where does that leave that poor kid?"

"I gave Catherine the file. I can't do anything else at the moment. We haven't entirely distanced ourselves from Rakovac yet. Although we know that he's left his penthouse apartment in Moscow and gone undercover. It would be better if Catherine stayed out of it until we see fit to make a final break."

"Better for you. Not better for Luke or Catherine. I can't blame her for being frantic to move now."

"Neither can I. But I can't help her to do it. I have to act for the good of the big picture."

"Screw the big picture."

He was silent a moment. "You're going to help her?"

"I haven't made up my mind. Though for heaven's sake someone should be helping her."

"That was aimed at me," he said. "If you decide to help her, limit it, Eve. Rakovac is an ugly customer, and he won't take kindly to you getting in his way."

Getting in the way of the viciousness of a man who would kidnap a two-year-old and keep him prisoner for nine years? "She only wants me to do an age progression. She doesn't trust your people."

"Imagine that," he said wearily. "Not that I blame her. But she's a desperate woman, and she'll take whatever from you she has to take to find her son. Watch yourself, Eve." He hung up.

She slowly pressed the disconnect button and stood gazing out at the sunlight glittering on the lake.

If she'd hoped to find a reason to throw Catherine out of the cottage, Venable had not given it to her. He'd only shown her a woman surrounded by an ideology where almost everything and everyone was expendable. She had told Eve the truth, and every action she had taken was perfectly reasonable. Eve would have done the same thing in Catherine's place. Any mother would give up whatever she had to surrender to protect her child.

But Eve had her own life, her own priorities. She didn't even know if she could help Catherine. Should she become involved in trying to —

"Of course, you can help her. Why are you fretting like this, Mama?"

Bonnie.

She glanced at the porch swing and saw her little girl in the Bugs Bunny T-shirt curled up with her legs beneath her. The sun was shining on her mop of red curls, and her smile was brilliant as that sun. Eve felt her heart warming as it always did when Bonnie came to her. She was always as real to Eve as the last day she had seen her.

"You don't know that I can help her, Miss Smarty. I'm not that good on age progression."

"No, but she has the right idea. You do make a connection." She suddenly chuckled. "It was funny that she was so quick to say that she didn't mean anything weird. People are so afraid that others are going to think they're not totally grounded in reality."

"It's always so strange to hear you talking like this. So grown-up . . ."

"I told you once that I couldn't stay seven forever. Nothing stands still, not even where I am." She smiled. "But you probably forgot it and are in denial because that idea is a little weird, too."

"Denying what isn't real is what keeps us sane, baby."

"You're sane, and yet you've accepted that a ghost comes and visits you."

Her ghost, her beloved spirit, her Bonnie. "That's different."

Bonnie nodded. "And it took you long enough to accept that I wasn't a dream or a hallucination or whatever. It's much more comfortable now, isn't it?"

"It will be comfortable when I can bring you home and find the bastard who killed you."

"Comfortable for you. I'm content right now." She leaned back in the swing. "It's over for me, Mama. Only the love is left."

"It's not over for me."

"I know." Bonnie's gaze shifted to the door. "And it's not over for her. She's hurting."

"Yes."

"Then why don't you go in and help her? Cindy won't care. She knows that time doesn't matter."

"It may matter to her parents."

"Go find Luke, Mama."

"I can only try to tell her what he looks like. I may not even be right."

"And you might be." Bonnie smiled. "I'll bet on you. I'll always bet on you. Why are you arguing with me? You know you're going to do it."

"Maybe." She smiled back at her. "And maybe I just want you to stick around a while. I hate it when you go away."

Her smile faded. "Me, too. But we have this. It's a lot, Mama."

Eve felt her throat tighten. "Yes, it's a lot." In the year following Bonnie's disappearance, her health and sanity had been spiraling downward, and she would not have survived another six months. But after Bonnie had begun to come to her, everything had changed. For years afterward, she wouldn't admit, even to herself, that Bonnie was not a dream. But she was with her, and that was all that mattered. "But it's not enough. I want more."

"Don't be greedy. It's not time. Mama," she said gently. "You have Joe, you have Jane. You have a talent that can help people like Catherine Ling. Now go tell her that soon she'll know what her Luke looks like right now."

"Is he still alive, Bonnie?"

She shook her head. "I don't know. I think he may be. Sometimes I know things, sometimes I don't." She frowned. "But there's darkness all around Catherine Ling. I hope it doesn't come from him."

"I hope so, too." She turned and headed for the door. "Since you're pushing me away from you, I guess I'd better see what I can do about —"

"I am pushing you away. I have to do it. But I'll always come back for you, Mama . . ."

"I know, baby." She glanced over her shoulder. "I was just . . ."

Bonnie was gone.

Good-bye, my love.

She paused a moment, letting regret and

memory flow out of her, then opened the door.

"Hello, you were gone longer than I thought." Catherine Ling was sitting before Eve's worktable with a laptop open before her. She glanced up, and her gaze warily raked Eve's expression, trying to read it. "I was wondering if you were going to come back or send in the cops."

"I don't think you were worried. You have too much confidence in yourself."

"I was worried." She smiled faintly before adding, "That I'd have to start again and find another way to get you. Honesty is all very well, but it doesn't work with everyone."

"No?" She crossed the room and stood looking down at the screen of Catherine's computer. "What are you doing?"

"Bones." Her forefinger traced the lines of the skull on the screen before her. "I accessed a medical site on the Net. This is the skull of a female child. I thought I'd familiarize myself with the final product that you need to work with." She pointed to a sliver of bone on the table before her. "That might be the bone beneath the orbital cavity."

Catherine was already driving forward, grasping at opportunities and concepts, Eve thought. She hadn't waited for Eve's decision. In the short time Eve had been gone, Catherine had started to work. "And it might not."

Catherine nodded. "I figured I'd try it there and be open to change." She lifted her gaze to meet Eve's eyes. "I'm always open to change, Eve."

Eve stood looking at her for a moment. Then she smiled and moved her desktop computer to the other side of the worktable. "So am I. You'd better be extremely careful about every movement you make with those bones. One sign of clumsiness, and I'll consider the arrangement blown."

Catherine tensed. "You'll do it?"

"I'll do it. I've warned you that I can't promise success, but I'll make a try. There are a good many things I'll need from you."

"Anything. How do we start?"

"By calling Joe and telling him that he's wasting his time." She pulled out her phone. "And that you're responsible for dragging him out of bed and sending him on a wild-goose chase."

She nodded. "I always accept responsibility. I'll talk to him. It's what I expected." She made a face. "From what I've heard, he's a difficult man. I don't look forward to it."

"Very wise." She was getting Joe's voice

mail. "But you have a reprieve. I'll call him back later." She hung up and focused on the program she was pulling up on the screen. She reached into the drawer beneath the table and pulled out her scanner. "Now let's get busy. Give me that photo of Luke."

Moscow

"She's left Colombia," Russo said as he hung up the phone and turned to Rakovac. "According to our informant, Prado, in the CIA, she boarded a flight out of Bogotá yesterday afternoon."

"Destination?" Rakovac asked.

"Houston, Texas. But she missed her connecting flight to Los Angeles." He smiled. "But a woman of her description boarded a flight to Atlanta an hour later, a last-minute booking. She's traveling under the name of Patricia Loring."

"Atlanta," Rakovac repeated. "Now what could the bitch be doing in Atlanta . . ."

"Venable could have sent her. There have been some communications between them, but Prado couldn't determine what they were about."

"Then we need a new man in Venable's camp. He knows that Catherine Ling is one of his top priorities." He leaned back in his chair, his brow furrowed in thought. "She could be making a move. I've been sensing that something was building the last few times I talked to her."

"You don't seem upset."

"No, I look forward to it." He suddenly smiled. "It's been going on too long. I'm growing bored. She needs to bleed a little."

"You're going to go after her?"

"Or let her come after me." He gazed at the framed photo of Catherine Ling he had on his desk. In all the years since he had taken her son, he had never put that photo away. It had served to remind him that he was the one in control, and she was only a victim to be punished. The bitch had almost taken him down. If he hadn't scrambled desperately to right his empire, he'd have been back in the sewer where he'd been born. "Beautiful, isn't she? If you can call a demon beautiful. I think it's time I brought her closer."

"Not a good idea," Russo said. "She's CIA. It's not safe. As long as you kept her at a distance, there was —"

"I wouldn't be where I am if I worried about safety," Rakovac interrupted. "You have to take chances to become what you're destined to be. You've always cringed at the bottom of the ladder, afraid to climb. That's why you answer to me."

Russo flushed. "And if you didn't have men like me propping up your ladder, you'd be crashing down on your ass. I've never seen why you snatched the kid. He's always been a threat to all of us. She's always been a threat."

Russo had surprised him. He didn't often lose his temper with him. "No, Catherine Ling ceased to be a threat when I took her son."

"It's gone on too long. You should have killed her instead of stretching out this idiocy. There's always the chance that the CIA will take action."

"Not as long as I give them what they want." He grimaced. "Or that they think that I'm doing it. It's merely a question of striking a balance."

"And how long can you do it? Venable isn't a fool. You haven't been spending enough time and attention on the business they're paying you for. He'll know that you're up to something."

It wasn't the first time Russo had spoken out against Rakovac's persecution of Catherine. Time to shut him down. "I'll do what I have to do. Stay out of my business." He gave him a cold glance. "You don't understand. I don't allow anyone to humiliate me the way Catherine Ling did. She came close to destroying me, and everyone knew it. I swore that I'd make her pay. And I've done it."

"Yes," Russo said. "But maybe it's time to end it." He paused. "Is the boy still alive?"

Rakovac smiled but didn't answer.

Russo's eyes widened. "Good God. You've killed him?"

He shrugged. "Perhaps. Again, that's my affair. She thinks he's still alive." He smiled maliciously. "Sometimes. It's the eternal seesaw. There's nothing more painful. I've made sure she's regretted that last mission in Moscow."

"But not enough?"

He shook his head. "Not while I can squeeze one more drop of pain from her. And after she's too numb to give me that pleasure, I'll take her blood." He gazed back at the photo. "But I have to find her first. Tell Prado to probe a little and find out if Venable made any phone calls to Atlanta recently."

CHAPTER 4

"I've scanned in Luke's photo." Eve looked up from her computer. "It's good that it's a frontal shot. It will help with the progression. But I need more than this."

"I know. Family members. I don't have much that you can use." She slipped from her stool. "I'll be right back. I left an envelope in my rental car." She ran out of the house and down the steps. She was back in a few minutes and handed Eve a large manila envelope. "The photos are all of my husband Terry's family. I don't know anything about my mother's background. I tried to trace my father, but I haven't been able to find out anything about him. Not even his name."

"That's not good."

"I tried," she said fiercely. "I can't help it that I was dropped into this world and everyone just walked away. It's not my fault, and it's not Luke's. Work with it."

"I will. It just makes it more difficult. What do you know about age progression?"

"Only that it's easier if you have a battery of photos from both sides of the family. I tried to give it to you. It just wasn't happening."

"The reason that we like to compare the child's photo with any available photos of family members is that there may be a resemblance to the features of a grandparent or uncle or another relative that's stronger than to the parents. And if we had a photograph of any of them at the same age as Luke, eleven, it could help."

"But maybe not. My husband always said Luke looked like me."

Eve gazed at the photo of Luke on the screen. Beautiful, faintly tilted dark eyes with long eyelashes. The lips appeared close to the same shape. She couldn't tell about the cheekbones. Luke had too much baby fat for her to be able to determine the shape.

"Well?"

"There is a strong resemblance, but we can't be sure that it will still be noticeable at his present age. The shape of the face changes."

"We can't be sure of anything. But it's something to work with."

Eve nodded. "But this is Luke at two.

When a child is born, the bones of the skull and neck are not nearly complete. The growth process doesn't complete until a person is twenty-five or older."

"So?"

"The proportional changes in the amount of the lower face are fundamental. Young children's faces grow downward and forward. The forehead changes from a bulbous look to an upright and flattened appearance. The lower half of the face drifts downward and either forward or outward. The upper and lower jaws are constantly increasing in size and changing form. They become more prominent and —"

"You're telling me all the difficulties. Can you override them?"

"I can only try." She opened the envelope and spread the photos on the table. "Which one was your husband?"

"The man in the brown bomber jacket. He doesn't look anything like Luke."

"I can see that." The man in the photo was tall, broad-shouldered, and had thinning gray hair. "He was quite a bit older than you."

"Sixty-two, but age doesn't matter."

Sixty-two to Catherine's seventeen.

"It doesn't matter," Catherine repeated. "Age is only a number. Venable sent me to

Terry as a mentor when I first joined the CIA, and he taught me, guided me, he even saved my life once. He was very good to me. That's the only thing that was important."

"Your relationship is your own business. I was just surprised."

"He was kind, we were partners, he gave me a child. Infinite riches. How could I ask for more?"

Didn't every woman deserve a young and heady passion at least once in her life? "He has a nice face." She went to another picture. "Who is the child?"

"Terry, at age six. The other picture is his mother, Gail. She doesn't look like Luke either. So you may be stuck with me. I was four when that picture of me was taken in Shanghai. My mother had to furnish it for the entry papers."

Eve picked up the photo of Catherine. It was amazingly similar to the photo on the computer screen before her. The child Catherine was thinner, her manner solemn and a little defiant, but the resemblance was unmistakable.

"Will it help?" Catherine asked.

"Yes, I think it will. I don't know how much." She bent forward and began to run feature programs on the photo of Luke before her. "Let me go to work."

"I won't bother you." Catherine was once more gazing down at Cindy's bones. "If I can do anything more to —"

"I'll let you know." Eve was staring at the lower part of Luke's face. Such an enchanting child, full of life and mischief. Some of the magic of early childhood would fade when she added years to his picture.

Catherine had missed that magic, she thought suddenly. How she must have loved this child. She would have regretted every year that passed and cheated her of those beloved changes. Eve had had Bonnie for seven years, and she had memories of every single one. Catherine had nothing past that second birthday.

Time to get to work.

Eleven. She had to clear her mind of that wonderfully engaging two-year-old and think eleven . . .

It was close to five when Joe walked into the cottage. Eve had called him back and explained briefly what had occurred since he had left, and he had been royally pissed. Now she took one look at his expression and murmured to Catherine, "You said you were ready to face responsibility for your actions? Here it comes."

Catherine sat up straighter on her stool, her gaze on Joe Quinn. "Will it upset you? I can handle him alone."

"Indeed?" Joe asked silkily.

"It won't upset me," Eve said. "It will interest me."

Catherine slipped from the stool and moved across the room to stand before Joe. "You're angry. I had to do it, you know. I had to get Eve alone to talk to her. You had to be removed."

"You're damn right I'm angry. You interfered with my life and my job. You broke into my home. You somehow managed to brainwash Eve into doing your job. Get the hell out of here."

"If that's what you want. But Eve is going to help me. We both know she always keeps her word. And I'm helping her, too. It will be easier for her if I stay here until it's done." She moistened her lips. "It won't be long. Eve says that two or three days, and she'll have the progression completed. I won't get in your way. I've brought a tent and sleeping bag. I'll camp out in the woods until she's finished. The minute she stops for the day, I'm out of your house and won't come back until the morning."

He stared at her without speaking.

"I've heard that she cares about you. She's

stayed with you a long time, so that must be true. I always knew that you could be the one who would get in my way. You might be able to persuade her to not help me." She looked him in the eye. "But I don't think you will. She hasn't had any luck finding her own child. She has a chance to help find mine. That would have to make her feel a sort of healing. I'd think that you'd want that." Her voice lowered. "I don't care how you feel about me. Yes, I'm selfish and self-serving, but I'm not hurting her. Just let me stay for a little while."

Joe didn't speak for a moment, and his gaze never left Catherine's face. "Eve?"

"Her son was only two when he was ripped away from her. He deserves to come home." She paused. "And he could be alive, Joe. Maybe for once the bad guy hasn't triumphed. She's right, I need this."

Joe muttered a curse and turned on his heel. "Okay, you've got it. Just don't let her pull you into anything else." He headed for the bedroom. "And you will sleep in your tent and stay out of my hair, Catherine. I won't have you insinuating your way into my house. Once the progression is over, you're out."

"You don't have to worry about that. Once I know what my son looks like, I'll be out of here and on the hunt." She turned back to the worktable. "Thank you, Detective Quinn."

Her only answer was the slamming of the bedroom door.

"When he cools down, I could ask him to let you sleep on the couch," Eve offered.

Catherine shook her head. "I'm lucky that he's being as generous as he is. I won't push my luck." She sat back down on her stool. "I've found three pieces that I think fit together." She picked up a tiny sliver of bone. "And I believe this one may be part of the nasal area. . . ." She looked up at Eve across the table. "Is it too early for me to ask how you're doing on the progression?"

"Much too early."

"May I ask about the procedure?"

Eve shrugged. "I work differently from most other forensic artists. Particularly when children are involved. I can't just dive in and combine all the changes that happen year by year and go to the final product. I have to do a complete progression at several growth stages and gradually build them to the present age. It's more work, and Venable's techs would probably say it's unnecessary. But maybe it's because I'm not as experienced as they are. It's necessary for me." She met Catherine's gaze. "So if you have any objections, voice them now, and we'll stop."

"No objections. Only one request."

"What request?"

"Will you save every stage progression you do of Luke for me?" She tried to smile, but her lips were trembling. "I want to see how he grew, how he changed. It will be like having a collection of school photos of him." Her smile faded. "School photos. Such an ordinary thing. It wouldn't have been ordinary to me, Eve."

"No, I can see it wouldn't," Eve said gently. "I'll save them and print them out for you. I won't be doing every year, but you'll be able to grasp the changes."

"Thank you." She looked down at the bones again. "I was just curious. I'll let you work now."

Curious and desperately reaching out for memories of which she'd been cheated, Eve thought.

Catherine changed the subject. "You know, this Cindy puzzle is every bit as difficult as I thought it was going to be." She grimaced as she looked back at the skull on her screen. "And I don't think it would help if I'd worked with skulls and bones for years as you have. It's just hit-or-miss."

Eve nodded. "Which is why I agreed to

let you try your luck. You have the same determination and motivation that I have. It's not based on the same foundation, but the result could be identical. I hope it will be."

Catherine was frowning, her tongue touching her upper lip as she tried another fragment of bone. "I hope so, too . . ."

Eve knew that Joe was not asleep when she took off her terry robe and slipped into bed.

"It's almost two in the morning," he said gruffly. "She's a demanding bitch, isn't she?"

"You know better than that." She cuddled closer to him. She loved the feel of him. Everything about Joe was warm and strong and hard. "No one pushes me but me. I wanted to get through the first transition to age three."

"Did you do it?"

"Yes. Actually, it was easier for me than for Catherine. She's going to have severe eyestrain from working on Cindy tonight. But she managed to get the shards of the upper-right cheekbone in place."

"I can't say I feel sorry for her."

"I know. I don't blame you. What she did was arrogant and done with all the finesse of a bulldozer."

"I won't say she was without finesse. It takes a certain amount of cleverness to be able to manage all the details of pulling the right strings at the precinct not only to set up a false crime scene, but arrange for me specifically to be called in for it."

"She's experienced. After all, she's CIA."

"And if there weren't a kid involved, you'd have kicked her out."

"Yes. I found I couldn't do it."

"Because she made you bleed, then gave you a bandage of hope to soothe the wound. I told you she was clever." He pulled her closer. "But there wasn't any way I could take that hope away from either of you. That's why I didn't toss her ass in the lake." His lips brushed her temple. "But it's still an option I'm leaving open."

"Me, too." But that option was gradually fading into the shadows the more she worked with Catherine Ling. "But I think she'd swim to the surface and be back on our porch an hour later. She's going to do anything she has to do to get her son back." She whispered, "I have to help her, Joe. I'll show you the photo of Luke tomorrow. I've never seen a sweeter, more beautiful child. So full of life. The more I work on the progression, the closer I feel to him."

"That's what I'm worried about."

She knew what he meant. It was a valid concern. She had told Catherine that she would only do the progression, and then go back to her own work. But she was being pulled deeper into Catherine's emotions, Catherine's obsession.

"She only asked me to show her what Luke looks like now. That's not so much."

"And I'll be right here to make sure that she doesn't try to persuade you to do anything else." He kissed her hard. "Don't close me away from you. I felt like an outsider when I came in tonight and saw the two of you working together. I could almost see the bond that was meshing, forming between you. I was jealous. And it scared the hell out of me. Because I can't fight it. I haven't lost a child. I can sympathize, but not empathize. I'm already working my way through your feelings for Bonnie. I'm not ready to deal with another lost child, whether he's dead or alive."

"I'm not asking you to deal with Luke."

"No, but it will happen if you become involved. I can't do anything else. After all these years, you should know that by now."

Yes, she knew it. They had been together since the week that her Bonnie was kidnapped, and he had been her salvation, pushing back the darkness. Since that nightmare period, they'd had a relationship as stormy as it was loving. At times she hadn't been sure it would survive. "Joe, if you —"

He kissed her again, smothering the words she had been about to speak. "No, I don't want to argue. I've had my say. I just want you to know how I feel."

"Duly noted." Her hands slid around him, and her nails bit teasingly into the back of his neck. "I like the way you feel. Emotionally . . ." She ran her tongue over his lower lip. "Physically." She pushed him over and climbed on top of him. "Sexually. Oh, yes, most definitely sexually."

He inhaled sharply as her hands moved over him. "Are you trying to distract me?"

"Hell, yes. You're being too intense. I'm dealing with enough intensity. Am I succeeding?"

He smiled as his hands closed on her breasts. "Without a shadow of a doubt."

Venable called Eve just after noon the following afternoon. "How is your collaboration with my pet she-wolf coming along?"

"Very well. And I don't have time to talk to you unless you have something to contribute." She gazed at Catherine. "Would you like to speak to Catherine?"

"No, I'd just like you to give her a message. Tell her that I kept my word. The Rakovac file should be on her e-mail."

"Tell her yourself. You may be fond of secrets and playing people against each other, but I like things out in the open. I'm putting you on speaker." She turned to Catherine as she pressed the button. "Venable says you have a document on your e-mail."

Catherine tensed. "The file, Venable?"

"I told you I'd get it for you," Venable said sourly. "And I put my ass on the line with the director to keep my word. He was having second thoughts."

"The entire file?"

"Surveillance on Rakovac from the week that your son was taken." He paused. "You're not going to be pleased. I told you at the time that we had no visual confirmation on Luke. I didn't lie to you."

"But he had to have some contact with him. I heard him crying on that first call. Rakovac mentioned things that he did in other calls."

"And we both know the bastard could have been stringing you along," Venable said bluntly. "Luke could have been killed right after that first call."

"No question. But if he wasn't, and Luke

is alive, there might be something in those surveillance records that will give me some direction."

"Well, go damn carefully. I don't want you blowing our relationship with him until we're ready to pounce. You owe me that much."

"Screw you. I don't owe you anything."

"I kept your son alive. I was always a presence reminding Rakovac how dangerous it would be to go too far. It had to have had an effect."

"Maybe. Neither of us knows whether that's true."

"But you're being positive. That's what this is all about." His voice harshened. "Look, you'll see by the info on the last section of that file that it's not only the Company that is working at parting ways. Rakovac is going down a path that's dangerous for all of us. He's left his apartment in Moscow and dropped off our radar. We're trying to find him, too. We're going to have to handle him very delicately until we get to a point where we can get rid of him."

Catherine's eyes widened. "You're going to kill him."

"It's quite likely it will be necessary. If we can't work it any other way."

"You can't do that. Not yet."

"It's not going to happen tomorrow. All I'm asking is that you keep it slow and easy and not cause us to have to move prematurely."

Catherine drew a deep breath. "I'll think about it. I can't promise. I've waited too long."

"Then I may have to work at slowing you down myself," he murmured. "I'll have to see what roadblocks I can toss in your path. I know you may not believe it, but I'm on your side, Catherine. I've always wanted the best for you."

"Listen to me." Catherine's voice was shaking. "You're telling me that there's going to be an explosion between you and Rakovac, and it might be soon. I know him. If Luke is alive and has even a tiny bit of security now, that will vanish in a heartbeat the minute Rakovac breaks with Washington. I have to get him away before that happens."

"But what if you're the one who causes it to happen?" Venable asked softly. "If you're clumsy, you might push Rakovac into making the break before any of us are ready. Slowly and delicately, Catherine."

"I can't —" She stopped. "I'll try to not rupture your precious alliance with Rakovac before you're ready. Hell, I may even act as a diversion. But you can't kill Rakovac until I've found Luke. Do you understand? My son could be lost forever."

"We've always tried to keep Luke safe for you," he said. "Eve, you can see that the situation is very difficult. I repeat, it would be wise of you and Joe to stay out of it." He added wearily, "No one is trying to victimize Catherine. We're just trying to do our jobs." He hung up.

"Slow and easy," Catherine repeated bitterly, as Eve pressed the disconnect. "When that's what I've been doing for nine years. And now he wants me to stand by while they kill Rakovac. Do you know how long I've wanted Rakovac dead? I would have found a way to kill him myself if I hadn't been afraid I'd lose my link to my son. It's not going to happen. I won't permit it."

"You're upset," Eve said quietly. "Why don't you go out on the porch and relax for a while."

"No." Catherine turned back to the worktable. "I have work to do. I promised you. We have an agreement."

"It won't hurt to take a break. Don't you want to read that file?"

"I'll do it after we finish for the day." She smiled grimly. "That phone call may have been one of the roadblocks Venable was talking about putting in my way. He knew it would upset me."

"And slow you down."

She nodded. "You heard more than you wanted to hear, didn't you? You may not like secrets, but it's sometimes safer to not be privy to them."

Eve shook her head. "I don't like cocoons. I'll take honesty every time."

Catherine stared at her for a moment. "I'm grateful, you know. Ask me anything. I'll do it."

Eve smiled. "I'll think about it."

Catherine nodded. "In the meantime, no secrets. I promise. It will be difficult for me. I've lived with secrets and deceptions all my life."

"Catherine, I don't want to invade your privacy."

She shrugged. "It's the only gift I can give you right now." She turned back to the worktable. "I'm better now. My hands aren't shaking any longer. I can go back to work."

But Catherine was still in an emotional tailspin. She needed a major distraction. "I'm not ready yet." Eve got up and headed for the kitchenette. "I want a cup of coffee. What about you?"

"I don't need it."

No, Catherine wouldn't admit to any

weakness. "But do you want it?" Eve asked.

Catherine hesitated, then slowly nodded. "Yes, thank you."

Eve nodded as she pressed the coffee button. "Drag your stool around to my computer. I might as well go over the transitions I've completed while we take a break."

Catherine's eyes lit with eagerness. "Are you that close?"

"I have two more transitions before I reach the final stage." She watched Catherine's cup fill. "But I'm far enough along that you may find it interesting."

"Oh, yes. I'll definitely find it interesting." She smiled ruefully. "I'm like a kid waiting for the gates of Disney World to open."

Eve crossed the room and handed Catherine her coffee before sitting down on her stool. "I only hope my work isn't as fantasy-based as Disney. I did the best I could."

"Show me."

"I was going to skip age three, but a lot happens in that year." She pulled up the first transition of Luke at age three. "Do you see that the eyes are slightly more elongated and less rounded? The interorbital distance is almost established. The cranium had expanded to accommodate the growing brain. Look at the teeth. The maxilla and mandible have become larger and widened to allow room for his deciduous teeth."

"Deciduous?"

"Baby teeth. The changes are subtle but important."

"He already looks different. Beautiful . . . but different."

"Your Luke was a baby. That doesn't last long."

"No."

Eve saved the transition and brought up the second one. "Luke, age five."

"Dear God."

"He doesn't have a button nose any longer, the bridge of the nose rises up and lifts some of the excess skin from the medial corners of the eyes. His chin has taken shape. His face continues to elongate, the nose lengthens. The growth pattern of the hair should have become established. I kept it fine and silky and as dark as yours. I figured that there was a good chance that would be a constant."

"Constant?" She cleared her throat. "There doesn't seem to be much else that's constant in this progression. I knew in my mind that he would change, but it's still coming as a shock."

"Do you want me to stop? You said you wanted to see all the transitions."

"I did. I do. But it's not school photos. It hurts." She swallowed. "Go ahead."

She brought up the next progression. "One more. Luke, age eight. The forehead has become less prominent and bulbous-looking. But the principal changes involve the nose. The bridge continues to rise, and the nostril size and nose width increase a little. The forms of the lower cartilages of the nose become apparent, and the tip takes shape. He now has a mixture of permanent and baby teeth, and his mouth has widened to accept them." She turned to Catherine. "That's all I have right now. I'll do one transition at age nine and the final one at eleven."

Catherine didn't answer, still staring at the photo on the screen.

"Catherine?"

"I've missed so much."

"So has he."

She nodded. "He won't have any memory of me, will he?"

"Perhaps. Some memories are said to go back to the womb."

"I don't give a damn about all that womb business. I just want him to remember that I love him. What could he think? One moment I was there, and the next I'd just disappeared. He wouldn't understand." Her voice was hoarse. "Sometimes I have nightmares of Luke running in the dark searching for me. I keep calling him, but he doesn't hear me."

Eve could feel her own throat tighten with pain at the words. It came close to her own experience with her own loss. She'd had dreams of Bonnie, lost, frightened, when her daughter had first been taken. She would wake up sobbing, reaching out desperately for her little girl, who would never return. "I can't tell you what Luke will remember. I only know that if you love someone enough, it goes on forever. Maybe he loved you that much, Catherine."

Catherine didn't answer for a moment. "Maybe. He was only two, just a baby. But maybe." She lifted her shoulders as if shrugging off a weight. "We have to get back to work." She stood up and took her stool back to her former position across the worktable. "When will you be finished?"

"Tomorrow, if all goes well." She finished her coffee and set the cup on the worktable. "And I believe it's going well. I feel as if I'm beginning to know your Luke."

"Better than I do. He's almost a stranger."

"This has shaken you." Eve asked quietly, "Do you still want me to save those progressions for you?"

"Of course. I want you to print all of them out and let me look at them and get used to each one. Yes, it hurts. But maybe it won't after a little while. I don't think that it will." She looked at Eve. "I had a dream, a memory. You're bringing that memory to life. It's like . . . birth."

"A midwife, I'm not," Eve said. "I'm just a professional doing my job. If I do a good job, then we'll both be happy." She looked away from Catherine. "Now quit slacking and get to work. Actually, you're doing a pretty good job with those bones. I couldn't do better."

"That's a rare compliment. It takes concentration and patience. I've developed both of those qualities over the years. I told you I'd be good at this."

"You are. Now let's both get busy. I want to at least start this progression before Joe gets home. I want to have dinner with him. I get caught up in my work too often, and it's not healthy for our relationship. Would you like to join us?"

Catherine shook her head. "I don't want to intrude any more than I have already. Your Joe Quinn would not appreciate it."

"You're probably right. He's not unreasonable, but he's stubborn. Sometimes it takes time for him to come around."

"I've heard a lot about him from Venable. The SEALs, the FBI, and he's supposed to be a straight shooter. I think I could like him." She shrugged. "If I ever got the chance . . ."

"I saw Catherine sitting outside her tent down by the lake," Joe said as he came into the cottage. "She was reading something and pretty deep into it. I don't think she even heard me drive up."

"I'd bet she was aware of everything going on around her. She's sharp, Joe." Eve glanced at him. His brown hair was tousled, and there were a few dark drops on his khaki jacket. "Has the rain started? It's supposed to be a downpour."

"It's only sprinkling, but the wind is up." He took off his jacket. "I thought you'd be working late again."

"Maybe after dinner. I wanted to spend some time with you."

"I'm flattered," he said. "And?"

He knew her so well. "I wanted to give Catherine time to get away by herself. She had an upsetting call from Venable today."

"News about her son?"

"Not directly. But she was definitely distracted when you drove up. Venable e-mailed her the Rakovac surveillance file."

She went to the oven and pulled out the casserole. "Get out the rolls, will you?"

He didn't move. "That report on Rakovac I requested came in this afternoon. He's a very nasty customer."

"I knew that from the moment Catherine told me about his kidnapping Luke. He would have had to be a monster. I didn't need an official report." She smiled at him over her shoulder. "Though I'm very interested in what you've found out."

"That's right, you believe everything Catherine tells you," he said dryly as he got the rolls out of the bread drawer and put them on a plate. "I shouldn't expect anything else. You're thinking with your emotions where she's concerned."

"No, where Luke's concerned." She put the casserole on the table. "But I don't think that she could lie to me if it was anything pertaining to her son. I'd know if it was the truth."

"That bond again," Joe said.

"Yes, I won't deny it. It wouldn't be honest, and I'm always honest with you, Joe."

"It's a dangerous bond, Eve." He sat down in his chair at the table. "It doesn't surprise me that Rakovac has been torturing Catherine for nine years. He's slightly unhinged, and he's become an expert at inflicting pain. He grew up in the Georgian town of Tiflis and joined the fighting against the Ossetians when he was only twelve. Not that he was into the cause itself. It was an opportunity to make contacts and pull himself out of the poverty into which he was born. He was involved in several ambushes and massacres. Some involving women and children. There's a story about him burying a mother and four children alive because the father wouldn't give him information. At nineteen, he went to Moscow and established himself with the mafia. He rose quickly in the underworld and bought, sold, and blackmailed himself into a position of power." He paused. "Power is everything to him. He's a complete megalomaniac. I can see that when Catherine came close to toppling him from the top of his mountain that he would go bonkers. He's probably enjoyed every minute of the torment he's put her through. Judging by his profile, he won't ever stop."

"Then who can blame Catherine for trying to put an end to it now." Eve sat down and shook out her napkin. "Particularly since Luke may be caught in the middle if the CIA and Rakovac part ways." She picked up her fork. "Venable as much as admitted that Rakovac may soon be a CIA target."

Joe gave a low whistle. "I can't think of anyone more deserving. But unless they manage to put him down with no advance knowledge, he could cause a hell of a lot of damage."

"That's what Catherine believes. She doesn't want Luke caught in the blast." She started to eat. "She's trying to find some clue to Luke's whereabouts in that file. Venable wasn't encouraging about it."

"And what if she does find something?" Joe asked. "What's it going to mean to you?"

"I'll be glad for her," Eve said quietly. "That's all, Joe. I'm helping her all I can with the age progression. The rest is up to her." She smiled. "You don't look relieved."

"I am . . . for now." He picked up his fork. "But I also know how events can change intentions. I wanted to hear you say it. I've been watching you weave back and forth like a cobra with a snake charmer."

She chuckled. "You're calling me a snake? Not complimentary. And Catherine is making no attempt to charm me."

"I wasn't referring to Catherine as the charmer with the power," Joe said quietly. "It's the boy. He's holding you captive with a fascination far stronger than anyone else could ever have."

She couldn't argue. Every moment she spent working on Luke's age progressions was drawing her close to him. She was always involved with her reconstructions, but this was different. This was like living with a child, watching him grow beneath her fingers. It was almost as if Luke were becoming her child. "I can't help it. I don't want to help it. I have the feeling the more I become involved with Luke, the closer I can make these progressions. There's nothing more important right now."

"Look, I understand." Joe leaned toward her across the table. "I even understand Catherine Ling. But I'm damn well going to stand between you and any involvement with Luke and Catherine. I won't have Rakovac bring you down, too." He leaned back. "That's all I have to say."

"And it's nothing that I didn't expect to hear." She tilted her head, studying him. "I think you're beginning to like Catherine."

He sighed. "Is that all you got out of my little speech? I don't know Catherine well enough to like her. I prefer not to get to know her that well. I admire her endurance and strength and cleverness. I'm wary of her desperation and total ruthlessness where her son is concerned. That's a mixed bag of emotions if I ever heard of one. Now may we talk about something else?"

She nodded. "By all means." She gazed out the window as rolling thunder came from the east. "The forecast is for rain all night. Catherine would be more comfortable in here."

"I'm sure she's accustomed to that tent. She's one tough cookie."

Eve didn't answer.

"Oh, for God's sake," Joe pushed back his chair. "Okay, I'll go get her out of her tent and bring her into the house." He headed for the door. "Heat up the casserole. She might as well have dinner with us."

CHAPTER 5

Catherine looked up warily from the Rakovac surveillance file as she heard the crunch of Joe's footsteps on the stony bank. She studied him, trying to decipher his mood as he came toward her.

No anger.

Impatience?

Maybe.

But not as obvious as she'd encountered in him before.

"It's starting to rain," he said curtly. "Eve is worried about you melting. You'd better come up to the cottage."

"I'll be fine."

"That's what I told her. She knows how tough you are, but she's instinctively protective. You probably counted on that when you came to ask her for help."

"Yes, I did. But not for me, for Luke."

"Whatever. Grab some clothes and come along." He glanced at her computer. "Eve said you were reading that Rakovac e-mail. Bring it with you. You can read it after dinner."

"I'm mostly scanning, hoping something will jump out at me."

"Good luck. From what I've found out about Rakovac, he's pretty clever."

"It's been a long time since he took Luke. He must have made blunders somewhere along the way."

"Then you can find them after we put Eve's mind at rest and we feed you and tuck you in. I figure we have less than five minutes before the rain starts. I've no desire to get soaking wet and have to change before dinner."

But he didn't really mind the weather, she could tell. The wind was blowing his hair back from his face and his tea-colored eyes were glittering in his tan face. He looked a little wild and stormy himself. "Then go back before you get caught."

He shook his head. "She wants you."

"And you always give her what she wants?"

"When I can. She doesn't ask much. I wish I could give her more."

"I think you probably give her a good deal. Does she do the same?"

"We have a relationship we both have to

work at. That's natural." He frowned. "Stop asking questions and let's get out of here."

She shook her head. "You don't want me. I won't put you in a position in which you're forced to accept me. That will just make you resent me more. I can't afford to have that happen."

"I'm not forced. I wouldn't be here if I didn't want to be. Spending a few hours with you isn't going to affect me one way or another." He paused. "And it will keep Eve from going right back to work and give her a little rest. That's always a plus."

She smiled. "It could be an uneasy evening."

He shook his head. "Not for me. And I think you probably got over being uneasy about anything when you left the cradle."

"Not very much later."

A lightning bolt streaked out of the sky, and a crash of thunder echoed across the lake.

Joe held out his hand. "Come, dammit."

She hesitated, then jumped to her feet. She disappeared into her tent and grabbed her duffel. A moment later, she was outside, and Joe was grabbing her elbow and running toward the cottage. The heavens had opened, and the rain was pelting them as they dashed for the porch. It felt strange having a man's hand helping her, supporting her, even in such a small thing. She had been on her own for such a long time, asking nothing, depending on her own strength.

She didn't pull away. It felt . . . nice.

"Okay?" Joe asked her, as they reached the front door. He wasn't even a little breathless, she noticed. He looked strong and reckless and was as charged as the lightning flashes across the lake.

"Of course." She pulled her arm away. "It's only a storm." She ran her hand through her damp hair. "I like it."

He nodded. "I thought you would." He opened the front door. "I would have been disappointed in you if you hadn't. Or rather in my own judgment. Eve sees you as a mother and victim. I see you as a warrior and a mover and shaker. I'd say we're both right. At any rate, we're already learning about each other."

"Yes." She couldn't deny that she had seen a new side of Joe Quinn in these last minutes. He was right, the learning process had begun.

And one of the things she had learned was that for the first time, she could see the magnetism that had drawn Eve to Joe and held them together these many years. She had experienced it herself as he had stood before her outside her tent. It had shocked and piqued her curiosity. It was the first stirring of physical interest she had experienced since Terry had died. It was odd that it had happened at this weird time and circumstance. Perhaps it was because her entire life was in a state of upheaval and change.

Yes, it was odd and completely unacceptable. Dismiss it. Whatever future relationship she was going to have with Joe Quinn, it would not be anything that would interfere with the bond she and Eve were forming. That tentative friendship was too precious and rare to risk being destroyed.

Joe gestured for her to precede him. "Go in. I'll find a towel so that you can dry your hair."

"You need one yourself." She walked past him into the cottage.

Eve looked at her with a smile. "You took long enough. I knew you'd give Joe an argument. But he always perseveres."

Catherine watched Joe disappear into the bathroom in search of that towel. "I can see that." She turned back to Eve and asked brusquely, "There are wonderful smells drifting from the kitchen. What can I do to help?"

■ ■ ■ ■

"It's still pouring," Eve said as she leaned back in the porch swing and gazed out at the veil of rain enclosing them. "See, Catherine. You're much better off here for the night."

"If you say so." Catherine lifted her cup of coffee to her lips. "I spent most of the last year in a tent in the jungle. I would have survived." She smiled. "But just surviving isn't macaroni casserole and a warm, cozy home. I enjoyed dinner. Thank you for having me. I should be grateful for the storm. I *am* grateful."

"That's saying something since I had to blast you away from that tent." Joe was leaning against the porch rail a few yards away. "More coffee?"

"Yes." Catherine jumped to her feet. "But I'll get it. You've waited on me enough for one day. I'm not accustomed to it." She headed for the door. "Joe? Eve?"

"Not for me," Joe said.

"I'll take another cup," Eve said. "I need the caffeine. I want to work an hour or two more tonight."

"Good. I'll join you." Catherine disappeared into the house.

"You'll probably both be working until dawn." Joe's gaze had followed Catherine as she'd gone into the house. "And through no manipulation by Catherine. Amazing."

"She's trying to be fair," Eve said. "It's difficult for her. She wants so desperately to forge ahead." She lifted her cup to her lips. "She didn't mention Luke or Rakovac once this evening." Catherine had spoken of her life growing up in Hong Kong, her years working for the CIA, her last job trying to rescue the Winters father and daughter. She had led a bizarre and colorful existence, and her recounting of it had been matter-of-fact and completely without self-pity. Eve had gotten an entirely different view of her. Tough, cynical, she certainly was, but there was a humanity that tempered that hardness. "It must have been difficult for her. I know that must be all that's on her mind now."

"But she's smart enough to know that overwhelming melancholy is hard to live with. Instead, we're seeing her as a complete, balanced person." He paused. "And, therefore, worthy of any help she needs."

"You're thinking she's that calculating?" She shook her head. "Bullshit. You're fighting it, but you don't believe she's that cold. Admit it, you like her."

He chuckled. "How could I help it? She made sure we both saw her tonight as warm and human, even vulnerable. Yes, I like her. But I won't discount the fact that she's clever as hell and has the potential for being a ticking time bomb."

"Neither will I," Eve said. "But you have to accept her as a complete package."

"Remember that when you're melting with sympathy. She's . . . complicated."

"Is that why you were watching her all through dinner? You've never appreciated the simple in anything."

"I was staring at her because she's very watchable. In case you haven't noticed, she's damn good-looking. She's a cross between Lucy Liu and Angelina Jolie with megawattage thrown into the mix. It's hard not to look at her."

"I noticed." But she felt a ripple of surprise that Joe had admitted to being conscious of that attractiveness when he was clearly so wary. "But I don't think that she's aware of it."

"Oh, she's aware of it." His lips twisted. "It's a weapon, and Catherine would know how to use it if it became necessary. She knows all about weapons. Perhaps it's just not a weapon of choice."

She nodded thoughtfully. "You may be

right. She's had to live in a man's world, and that kind of weapon would end in a sexual battle. I can't see her using sex to beat out an opponent. She'd regard it as beneath her."

"You think you know her that well?"

She shrugged. "As well as I can under the circumstances. We all have instincts about people. My instincts say that she saw her mother as a sexual victim and she would never want to engage anyone on that particular battlefield. And growing up in the streets, she must have been exposed to all kinds of vice. It just shows how strong she is that she overcame that twisted background enough to marry and have a child." She added softly, "A beautiful child, Joe. The older he gets, the more he looks like Catherine. I'll show you the progressions if you like."

"I'll wait until you finish. You're already besotted with the kid. That's almost more dangerous than your liking for Catherine."

"But you said you liked her, too." She smiled. "And that logical, analytical mind of yours would like to take her apart and put her back together again to see how she ticks."

"That leads to thoughts of ticking bombs." He inclined his head. "I'm curious, and I don't mind being the one to defuse her. Better me than you."

"I'd mind. I don't want either you or her to be hurt."

He lifted his cup to her in a half salute. "As you command. Then I'll try to restrain my curiosity . . . within limits."

"Curiosity?" Catherine stood in the doorway with a carafe of coffee in her hand. "Have you been talking about me, Joe Quinn?"

"Yes. Though Eve and I do have other things to discuss than you."

"But I'm the new comet on the scene." She came toward them and filled Eve's cup. "And I'm a very flashy comet. I've disturbed your lives, and naturally I'd be the center of attention." She filled her own cup and set it on the swing before turning to Joe. "Go ahead. Ask your questions. I promised Eve I'd have no secrets from her." She crossed to stand before him, and said challengingly, "Try me."

He smiled faintly. "What bravado. Wouldn't you be deflated if I said I just wasn't interested?"

"But you are. I overheard the word 'curious.' " She topped off the coffee in his cup and turned back to the swing and sat down beside Eve. "You're a detective. You have an inquiring mind. It goes with the territory. I tried to be open with you at dinner. Not enough?"

"I found myself wondering about a few things."

"What?"

"Your relationship with Venable and the CIA. Why are you still working with them? They wouldn't help you search for your son. You should have been furious with them."

"I was. I still am. They did try to find him, but when they couldn't locate him, they refused to go any further. They wouldn't go after Rakovac." She took a drink of her coffee. "I resented it with all my being."

"But you still continued to work for them."

"Because I knew my time would come." She gazed at him. "And, bitter as I feel, I understand who they are and where they're coming from. When I'm able to think about it sanely, it's exactly what I'd expect from them. Venable thinks that he recruited me all those years ago. He's wrong. I went after that job with all the determination I put into everything I do. I had a choice. Either continue in the path I'd started or walk a different road. I was tired of fighting the scum on their level. I wanted to be one of the good guys."

"There are those who would give you an argument about the CIA's good-guy quotient."

"Because they haven't been on the other side. How do you keep to some idealistic set of rules when your opponent has no rules? It's a complicated world, and someone is always trying to destroy it in one way or the other. The only thing we can do is try to keep it intact. That way it has a chance of building itself back into something worthwhile." She shrugged. "Sometimes it gets dirty and ragged while we're doing it. That's too bad, but it happens. Sometimes, important, personal things get pushed aside."

"Like your son," Eve said.

She nodded. "But there's no way in hell I can see past Luke to the big picture. He *is* the big picture." She glanced at Joe. "You were FBI at one time. One of those white knights bound by law and rules and structure, but I'd bet there were times when you felt like breaking every one of them." She leaned forward, her gaze fixed intently on his face. "Am I wrong?"

He was silent a moment. "No."

"And you had the U.S. courts backing you."

"Sometimes."

"Well, most of the time the CIA has backing when it's a popular cause and none when it's a less publicized mission to some Podunk country most citizens never knew existed. But we do our job anyway."

"We? In spite of everything, you're still aligning yourself with them."

"They would have helped me if they could. Hell, Venable might not have freed Luke, but he might have saved his life." Her lips twisted. "They are good guys. They just wear black hats."

"Interesting reasoning," Eve said as she looked at Joe. "Complicated enough, Joe?"

"Actually, I understand her viewpoint perfectly," he murmured. "I'm sure the complications are all under the surface."

"Any other questions?" Catherine asked.

"I'm thinking," Joe said. "There may be something I'd like to —"

Catherine's cell phone rang.

"Excuse me." She pulled the phone out of her pocket. "It's probably Venable wondering if I read —" She inhaled sharply as she gazed at the ID. "No, it's not Venable." She moistened her lips. "It's Rakovac."

"Are you sure?" Joe asked. "Criminals don't usually broadcast their IDs on —"

"Oh, it's him. He always wants me to know and dread what's coming."

Fear. Eve could see the tension and fear in every line of Catherine's body. "Would you like us to leave?"

"No, I told you, no secrets. Rakovac couldn't be more a part of my life. You might as well meet him." She pressed the speaker amplifier. "Hello, Rakovac. I haven't heard from you for a while."

"Have you missed me? I've missed you." Rakovac's mocking voice was deep and only faintly accented. "Don't think because I've not been in touch that you've been forgotten. These years have woven you into the fabric of my life." He paused. "You and Luke."

"Why are you calling?"

"Because I sense that you're not being your usual meek self. I thought it was time you and I had a talk and reestablished my position in your life."

"I know exactly what your position is. You're the devil who needs to be sent straight back to hell."

He laughed. "I don't mind being compared to Satan. He has power, and he knows how to manipulate things to suit himself. I'm glad you've noticed how clever I am in that area. But you usually hold your tongue. Another sign that there may be a rebellion in the wings."

"Why are you calling?" she repeated through set teeth.

"You know I always keep track of you. That was an amazing rescue of the Winters girl. I've been wondering if you managed to reap a reward from your friend Venable."

"You know he won't touch you."

"I've made sure of any dire consequences. But you're such a valuable tool for him. He might have given you a small gift in return."

"What are you getting at?"

"Isn't there a song about a rainy night in Georgia?"

She stiffened. "I don't know what you mean."

"Yes, you do. You just had a cozy dinner with your newfound friends. Do you really think that Eve Duncan can help you, Catherine?"

Her gaze flew to the darkness beyond the porch. "You have someone here watching me?"

"Of course, I always keep my eye on you. And no, there's no use trying to track him down. I pulled him out as soon as I had the information I wanted. Now tell me about Eve Duncan."

She was silent a moment. "I hired her to do an age progression on Luke. I'm a mother. I want to know what my little boy looks like."

"Touching. What a sentimental motive."

"Every mother is sentimental about her child. You've played on that emotion for years. You shouldn't be surprised."

"Oh, I'm not surprised. I knew when I took your cub away from you that even a tigress loves her offspring. That's why you've given me such joy. Strike at the child, and it makes you go through a living hell."

"I wanted to see what he looks like," she repeated.

"But perhaps not for sentimental reasons. Are you thinking of taking my toy away from me?"

"You've seen that I have no chance of doing that. After all this time, why would I even make the attempt?"

"Desperation?"

"I'd never risk Luke. You've told me enough times what you'd do to him if I tried anything."

"Perhaps. Sometimes one can become calloused and numb to a constant threat."

"I'm not numb."

"No, I keep you raw and bleeding, don't I? But I find it interesting you chose Duncan to do the age progression. Her fame lies in another direction."

"She's very good."

"But she's better with her skulls. I've decided that it must have been fate that led you to her."

"Fate?"

He said softly, "You'll have need of a reconstruction, not an age progression."

Catherine inhaled sharply. "You're lying."

"No, I killed Luke when he was five years old. Venable was getting too persistent about releasing him, and I grew angry. No one can tell me what to do. I shot your son in the head and buried him in the woods. He was frightened and crying. He knew about guns and what they could do. I'd had him taught about them from the time I took him."

Catherine closed her eyes. "I don't believe you. You've told me you've killed him before, then said you were lying. You're just trying to hurt me."

"It's a possibility." He added maliciously, "But you can't be sure. You haven't talked to him. You have only me to rely on for any information about Luke. I control him. I control you."

"He's alive. I know it."

"He's buried in the woods. If it suits me, I may dig him up and send his skull to Eve Duncan. I'll have to think about it."

"You bastard," Catherine whispered.

"Or send word to Venable where he can find him. Why shouldn't he do the work? He and his cohorts in Washington have been irritating me lately."

"You're lying."

"What if I'm not? I think you'll have nightmares tonight envisioning Luke scared and crying right before I shot him." He chuckled. "Go ahead. Work on that age progression. But don't take it past five years. It would be totally futile." He hung up.

Eve reached out. "Catherine, I know —"

"Don't touch me. Not yet." She huddled sidewise, leaning on the arm of the porch swing. "I'm . . . hurting." Her voice was shaking. "I'm sorry. I don't like you to — Give me time . . ."

Good Lord, she was hurting, Eve thought. Her back was arched, and Eve could almost feel the vibrations of the agony she was emitting.

"Is there anything I can do?"

"No."

"Screw it." Joe was suddenly kneeling before Catherine, taking her in his arms. "I will touch you. Stop trying to handle it on your own. You need us."

"I don't —" She suddenly collapsed against him, her arms clinging desperately. "I'm sorry." Her voice was muffled against him. "You'd think I'd be able to handle it by this time. But he knows just where and how to — I've got to stop this. It's what he wants, what he expects." Her voice was shaking. "He was lying, you know. Every now and then, he'll tell me he's killed Luke. I think he saves it for when he's feeling in the mood for a particularly savage turn of the knife. But he has to be lying, doesn't he? But I don't know. I don't know."

"No, you don't know," Eve said quietly. "But you have a chance of its not being true. He's such a bastard that I can't imagine that he'd give up the value of a live hostage with whom he can taunt you for the momentary pleasure of a kill."

"That's what I tell myself. Sometimes I believe it." She drew a long, shaky breath and pushed Joe away. "I'm okay. I'm sorry I fell apart like that. Thank you."

He leaned back on his heels. "You're welcome." He gazed searchingly at her face. "You're pale, drained. I think you need to drink that coffee."

"I agree." She picked up her cup. "Or something stiffer." She glanced at Eve. "He was particularly ugly tonight. He didn't like me coming to you."

"Tough. I don't know how you kept from blowing up at him."

"Think about it. He taught me well to hold my tongue. Every time I'd grow angry and say something he didn't like he'd threaten Luke. That was one of the hardest things to bear." She took a long drink of coffee. "And one he enjoys the most. He told me once that as long as he holds Luke, I'm his slave. He loves the control over me."

"And he evidently embroiders his stories of Luke in detail," Joe said. "A five-year-old familiar with guns. Unusual."

"He meant that he'd threatened Luke with weapons."

"Is that what he meant? Or was it something else?"

Catherine shook her head. "He lies. I can't tell what's true and what's not." Her grip tightened on the cup. "Except about Luke's being dead. He's not dead. Why would he worry if I found out what my son looked like? Why would he try to discourage me?" She added bitterly, "And, yes, I know there's no telling why Rakovac would do anything. The son of a bitch is crazy."

"According to the dossier I pulled on him, he may be a little unbalanced, but he's clever," Joe said. "And I think he had a purpose other than wanting to toy with you."

"I do, too," Eve said. "And I believe I'll

thumb my nose at him and finish that progression ASAP." She finished her coffee and stood up. "I'll start the dishwasher, then hit the computer."

"I'll go with you," Catherine said quickly.

Eve shook her head as she moved toward the door. "Give yourself a few minutes. Your hands are shaking. I don't want you touching Cindy yet."

"Yes, ma'am," Catherine said.

Eve suddenly grinned as she paused at the door. "When was the last time you said that?"

"Never," Catherine said. "I'm not very obedient, and I don't know many women."

"I thought so. It sounded a little awkward." Eve went into the house.

"She's right." Joe was smiling with amusement. "You're very articulate, but that did sound awkward."

"This entire situation is awkward for me," Catherine said. "I had to beg Eve to do this progression for me. I've never begged anyone for anything before." Her lips twisted. "Except Rakovac. I begged him to return Luke. He laughed at me."

"And Eve listened and helped you. Do you resent her having that kind of power over you?"

"No, of course —" She stopped. "Maybe. I don't have a generous spirit. I want it all. I want to keep my pride and still get everything I want."

"That's understandable. I'd say everyone has that philosophy."

"Do you?"

He thought about it. "I have almost everything I want. A job I like, my adopted daughter, Jane, Eve . . ."

"Almost," she repeated. "What else, Joe?"

He didn't answer.

She tilted her head, studying him. "Maybe . . . an Eve with no obsession about finding her daughter's killer?"

"I didn't say that."

"Because you'd never be disloyal to Eve in any way. Still, you might consider that a breach in the relationship if she closes you out. I can see how you might come to resent it. Obsession is a terrible and all-consuming thing." She shrugged. "Who should know better? I'm just as obsessed as Eve. Though I'm lucky, I'm alone. I don't have to worry about anyone else."

"Really? Are you lucky, Catherine?"

She gazed at him standing there, leaning against the railing. Slim hips, broad shoulders, tea-colored eyes staring intently at her; mature, intelligent, with a quietness that could mask power and leashed recklessness.

"Are you lucky to be alone, Catherine?" he repeated.

She had a sudden memory of Joe holding her, warm, strong, absorbing all the pain that Rakovac had inflicted.

"No." She jumped to her feet. "But I don't know anything else, and at least I'm not hurting anyone." She avoided his eyes as she headed for the door. "I've got to help Eve. Thanks for being there for me tonight. I'll try not to fall apart again."

"No problem."

She had an inkling there was definitely a problem. Being with Joe Quinn was making her aware of what she was missing. Eve and Joe had a relationship that was like a deep, strong river and yet Catherine could see the exciting rapids that still ran through it. She had never known a relationship with that intensity. She had loved Terry, but it had been a comfortable affection comprised of gratitude and common likes and dislikes. They had both wanted a home and child and passion had not been that important.

Eve and Joe had passion. A passion for each other and a passion for their life together. They didn't display it blatantly, but every glance revealed it.

She wanted that passion for living. She

was tired of just surviving.

Good Lord, was she jealous?

No, that would mean she wanted to take something from them to keep for herself, and she would never do that. This emotion was a sort of poignant wistfulness all the more powerful for the unexpectedness of its appearance in her life.

She would not steal, but perhaps she could watch and learn.

Joe was no longer looking at her. He had moved to the steps and was starting down them. Wind was whipping his clothes to his body, and he was drenched in seconds.

"Where are you going?" she asked, startled.

"I thought I'd take a look around to see if I can locate Rakovac's scout."

"He said he pulled him once he reported."

"Why should I believe he's telling the truth any more than you do?" He smiled recklessly. "I think I'll see if he lied about that, too. I'm probably going to bat zero, but I'll at least be able to work off some stored energy. I don't like the idea of someone out there on my property."

Before she could respond, he had vanished into the heavy veil of rain.

CHAPTER 6

2:35 a.m.

"You're tired," Eve said. "Why don't you go to bed?"

"Not until you do." Catherine looked up. "I have almost a quarter of this face done. I didn't think I'd get this far so quickly. I'm very proud of myself."

"That's two of us. I'm proud of you, too. I wasn't sure that you'd be able to do it. It's one hell of a difficult job."

Catherine nodded. "It takes concentration." She smiled. "And study. I know more than I ever wanted to know about the bones of the human face." Her smile faded. "You say Cindy was buried at least ten years ago. Does it take that long in the ground to turn a body into . . . this?"

"It depends on the circumstances and conditions. Sometimes shorter, sometimes longer." She studied Catherine's face. "You're thinking of what Rakovac said about killing Luke and burying his body in the woods."

"I try not to remember. But I do. How can I help it?"

"You can't. It's impossible." Her lips tightened. "What a sadistic bastard. What other things has he taunted you with over the years?"

"Do you want a list? Sometimes it amused him to tell me how he tortured Luke. He made me listen as he described the most horrible atrocities imaginable." She shuddered. "I nearly went crazy. The only way I could survive was to tell myself over and over that it was all lies. That he wouldn't have dared to do anything to Luke while Venable knew he was holding him. It might have disturbed the status quo of their relationship." She added hoarsely, "I had to believe that, or I would have slit my throat. I kept thinking if I were dead, there wouldn't be any reason for him to hurt Luke. And then I would think if he was still alive, I had to live, or Rakovac would have him forever." She shook her head and glanced back down at the bones in front of her. "But you don't want to hear this. I've been moaning since I came into your life. I didn't do it to make you feel sorry for me. Being who you are and what you've been through, that's a given. That's just my life right now."

"You didn't offer," Eve said. "If I hadn't wanted an answer, I wouldn't have asked."

"Let's change the subject. How long before I see my Luke?"

"I'll start the last transition tomorrow. I can't wait either."

She nodded. "He's got you, hasn't he?" Her face was suddenly luminous. "You can see what kind of wonderful little boy he is. I used to look at him when he was sleeping and think how lucky I was to have a child like Luke. He was different from other children, full of love, full of mischief, smart. I know every mother thinks her child is special, but it's true. He was only two, and he spoke like a five-year-old. And he was beautiful, you can tell how beautiful he is."

"Yes, he's very beautiful," she said gently. "He must be a good deal like you."

She shook her head. "He's nothing like me. There may be a little resemblance, but inside he's different. From the time I was a toddler, I was always looking for the way to fight my way to the top. I didn't care how. I had to survive. From the moment he was out of the cradle, Luke was always caring and giving."

"Because he had a mother who adored him, and was surrounded by love."

"People are born with souls. His soul was special. Sometimes he seemed to be lit from within."

Like the face of Catherine when she spoke of her son, Eve thought. "I'm sure he's all you say he is."

Catherine suddenly smiled. "You're being very soothing. I know I'm besotted. But it's true. It's all true. He was like —"

A banging at the front door.

Eve's gaze flew across the room. For heaven's sake, it was after two in the morning.

"Don't answer it." Catherine was gliding across the room to her duffel. "Rakovac had someone here watching. Maybe his orders weren't only to watch."

"Joe said he thought that Rakovac's man had taken off. He saw the tire prints. If he was still out there, Joe would have found him."

"Oh, I believe Joe is very efficient. But Rakovac's men are good. Better to be safe." She drew her gun out of the duffel and headed toward the door. "Stand back. I'll take —"

"You can see the front of the porch from the window left of the door," Eve said as she slipped from her stool. Her heart was pounding, hard. "Just stay away from the glass in case someone decides to take a shot."

"I'm not stupid," Catherine said. "Go wake up Joe. We may need him."

"I'm not leaving you alone," Eve said. "This is my house, and I should be the one repelling intruders. And Joe's a light sleeper. He probably heard that pounding. It was loud enough."

"Have it your way," Catherine was to the left of the window carefully moving the curtains, her gun ready. "Just don't come close to the door. A spray from an AK-47 could blast it off its hinges."

"I've seen what one can do. I'm not about to go in harm's way. What do you see out —"

"Oh, shit." Catherine dropped the curtain, strode to the door and jerked it open.

"What the hell are you doing here?"

Eve frowned in puzzlement as she moved forward to get a glimpse of the person at the door.

Not person, a young girl. A small, fair-haired girl in blue jeans and pine green sweatshirt dotted with dark drops of rain.

"I had to come," the girl whispered. "I couldn't stay with my mother."

"What am I going to do with you?" Catherine said helplessly. "You can't stay here,

Kelly. You shouldn't have come."

"Who is she?" Eve came to the door to stand beside Catherine. The girl wasn't as young as she had first thought. She must be at least entering her teens. She was just small and extremely fine boned. "What is she doing here?"

"She's Kelly Winters." Catherine was glancing down the road. "See those taillights about a mile away? I'd bet she was dropped off on your doorstep." Her lips tightened. "Only it's meant to be my doorstep."

Kelly Winters. The young girl who had been kidnapped that Catherine had told her about, Eve realized. No wonder she appeared so fragile and haunted. "Well, I don't care what was meant or not meant. This is my home, and I won't have her stand out there in the rain while you decide what to do with her." She held out her hand to the girl. "I'm Eve Duncan, Kelly. Come in."

Kelly's gaze was fastened on Catherine. "May I?"

"Oh, for Pete's sake." Catherine threw up her hands. "Okay. Come in, but you can't stay. You shouldn't even be here."

"I'm glad that's decided." Joe was coming up the porch steps. He was barefoot, without a shirt, soaked to the skin, and clearly in a foul mood. "Get her inside."

"You slipped out the bedroom window and came around the front?" Eve guessed.

"It seemed the thing to do at the time. I didn't realize that it was only a kid who was trying to get in from the storm." He held up his hand as Catherine started to speak. "At the moment, I don't care why she's here. Now that I know that it's not one of Rakovac's men or a midget with bombs strapped to her chest, I'm opting out. I just want to get her inside and hit a hot shower and get on some dry clothes. She's your problem. Settle it yourself. Preferably before I get out of the shower." He strode past Kelly and went into the house.

"He's angry," Kelly said.

"He's disappointed," Eve said. "Joe has the instincts of a gladiator. For the second time tonight, he was all primed to step into the arena and take care of a massive threat. Instead, it turned out to be you. He'll be fine after he relaxes and lets the adrenaline stop ruling him."

The girl shook her head. "I didn't want to make him —"

"Kelly, be quiet and come in." Catherine pulled her inside and shut the door. "It's done. Now all I want is to know what's happening. Who dropped you off and ran like a thief in the night? Venable?"

She shook her head. "Agent Dufour. But Venable told him to bring me."

"Why?" Catherine shook her head. "And why am I even asking? He's manipulating the situation to suit himself. He thought if he'd throw you into the fray, that I'd —"

"No." Kelly shook her head. "I made him do it. I told him I'd run away if he didn't tell me where you were."

"And Venable couldn't handle the threat from one small girl?" Catherine asked. "I don't think that's true." She turned on her heel and went into the kitchenette. "Where's the cocoa, Eve? Do you have any around here? She needs something hot and sweet. She's shivering."

"I'm okay," Kelly said. "I'm only a little wet. I had to run from the car to the porch."

"The cocoa's in the first cabinet. It's instant. Use the hot water from the coffee-maker," Eve said. She smiled slightly as she watched Catherine take down the box. There was frustration and anger in every line of the woman's body, but even through the aggravation, she was still trying to take care of the young girl. "I'll get her a towel for her hair." She headed down the hall to the linen closet. When she returned with the towel, Kelly was sitting at the bar, a mug of chocolate in front of her and a warm throw around her.

"I'll do it." Catherine took the towel and enveloped Kelly's head with the cloth and rubbed vigorously but gently. Then she stepped back and threw the towel on the barstool. "Now drink your chocolate."

Kelly didn't touch the mug in front of her. She just sat there staring at Catherine.

"Don't sit there looking at me," Catherine said. "I told you that I can't help you. I'd take you in if I could, but you came to me at the worst time possible. Hell, the whole world wants to help you, Kelly. I'm the wrong one to pick."

"I'm not going to get in your way. I won't be any trouble. I'll help you." She paused. "We need to help each other."

"You can't help me."

"Yes, I can." She hesitated. "I'm smart, Catherine. Very smart. That's why my mother doesn't want me around. Daddy said that she had an idea of what she wanted in a daughter, and I wasn't it. I make her uncomfortable. I try to hide it, but sometimes it tumbles out. But maybe you can use me." Her lips firmed. "No, not maybe, I'll make sure you can do it."

"You can't help me," Catherine repeated.

"Venable told me that you're looking for your son. He told me all about it. I'll help you find him."

Catherine muttered an oath beneath her breath. "He had no business telling you anything. You're a kid, for heaven's sake."

Kelly shook her head. "I don't feel like a kid."

"That damn Munoz. I told you that you shouldn't let what he did make you —" She shook her head. "What am I saying? It's your father. His death alone was enough to make a big change in you." She shrugged. "And you may not feel like a kid, but it's the responsibility of the adults around you to recognize that you still have the right not to have to confront adult problems."

"Do I have that right?" Kelly gave her the ghost of a smile. "Did you, Catherine? Not according to what Venable told me."

"Did he give you my life history?" Catherine asked in disgust. "I can see him doing that. He wouldn't care that you have problems of your own."

Eve could see Catherine's irritation growing by the moment. She wasn't angry at Kelly so much as the situation, but Kelly might misinterpret. Time to step into the picture. "Kelly, you were supposed to go to your mother's after you left the hospital. What happened? I can't believe she wouldn't be concerned."

"She was concerned," Kelly said. "But she didn't want to deal with me. After the social worker explained what had happened and all the care and attention she should pay me for the next few months, she panicked. She set her secretary to trying to find a good rehabilitation home to stash me in for the next few months." She added quietly, "She's not a monster. It would have been a fine, luxurious rehabilitation home with wonderful psychiatrists. But I wouldn't have been able to take it. And there's no way I could persuade her not to send me there. She's always sure she's right when she wants something badly enough."

"Bitch," Catherine said.

Kelly shook her head. "No. You don't understand. She doesn't mean any harm. She just wants me to go away."

"She's your mother," Eve said.

"Maybe the stork got the babies confused." She met Eve's gaze. "Don't pity me. Because sometimes I want her to go away, too. Does that make me a terrible person?"

"It makes you human," Eve said gently.

She nodded. "That's what Daddy said. But Daddy was angry with her most of the time himself, so I couldn't be sure."

"Be sure," Catherine said. "So you called Venable, and he came and picked you up?"

"He didn't want to do it. He argued with me. He even hung up on me. But he called back. He said he'd thought about it, and my place was with you."

"After he realized that you'd be the perfect roadblock to my plans," Catherine said dryly. "He threatened to do everything he could to stop me from upsetting their plans for Rakovac. Then here you come, and it's a golden opportunity."

Kelly nodded. "You're probably right. He was kind to me, but I think he may be a devious man. But I didn't care, he gave me what I wanted."

"A trip to Atlanta and the chance to be dumped on Eve's doorstep."

"Yes, and he promised to talk to my mother and convince her that he'd placed me in a secure home where I would receive excellent therapy." She smiled wistfully. "It won't take much to convince her. It's what she wants to hear."

"Eve's home may be secure, but I'm leaving it within the next few days," Catherine said. "And I'm as far from being a therapist as I could possibly be. I'm pretty screwed up myself right now. I could strangle Venable."

"You're not screwed up. You're one of the sanest people I've ever met."

"Your experience is limited." She pushed the mug closer to Kelly. "Drink your chocolate. Then we'll talk about where you're going to spend the next six months."

"Here, with you."

"I can't take care of you."

"I don't want you to care for me. I want breathing space until I can figure a way to run my life myself." She lifted her chocolate to her lips. "I think the best thing for me would be to go and stay at school. I attend the College of William and Mary in Virginia. Then no one would have to bother with me."

"A college?" Eve said. "But you're only fourteen."

"I'm very smart. All the professors decided that I should be at a think tank. Some of them wanted to send me to Harvard, but Daddy said he didn't want me at a place with that high, edgy profile. He thought the pressure would be less on me in a Southern school. I like it okay there." She paused. "Daddy told me that I was going to be all right as far as money was concerned. He set up some kind of trust for me. But public opinion matters to my mother, and she wouldn't let a bank be my guardian. I'm too young, and she'd get a lot of bad press. But if enough time passes, maybe I can work it out."

"Then perhaps Venable could persuade your mother to send you to school instead of a rehabilitation home," Catherine said. "I'll get on the phone and talk to him."

"It won't do any good. She won't give in while there are still media stories about me. And you said that Venable wants me here. He's not going to help you."

"No, heaven forbid that he gives me a break." Catherine drew a deep breath. "Kelly, being with me wouldn't be good for you. If I thought anything else, I'd take a chance and let you stay with me. But it might even be dangerous. Venable knew that, and he still sent you. I can find you a safe place. I know a lot of people who owe me favors."

Kelly smiled slightly. "Did you save their lives, too?"

"Look, I'm not some saintly do-gooder. I only went into Munoz's camp because Venable and I had made a deal."

"I don't care. And I don't think you're a saint. I made Venable tell me all about you. He told me about Eve, too, so I wouldn't be upset seeing bones from her reconstruction lying around."

"Then, blast it, why did you come to me?"

"I like you," she said simply. "I feel . . . at

home with you. I don't have to pretend. You don't pity me, and if you find I can help, you'll let me earn my way. That's important to me right now."

Catherine stared at her helplessly. "Kelly."

"Let her stay the night," Eve said quietly. "It's no use arguing with her. You're not going to toss her out in the rain. You've both had your say. Now you can both let everything simmer until morning."

"Let? Me? This isn't even my house. I'm not going to impose her on you. If she stays, we'll both go down to my tent for the night."

"You will not," Eve said firmly. "It's raining. Rakovac's man may still be wandering around out there. I'd worry too much to sleep, and I'm much too selfish to permit you to do that. You can have the guest bedroom, and Kelly can sleep on the couch." She turned to Kelly. "I presume you brought a suitcase."

Kelly nodded. "It's on the porch." She got off the stool and headed for the door. "I'll go get it."

Catherine turned to Eve. "I never meant this to happen."

"I know. Life has a way of slipping in the unexpected just when we have everything neatly planned." She looked after Kelly, who had gone out on the porch. "But it may not be safe to send her away now. If you're still under surveillance, Rakovac will probably soon know about her and that she followed you here. Maybe he'll think you have affection for her. Couldn't that be dangerous?"

Catherine nodded. "Yes, dammit."

"Then you have a big problem, and you'll have to work with it." She smiled at Kelly as she came back into the house. "Catherine will show you the bathroom while I make up the couch for you."

"Thank you." Kelly hesitated. "I don't want to be a bother, Ms. Duncan. I had to come, but I never meant you to have to —"

"Eve," she interrupted. "And I wouldn't have told you to stay if you weren't welcome. But it's late, and we all need to get to sleep. We'll settle everything in the morning. Good night, Kelly."

"Good night, Eve." Her voice was low and uneven. She turned to Catherine. "I'll make it right. I promise. Just give me a chance."

"Tomorrow." Catherine led her across the living room toward the bathroom. "I'm not about to give you any encouragement. I like you, I want to help you, but you're going to be a headache, and I have to find a remedy." She opened the door of the bathroom and turned on the light. "I'll see you in the morning. Try to get some sense into your stubborn —" She broke off as she saw Kelly's expression. She was not crying, but she was very close. "Don't look like that." She pulled her close in a quick, hard hug and let her go. "Your mother is an idiot and doesn't deserve you. Which doesn't mean I'm going to give in to this idiocy. I just thought you should know that I'm your friend, and I'll find a way to get you what you need." She turned away. "Not necessarily what you want."

"They're one and the same," Kelly said unevenly. "And I think you'll see that you need me, too. I can help you find your son. I'm smart. I see patterns. Just let me show you."

"No, you may want to help, but I'm alone in this. Good night, Kelly." She shut the bathroom door and turned and went back to Eve. "Do you need help making up that couch?"

Eve shook her head. "It's almost done. The couch practically makes into a bed with the press of a button. I'm not much of a housekeeper, so I made sure everything around me is easy. Life is too difficult to have to work at the little things." She stepped back and put a blanket on the foot of the bed. "That should be comfortable. Not that the poor kid will notice. She was almost numb with exhaustion."

"She wasn't too exhausted to manipulate her way into staying here tonight."

"She tried to be honest with you."

"I know," Catherine said wearily. "Probably because she knew that I wouldn't accept anything else." She shook her head. "Or maybe not. Maybe that's her nature. I'm pretty cynical. I haven't known her for long."

"Long enough for her to trust you."

"She would have trusted the devil himself if he could have gotten her away from Munoz."

"Possibly," Eve said. "But I prefer to think the kid has excellent instincts. What is all this patterns business?"

"I'm not sure. Venable only said that she was brilliant and disturbingly inquisitive." She reached for her phone and put it on speaker. "But I'm going to find out."

"Good morning, Catherine." Venable didn't sound in the least drowsy in spite of the hour. "Did you like the little surprise package I left for you?"

"No. I don't like you using her or using me. I want her out of here."

"Actually, I had the feeling that she was using me. But it suited me to give her what she wanted. At any rate, she's now your problem. Deal with her."

"I could strangle you, Venable. She's a kid. Even you wouldn't want to throw her in Rakovac's path."

"Then perhaps the two of you had better keep a low profile and leave Rakovac to us." He paused. "If you send her back to me, I can't promise that she won't run away. She was determined not to let her mother shove her into that rehabilitation home. Besides, there's a slight chance she might be able to help you find Luke."

"She's a kid," Catherine repeated flatly. "I don't care how intelligent, she can't offer me anything that I'd want to use."

"Don't be too sure. Did she tell you about the patterns?"

"Briefly. Not enough. You tell me."

"Kelly's thinking processes are different from anyone else's. When she was a toddler, they found she was a whiz at mathematics."

"And how would that help me?" Catherine asked impatiently.

"It was only the start. The educators began testing her, and they found that if they gave her a piece of a puzzle, she could construct the entire picture."

"What kind of puzzle?"

"Any puzzle. Astronomy, mathematical, situational. You name it. She can see it all and project the ending. Her professors at William and Mary think that Einstein must have had that kind of brain. She's incredible. That's why her mother is so uneasy with her. Kelly can probably read her like a book."

"Is that any reason to push her away? All the more reason to hold her close and help her work it out. It must have been frightening for her."

"Yes, some puzzles aren't pretty, are they? But Kelly had her father, and after his divorce, he was very protective of the girl." He added dryly, "Believe me, I know. He wouldn't let us near her."

"Why would you — Of course, an ability like that would prove very valuable to the Company. I'm surprised you don't want to whisk her away to one of your training camps."

"I admit I was interested enough in what I heard about her to go to her school and talk to her professors. As I said, she's very promising."

"She's a kid, Venable."

"I didn't do anything, did I?"

"Because she had her father to protect her."

"I might have been able to get around him. And now her father has been removed from the equation." He added quickly, "Not that I've been thinking about it. It wouldn't be practical. All that media attention has spoiled her for any confidential use."

"Otherwise, you'd do it."

"Possibly." He went on brusquely. "That's not important since I can't implement it. What might be beneficial is having her concentrate on your problem. Doesn't it seem fitting that your Luke's kidnapping should be resolved by another child who was also a victim?"

"Fitting and completely nuts."

"Don't be hardheaded. I think it would be poetic justice." His tone became grave. "You may not believe this, but I sent her because I wanted to give you a chance before there are no more chances. Use her, Catherine. Use everything you've got." He hung up.

"He sounded dead serious," Eve said. "And foreboding."

Catherine nodded. "Something ugly is going on with Rakovac. I'd bet that the situation is heating up." She slowly put her phone in her pocket. "And Venable was trying to warn me that Luke may not have much time before the blowup."

"And what can you do that you're not doing?"

Catherine shook her head. "I don't know. Move faster. Get really desperate and take a stab at using Kelly?" She looked at Eve. "The only thing I do know is that I have to know what Luke looks like so that I won't get the wrong kid when I go after him. You'll be finished tomorrow?"

"If everything goes right." She didn't speak for a moment. "I could keep Kelly with me after you leave."

Catherine's face lit. "You'd do that?" She grimaced. "Not that I'll be able to get her to stay. She seems pretty determined. Still, thanks for the option." She sat down in the chair. "Go on to bed. I'll wait until Kelly gets out of the shower and tuck her in."

"Good." Eve yawned and started down the hall. "I'm ready for bed, and I still have to explain Kelly to Joe before I go to sleep. Try to get a few hours' sleep before morning."

"I will."

"And don't lecture the girl. She's been through enough tonight."

"Whatever you say."

Eve glanced back at her over her shoulder. No, Catherine wouldn't be giving that child a hard time. She was a strange combination of toughness and vulnerability, and Eve wasn't sure which was stronger. But Kelly seemed to tap into that same reservoir of emotion that Catherine reserved for her Luke.

It wasn't something that she should be worrying about, Eve thought impatiently. Both Catherine and Kelly had been catapulted into her life, and she would do the best she could for them, but after tomorrow her involvement would probably be over.

Why didn't she believe that?

And why wasn't she relieved?

The bitch had been frightened, Rakovac thought, as he stared thoughtfully at the photo on his desk. He had felt the jolt of familiar satisfaction at Catherine's panic and shock. It was always like that when he twisted the knife. He tried to ration the extreme cruelties so that she would not become calloused, but there was no doubt that this time she had needed the flick of the whip.

Her use of Eve Duncan was not to be tolerated. She must stay groveling at his feet until it suited him to step forward and crush her.

"You just received a call from Ali Dabala." Nicholas Russo came into the office. "He wants to know when he can set a date."

"Let him wait. I've given him a tentative.

The fool has no grasp of the importance of details. He doesn't realize that one false step and his men will end up in Guantanamo."

"He has a grasp on the huge amount of money he's paid you," Russo said. "He's being pressured by Al-Qaeda."

"I'm fully aware of that, Russo."

"Then why are you still playing games with Catherine Ling?" Russo frowned. "You have no time for this."

"There is always time for the pleasures of life." Be patient. He still had use for Russo. As usual, Russo was dressed in an immaculate suit made by his favorite London tailor, and he was beautifully groomed from the top of his brown hair to his polished shoes. He was a good front man. Yet it was difficult to be patient. Lately, Russo had been very critical and overbearing, and Rakovac was well aware that Russo had always been slightly contemptuous of Rakovac's lack of proper schooling and rough background. He added softly, "What I don't have time for is a man who questions my authority. You're acting like a frightened rabbit. Dabala is no more a threat than a hundred others I've dealt with over the years. The only difference is the money. I'm charging him enough to set up my own little kingdom on an island off the Brazilian coast. If you're efficient and do everything I tell you, then you'll have a place there." He shrugged. "If you're not, I'll toss you to Dabala and let him deal with someone who is a possible informer."

"You know I won't inform. I've been with you too long."

"And become rich. But we've never reached that level in the stratosphere where money can buy anything. But it's only one more step, Russo."

"A huge step. This is different. They'll never stop searching for us."

"And never find us. That's why the money is so important. It can buy plastic surgeons, documents, politicians who turn blind eyes. All of those little luxuries that make a man feel safe and content."

"They won't turn a blind eye. Not to this. They'd be too afraid."

"Russo."

"All right, I'll be quiet. But you may be sorry that you didn't listen to me." He turned on his heel. "Dabala said that if you didn't call him, he'd come to see you. You don't want him to lead the CIA to you."

"I'll call him." He watched Russo leave the room. The CIA might be aware something was going on but couldn't be permitted to know anything concrete about his deal with Dabala until he was ready to leave. Washington might accept nearly any corruption from him as long as he was a constant source of information, but even a hint of this business would cause them to bolt in panic. They were extremely sensitive to any Middle Eastern activity, and Rakovac had been careful to keep away from that contingent during their partnership.

But the Middle East was where the real money lay, and fanatics cared nothing how much it cost to grease the way to paradise. Naturally, he'd had to turn to them to find a way to his own paradise.

But paradise had its own restrictions, he thought regretfully. He wouldn't be able to make those delightful calls to Catherine after he made his exit. It would be too dangerous not to break all ties to the outside world. The delicious game he had played all these years must be brought to an end. He reached out and touched Catherine's throat in the photo. She had a lovely throat and many times when the anger had come to the surface, he'd wanted to slit it. Passing fancy. The mental torture he inflicted was much more enjoyable.

Oh, well, if he was going to end the charade, he would do it with style and ferocity. He had to have a plan that would be the crowning blow to his revenge on Catherine. It couldn't terminate with just a final burst of agony from a sniper bullet. He'd bring her close to him so that he could watch every nuance of her pain.

And not only Catherine. That wouldn't be in keeping with the grand finale.

"Who first?" he murmured. "Maybe a warning to punish you and show you what's to come?" His finger moved to caressingly touch the lips of the woman in the photo. "Yes, that's an excellent idea, Catherine. Let's start with Eve Duncan."

CHAPTER 7

Eve's eyes flew open.

What had she heard?

It had been a small sound, but enough to disturb her restless slumber. She checked the bedside clock — 5:42 A.M.

Probably nothing. The sound hadn't been loud enough to wake Joe. She wasn't accustomed to having guests in the house. She and Joe led an intensely solitary life.

She lay there, listening.

Movement? The creak of the couch in the living room? Kelly was only a young girl to have gone through so much. Perhaps she was having trouble sleeping in a strange place.

Eve obviously wasn't going to be able to go back to sleep until she checked on her. She carefully moved away from Joe and slid out of bed.

"Eve?" Joe asked sleepily.

"Shh, I'll be right back." She glided

toward the door. "I'm having trouble sleeping."

"I know a therapy for that."

She chuckled. "I'll discuss that with you when I come back."

"Do that . . ."

He was dozing off as she quietly closed the door behind her.

The hall was dark, but there was a light in the living room. Bright light.

She moved quickly down the hall.

No Kelly.

The couch was vacant, the covers tossed to one side.

Where the hell was —

"I didn't mean to wake you." Kelly was perched on the high stool at the desk usually occupied by Catherine. She was dressed in loose blue-striped pajamas, and her bare feet dangled above the floor. Her blue eyes were wide in her pale face, and she looked even younger than she had earlier in the evening. "I'm sorry. I couldn't sleep."

"I had trouble, too." Eve stiffened as she saw the sliver of bone in Kelly's hand. "Put that down."

Kelly quickly put the bone back on the table. "I'm sorry," she said again. "I didn't hurt anything. I didn't think you'd mind if I —"

"I do mind. This is my work, and it's not something to play with." She strode across the room. "Those bones are fragile, and I don't need any more breakage than what's already here."

"I didn't break anything. I was just —" She shook her head. "I only wanted to help."

"You should have asked me, and I would have told you not to —" She stopped as she looked down at the table. "Dear heavens."

"I didn't do anything wrong."

"Take it easy. I can see that you didn't." She was still staring at the bones on the worktable. "When we went to bed, Catherine had only a quarter of Cindy's face put back together. Now you have at least two-thirds of it completed. How?"

"I couldn't sleep. I needed something to do." Kelly moistened her lips. "There was a program pulled up on the computer. It seemed clear what you wanted done."

"So you did it."

She nodded. "It wasn't difficult. It was just a puzzle."

A puzzle that would have taken Eve days to solve. A puzzle that Catherine had strained and worked at for a full day. "How long did it take you?"

She shrugged. "A couple hours, I guess. I don't want to do anything that would make you angry. I won't touch it again."

"You shouldn't have touched it to begin with." She held up her hand as Kelly opened her lips to protest. "No, you didn't do any harm, and you might have done some good. But that doesn't mean you can interfere with my work without permission. That's not going to happen. Understand?"

Kelly nodded. "I just had to do something to unwind. I thought your puzzle might wear me out. Sometimes they do."

"And did it?"

"No."

"Why not?"

Kelly hesitated. "It wasn't hard enough," she said simply.

And the girl had not wanted to hurt Eve's feelings by telling her that that poor broken skull that had been a nightmare prospect to Eve had not even challenged her. "Catherine was finding it hard enough," she said dryly. "And I wouldn't have had an easy time of it."

"Mr. Venable says you're very clever," she said politely. "I'm sure it's just that I'm good at patterns."

"Kelly, are you patronizing me?"

She frowned, distressed. "Oh, no. I didn't mean that you —" She nibbled at her lower lip. "I said the wrong thing again. You can see why my mother doesn't want to be around me."

"No, I can't see any such thing. My ego isn't that fragile."

Kelly smiled tentatively. "Sometimes I do offend people. It was terrible when I was younger. But even now I forget every now and then. I'm glad that you aren't angry."

"I'll be mad as hell if I examine that skull and find that those shards don't match exactly."

"They'll match." She added quietly, "I'm never wrong, Eve."

"And modest, too."

She shook her head. "They tested me so many times. I hated it. But even when it seemed I might be wrong, in the end it always turned around. After a while, I refused to do it anymore. I didn't want to know more than anyone else about what could happen."

"Why not?"

"It could be . . . sad. Some patterns don't lead to good endings. I didn't want to think about it." She glanced down at the bone fragments. "This wasn't a good ending, but I can't do anything about it. Except maybe give you something that you want. You were kind to me. I wanted to please you. I'm sorry it didn't work out well."

"It didn't work out terribly either." She smiled. "Now get to bed and get a few hours' sleep. Joe has to leave for the precinct in an hour, and I'd like you to be asleep by the time he has to come through here."

"I'm causing him trouble, too."

"Inconvenience," Eve corrected. " 'Trouble' is too strong a word. It takes a lot for Joe to consider it trouble. He just can't get a handle on the situation, and it makes him upset. Now jump into that fine bed I made up for you and try to keep yourself from working on Cindy's bones."

"Okay." Kelly headed for the couch. "Are you going to tell Catherine?"

"Yes. I could hardly keep it secret once she saw the progress you've made." She pulled up the blanket around Kelly's shoulders. "It's pretty clear you —" She stopped and gazed down at the girl. "Or is that the aim of this exercise? Did you want to give a little demonstration of how much you can help Catherine?"

Kelly stared up at her. "Maybe. Partly." She shook her head. "No, probably. I didn't think it through, but I wanted her to know that I wouldn't be a burden."

"Kelly, Catherine was telling you the truth," Eve said gently. "It's the wrong time for you to be with her. Why can't you understand that? I know that she saved your life, but you have to stand back."

She was silent a moment, then looked away. "I can't do that. Ever since they found out my brain could do this weird stuff, they've been telling me that it was a good thing. That I could be another Einstein or help people in a hundred different ways. But when Daddy and I were in Munoz's camp, I tried to put together what might happen, what we should do to keep alive."

"And you couldn't do it?"

"No, I could do it," she whispered. "Munoz kept threatening Daddy, talking about how he was going to rape me if the government didn't do what he wanted. Daddy nearly exploded whenever he'd do that. He got so angry . . ." She shook her head. "It was going to happen. Munoz's anger and threats, Daddy's anger. Something bad . . . I could see it coming. It was a pattern, and I was in the middle of it." Her eyes were glittering with tears. "I tried to talk to Daddy and tell him that nothing Munoz did to me would matter, that he mustn't ever fight him. He wouldn't listen. I tried to think of a way to get away, to break the pattern, but I couldn't." Her voice was shaking. "They kept telling me how smart I am, but they lied. I'm stupid. Stupid. I couldn't think of any way to stop it."

"Stop this." Eve's hand covered Kelly's on the blanket. "You were in a no-win situation. Just because you can see patterns doesn't mean that you can change them."

"Then what good is it?" she said fiercely. "I can't turn it off. It's with me all the time. There should have been a way that I could have stopped Daddy from trying to —"

"What way?" Eve asked. "He loved you. You help people you love."

"I couldn't help him."

What can I say? Eve thought helplessly. There was no arguing with that statement. The girl had obviously wrestled with this painful truth since her father's death, perhaps even before. "No." She paused, seeking for a way to soothe that pain. "He didn't want your help. He thought he was doing the right thing. It wasn't your responsibility. You might just as well say it was Catherine's fault because she didn't get there in time."

Kelly shook her head.

"She doesn't want your help, Kelly."

"She has to take it. I have to know —"

"Know what?"

"First, I wanted to go to Catherine because I felt as if she understood — but the minute Venable told me about Catherine's son, I knew that I might have another chance." She moistened her lips. "If I help her, if I can work out her pattern with her son, then maybe this quirk I have isn't stupid and worthless. Maybe I'm not worthless."

"There's no doubt in my mind."

"There's doubt in mine." Her hand tightened on Eve's. "I should have been able to save Daddy. Will you help me convince Catherine to let me stay with her?"

"No, that's up to you." She straightened and turned away. "The most I'll do is tell her what you've told me and let her judge." She turned off the light. "Good night, Kelly. I'll see you in a few hours."

"Good night." In the darkness, Kelly's words were a breath above a whisper. "I was wondering . . ."

"Wondering what?"

"As you work on those skulls, do you see a pattern, too?"

A pattern of darkness and murder and violence. A puzzle that she hoped to solve every time her fingers touched the skulls. "Only in my imagination, Kelly."

Kelly rolled over and huddled under the blanket. "You're lucky."

It was after ten o'clock when Catherine got

out of the shower, dressed, and strode into the living room. The couch was neatly made up, and Eve was sitting at the bar drinking a cup of coffee. "Where's Kelly?"

"Out on the porch. I told her to go get some sun." She poured Catherine a cup of coffee. "I wanted some time alone with you."

"Why? I told you when you came to my room last night that I couldn't be either a sister or psychologist to Kelly. Not now."

"You were upset then, and you didn't want to deal with her." She lifted her cup to her lips. "But I think you're going to find that you have no choice."

"I have a choice."

"Go over to the worktable and look at that work she did on Cindy's skull last night."

"I don't want to look."

"Are you being stubborn?"

"Yes." She was silent a moment, then burst out, "Dammit, I'm not like you. I'm harder, more ruthless. Even though I don't want her involved, I'm capable of ignoring what's good for her if I decide she could help me find Luke. I don't want to make that decision."

"You could limit her input, find ways to keep her on the sidelines."

"Anyone close to me may be a target if

Rakovac decides to make a move. She's fourteen years old." She shrugged. "Besides, all that pattern business could be crap. I prefer to believe that it is."

"And I prefer to believe that it's not. You have to face the possibility. Stop hiding your head in the ground. Go look at Cindy."

Catherine hesitated, then turned and strode across the room to the work desk. "Maybe I'm wrong. Maybe you are as ruthless as I am. I thought you — Oh, shit." She was gazing down at the skull fragments put together by Kelly. "She did this in a couple hours?"

Eve nodded.

"Hell, I know how difficult — I nearly went blind straining to tell those pieces apart." She murmured, "Incredible."

"Two hours."

"But this was a physical puzzle, it doesn't mean she'd be that good at anything more abstract."

"Like finding a lost boy?" Eve nodded. "That's right. We have no proof. Other than Venable thought she was promising enough to be interesting to the CIA."

She shook her head. "Too vague." She studied Eve's expression. "Why are you trying to convince me to use Kelly? I thought you'd be against it."

"I want you to bring your Luke home." She smiled. "I've grown attached to him. It doesn't seem to me that you have a plan that is even close to being foolproof."

"I'm working on it."

"I know you are," Eve said quietly. "But Kelly is offering you an opportunity that could be . . . hopeful. I think you should explore the possibility. Face it, she's going to be hard to get rid of, so let her help you, but keep her out of the line of fire. As I said, I'd be glad to have her stay with me."

Catherine frowned, then shrugged. "I'll think about it." A faint smile curved her lips. "And I thought I was obsessed. Luke *has* you, and you've only seen his photo."

"What do you expect? I've been watching him grow up before my eyes," Eve said. "Or should I say within my computer?" She turned and headed for the door. "Let's bring Kelly in and have breakfast. I want to get back to work on him."

Kelly was sitting on the swing, and her expression became wary as she saw Catherine. "Am I in trouble?"

"Yes and no," Catherine said. "You shouldn't have touched Eve's work without her permission. But since she's forgiven you, I don't have the right to be angry."

Kelly looked relieved. "I just thought I'd

get it done for you."

"Since I was being so slow and inefficient," Catherine said dryly.

Kelly shook her head. "I think you did a fine job since you were going at it blind."

"Blind?" Catherine asked curiously. "Do you actually see where you're going when you start working on a pattern?"

"Sometimes. Sometimes I have to jump from piece to piece and hope it comes to me as I travel." She turned to Eve. "Is that how it is when you do a reconstruction?"

"In a way. During the last stage of the reconstruction." She looked at Catherine, and said meaningfully, "But it's much better to not go at any endeavor blind if there's any way around it."

"Point taken," Catherine said. "But not necessarily accepted."

Kelly was focused and oblivious of the undercurrents. "I knew where I was going with the skull the moment that I saw the pieces," she said. "That's why it went so fast."

Catherine gazed at Eve, then back at Kelly, and finally said, "Then, in the name of speed and efficiency, I think you should finish what you started."

Kelly's face lit. "You'll let me help?"

"Only with the bone fragments. And with

Eve's permission."

"She has it." Eve made a face. "Though I can't believe I'm saying that. I never let anyone touch my work, and now I've let both of you help me. But it's only under my strict supervision."

Kelly's gaze was on Catherine's face.

"Are you sure?"

"Yes. The idea was to free Eve to work on the age progression. I'm not going to be hurt because you're doing it better than me. I can spend the time reading the Rakovac e-mail surveillance report."

"Come in and eat breakfast, Kelly," Eve said. "You haven't had anything but orange juice since you got up this morning."

"And I think I'm hungry." Kelly's voice was surprised as she stood up and moved toward the door. "I haven't wanted to eat since — a long time."

"That's obvious," Catherine said. "A breeze could blow you away." She stepped aside so that Kelly could enter. "You're not going to be any good to anyone if you let yourself get weak and puny."

Kelly nodded. "I'll remember. I won't disappoint you."

"Disappoint? Kelly, it's only the bone fragments," Catherine said.

"I won't disappoint you," Kelly repeated.

Catherine gazed at her in frustration. "Kelly, I'm not going to —"

"Breakfast," Eve said firmly, and whisked both of them inside the house.

"What's wrong, Kelly?" Catherine had been studying Kelly's expression from where she was sitting reading the e-mail report on the couch across the room. "You've been working for five hours on that skull. You only had a little left to do. I thought you'd be finished before this."

"I'm almost there," Kelly said absently. "These fragments are much more delicate. I didn't want to risk breaking them."

"Good decision," Eve said grimly as she glanced up from her computer. "I would have been most displeased with you. So displeased I would have felt like breaking *you* into fragments."

Kelly shook her head gravely. "I told you I wouldn't disappoint you. I'll be done in a few minutes."

Eve leaned back in her chair. "Then I'm ahead of you."

Catherine sat up straight on the couch. "You're done with the progression?"

"Yes, do you want to see it?"

"Of course." She jumped to her feet and was across the room in seconds. "Show me."

"I only had another two steps to go from the last transition." She pulled up a photo on the computer. "Luke at nine. You'll see the face has elongated a little. The chin is a trifle more square. The bridge of the nose is continuing to rise up, and the nostril size and width have increased. His permanent teeth are fully down." She tapped the screen. "At this stage, the teeth seem too big for the face. But that's entirely natural."

"Is it?" Every time Eve brought up a transition, it came as a shock to Catherine. This was no exception. A shock and a sharp pang.

Eve's gaze was on her face. "Are you ready for the last one?"

"Luke at eleven?"

Eve nodded. "Luke as he is now."

Catherine was experiencing an odd mixture of eagerness and dread. Foolish. This was what she wanted, what she needed. "By all means." She swallowed hard. "Luke as he is now."

Eve accessed the final progression.

For an instant Catherine felt her breath leave her body. "He's . . . beautiful."

"At this age, he'd already have a masculine resentment of that particular description," Eve said. "I'm sure he'd prefer 'handsome' or 'good-looking.' "

"Yes." Catherine couldn't keep her gaze from the boy's face. "But he is beautiful."

Eve nodded. "I think so, too," she said softly. She tapped the computer screen. "Luke at age eleven. You'll notice the chin is now square and masculine. The bridge of the nose is still higher. His ears are a little too large for his face."

"They are not," Catherine said quickly. "They're fine."

"Have it your way," Eve said. "But you will agree that he's lost almost all his baby fat, and the look of childhood has almost disappeared. The forms of his face are harder, more defined. He's a juvenile now." She paused. "On his way to becoming a man."

Catherine blinked hard. "Yes, I'll agree that's true." She drew a long shaky breath. "Could you put all the transitions up together so that I can see the progression?"

Eve nodded. "No problem."

"May I see him?" Kelly was at Catherine's elbow, her voice tentative. "Please."

"Okay." Catherine stepped closer to Eve so that Kelly could see the screen. "That's my son, Luke."

Kelly studied the photo. "He's beautiful."

"Are you saying that because you think that's what I want to hear?"

"No." Then she smiled. "Yes. But it's true. He looks like you, Catherine." Her gaze was on the collage of photos Eve had just brought up on the screen. "All those transitions look so different, but for some reason I'd know they were the same person. Why is that?"

Eve's forefinger went to the area around the eyes. "Some of it is here. Most people maintain a certain 'look' throughout their lives. It's a certain 'something' that causes others to recognize someone even through age and changes. I tried to incorporate that quality in all the photos. Sometimes it's ephemeral or hard to discern, but in Luke's case, I thought it was centered around the eyes and lips."

"Patterns," Kelly murmured.

"I never thought of it that way, but it doesn't surprise me that you do."

"If it's eyes and lips, then you're talking about expression," Catherine said.

"Sometimes," Eve said. "Luke has a dimple in his left cheek, and his eyes are alert and full of vitality. He may have retained that tremendous joie de vivre." She paused. "Or he may have lost it if life was hard. But either way, there will be traces of that lifelong look. If you look at photos of JFK, you'll see what I mean. From childhood on, he had that unmistakable, recognizable look." She glanced at Catherine. "Have you seen enough?"

No, there would never be enough. "It's as close as you can come?"

She nodded. "I did the best I could. I think it may be a good best."

"So do I." Catherine cleared her throat. "Will you print it out? I'd also like you to send it to my cell phone."

"Done."

She didn't speak for a moment. "You know I can't thank you enough. I owe you. Ask me anything, and I'll do it."

"Find Luke," Eve said. "Bring him home alive and well."

"I will," she said fiercely. "But that's for me. I have to pay you back. Name it."

"I'll think about it." Eve slipped from her stool. "But in the meantime, you can make me a cup of coffee." She flexed her neck and back. "I'm stiff as a board."

"I'll do it." Kelly was already halfway across the room. "Catherine?"

"Yes." Catherine wrinkled her nose. "You persist in taking away my jobs."

"Pushy." Kelly smiled over her shoulder. "Daddy used to say I was —" She broke off as she went behind the bar of the kitchenette. "He was right."

"Nothing wrong with a little assertiveness, Catherine," Eve said. "I believe both you and I are prone to be a little forceful."

"True." Catherine sat down at the bar. "But I understand there should be a balance."

"Have you ever found it?"

Catherine smiled. "No." Her smile faded. "I mean it. I'll find a way to give you whatever you want. But in the meantime, I know you want me out of here, and I'll oblige as soon as I can get my things together. I know a lot about the art of disappearing. In a few hours, you'll find it hard to remember I was here."

"I'll remember." She took the cup of coffee Kelly set before her. "You're hard to forget. So is Luke." She smiled at Kelly. "And so is our young friend. Have you found anything in that report to give you any insight into where Rakovac might have hidden Luke?"

"No, not yet."

"Then what are you planning to do?"

"As I told you, I have friends in Moscow. I'll do my own surveillance, and I may twist some arms." Her lips tightened. "I'll do anything I have to do. I just hope there's something in that report that will give me a start. It contains years of surveillance reports I'll have to comb through."

"Let me do it," Kelly offered.

"No," Catherine said emphatically. "After I finish this coffee, we're going to have a discussion about where you're going to go until you can make other arrangements."

"I'm either going with you, or it's none of your business where I go," Kelly said quietly. "You can discuss all you please. I won't impose on Eve, and I won't —"

Catherine's cell phone rang.

She stiffened. "Rakovac."

She punched the button. "What do you want?"

"You're being rude. You know I don't tolerate that, Catherine. I wonder why you're suddenly so brave."

She should back down. It wasn't safe for Luke. "You just called me. What else could you have to say?"

"A good deal. I've decided it's time to bring our relationship to a close. I can't tell how I'll regret having to do that, but circumstances are crowding me."

She didn't like where this conversation was going. "What circumstances?"

"A change of lifestyle. I'm afraid you have no part in it." He paused. "Neither does your obsession for your son."

Her heart was starting to pound. "Then

let him go."

"I can't do that. You'll have to come and get him."

"What do you mean?"

"I've been busy since I last called you. I paid a visit to your Luke's grave and had him dug up so that I could give you a little challenge."

"You're lying."

"Why won't you believe me? He was five years old when I shot him." He paused. "Is your friend Eve Duncan there with you?"

"Yes."

"Good, because the challenge is for her, too. She's being such a help to you. I'm going to let her do the final rites."

Catherine was beginning to feel sick with panic. Nightmare on top of nightmare. "She has nothing to do with this. It's only a job to her."

"But I've been investigating her background, and I believe she can't be a part of something without becoming personally involved. She annoyed me by deciding to interfere in our private affairs."

"It's over. I'm leaving here."

"With your precious age progression to speed you on. It's bogus, Catherine. What a pity. All her work for nothing." His voice lowered. "But I have more work for her to do. Providing that she chooses to set your mind at rest. I have a skull for her to work on. Ask me to whom it belongs."

"Why? You'll tell me, and it will be a lie."

"Will it? Come and find out. Come play hide-and-seek. It's a splendid game, the final game. Find out if I'm lying about your son. You'll get a prize if you do."

"What kind of prize?"

"A quick death . . . maybe. As for your interfering friend, Duncan, I may let the people she cares about live."

"Not Eve?"

"I'm trying to be honest with you. I want her dead. Her lover, Quinn, and daughter, Jane, are negotiable." He added maliciously, "One way or another, you'll know your son is going to be in his grave by the end of the month. I make you that promise. Now all you have to do is find out if he's there already, or if I have to kill him to keep that promise."

"He's not dead. You wouldn't do it."

"You're gambling. Come and find out for yourself. I'll give you a series of clues that will lead you to your son. The first is in the photo I've just sent you. I have a passion for photos, they keep the memories fresh. Access it when you hang up."

"Wait. Don't —"

He had already hung up. Her hands were shaking as she quickly accessed the photo in her phone.

It was the photo of the skeleton of a child lying on a pile of earth beneath a twisted tree. The bones were stained with dirt, and a hole gaped in the center of the skull.

She made a whimpering noise deep in her throat. She closed her eyes a moment as the waves of pain hit her.

"May I see it?" Eve took her phone and gazed at the photo for a long time.

"Eve?"

Eve drew a shaking breath. "Damn him. It could be a fake, but it appears to be authentic."

Catherine's eyes flicked open. "How old?"

"Hard to tell."

"Five?"

"Possibly."

"It doesn't matter. It's a fake. He's just doing it to hurt me."

"Well, he succeeded, didn't he?" Eve's face was drained of color as she stood up and moved jerkily toward the door. "I'll be right back. I need some air."

Catherine stared after her in bewilderment.

"It's the photo," Kelly said quietly. "The skeleton. She's thinking about her daughter.

It's hurting her."

Of course, Catherine realized. She had been too deep in her own pain to think of Eve's. But Kelly had read those signs.

"I'm on the outside," Kelly said, as if reading her thoughts. "Sometimes it helps. Should we go after her?"

"No." Catherine's gaze shifted back to the photo. It couldn't be Luke. Oh God, don't let it be Luke. "She wouldn't thank us. She'll be back when she's ready."

CHAPTER 8

Eve walked quickly, feverishly, down the path toward the lake.

Those bones, those poor pitiful bones.

A child tossed carelessly into the earth naked and alone.

She would not cry. Too late. She could feel dampness on her cheeks.

Stupid. Lord, how many skeletons had she seen in her career? Why had this one struck such an agonizing resonance? She should be harder, more calloused.

"That's never going to happen, Mama."

Bonnie.

Eve looked ahead on the path and saw Bonnie leaning against a pine tree forty feet away. The sunlight was tangling in her red curls, and she was smiling.

"Someday it might," Eve said. "I can't go on bleeding inside every time I see a skeleton. It's not professional." She wiped her eyes.

"And I'm very professional. Bonnie."

"Yes, Mama."

"Stop smiling. No, don't." She stopped on the path. "I need to see you smile. Why are you here?"

"Because I wanted to be here. Because you wanted me. Isn't that a good reason?"

She drew a shaky breath. "It's a wonderful reason. But I think that you have another agenda."

"Agenda." Bonnie chuckled. "Now that's a very professional word. Yes, I have an agenda." Her smile disappeared, and she said gently, "My agenda is to help soften the pain. That photo rocked you and sent you reeling back to what you felt when I was taken. It hurts me when you feel like that, Mama. I want it to go away."

"Rakovac doesn't want it to go away. Those bones . . . such a small child." She whispered. "Like you, baby, such a little girl."

"But it's over, Mama." She paused. "For me. I keep telling you that. I know it's not for you. And maybe not for Luke. Don't think about me. Don't let that picture make you sad. Or if it does, not for me."

"Don't be silly. Of course it made me sad." She swallowed. "But now I'm getting angry."

"Good. That's much healthier."

"And you're being very wise and superior.

I'm not sure I like it."

"You like it. You like everything about me."

"You're very confident, young lady."

"I have a right to be. My spirit status allows a few privileges. Now go in and talk to Catherine. You're feeling a little better, but she's still hurting. She's been hurting for such a long time."

"I know. That doesn't mean I can solve her problems." She turned and headed for the cottage. "Or that I've even decided to try."

"That's true," Bonnie said. "I'm sure that it will at least take you until you reach the front porch to think it all out and come to a decision."

"Brat." Wonderful, beloved brat.

"Be careful, Mama . . ."

She didn't have to look behind her to know that Bonnie was no longer there.

No sadness. Bonnie didn't want it. Not for her.

But the sadness was still there, and the anger.

Oh yes, the anger.

"Are you okay?" Catherine asked, as Eve came in the door. "I'm sorry. I didn't mean to upset —"

"I'm fine," Eve interrupted. "I just had to

get away and do some thinking." She went over to the sink and got a glass of water. "And I was upset. I'm still upset."

"I told you, the photo has to be a fake. He'll do anything to hurt me."

"Or to lure you to come into his web and find out for yourself if it was a fake," Eve said. "I'd say that was the principal reason for that photo. Shock value, then to draw you to him. He even said as much."

"But he also threatened you, Eve." She shook her head. "I never meant that to happen. I wanted your help. I didn't want to lead him to you."

"I realize it wasn't deliberate." She smiled crookedly. "Although we both know that you would have probably run the risk even if you'd known that he'd be on our doorstep. That's the way obsession works. Take it from someone who knows."

Catherine hesitated. "Yes, but I would have protected you. I wouldn't have let him hurt you. I won't let him hurt you now."

"It's not up to you. Not any longer." She took Catherine's phone again and gazed down at the pitifully macabre skeleton in the photo. "I *hate* this. I don't care if it's your Luke or some other helpless child. I hate it. I hate the brutality of the act and the use of this child's murder to help Rakovac get what he wants. These monsters think they can kill and kill and kill again. Not this time." Her lips tightened. "I'm not going to let it happen." She glanced at Catherine. "We're not going to let it happen. I don't want to hear any more bullshit about you protecting me. Whatever happens, Joe and I will take care of ourselves and Jane."

"You're shutting me out," Kelly said. "Don't do that. Let me help."

"Kelly, I don't even know what I'm going to do yet," Catherine said.

"She knows." Kelly nodded at Eve. "Don't you, Eve?"

Eve nodded. "I know I'm going to talk to Joe. That comes first. I know we're going to examine this photo that Rakovac says contains the first clue in his damn game. We're going to find it and try to figure a way to push him to the next step without getting killed." She met Catherine's eyes. "And then you're going to find a way for us to get into Russia without Rakovac's being aware that we're there."

Catherine went still. "You're actually going with me?"

"Hell, yes. I'm going to find out if that child is Luke. If he's not, I'm going to find out who he is and who killed him." She tapped the photo. "This wasn't only a gauntlet tossed down for you, Catherine. Rakovac has obviously studied me, too. He knew seeing that skeleton would hurt me and make me think of Bonnie. He says he wants me to do a reconstruction and find out if that poor kid is Luke?" Her jaw set. "Well, I'm going to do it and find a way to make it boomerang and send him straight to hell."

Catherine stared at her in surprise. Then she started to laugh. "I didn't think that you'd react like this. Where's all your cool, professional reasoning?"

"He shouldn't have sent that photo. I'm going to call Joe. You start thinking of contacts in Russia that can help us." She turned to Kelly, and ordered, "You finish Cindy."

"I want to —"

"I don't care what you want," Eve said. "We have enough to worry about, saving one child. You're not much more than a child yourself. We're not going to have you put in danger or getting in our way while we're doing it."

Kelly gazed at her for a moment, then turned and sat down at the worktable. "You're wrong. But I'll do what you wish. I'll finish Cindy."

"Thank you." Eve whirled and went out

on the porch again to make her call to Joe.

"Am I going to be able to talk you out of it?" Joe asked tersely.

Eve braced herself. "No. It has to be done."

"And, of course, you have to be the one to do it."

"I have to help. He can't be allowed to go on. If you could have seen that photo —"

"I don't doubt that it was enough to send you into a tailspin." Joe was silent a moment and gave a low curse. "I knew it. I could see it coming."

"I need you to protect Jane. You don't have to be involved."

"Of course I'll see that she's protected. And you know damn well that I'm going to be involved," he added. "And I'm curious to know why Rakovac has suddenly decided that his persecution of Catherine has to come to an end. He's obviously enjoying it. After all these years, it would have to take something monumental to cause him to stop. What does Venable say about it?"

"Catherine hasn't told him about Rakovac's latest call, but Venable's attitude has been . . . vaguely noncommittal regarding what's been going on between Rakovac and the CIA."

"Other than that they might have to take Rakovac out. That's a pretty radical action. I believe we'll have to probe a little into Venable's reasons. The situation may be even more volatile than he's telling you."

"That wouldn't surprise me. He appears to be alternating between trying to keep Catherine from interfering and a genuine concern about the boy."

"He probably is concerned. As much as he permits himself to be. I've worked with him before, and he's not a bad guy. Just all CIA."

"He'd have to be to let Luke be held by that bastard all these years just to keep international relations on an even keel. I can't understand him."

"No, you wouldn't be able to fathom that kind of thinking," Joe said. "But evidently Catherine understands, even if she doesn't condone." He added, "I'm going to call Jane and tell her what's happening. The last we heard from her, she was in London. Right?"

"Yes. But warning isn't enough, Joe."

"No, I'll also call on Venable and get him to assign her protection. And, remember, Jane has friends in Scotland who will look out for her if they're put on the alert."

Yes, she did, Eve thought. And some of those friends were more lethal than Rakovac could ever hope to be. John MacDuff, Jock Gavin, and Caleb were formidable. "Then by all means give them a call. I want her surrounded." She paused. "And she's so damn stubborn."

"Just like the company she keeps," he said dryly. "You're sure that I can't talk you out of this? If you want the kid out, I'll go in and get him by myself."

"And run the risk of getting him killed. Rakovac wants Catherine, and if we can tease him with an occasional glimpse, we might be able to strike a balance that will let us grab Luke without sacrificing Catherine."

"And is she agreeing to stake herself out?"

"We haven't discussed it. It's my take on the best way of handling him. But Catherine wouldn't blink about doing anything that had a chance of working. She's desperate. I'm hanging up now. I've got to go back in and see what we can do about finding a place for Kelly to go."

"At least you're not planning on taking her with you," Joe said. "That would not be smart."

"Actually, it might be very smart, but not in the least humane. She's fourteen. Call me after you've talked to Jane." She hung up.

She felt immensely relieved. Joe would make sure that Jane was safe, and that was the most important thing. He'd be on Venable, probing, demanding and digging until everything was out in the open.

"Eve?"

She turned to see Catherine standing in the doorway. "Joe is taking care of making sure that my adopted daughter, Jane, is safe."

"Good." She came out on the porch. "Is he angry?"

"No, he said he knew it was coming." She shrugged. "Joe knows me very well."

"That must be nice. Comfortable."

"And sometimes not so comfortable." She smiled. "But, yes, I wouldn't have it any other way. We've gone through far too much together to have to do it all again. What a headache that would be." She changed the subject. "So when do we leave?"

"Tonight. Just after midnight. There's a private airport outside Gainesville, and we'll take a private jet to Rome, then change planes and go on to Moscow."

"Private enough to keep Rakovac from knowing that we're invading his turf? He seems to keep an eagle eye on you."

She nodded. "I can do it. I only tried to keep him in the dark when I went in to make an attempt to locate Luke. Otherwise, I let him track me. I figured it made him feel powerful, and it didn't hurt to feed his ego. My aim was always to keep his volatility in check."

"And when we reach Russia?"

"I know a man who may hate Rakovac more than I do. Alex Kelsov fought with Rakovac before he went to Moscow and became big in the mafia. Rakovac betrayed Kelsov to the Russian secret police, and he spent three years in a prison in Siberia. He was lucky not to have been executed. But Kelsov was always a major deal maker and slippery as an eel." She made a face. "He still is. He may want to bring Rakovac down, but it's still going to cost me."

"What?"

"It depends on what Kelsov wants at the time. Whatever it is, I'll give it to him." She paused before saying soberly, "Rakovac meant what he said, you know. He'll try to kill you."

"But not for a while. He impressed me as a man with a plan. This has been going on too long for him to let his revenge just dribble away into nothingness. He wanted to punish you so badly that he was willing to risk his Washington connection."

"You can't be sure that he won't make a

move. He's not predictable."

Eve shrugged. "Then we'd better move fast." She started for the door. "I'll pack a bag for both Joe and myself. What arrangements have you made for Kelly?"

"Nothing yet. I haven't had time," Catherine said. "Whatever I decide, it's not going to be easy convincing her to go."

"Then you'd better start." She held out her hand. "Give me your phone. I want to print off a copy of that picture Rakovac claims is Luke's skeleton."

She gave her the phone. "Why?"

"I want to send it to an institute in St. Louis that may be able to give me a definitive analysis on the skeleton and location."

"You mean if it's a fake or not?"

"Yes, and if they can zero in on the skull and determine if it was a bullet that shattered it."

"Could you compare the photo of the skull to any of the transitions and see if there is a match?"

"Possibly. But it would take time. According to Rakovac, we have no time. We'll take what we can get. I'm more interested in that twisted pine in the background. And the moss on the leg of the skeleton. They might lead us somewhere." She entered the house to see Kelly bent over Cindy's skull. "How is it going?"

"Well." Kelly didn't look up. "I'll be finished soon."

"Good." She hesitated. "You didn't have to do this. I appreciate it."

"But not enough to let me really help you."

"Kelly . . ."

"It's okay, I understand. I told you I'd finish Cindy, and I'm doing it." She finally lifted her gaze to look at Eve. "I heard you talking to Catherine about wondering where you're going to send me. You don't have to worry about that. I've already taken care of it."

Eve's brows rose. "Indeed?"

"I called Venable and told him that he had to send someone to pick me up. He said he'd do it right away." She looked back down at the bone shards. "I think it will be Agent Dufour. He sent me with him before."

"You're suddenly being very cooperative."

"And you're suspicious." Her smile was a little sad. "I'm not stupid, Eve. I know I'm not going to be able to convince you and Catherine that I should go with you. I have to move on. Agent Venable told me that if my being with you didn't work out, he'd see that I was settled somewhere I'd be comfortable for a little while."

"That's better than we could offer," Eve said.

"Yes." She looked back down. "When you finish the reconstruction of Cindy, will you send me a photo? I kind of feel like I know her."

"You do. You've been a big part in helping me to bring her home."

"I hope so. Home is important." She grimaced. "Not that I know that from experience. Daddy was always planning on buying a house and settling down in Boulder, Colorado, with me, but his company kept sending him out of the country. And I was always away at the college. They always arranged for me to stay with really nice families near the campus, but that was their home, not mine." She changed the subject. "You know that Rakovac sent you that photo to make you angry, don't you? He wanted to hurt Catherine, but he wanted to make you come with her."

"And why would he want me to come? I'm not really important to him."

"Catherine is alone. She has no family. She's the only one he can hurt. He wants more than that. What good is a Fourth of July explosion if you don't have someone to see it?"

"Then I'm supposed to be the witness?" She shook her head. "No, I believe he'd rather tie me to one of the rockets."

"It could be both or either."

"That's what this so-called pattern is telling you?"

She shook her head. "You haven't let me study him enough to see a pattern. I can only guess from what I've been told."

And it was a pretty good guess, Eve thought. Venable was right; Kelly was incredibly intelligent, and her instincts were unsettling. Kelly looked to be such a delicate child in appearance that it was disturbing to hear her speak as if she were a woman in her thirties. Perhaps her training with her patterns had caused her to leave that childhood behind. Then the nightmare that had happened to her in Munoz's camp had been the final blow.

"You're pitying me," Kelly said. "Don't do it. I don't need it." She placed another shard carefully on Cindy's temple. "How are we going to glue these pieces together?"

"I'll do it before I leave tonight. I use a special epoxy."

"After you go over her with a fine-tooth comb and make sure I didn't make any mistakes."

Eve nodded. "That's my job. But I don't

think you did. I believe both you and Catherine did a remarkable job."

Kelly nodded. "It's all you allowed me to do." She added soberly, "Take care of Catherine. Someone has to do it. I should be the one, but she won't let me."

"I know you feel that you owe her, but Catherine's capable of taking care of herself."

Kelly looked away. She repeated, "Take care of her."

"I'll do my best." She turned and moved toward the bedroom. No matter what Eve promised, it would not be enough for Kelly. The girl and Catherine had forged a strange and powerful bond, and Kelly had the added urgency of proving to herself that her abilities could make a difference. Eve couldn't blame her for her persistence. She was even surprised she had finally given up. "Good luck, Kelly."

"Good luck to you. You'll need it more than I do." She gave her a ghost of a smile. "Since you don't have my valuable assistance."

"We'll survive," Eve said over her shoulder. "And so will you. The only one who's not going to come out on top will be Rakovac."

■ ■ ■ ■

Agent Dufour arrived at the cottage at four thirty that afternoon.

Kelly watched the dark blue sedan drive up the driveway and turned to Catherine. "You won't change your mind?"

Catherine shook her head. "I'll be in touch when we get back. Let Venable help you. Don't do anything on your own. Okay?"

Kelly didn't answer. "Good-bye." She gave Catherine a hug. "Be careful." She turned and ran down the steps and jumped into the sedan. She didn't look back as Dufour pulled out of the driveway.

"Venable had better take good care of her," Catherine said. "She's so damn vulnerable, and she's just a kid."

"I was just thinking this afternoon how grown-up she seemed," Eve said. "And she trusted Venable enough to call him when she knew she wasn't going to be able to go with us. Should she trust him, Catherine?"

"In most cases."

"Not in the case of your son."

"Luke was standing in the way of Venable's saving the world for democracy," she said sarcastically. "Kelly isn't in that position.

He tried to use her as a roadblock, and it didn't work. Now he'll do what he can to keep her happy. He knows he'll answer to me if he doesn't." She watched for another moment until Kelly disappeared from view. Then she turned to go back into the cottage. "While you finish using that epoxy on Cindy's face, I have to make a couple more calls before we leave for the airport. Is Joe coming back here?"

"No, he's meeting us at the airport. He said he had a few things to do himself."

"With your daughter, Jane?"

"No, he said that's all taken care of. He's satisfied that she's safe." Eve opened the door. "And Joe doesn't make mistakes about the people he cares about."

"I noticed that he's very . . . protective and comforting."

Eve remembered how Joe had taken Catherine into his arms to comfort her after that phone call from Rakovac. "Yes, he can be pretty wonderful."

"You two are good together. It's nice to see that in a couple. I think most people stay together just so they won't be alone."

"Is that what you've found? Is that why you married?"

"No, I didn't care about being alone. I never knew anything else. But Terry wanted it, and I wanted him to be happy. He'd been good to me. I'm glad I did marry him. He gave me Luke and those years were wonderful for both of us." She pulled out her phone. "He was a great agent, too. He'd been with the CIA for years, and he knew everyone and had contacts everywhere. He worked with Kelsov even before we married." She dialed quickly. "Go on, get to work. We need to leave here in another two hours."

Joe was waiting at the hangar when Catherine and Eve pulled into the airport.

"You're late. I was beginning to wonder."

"Eve wasn't going to leave until she finished doing as much as she could on Cindy," Catherine said. "And I wasn't about to hurry her." She turned as the pilot came down the steps of the Learjet. "Hi, Dorsey. Ready to go?"

"As ready as I'll ever be," the stocky, thirtysomething pilot said dryly. "Since every trip with you puts my license in jeopardy."

"Complaints. Complaints." She turned to Eve. "Eve Duncan, Joe Quinn. This is Dorsey Hodges. He used to work for the Company but decided he liked the good life better than risking his neck."

He smiled and nodded. "So Catherine

wants to make sure I don't become bored with the good life by putting it constantly at risk." He waved at the steps. "Get on board. Let's get moving. I have a job in Key West in two days."

"I may need you longer," Catherine said.

His smile faded. "Then I'll reluctantly tell Key West to take a flying leap. You know I'll always be there for you, Catherine." He turned away. "I've found ways to get around Homeland Security, but I hope your friend Kelsov is going to be able to handle any problems on that end. I've no desire to end up in Siberia."

"Neither does Kelsov. He's been there, done that." She ran up the steps. "You're safe, Dorsey."

"Is he?" Joe asked, as they followed her into the plane. "You seem to be confident of your Kelsov."

"Dorsey's safer than on other jobs I've asked him to do," Catherine said as she sat down and fastened her seat belt. "Sit down. I've printed out copies of the skeleton photo. After we take off, we can go over them and see if we can identify Rakovac's so-called clue he planted in it."

"If there is a clue," Joe said.

"I think that there will be," Eve said as she sat down beside Catherine. "He was too smug, too excited. He was proud of himself."

"Call me when you're ready." Joe moved up the aisle. "I think I'll go up to the cockpit and get to know Hodges better. You never know when you're going to need a little airpower."

Eve watched him go up the aisle. Trust Joe to try to delve into the alluring mechanical world of this jet. He always liked to take things apart and put them back together again. It was a part of that insatiable curiosity.

"You can still back out," Catherine said quietly. "Just walk off the plane."

Eve shook her head. "I can't do that." She smiled. "Luke's waiting."

"Is he?" Catherine asked. "I hope so."

So did Eve. But Catherine didn't need her to be anything but positive right now. She would close out all her own fears as long as it was possible. "Luke is waiting for us," she said firmly. "Now dig out those prints of the photo, and let's see if they can tell us what carrot Rakovac is dangling in front of us."

It was difficult analyzing the photo of the skeleton, Eve thought. She had to close out the thought of the child and concentrate on the surroundings, and that was almost impossible for her. Seeing the skeleton filled her with such a wild combination of anger and sadness that it interfered with any type of logical reasoning.

"Okay?" Joe asked quietly.

She nodded jerkily. "There's nothing okay about this, but I can't let it get to me." She glanced at Catherine, who was across the aisle from them. "I can imagine what she's going through right now."

"The photo," Joe prompted.

Concentrate.

"The skeleton is almost certainly that of a five-year-old male. I can't judge how long he's been buried without examining the actual bones." She added, "Or if he was actually buried in that grave. Perhaps Rakovac staged it. But if he did, then he still would have had to plant some kind of clue to draw us into the web."

His gaze narrowed on the photo and began to take it apart. "A pile of dirt that resembles a makeshift grave. The dirt is moist, lumpy, and appears to have a slight green cast. There are trees in the background. Pines?"

Eve nodded. "No help there. Pines are everywhere."

"Then the skeleton itself." He turned to

Catherine. "Rakovac said he shot him in the head?"

"Yes." She moistened her lips. "But he lied. This isn't Luke."

"But that shattered entry is consistent with a bullet wound," Eve said gently. "I got a preliminary report from the St. Louis Institute just before I left the cottage. They blew up the shot and examined the pixels under the microscope. It had to be a large-caliber bullet that would cause that much damage on such a small skull."

Catherine flinched. "It's not Luke."

"It was a helpless, five-year-old boy," Eve said tightly. "At the moment, that's all that I can see; everything else is blurred."

"I'm sorry," Catherine said. "I'd be as angry as you under ordinary circumstances. The killing of any child is terrible. But there's nothing blurred about my thinking right now. It's clear and sharp and all about Luke."

Eve nodded. "Then try to focus some of that sharpness on the photo. Is there anything about it that's in the least familiar?"

Catherine looked down at the photo. "Nothing. It's just . . . horrible."

"What is this patch of earth on his thigh?" Joe was examining the skeleton more closely.

"I think it's moss," Eve said. "It's clumpy

and moist like the rest of the dirt. I guess that's why it clung to the skeleton when it was exhumed."

"Did you e-mail it to your friends at the St. Louis Institute and see if they can identify it and place it at a specific location?"

Eve nodded. "It seems to be an odd color, but I can't determine much about it without putting it under intense magnification."

"Maybe that's Rakovac's carrot," Joe said.

"That's what I thought. Long shot." Eve flipped open her computer and began typing in the message to go with the e-mail. "But it's all we have. I'll ask them to put a rush on it."

"How long?" Catherine asked.

Eve shrugged. "It depends on how close they can come to identifying that soil sample from the photo. In the meantime, we'd probably better keep looking for any other leads."

Catherine nodded. "It's not as if we have Langley." She made a face. "I've seen them call in a satellite to measure the angle of the moonlight and come up with a probable location."

"Were they right?"

"Yes, but it took them four days. We don't have four days. And if I asked Venable to do it, I couldn't be sure that he'd feed me the right information. It would depend on the state of their negotiations with Rakovac. We'll try your St. Louis Institute first." She pulled up the Rakovac surveillance file. "And while we're waiting, I'll see if I can glean anything from this report."

"Akron, Ohio." Venable punched a yellow pin on the city on the map of the U.S. on the wall. "Are we sure, Bradley?"

"Hell, no." Agent Eric Bradley scowled as he stared at the map. "We're not sure of anything. It could be another red herring. But my informant says that Akron is a possibility." He shook his head. "But we still don't know who the contact is." He cursed. "Or if there is one in Akron. It's another damn blank. If they're getting ready for a hit, why can't we get someone to talk?"

"Because whoever is handling the money trail is smart and has the manpower to cover his tracks."

"Rakovac?"

"I'd bet on it."

"Then find him and get rid of him."

It was the solution Venable had been considering, but it might be too dangerous. "And what if everything is in place and goes forward even after we kill him? We don't know how far along he's come with Ali Dabala. No, we have to know names, dates, cities."

"I've tried, Venable."

Venable knew Bradley had tried, and he was a good man. He had used every resource available and had gathered an amazing amount of information.

But not enough.

Venable felt a tightness in his chest as he gazed at the map. So many colorful tacks. It looked like a cell-phone commercial. Yellow tacks for possibles. Red tacks for probables. So many cities. So many people . . .

Damn Rakovac.

"What next?" Bradley asked.

"What do you think? Go back and get the information."

Bradley hesitated. "The last timeline we have is between four and seven days. There may not be enough time."

"Then stop wasting it."

Bradley shrugged and strode out of Venable's office.

Venable's gaze returned to the map.

Four to seven days.

And the chances were that Bradley wasn't going to be able to find out anything more than he had already.

Dammit, he had to *know.*

Stop hesitating. Do what had to be done. He couldn't afford to be soft. He had to balance the good of the majority against the good of a few. He had lived all his adult life making decisions like this one. This would only be one more.

He reached for his phone and dialed a number. Voice mail. "Dufour, call me back. I need to speak to you. Pronto."

Chapter 9

Navrodas, Russia

The airport where they landed was located in a deserted area, with only three hangars and a runway that was bumpy and full of potholes.

Eve felt as if her teeth were being jarred out of their sockets by the time the jet came to rest at the end of the runway. "Not exactly a smooth landing."

"Beggars can't be choosers," Catherine said. "It's within sixty miles of Moscow. The mafia built it over two decades ago, but they moved up in the world and abandoned it. It's been deserted for at least seven years."

"Totally deserted?" Joe asked. "Rakovac is still heavily involved with the mafia. It's not watched?"

Catherine shook her head. "It's safe, or Kelsov wouldn't have brought us here. Believe me, he's trying to stay off Rakovac's hit list until he's in a position to take him down." She glanced at Eve's computer. "No word from your institute?"

"Not yet."

"Backlogged?"

"Always. But I put an *urgent* on the request. They know I don't push unless there's reason." She was unfastening her seat belt. "And I've done a few favors for them."

"More than a few," Joe said dryly as he stood up. "Now tell me about this Kelsov. How much can we trust him?"

"All the way if it concerns taking Rakovac down," Catherine said. "On every other front, he's a wild card. He's very smart, violent, and, on occasion, reckless. In most cases he sticks to his word, but I've known him to change horses in midstream." She shrugged. "He's a survivor. A survivor has to make certain adjustments."

"But she likes him." Dorsey Hodges had come out of the cockpit. "Enough to risk my neck whenever she decides she has to make a foray here to find her Luke." He smiled at Catherine. "I, on the other hand, find him a little too barbaric for my taste. By the way, I don't see a sign of him."

"He was fighting and killing for the Georgian Republic in their fight with Ossetians and Russia when he was twelve. He was doing hard labor in Siberia by the time he was seventeen. I'd say that would foster barbaric tendencies." Catherine was looking out the window. "And here he comes."

"You'd think he'd be here waiting," Dorsey said. He opened the door and pressed the button to lower the stairs. "But then we don't think alike."

"No." Catherine had started down the stairs. "But there's no rule that says you have to. As long as the job gets done." She was waving at Kelsov. "You've upset Dorsey," she called. "He thinks that you should have been here to whisk us safely away when the wheels touched down."

"I was almost on time." Alex Kelsov stepped out of the dark gray Mercedes. "I had a poker game last night, and I didn't want to walk away a complete winner. It's always better to lose a little to keep the tempers from flaring." A brilliant white smile lit his tan face. "It takes time to lose convincingly."

Lord, he's big, Eve thought. Kelsov must have been at least six-five with broad shoulders, brawny arms and thighs, and tight waist and butt. Dressed in a white crewneck cable sweater and dark jeans, he looked vaguely nautical. He was probably in his late twenties but he appeared younger.

His hair was dark chestnut and worn a little long. His dark eyes were set deep in his craggy face, and his big white teeth and wide lips added boldness to his features. Not that he needed any additional boldness, Eve thought. Everything about his expression and body language spoke, no, shouted, of confidence and vitality.

"I imagine it takes longer to win convincingly," Catherine said dryly. "Did you cheat, Kelsov?"

"Not this time. It wasn't that kind of game." He strode forward, picked her up, and gave her an enormous hug. "It's good to see you, Catherine. I've missed you. Life is always more interesting when you come to visit me."

"Put me down, Kelsov," Catherine said. "You only do this to put me at a disadvantage."

"Nonsense." He swung her around, then set her on her feet. "I do it because you're a beautiful woman, and it gives me the opportunity to touch you."

"And?"

He grinned. "And it's not often I can feel superior around you. A man must do whatever he can to keep his ego intact." He looked beyond her to Dorsey Hodges. "Are you slipping? That landing wasn't all that smooth."

Dorsey said between set teeth, "If you'd arrange to bring us into a decent airport, I might be able to —"

"He's right, Kelsov." Catherine stepped into the conversation. "Stop baiting him." She turned to Eve and Joe. "Joe Quinn, Eve Duncan. I told you about them. This is Alex Kelsov."

"Delighted. I was a little uneasy until I did a little checking, but I think I can tolerate you." Kelsov gave them another brilliant smile as he inclined his head. "If you don't get in my way."

"I'm not sure that we can tolerate you," Joe said. "But there are always solutions if we can't."

"Oh, yes," Dorsey said, half-beneath his breath.

Kelsov's smile didn't waver, but his expression became thoughtful. "That is true. There are always solutions." He turned back to Catherine. "Do I take you to my farmhouse or do we have a destination?"

"The farmhouse. We should have word soon."

"Is this farmhouse safe?" Joe asked.

"Of course," Kelsov said. "I don't make mistakes like that. I know Rakovac has his people crawling from beneath every rock."

Catherine turned to Dorsey. "Stay nearby. I'll let you know when I need you."

"Anytime." He turned toward the plane. "Good luck, Catherine."

"She has me," Kelsov said as he strolled toward the car. "Luck isn't necessary."

"It's not that kind of game?" Catherine asked. "I think that I'll take any kind of luck I can get." She waved at Dorsey as he climbed the steps. "Thank you, Dorsey."

He shook his head. "After what you did for me, I'm still way behind." He smiled and disappeared into the plane.

Catherine turned toward Eve. "Kelsov isn't usually this abrasive. He and Dorsey rub each other the wrong way."

And Eve had an idea that conflict swirled around Catherine. And, why not? She was an extraordinary woman who was also stunningly attractive. Even with no encouragement from her, it would be natural for them to gravitate toward her. Even Joe had noticed how beautiful Catherine was.

Lucy Liu combined with Angelina Jolie.

"I can see how they'd be a little antagonistic. They seem to be direct opposites."

"You're right. Dorsey is smooth and civilized. Kelsov is rough-diamond flamboyant." Catherine shrugged. "But they work well together when they have to. That's all that's important."

"Come. Don't dawdle," Kelsov called to them from the driver's seat. "I've called ahead to Natalie, and dinner will be waiting for us. Catherine, sit up here with me and tell me how we're going to cut Rakovac's throat."

"I told you on the phone, Luke comes first." She got into the passenger seat. "One move from you that puts Luke in danger, and I'll cut your throat."

"My gentle dove." Kelsov threw back his head and laughed. "How I've missed you."

"Interesting," Joe said in a low voice as he opened the door to the backseat for Eve. "Rather like Kate and Petruchio in *Taming of the Shrew.*"

"I'd lay odds there's no taming going on." Eve got into the car and pulled her computer out of her case. "I've got to check my e-mail. The institute should have answered me by now."

"Institute?" Kelsov asked as he started the car. "From what I read about you, I thought you worked alone. Brilliant forensic sculptor closeted away doing her magic."

"It's not magic."

"Sometimes it is," Catherine said quietly. "Skill can do magic. So can dedication."

"Then you should have enough magic to

be able to hurl lightning bolts, Catherine," Kelsov said. "I've never known anyone with more dedication."

"I have." Catherine glanced over her shoulder and met Eve's gaze. "Perhaps not more, but just as much." Her gaze shifted to Kelsov. "And what about you, Kelsov? I wouldn't be able to use you if you weren't obsessed with Rakovac. I can't see you risking your neck just to help me find Luke."

"I might." He smiled. "Though that wasn't my attitude in the beginning. All I could think about was pure revenge. You were a stranger, and we used each other. But I've grown to know you, Catherine. These days, it's difficult for me to separate my obsession from yours."

"I imagine that if you had an opportunity to put Rakovac down, it would all become very clear to you," she said dryly. "Don't try to tell me anything else."

He stared at her for a moment before he said, "I might, if I thought I could make you believe me." Then he chuckled. "But that won't happen, so I'll hold my peace."

" 'Peace'?" she repeated. "You and that word are strangers to each other. How is Natalie?"

"She's well. As well as she can be. She'll be much better once I kill Rakovac." He changed the subject. "You said you had Rakovac's surveillance file. Is there anything in it that will help us?"

"Not so far as I can tell. I still haven't finished."

"Who is Natalie?" Joe asked.

"Natalie Ladvar," Catherine said. "Another one of Rakovac's victims. We found her two years ago in a town near what was his headquarters at that time. Sixteen years old and the daughter of one of Rakovac's men. Rakovac thought she'd amuse him for a few months, so he raped her and set her up as his mistress. She decided she didn't appreciate the honor and took off. He was insulted and found her and brought her back." Her lips tightened. "He kept her prisoner for six months, and she can't even talk about the torture he put her through. When he decided he was finished with her and let her go, she was almost a zombie. We found her in the brothel where he'd sold her. I thought she might be able to tell me something about Luke, so Kelsov went in and got her."

"And?"

Catherine shook her head. "I told you, she was a zombie. She couldn't even talk." She made a face. "But we couldn't just let her go back there. So Kelsov took her home with him."

"At Catherine's orders," Kelsov said.

"You didn't argue," Catherine said. "So shut up. If I hadn't told you to do it, you would have done it anyway. And you never tried to get rid of her."

"She doesn't talk much, and she cooks pretty good."

"After you worked with her for a year."

"Which just demonstrates how much I hate to cook."

"That must be it." She glanced back at Eve. "Anything from the institute?"

Eve shook her head. "Not yet. I'll e-mail them again."

"Wait until we reach the farmhouse," Kelsov said. "The reception is better." He turned a curve in the road and nodded. "It's just ahead."

The house he'd indicated was a small stone building that was set far back from the road. An equally small barn was situated to the rear of the house. A brown-haired woman opened the door as they drove up the driveway. She was small, thin, dressed in brown pants and a loose white shirt, her hair pulled back in a loose ponytail. If this was Natalie, she appeared far older than her eighteen years. Eve had expected her to be the zombie Catherine had called her, but she only appeared to be pale and withdrawn. Her enormous brown eyes weren't terrified, only uncertain.

"You lied," Catherine murmured. "She *is* better."

"I worked with her. I couldn't leave her like that. Rakovac would love it if he'd totally destroyed her. I wasn't having it."

"And that's the only reason you helped her? I don't think so."

"Don't make the mistake of thinking I'm getting soft," he said quietly. "I'm a selfish bastard intent on getting exactly what I want. I'm just no monster. In comparison, I look pretty good to her."

"Better than good." Catherine got out of the car and moved toward the girl. "Hello, Natalie. Do you remember me? I'm Catherine Ling."

Natalie nodded. "I remember. You were with Kelsov when he took me from that place." She tried to smile. "Though Kelsov says I shouldn't remember anything about that time if I can help it."

"You should pay no attention to him," she said. "Don't dwell on it, but it will always be with you. You can't ignore it, or it will sneak up on you when you least expect it." She studied her. "You're looking well."

Natalie nodded. "I looked in the mirror

one day last week, and I could almost see . . . I looked alive."

"You are alive," Kelsov said roughly as he got out of the car. "Stop talking foolishness. Would I have wasted all my time on you if you weren't alive and worthwhile?"

"No." Natalie smiled faintly. "And because your time is so important, I must be very worthy." She started to turn away. "Dinner is ready. I made stew that —"

"Wait." Catherine gestured to Eve and Joe, who had just joined her. "Joe Quinn, Eve Duncan. This is Natalie Ladvar. They're trying to help me, Natalie."

Natalie inclined her head. "I'm very happy to meet you. I hope you can help Catherine. I couldn't do it. She wanted me to tell her about — but I couldn't — I might have known something, but by the time she came to that . . . place, it was gone."

"We'll help her," Eve said gently. "Everything is all right, Natalie." She stepped forward. "And it will be better when I try that stew. I'm very hungry."

Natalie smiled. "Then please come in. Kelsov doesn't bring company very often. This stew is what you might call a test case."

"Your test case was a complete success," Joe said as he lifted his napkin to his lips.

"You're quite a cook."

"My mother taught me before she left us." A shadow crossed her face. "But I forgot how to do it. I forgot a lot of things."

"It's coming back to you," Kelsov said. "And if it doesn't, sometimes new is better."

"He always says that," Natalie said as she rose to her feet. "Go into the living room while I stack the dishes. I'll bring coffee."

"I'll help," Catherine said.

Natalie shook her head. "It's my job. I have to pay for my keep some way." She started to stack the bowls. "Kelsov says it's important for me."

"And she believes me. She doesn't realize it's because I've always wanted a slave," Kelsov said, straight-faced.

"Yes, I believe you." She didn't look at him as she turned toward the huge country sink. "I'll always believe you."

Kelsov rose to his feet. "You see what I'm up against? I'm such a good liar, and it's all wasted." He turned and led them from the small kitchen to the adjoining living room. "How can I fight her?"

"You can't," Eve said as she dropped down on the faded easy chair by the fire. "Why would you want to? She's very fragile."

"If I treat her too gently, she'll never come into her full strength," Kelsov said. "That bastard took her when she was only a kid, and what he did stunted her. It wasn't only the mental and physical torture. He made her feel so helpless, she withdrew into herself." He sat down and stretched his long legs out before him. "So I pull her out of the shell. Sometimes it hurts her, but that's too bad. It's got to be done even if she hates me."

"I don't think that's going to happen." Eve had watched the strange interaction between the two of them at dinner. Close. So close. Natalie had been very quiet, but Eve was sure she had not missed a word or gesture that had issued from Kelsov. Kelsov had spoken very seldom to Natalie, and he had clearly been trying to avoid showing any concern, but his attitude had been watchful, protective. "Would she be better off in a rehabilitation center?"

"Yes. God knows, she shouldn't be around me. I probably remind her of Rakovac and all the men who abused her. I drink too much on occasion, I don't bring women home, but she knows I have them." He grimaced. "And Catherine will tell you that I'm not a gentle man."

But he was gentle with Natalie. "Then

why not get her to go where she wouldn't be exposed to you?"

"I tried that a month after she came to me. A nice little rest home in the Alps." He shook his head. "She tried to commit suicide the night I left her. I won't do that again."

"You didn't tell me that," Catherine said.

"It wasn't your business any longer. You turned her over to me. She was mine."

"It's not safe for her. Rakovac hates you. He hasn't tried to hunt you down since you've been keeping a low profile. But he could find out she's with you and come after her. Send her away. She's stronger now."

"I won't do that again," he repeated. "We'll get through this together. Sometimes you can't pick and choose. You have to accept the inevitable and make the best of it."

"She's doing so well. I'd hate to have —"

A gentle ping from Eve's computer on the console across the room.

"E-mail!" Eve jumped from her chair and was at the bureau where she'd left the computer in seconds. She flipped open the laptop as she carried it back to the chair. "It's about time."

"The institute?" Joe asked.

She nodded absently as she pulled up the message. "And it seems to be fairly inclusive by the size of it." Her gaze was flying over the e-mail. "The twisted tree near the grave appears to be pine. Under intense magnification, they discerned another tree in the background that they're sure is birch. The earth is slightly damp and suggests either recent rainfall after the exhumation or that the grave is located in a marsh." She leaned forward. "They're leaning heavily toward the latter because of the piece of fungus on the left thigh."

"The moss?" Catherine asked.

"Only it's not moss, it's lichen. Which is usually a cross between alga and fungal filaments."

"And does it exist in a marsh?" Catherine was suddenly beside her, looking down at the e-mail. "Birch and pine are found in marshes."

Eve nodded. "There are over twenty thousand different kinds of lichen known, but that gray lichen with orange markings is from a peat bog. And it's not that common, thank God. It exists in several places in northern Europe, but in Russia it's been found only near the Caspian Sea and in the marshes of the Ivanova region."

"Ivanova," Kelsov murmured. "Oh, yes, I know those marshes."

Catherine's gaze flew to his face. "And

that means Rakovac would know them."

"Like the back of his hand." Kelsov's lips twisted. "I can still feel the chill of the nights we spent in those marshes. Russia had given refuge to our enemies, the Ossetians, and a large number settled there. We went after them. I killed my first man near there and threw his body into a peat bog. I was twelve, and I had nightmares for years of watching that yellow mud suck him down."

"So if Rakovac was going to hide a grave, it could be near there?"

"Much more likely than the Caspian Sea," Kelsov said. "But that marshland area extends for miles. The grave won't be easy to find if he didn't decide just to throw the skeleton into the bog instead of returning it to the grave."

"I think he buried the skeleton again," Eve said. "He kept taunting me about working on Luke's skull. I'd have to have access to it if I'm to do a reconstruction. He wants me to find it. Or, at least, he wants to dangle it in front of us. If Rakovac can kill us, then he'll probably do it, but I think he'd prefer that he stretch it out a bit."

"Yes, he would," Natalie whispered. She was standing in the doorway, carrying a tray, and her face was parchment pale. "He likes to take his time and make you hurt."

"I'll take that." Joe was on his feet and taking the tray. "Sit down. I'll pour you a cup of coffee."

"No, I'll do it. My job . . ."

Kelsov pushed her into a chair. "You're officially on vacation." He poured a cup of coffee and put it into her hands. "But only for the next twenty minutes. Then you're back on the clock."

She lifted the cup to her lips. "I'm sorry." She took a deep drink of coffee. "You've found him?"

"We're close. We think we can find the place where he'll set up an ambush. We might be able to turn it on him."

She shook her head. "That's not good. You're not sure. You have to be sure with him. I had no plan. I just ran. I should have had a plan."

Such simple words but threaded with pain, Eve thought. Through this woman, her vision of Rakovac was becoming vividly alive and hideous. "We'll have a plan. First, we have to see if we can find that grave." She looked at Kelsov. "Do you have any contacts in that area who might be able to tell you anything?"

He nodded. "If they're not too afraid to talk. Rakovac still has both friends and enemies in that area."

"Can you call them?"

He shook his head. "I have to see them in person. It's the only way I can judge whether they're lying to me. I have friends and enemies there, too. Most of them in the village of Svedrun, near the marsh. I can't always tell which ones have crossed over to Rakovac's camp. Time and money change everything. Men who swore that they'd hate Rakovac to the day they died for betraying me are working for him now." He shrugged. "I think I'd know if they were lying to me if we were face-to-face. I'll have to see." He poured coffee into the cups on the tray. "I suggest we drink our coffee and head for bed. We'll start out for Svedrun in the morning."

"I'm coming with you," Natalie said.

He shook his head. "Not this time." He lifted his cup. "I promised you that I'd give you Rakovac, but we're not close enough."

"I want to —"

"No," he said. "Don't argue, Natalie."

She opened her lips to protest, then closed them again.

Catherine turned back to Eve. "Is there anything else?"

Eve glanced down at the e-mail. "Just references and sources they used. The institute is nothing if not meticulous."

"But efficient," Catherine said. "Why can't we leave tonight, Kelsov?"

"I have a few calls to make to prepare the way. I want to switch cars halfway to Svedrun. I don't believe my vehicle has been traced to me, but I don't want to take chances when we're going into what might be Rakovac territory. As I said, he has spies and contacts all over Russia." He paused. "I know you're in a hurry, Catherine. But I won't risk our necks unless I have to do it." He turned to Natalie. "Show Eve and Joe to my bedroom. Catherine can sleep with you. I'll bed out here on the couch tonight. Tomorrow I'll put up a cot in the barn."

Natalie got to her feet. "I'll bring you some linens." She looked at Eve and Joe. "If you'll follow me?"

Eve closed the computer and got to her feet. "Thank you." She asked Kelsov, "What time in the morning?"

"Six." He turned to Catherine. "Is that good enough?"

"If it has to be." Catherine moved toward the door. "You go with Natalie, Eve. Kelsov, come and help me bring in our suitcases."

"I'll come out and help," Joe offered.

Catherine shook her head. "Get Eve settled. Kelsov is always bragging how strong he got working in that labor camp in

Siberia. Let him prove it. I'll load him down like a pack mule."

"I believe she's a bit irritated because I'm asking her to wait for morning," Kelsov said as he followed Catherine. "But it's no punishment. I'm far stronger than any pack mule."

"I told you he bragged a lot," Catherine said as she opened the front door. "I'll have your cases to you in a few minutes."

Natalie stared after her an instant before she opened the bedroom door. "She's so . . . strong. Not in body, but in other ways. As strong as he is. He likes that." She stepped aside and gestured. "I changed the linens when Kelsov told me he was bringing guests. There's only one bathroom in the house, and it's off the living room. Tell me if you need anything."

"We'll be fine, Natalie," Eve said. "Catherine will bring us a toothbrush and anything else we need." She glanced around the room. It was very simply furnished, with only a double bed covered with a dark cotton spread and an oak nightstand. Everything in the room appeared spotlessly clean. "It looks very comfortable. Good night." She turned to Joe after Natalie left the room. "You were quiet at dinner. What were you thinking?"

"I was thinking I don't like this damn lack of control." He made a face. "Kelsov is a little too domineering for my taste."

"And you don't trust him."

He shrugged. "He's an unknown quantity. Catherine trusts him . . . within limits. I'd just as soon make my own judgments."

"You always do. But he seems to be in control at present."

"Then it might be a good idea to do something to shift the balance."

Eve's eyes narrowed on his face. "We do need him, Joe."

"I'm not saying that I'm ready to eliminate him from the picture." He smiled. "I'm just analyzing the situation, Eve."

But Joe was probing, weighing options, and that often translated into action. She had known when she had first seen Kelsov that Joe would be wary of him. He didn't entirely trust arrogance or flamboyance, and Kelsov certainly had both.

"Stop frowning." He touched her cheek. "I'm not going to cause any trouble. I'm just going to keep my eye on Kelsov." He turned toward the bed. "Now I think I'll stretch out. You use the bathroom first, and I'll bring you your robe when Catherine comes back with the cases."

■ ■ ■ ■

"We think Catherine Ling has left Atlanta," Russo said as he came into the study. "Or, at least, Duncan's lake cottage. Our agent was able to get close again earlier today, and the cottage appears to be deserted."

Rakovac leaned back in his chair. "No Duncan either?"

Russo shook his head. "And he checked with the ATLPD, and Joe Quinn has taken a leave of absence."

He smiled with satisfaction. "Then I believe we can assume that Catherine has taken the bait and jerked Eve Duncan into the whirlpool with her. We should be hearing something from our Catherine shortly." And that meant that the final stage of his personal game had been put in place. But it had to coincide with the grand scheme with Dabala for the timing to be perfect. "Did you check the bank? Has Ali Dabala sent the first installment?"

Russo shook his head. "He said he and his group want to see proof of your efficiency. It's a lot of money. How does he know that you won't disappear and leave him looking the fool?"

Rakovac scowled. He'd known that Ali

would balk at the down payment, but he'd hoped he was desperate enough to come through with it anyway. Evidently, that wasn't going to happen.

"What are you going to do?" Russo asked.

"Give him what he wants. It's not as if I'm not prepared." He flipped open his desk drawer and pulled out the schedule. Ten positive hits. Three alternates if those didn't come through. Two other cities far from the main target area.

One in Istanbul, Turkey.

One in Lima, Peru.

He pondered the two cities. It felt a little godlike to be able to lift his finger and decide if thousands of people were going to die.

Russo moistened his lips. "Which one?"

"Either would do. They're both on different continents from the U.S. and wouldn't arouse too much outrage. The Americans always claim to be horrified at another country's disasters, but if it doesn't touch them, they have a certain remoteness. They wouldn't recognize it as a threat to them."

"Venable would recognize it."

"But he wouldn't be able to convince anyone else."

"So which one?"

His hand hesitated over the Istanbul page,

then flipped open the Lima file.

The face in the photo was of a man his late forties, slightly plump, with silver frosting his temples.

"Pedro Gonzalez," Rakovac said. "Gate agent. Vantaro Airlines. Wife and three children. Are we ready for him?"

"We're ready."

"Then tell Dabala to get one of his men down to Lima, and we'll have his documents and his flight arranged. All he has to worry about is whether his man has the nerve to pull the trigger. Or, in this case, go to his precious paradise." His lips tightened. "And the minute it happens, I want a wire in my bank account for the $3 million."

Russo nodded and hurried from the room.

Rakovac closed the file, and his gaze shifted to the photo of Catherine Ling. "It's starting," he said softly. "I'd love to stretch our finale out to the limit, but I may be getting pushed. Do hurry along, won't you?"

Joe's eyes flicked open.

A car was starting outside the house.

He stared into the darkness, listening.

Unmistakable.

He checked his watch — 3:05 A.M.

He slid silently and swiftly out of bed, careful not to wake Eve. He grabbed his gun from his case and moved out of the bedroom and through the living room.

No Kelsov on the couch. Only a carelessly thrown blanket on the floor beside it.

Joe was out of the house in seconds.

But the car was already moving down the road, and he could only see the red taillights.

His hand clenched on the handle of his gun.

"Where the hell are you going, Kelsov?" he muttered.

They had no other vehicle, so he couldn't go after him, and again he felt that irritating sense of helplessness. It had to stop.

Was Kelsov betraying them?

He had no idea, and that made him even angrier. It was definitely a surreptitious and suspicious move, but this was Kelsov's territory, and sometimes actions weren't what they seemed. The only thing he could do was wait and be on alert for any danger to Eve and Catherine. But he was going to have a few choice words for Kelsov when he returned.

No, he was too pissed for words. Action. Definitely action.

The decision caused the adrenaline to start pumping through his body. He felt alive and purposeful for the first time since they had landed at that airport. He'd check the barn and surrounding woods to make sure there weren't any surprises waiting. Then he'd stake out the cottage and wait for Kelsov.

He turned on his heel and went back into the house to get dressed.

Chapter 10

The first dim light of dawn was starting in the east when Joe saw the headlights of Kelsov's Mercedes.

One car.

No one following him.

But he had been gone almost two hours.

Forget it and approach him diplomatically at a later time?

Hell, no.

He faded into the shadows beside the door.

The car slowed and came to a stop in front of the cottage.

Kelsov got out and came around the front of the car, but didn't come toward the door. Now he was beside the passenger seat and moving —

Someone was in the backseat!

Joe leaped forward and brought him down.

Kelsov rolled over and was reaching inside his jacket.

A knife.

"Oh, no." Joe flipped him over and his arm encircled his neck, using him as a shield against whoever was in the car.

"Let him go." The muzzle of a gun was pressed to the back of Joe's head. "Hurt him, and I'll shoot you."

Natalie. Her voice was shaking but the gun she was holding was not.

"No. Put down the gun. I won't break his neck if he stops struggling."

"Screw you," Kelsov said.

"Stop it." The back door of the car swung open. "All of you. Stop it. Joe, he's not doing anything wrong. Let him go."

"Kelly?"

The girl got out of the car. Her face was pale and she was shaking. But she was standing with hands clenched, her gaze on the other woman. "And you, you're shaking so badly that you could blow his brains out by accident. Kelsov, tell her to put it down."

"Some accidents are sent by God."

"And how would she feel?"

He was silent. "Put it down, Natalie."

She didn't move.

"Joe," Kelly said.

He reluctantly released Kelsov.

Natalie stepped back, but she didn't lower the gun.

Kelsov sprang catlike to his feet and whirled on Joe.

Joe blocked the first karate chop and kicked Kelsov's legs out from under him.

"No!" Catherine was standing in the doorway, an automatic weapon in her hand. "Freeze. Or I'll shoot you both in the knees. It's not something I want to do since I may need you, but I'll do it."

Natalie swung the gun in her direction.

"No, Natalie!" Kelsov dove forward between her and Catherine. He took the gun away from her. "It's okay."

"No, it's not okay," Catherine said. "What is happening here?" Then her gaze fell on Kelly standing beside the car. "Oh, for Pete's sake."

"Hello, Catherine," Kelly said.

Catherine whirled on Kelsov. "What's she doing here?"

Kelsov shrugged. "Venable called me tonight just after midnight and told me she was on her way and to pick her up at the airport."

"Dammit, why didn't you tell me?"

"He told me you wouldn't like it."

"But you did it anyway."

"It's a tough world. Venable is valuable to me, and he doesn't like me helping you. I have to strike a balance. I do a few things he considers as favors, and he turns a blind eye to a few things that tend to annoy him. It didn't seem much of a favor just doing a pickup and delivery." He turned and glanced at Kelly. "But he didn't tell me she was just a kid."

"But, again, you would have done it anyway."

He nodded. "It's a tough world," he repeated. His expression hardened as he looked at Joe. "What the hell do you think you were doing?"

"Taking down a threat. What was I supposed to do when a prick like you sneaks out of the house in the middle of the night? Catherine may trust you, but should I?"

Kelsov glared at him. "It doesn't matter. It's my —" He stopped. Then he slowly shook his head. "Not unless you're a fool. Put away the gun, Catherine. I'm not going to kill him tonight." He took Kelly's wrist and pulled her forward. "Here's your package from Venable. Delivered as promised." He turned to Natalie. "Suppose you go in and make us coffee. The task is a little mundane and tame compared to bluffing Quinn with a threat to send him to meet his maker, but we could all use —"

"I was not bluffing," she said simply as she turned toward the door. "I could not let you die." She went past Catherine into the house.

"I'm sorry I caused all this trouble," Kelly said. "Venable said it would be no problem getting me here." She smiled unsteadily. "He said all the trouble would come later. I guess he was wrong."

"I guess he was." Catherine stepped aside. "Come in and tell us why the hell Venable dropped you in the middle of Russia like some kind of atomic bomb."

"He said he had to do it. He didn't want me to come, but he —"

"Not out here." Catherine pulled her into the house. "Good heavens, Kelly, how could you do this? I thought when you left the lake cottage that you'd be safe."

"I know you did." She glanced at Joe. "I didn't mean to cause you any trouble. I didn't know Mr. Kelsov wouldn't tell anyone he was picking me up."

"Then it was his fault, not yours." He smiled. "And the night wasn't all that bad. I enjoyed parts of it."

"I bet you did," Catherine murmured.

"But now I've got to go and wake Eve and tell her what —"

"Wake?" Eve said grimly. She was standing in the bedroom doorway. "I think you should have done that some time ago." She glanced around the room. "I seem to be the only onc who was sleeping." She shook her head as she looked back at Kelly. "I can't believe it."

"You thought you got rid of me. I must be the bad penny."

"Not bad," Catherine said gruffly. "Just damn stubborn." She looked at Eve. "Venable sent her."

"Not again? Not here?"

"Don't ask. I don't know." She took Kelly's elbow and led her toward the table. "But we'll find out. Sit down. I'll get you a cup of coffee."

"Thank you." Kelly leaned back in the chair and gave a deep sigh. "I was scared. I was afraid that woman would shoot Joe."

"Shoot Joe?" Eve sat down across from Kelly. "I believe I missed more than I thought. Talk."

"Give her a moment," Catherine said.

Eve nodded. "We're standing around staring at her as if she's a murder suspect, and we're cops giving her the third degree."

"More like a murder victim," Catherine said as she put a cup of coffee down in front of Kelly. "If Rakovac comes knocking on our door. Why, Kelly?"

Kelly didn't speak for an instant. "The

same reason I've been giving you since I came to the lake cottage. I want to help you."

"I'm not even going to discuss that," Catherine said. "I've already told you my feelings. What I'm really asking is why Venable gave in to you and sent you here? I can see his reasoning when he sent you to the lake cottage, but he's no reckless fool, and he does have a conscience. There's no way he should have sent you into the line of fire no matter how much you begged and pleaded."

"I didn't beg or plead." She sipped her coffee. "I didn't get the chance. I called him right after I left the lake cottage. I was going to try to persuade him to talk to you, but every time I tried to get through to him, I got his voice mail. I thought he was trying to avoid me. Then later in the evening he phoned Agent Dufour at the motel where he'd taken me and told him that he needed to talk to me."

"He called you?" Joe repeated. "Why?"

Kelly's gaze never left Catherine. "Because he's not like you. He believed that I could help you. He said to tell you that he had no choice. He said desperate situations require desperate measures."

"And you're the desperate measure?

That's bullshit. Even Venable wouldn't send a kid into a situation like this."

"He did, didn't he?" Kelly cradled her cup in her two hands. "So that must mean you're wrong. This hot coffee feels good. I'm a little chilly. Could I get my suitcase and find my sweater?"

"Why didn't you say so?" Catherine took off her terry robe and draped it around Kelly's shoulders. "Didn't anyone tell you that Russia was colder than Atlanta? No, they just bundled you onto a plane and sent you off."

"They were in a hurry. Venable said that he didn't know how or in what direction you'd be traveling once you reached Moscow. He wanted to make sure that I'd be able to hook up with you. He said it would be safer for me."

"How considerate," Eve said dryly. "But he sent you anyway."

"Desperate measures," Kelly said. "And I told him I'd take the chance of missing you. He said that if I didn't find you, he'd set me up somewhere else safe to work. I told him it wasn't a deal unless I could be with you."

"A deal?" Catherine said.

Kelly met her gaze. "He said you might think he was putting another roadblock in his way, but it isn't true. He wants you to find Rakovac now, and he doesn't care how you do it. He said the time was over for being diplomatic."

"Interesting," Kelsov said. "Does that mean he's going to help us nail the bastard?"

"He would if he could." She smiled tentatively. "That's why he sent me. He said it was urgent. None of his agents have been able to find Rakovac, and he has to find him soon."

"Urgent?" Catherine said. "How soon?"

"He's not sure. A week or ten days. He doesn't know how much time he has left. That's why we have to get to Rakovac."

"And why is he suddenly so urgent?" Joe asked.

She shrugged. "He wouldn't tell me. He just said that you have to let him know when you find him." She paused. "I have to let him know. He made me promise."

"Part of your deal?" Catherine asked. "And what are the other details of this deal?"

"I'm to figure out where he's hidden your son. If Luke is still alive, at some point Rakovac will be near him." She moistened her lips. "But you mustn't kill Rakovac. He should have either a journal or computer file in his possession. Perhaps both. Venable said he probably won't have it on him. You may have to follow him back to his office or residence. But Venable has to have that file."

"Why?"

"He wouldn't tell me. But he said that Rakovac mustn't die until we get the file." She paused. "That you wouldn't want him to die."

"I can't think of any circumstance where I wouldn't want Rakovac to die . . . after I find Luke."

"Venable said that you . . ." She trailed off. "I've given you his message. That's all I can do. He'll have to convince you to pay attention to it." She took a sip of her coffee. "All I care about is that I'm here with you."

"Why did he send her?" Kelsov asked. "I still don't understand. Does she know something about Rakovac that we don't?"

"No, she's a whiz kid who sees patterns where no one else does. Sort of a juvenile Einstein," Catherine said. "She thinks that she can find Luke . . . and Rakovac. Evidently, Venable believes that she can, too."

Kelsov gave a low whistle. "Venable isn't a gullible man. I'd listen to him. How is she supposed to do this?"

"A good question," Joe said.

"The Rakovac surveillance file," Kelly said. "The one you wouldn't let me read,

Catherine."

"And now I'm supposed to turn it over to you?"

Kelly shook her head. "Venable sent me my own copy."

Of course he would, Catherine thought in frustration. "And that's going to send you down the right path?"

"Perhaps. Or maybe I can talk to people who know him and try to see which way he would go in certain circumstances." She met Catherine's gaze. "I'm not going to get in your way. I know that's what you're afraid of."

"Dammit, yes, I'm afraid you'll get in my way." She knelt by Kelly's chair and brushed the girl's fair hair away from her face with rough tenderness. "And I'm more afraid you'll get in Rakovac's way. Let me call Venable and get him to pick you up and take you back to the U.S."

"It's too late. We made a deal." Kelly smiled. "And he wouldn't come and get me. He told me I was on my own. I think he considers me . . . expendable. Isn't that the word?"

Catherine's lips tightened grimly. "That's the word."

"He's very worried about something Rakovac is going to do. I'm not very important in comparison."

"Well, you're important to me." She gave Kelly a quick hug and sat back on her heels. "We're leaving this morning to try to find the grave you saw in that photo. Can I convince you to call Venable and tell him to come and get you?"

"No."

"Then will you stay here with Natalie and work on the file? That's what you promised to do, and you can't do it trailing after us through a swamp."

Kelly shook her head.

"Use your head." Catherine took her shoulders and gently shook her. "This is the only way you're valuable to me. Now stay and do your job."

"I don't know what will happen to you in that swamp."

"Neither do I. But I have a better chance of surviving if I don't have to worry about taking care of you. You can see that."

"Yes." She was frowning. "But I don't want to see it." She looked at Eve. "What's going to happen in that marsh?"

"We're going to try to find that grave and dig up the skeleton again," Eve said.

"Won't Rakovac have left someone to watch the grave?"

"More than likely. We'll have to take action to avoid them."

Kelly's gaze went to Joe. "I can't see him avoiding anyone."

Joe smiled. "You think I'm confrontational?"

"You climbed out a window and went hunting the night I came to your house."

"I was defending my turf."

"You looked like you were enjoying yourself." She glanced back at Eve. "What happens next?"

"After we find the skeleton, I do a quick examination to see if there's even a possibility that it might be Luke."

"And if there is?"

She hesitated and glanced at Catherine. "I take the skull."

Catherine inhaled sharply. She had known that would be the procedure. There was no way they could remove the entire skeleton. But the thought of wrenching the head off any skeleton that might be Luke's was painful. She steadied her voice. "Of course she does. It's the only way to handle it. She'll have to bring the skull back here and do the reconstruction."

"And I can't help you do that?" Kelly looked at Eve. "Is she right?"

Eve nodded. "You don't need me to tell you that."

"I guess I don't." Her glance shifted back to Catherine. "Okay, I'll stay here and work." She added fiercely, "But you come back. Don't let anything happen to you." She looked at Natalie. "I guess you're stuck with me. I'll try not to be any trouble."

Natalie nodded but turned back to Kelsov. "Is that what you want?"

Kelsov was already moving toward the door. "Take care of her. Answer any questions she asks." He glanced back over his shoulder at Kelly. "You say you might need to contact people who have known Rakovac for a long time. That's me, and that's Natalie. I'm not going to be around and Natalie is going to find it difficult to answer any questions. You'll just have to make do." He looked at Catherine. "I'll put gas in the car. You, Eve, and Quinn get ready to move out in the next forty minutes."

"I'll be ready." Catherine got to her feet. She brushed a light kiss on the top of Kelly's head. "I think you'll be safe here. Kelsov assures me that you will be. But if you or Natalie gets spooked for any reason, grab that gun Natalie was brandishing around, take off and call me. Do you understand?"

Kelly nodded. "Yes, can I help you get ready?"

"No, just hang out and keep out of the way until we leave, then take a shower and get a nap. You probably didn't get any sleep on the way here."

Kelly smiled. "I was too nervous. I don't like you to be angry with me, and I knew you would be."

"But it didn't stop you."

Her smile faded. "You need me. And Venable says he needs me. That's reason enough to bring me here. Maybe I'll be able to prove to myself that I'm worth something after all."

"Don't talk nonsense. You're worth more than practically anyone I've ever run across." She turned away. "Just keep yourself safe."

"No problem. I'm stuck here in this house with my computer. My big threat is going to be a bad headache or eyestrain." She leaned back in the chair. "I'll try to have something for you when you come back. But I hope you come back so soon that I won't have time to get anything together."

An hour later, Kelly and Natalie stood outside the house and watched the Mercedes disappear around the corner of the road.

Kelly's nails dug into her palms. She should be with them. Catherine had saved her life, and now she couldn't do anything to make sure that Catherine didn't die in that swamp. It was all very well for Catherine to say that analyzing the patterns was the only way that Kelly could be valuable to them. It was a very sterile and cerebral path when she wanted to be slogging away with them in that swamp, trying to find that skeleton.

"I want to go, too," Natalie said quietly.

"Then why didn't you argue? You didn't say a word when they just assumed that you'd be staying behind."

"I never argue with Kelsov."

"Why not?"

"I have to stay with him. He might send me away."

"Then it would be his loss. From what little I've seen, you seem to run this house and keep everything ticking."

"I have to stay with him."

"Anyone would be happy to have you work for them." She smiled. "Particularly since you're willing to protect them by shooting anyone who threatens them."

"But I wouldn't be happy." She turned away. "Catherine said you need a shower and rest. I'll make up Kelsov's bed for you." She looked back over her shoulder. "Can you really do what Catherine said? It sounds very strange. Can you find Rakovac?"

"If I have enough pieces to the puzzle. Will you help me?"

"You mean talk about Rakovac." Natalie was silent. "It will . . . hurt me."

"I don't want to hurt you."

"But Kelsov wants me to talk to you."

"That doesn't mean you have to do it. The report Venable gave me may be enough."

"But you're not sure."

"No, I'm not sure." She shrugged. "But I'm very good at this, Natalie. My brain is kind of . . . kooky. And I've been doing this since I was a little girl. Sometimes I see a pattern right away. Sometimes it takes me a long time, but it always comes."

"Always?"

She nodded. "There are times when I wish it didn't. Sometimes it scares me."

"I can see that it might. It would scare me to know where Rakovac was. Right now, he's like an ugly storm in the distance. But if I knew where he was, then he'd be real to me again." She whispered, "And I'd know I'd have to go and find him."

"There seem to be plenty of people who are willing to do that for you."

"Yes, but I have to do it. I'm frightened, but it has to be me."

"Why?"

She was silent. "Because I think that's the only way the nightmares would stop."

Kelly knew about nightmares. "Maybe it would help to talk." She made a face. "I sound like one of those psychiatrists that those social workers wanted to send me to. Don't do anything you don't want to do. What do I know? I'm just a kid. I know about these patterns and not much else. And even when I can figure out where those patterns are taking me, I can't do anything about it." She turned and headed for the door. "But I'm going to do something this time. I'm not going to let it beat me. And you shouldn't either. Stand up to Kelsov and tell him that you'll do what you want to do."

"That's not easy."

"I know. We'll both have to work at it. Come on, I have to get some sleep, so that I'll be fresh to start to pull up those files."

Lima, Peru
Santa Theresa Cathedral
2:55 p.m.

Holy Jesus send me a miracle.

Pedro Gonzalez's hands clenched on the rosary his wife had given him for his birthday, his gaze fixed desperately on the gold crucifix above the altar.

Save us all.

Save me from condemning my soul to hell.

Why was he here? Even God would not forgive the sin he was going to commit.

Yet Jesus had forgiven the world that had crucified him.

Forgive me. Forgive me. Forgive me.

Did God even hear him?

The tears were running down his cheeks as he buried his face in his hands.

The bell was tolling.

Three o'clock. He would have to leave. It was almost time.

Blessed Savior, let it not happen.

Holy Mother, save us all.

But there was no answer, no divine intervention.

His soul was doomed.

Svedrun, Russia
Ivanova Region

They reached the village of Svedrun late that afternoon. It was a barren, brown, marshy flatland that reminded Eve of the marshes she'd seen in England. She shivered. "It's very dreary. It's not like the swamps we have in the South. No cypresses growing out of the water. Just birches and pines. Our swamps are more . . . lush."

"And complete with alligators," Joe said.

"I'll take a little less lushness and no alligators."

"What do we do now?" Catherine asked Kelsov. "Who is your contact here?"

"I'm probably safest with Valentin Bravski. At one time, he hated Rakovac. I've just got to hope he still does." He got out of the car. "You wait here. I'll see what I can find out."

"You're just going to walk into the village?" Joe asked. "Is that smart?"

He shrugged. "Bravski lives on the edge of the village and I just have to make sure no one else sees me."

"That's not easy when you're ten feet tall," Catherine said dryly.

"Not quite ten feet," Kelsov said. "And I usually manage to be fairly inconspicuous if the need arises. Give me one of the photos of the grave site."

Catherine dug in her backpack and handed him a photo. "You think he'll recognize the area?"

"I have no idea. But he knows the marsh better than anyone else I know. We have a chance. Wait here." He disappeared into the trees.

Eve got out of the car and stood looking down at the village. "There's not much activity. It looks almost deserted."

"Deserted by the young," Catherine said.

"That's a problem with these small towns and villages in Russia. The young people don't want to live here in the country. As soon as they're old enough, they take off for the city. You can't blame them. Would you want to live in that village?"

Eve thought about it. "It's depressing. But with a little effort, you could change things. Most places are what you make of them."

"And Eve lives in her own world anyway." Joe got out of the car and came to stand beside her. "She'd take what she needed and be content."

Catherine glanced at him. "What about you?"

"I'm more restless. Contentment is boring."

Eve smiled. "He'd be whipping the entire village into shape. Forming co-ops and establishing a police force."

"Maybe," Joe said. "It's likely. If it was worth my while." He looked at Catherine. "I believe you'd do the same thing. You're restless, too."

"I could settle," Catherine said. "After I find Luke. But not here. In the U.S. And I'm going to build strong walls around him to keep him safe."

"And he'll run away like those kids who deserted this village."

"He won't want to run away," Catherine said. "I'll make him happy."

"That would be my first instinct, too," Eve said. "But you're going to have to be careful. You don't know what he's gone through . . . or what he's become."

Or if he'll be alive to surround with all that love and protection.

In this somber place, it was difficult to take an optimistic viewpoint of Luke's situation.

Catherine must have felt that same overwhelming sense of depression for she abruptly turned away. "Let's get back in the car. There's no sense standing here staring at that stupid village. There's no telling how long it will be until Kelsov gets through with questioning Bravski."

CHAPTER 11

Kelsov didn't return for another three hours, when darkness was beginning to fall.

"It's about time," Catherine said. "Did you find him?"

"Do I detect a hint of nerves?" Kelsov asked as he got into the car. "That's not like you. You're always so cool."

"Cut the sarcasm," Catherine said. "Did you find Bravski? Was he still there?"

"Yes, I found him. No, he wasn't quite there. Not all there. He's taken to the bottle. He was always fond of his vodka, but it's become a passion."

"He couldn't tell you anything?" Joe asked.

"I didn't say that. It just took me a little longer to get him sober and coherent. And willing to talk."

"But you did it?" Eve asked,

"Yes, Bravski was more than willing after I began to talk about Rakovac. Even through an alcoholic haze, he still hates his guts. And thanks to the vodka, I could be certain that he was telling the truth. It's difficult for a drunk to be too deceptive."

"The grave," Catherine prompted.

"He said he didn't know anything about it."

"Shit."

He held up his hand. "Wait. He did recognize the tree formation. He said he'd seen that intertwined birch and pine about six miles into the marsh."

"Good," Eve said. "Let's go."

"Wait." Joe's gaze was narrowed on Kelsov. "This is a very small village, and everyone must know everything that's going on. Even the town drunk. I can't believe that someone didn't know that Rakovac was in the area the night that photo was taken."

"I didn't say that," Kelsov said. "Everyone knew that he'd come back. They just preferred to turn a blind eye. It was safer. They'd had experience with Rakovac and didn't want to have anything to do with him." He grimaced. "After he betrayed me to Moscow, he did a little more work for the government. He came back here and executed a number of revolutionaries who were hiding out here in the marshes and surrounding villages. He hunted them down and killed anyone who sheltered them."

"Then I can't see why they wouldn't want to take him down," Catherine said.

"Fear. Rakovac is good at spreading fear. I understand he set examples to discourage anyone from coming after him. You should know how clever he is at manipulating the emotions."

"Yes, I know how clever he can be," Catherine said. "Okay, they knew that Rakovac was here. Is he still here?"

Kelsov shook his head. "Bravski doesn't think so. But he left at least two men in the marsh. Maybe more."

"To see if the trap is sprung," Eve murmured.

"That's reasonable," Kelsov said. "Which means that they have to be taken out before we can dig up that skeleton." He glanced at Joe. "Care to go hunting?"

Joe's brows rose. "You trust me?"

"I don't have to trust you. You don't have to trust me. We just have to trust that we can both get the job done. If you could take me down, I can trust you to do the same with Rakovac's men." He met Joe's eyes. "Do you think I can do the job? I was damn clumsy when you jumped me. I'm not usually that inefficient."

Joe studied him, silent. "I think you could

be fairly lethal if your ego doesn't get in the way."

"It never gets in the way where Rakovac is concerned."

"And now that you've completed your bonding, let's go find that grave," Catherine said impatiently. "I have to *know.*"

"I'm surprised you're not wanting to go hunting with us," Kelsov said.

"I could probably do it better," Catherine said. "But I have to make sure that Eve is safe and gets to that skeleton. That's all that's important."

"You're damn right that's important," Joe said grimly. "You'd better guard her as if she were your precious Luke."

"Joe, this is my choice," Eve said quietly. "No one is responsible for my safety but me."

"Wrong." Joe's gaze never left Catherine's. "I'm not reasonable about this. Keep her safe, or I'll come after you."

"I understand."

She did understand, Eve thought. Staring at the two of them she could see that there was an understanding between them that was forged not by years, but by spirit. She hadn't realized until that moment how similar they were. The same recklessness, protectiveness, toughness, perhaps even the same philosophy. It came as a slight shock.

Then Catherine turned to her and smiled. "It's okay, we're not going to be at each other's throats. You don't have to worry." She turned to Kelsov. "How do we get to this area?"

"Bravski drew me a map." He pointed to a crooked symbol. "That's the pine. We can drive through the marsh until we're about two miles away. Then we'll go on foot the rest of the way." He started the car. "But you'll give Quinn and me an hour head start. We'll call you if there's any mound that might be a grave near it and if it's safe to go after the skeleton."

Safe?

Eve was sure there wasn't going to be anything safe about this night.

Jorge Chavez International Airport
Lima, Peru

"You're late." Juan Martinez scowled as Gonzalez came up to the gate. "It's almost time to board the flight. They sent me to take over for you. I'm missing my lunch break."

"I'm sorry," Gonzalez said as he went behind the desk. "I was sick."

"You still look sick." Martinez's gaze raked Gonzalez's face. "You're pale. Go home. I can handle this."

Gonzalez shook his head. "I'm better now. Go on and have your lunch. What's the count?"

"Two hundred thirty-five."

Gonzalez closed his eyes. "So many?"

"Are you sure you're all right?"

His eyes flicked open. "I'm fine." It was a lie. He'd never be fine again. "Go on."

Martinez hesitated and turned to go. "Call me if you need me."

"Thank you." He began to call the flight.

First class first.

He'd be in seat 3C.

What did death look like?

He began to take the boarding passes.

Seat 3C was third in line. Camarez was on the boarding pass.

Dark hair, swarthy skin, dressed in a gray suit. He smiled pleasantly at Gonzalez. "It's always a pleasure to fly your airline. Everyone is so cooperative."

Excellent Spanish, not a hint of nerves. Was he on drugs?

"My case," Camarez said. "I believe security sent it up here?"

Gonzalez stared at him. He could say no. Dear God, he wanted to say no.

He reached beneath the desk and pulled

out the black briefcase and handed it to Camarez.

"Thank you." Then the man was gone, hurrying down the jetway to the plane.

No!

Don't run after him.

He couldn't stop him. He had to finish boarding the flight and walk out of the airport.

Martinez would tell everyone that he was ill. No one would be suspicious.

Just finish boarding the flight and walk away.

Don't look at the passengers getting on the flight. I don't want to remember the faces.

I've made my choice.

God had not saved them all. He would have to do it himself.

I just must not look at their faces.

Joe jumped out of the car and into the knee-deep mud at the side of the road. "Let's go, Kelsov. I'll take the guard on the road, then move into the trees. You move east deeper into the marsh."

Kelsov was already slogging through the mud and disappeared into the trees.

Joe glanced at Eve. "Stay in the car. Don't get impatient. I'll let you know when it's safe to go."

"We'll stay unless you're too long," Eve said.

Catherine nodded. "And then we come looking."

Joe shrugged. He hadn't expected anything else. "I'll let you know," he repeated, and moved away from the road into the thicket.

Stay close to the road but out of sight.

Bravski had said he'd seen one of Rakovac's men on the road several yards north of the twisted pine. That didn't mean he'd not change his sentry position, but it was reasonable to put a man on the road in case of an approach by auto.

Move silently.

It was easy enough to move through the heavy water and mud with no noise. The problem was usually to not disturb the birds and other animals. That was why he had to creep through the marsh; slowness was of the essence. But he knew how to negotiate swamps. He had done it so many times before. It was bringing back memories of those missions in North Korea when he was a SEAL.

Good. He needed that mind-set.

That was no problem. He was already feeling the surge of adrenaline and the revving of the fierce hunting instinct that was purely primitive. He had loved his stint in the SEALs. He had left the service when he realized he loved it too much. He knew that hunting instinct had to be channeled, or he'd become a savage.

As he was at this moment.

He felt his blood pounding through his veins and his brain open and hyperalert as he searched for the prey.

And there he was.

A tall, burly man carrying an automatic rifle as he stood on the road. He looked bored.

He wouldn't be bored for long.

Joe moved several yards past the sentry before he started to edge closer to the road.

Slowly.

He took his knife from his holster.

No sound.

Closer.

He had to be almost on top of him before he came out of the water. There was no way to disguise that sound.

Position.

The sentry was oblivious, staring into the marsh.

Joe tensed, gathering his muscles for the spring.

Be swift. Be catlike. Then the knife before

the man knew the threat.

Now!

He leaped out of the marsh.

The guard cursed and tried to swing the rifle around.

Too late.

Joe's knife entered his heart.

He fell to the road.

Get rid of the body in case one of the other guards in the thicket saw him lying on the road.

If they hadn't already.

Joe pulled the dead man to the edge of the road and pushed him into the marsh. Then he jumped in after him.

One gone.

Go after the other two.

He could feel his heart beating hard as he moved through the mud. He felt complete, invincible. No one could stop him.

"Quinn."

He whirled, knife ready.

"Easy," Kelsov whispered. He warily backed away. "I'm on your side. Particularly after watching you take down that guy on the road."

"Have you located anyone else?"

"One man right after I entered the thicket. He was in a tree. Didn't want to get his feet wet. I made a few noises, and he reluctantly decided he had to come down and investigate."

"Dead?"

He nodded. "But there's supposed to be one more."

"Then let's stop talking," Joe said impatiently. His gaze was raking the trees around them. The hunt hadn't ended. There was still prey to be had.

Kelsov's eyes were narrowed on his face. "You're enjoying this, aren't you?"

Joe didn't answer. He was moving deeper into the marsh. "If you're coming with me, shut up. I'm not going to get killed because you're running your mouth."

"Oh, I'm coming along." Kelsov waded after him. "I wouldn't miss it. You put on quite a show."

"Where are they?"

Eve's gaze searched the darkness. She could hear the sounds of insects, birds, and night creatures. She was accustomed to those sounds at the lake cottage, but swamps were always different. The sounds were heavier, more exotic, alien. Joe and Kelsov had vanished into that alien growth more than forty-five minutes ago. "I expected to hear something."

"If you had, then they might really be in

trouble," Catherine said. "Silence is good. Kelsov knows what he's doing. I've been with him in situations like this. And I don't have to have been with Joe to know that it would be hard to put him down."

Again, that sense of bonding, Eve thought. But she was in no mood to accept it as comfort. No one knew Joe's skills better than she did, and she was still scared. "I don't like —"

Her phone vibrated.

"Get moving," Joe said. "Three down. There's a mound by the pine tree. Kelsov is bringing the car closer. One of the men we took down had recently made a call, and I don't know how much time we have. I'll meet you at the grave." He hung up.

"Come on, Catherine." Eve was already moving through the marsh as she hung up. She adjusted the straps of her backpack. "Quick."

"I'm coming." Catherine was running after her. "Your backpack is bigger than mine. Do you need any help? What's in it?"

"Just that small shovel Kelsov gave all of us."

"Then why is it —"

"I had to bring something else." Catherine wasn't going to give up. Eve added, "My tools and forensic case."

Catherine was silent a moment. "Of course, you might need them. I guess I didn't want to think about them. Not connected with Luke. It seemed . . . cold."

And Eve hadn't wanted to bring it up either. Scalpels and forensic cases to deal with the dead were necessary but chilling to anyone who didn't work with them every day as Eve did. "Truth is often cold. But it has to be faced."

Four minutes later, they'd reached the twisted tree.

And that mound of dirt heaped before it.

Catherine stopped, took a deep breath, then strode toward it. "You keep watch. I'm stronger. I'll do the digging."

"Hell, no." Eve ran after her. "Joe said we had to move fast. I'll help."

"Rakovac didn't even try to disguise that mound of dirt," Catherine said as she took the shovel from her backpack. "Why should he? He wanted us to find it." She started to dig. "It shouldn't take long. The earth is soft, damp . . ."

Eve remembered how soft and damp that earth had appeared in the photo. How hard and brittle the child's bones had looked in contrast.

Blank it out. She would be seeing those bones soon enough. She dug into the earth.

"Be careful."

"Give me that." Joe was beside her taking the shovel. "Catherine and I can do this. Your job begins when we reach the skeleton."

Joe was being protective as usual, but it made Eve feel helpless as she watched them work together. They were both so strong and quick and decisive. Even though they were digging cautiously, every motion had purpose and meaning.

She needed to be part of that purpose. She took a step closer to take back the —

"I think I've reached something," Catherine said. "The bastard must have tossed just enough dirt to cover him." She was slowly moving the earth now. "Be careful, Joe."

"I'm not going to damage him," Joe said gently. "But we have to move fast, Catherine."

"I'll help." Eve was kneeling beside the grave and shifting the wet earth away from the bones with her bare hands.

Damn Rakovac.

Poor child.

Lost child.

Let this child not be Luke.

"We can't reach Calbre," Russo said as he came into Rakovac's office. "Ten minutes ago he tried to phone in but was cut off."

"Calbre was in charge of guarding the grave at Svedrun?"

Russo nodded. "There's been no trouble since we left there."

"Evidently there's trouble now." Ah, clever Catherine. He hadn't expected that she would be able to put together the pieces quite so soon. "Have you been able to contact any of his men?"

"We've made the attempt."

"That means you've failed."

"I can have someone there in the marsh in thirty minutes. We have people we can call on in a small town just outside the marsh."

"You haven't done so?"

"I was waiting to ask our position in the matter. It has to be Catherine Ling. Your reactions haven't been predictable where she's concerned."

"Our position is to kill Catherine Ling if we can, as well as anyone who is helping her. I expect that she has very good help if they've been able to get this far along." Joe Quinn. Eve Duncan. Who else? Kelsov had been a thorn in his side since he had been released from prison and had helped Catherine in the past. Yes, Kelsov was probably with her, too. "Is that clear enough, Russo?

Now I'd suggest you make that call."

He smiled as Russo left the room. The man didn't understand the subtleties of the game. No, Rakovac didn't want Catherine to die yet, but there would be no satisfaction in the finale if the threat was not genuine. Let her run from the hunters, and he would accept it if he was cheated.

But he would not be cheated. He believed in fate. It was meant that she be killed by him in the most painful way possible.

He looked at the photo of her on the desk.

"Run, Catherine," he said softly. "Run until you drop. I'll be there to pick you off as you fall."

His cell phone rang.

He glanced at the ID. It was the call he'd been waiting for.

Lima, Peru.

So small, Eve thought. The bones of a child were so delicate, so easy to break. Her Bonnie was only a little older when she'd been taken. Had her body been flung carelessly into the ground to become —

"Eve."

She tore her eyes from the little boy's skeleton to look at Joe.

Empathy.

Tenderness.

"I know," he said. "But we need you to hurry."

Yes, no time for pain. No time for memories or comparisons. She jerked her attention back to the task she had to do. "I need more light. Catherine, get the lantern out of my backpack." She crawled closer to the skeleton. The pelvis and teeth definitely indicated a male of four or five. Bones appeared aged and weathered, but probably preserved by being buried near the peat marsh. The skull . . . Rakovac had said that he'd shot the child.

"The light," she said impatiently. "I have to examine the skull, Catherine."

"Sorry," Catherine said hoarsely. "Here it is."

The lantern was shaking as she gave it to Eve. No, it was Catherine's hand that was shaking. Her gaze flew to Catherine's face. It was pale in the lanternlight, and her lips were trembling.

"Sorry," Catherine said again. "I didn't think I'd fall apart like this. He's so little."

"Yes, that's what I was thinking." And Catherine had the additional heartache of thinking this might be her son. "I'll be as quick as I can."

She shined the beam of light on the skull. "Bullet hole. Very clean. More clean than the photo indicated. It's lucky it didn't shatter the skull or we'd be spending a lot of time just in the initial reconstruction. It should be a relatively easy job."

"You're going to do it?" Catherine said.

"That's why I came, isn't it? The boy is four or five years old. I can't determine exactly how long he was buried here because of the marsh preservation, but that could be correct, too."

"He lied. It's not Luke."

"I hope you're right. But it could be Luke. Are you going to walk away and never be sure? I'm not. Joe, get my case."

"You're going to take his skull," Catherine said. She drew a deep breath. "Okay, what can I do to help you?"

"Nothing," Joe said. He pulled Eve to her feet. "Go to the car. Both of you. Yeah, I know. You want to be professional and do your job. And Catherine wants to prove that she can take it and help you. Well, it's bullshit. You can't be careful about taking that kid's head. We don't have time. I'm the only one who won't agonize over doing what has to be done." He took her lantern and case. "Now get the hell out of here. I don't want you remembering how I did it."

She hesitated.

"Go." He turned back to the skeleton.

"And take Catherine with you. I don't want her stabbing me in the back when she sees what I have to do to this poor kid."

Oh, no, he was so tough. He wouldn't agonize the way she and Catherine would.

The hell he wouldn't.

But he was right, she'd take too long because she couldn't bear to be rough. She took Catherine's arm and pulled her toward the road. "Come on, let's get out of here. I have my orders. I have to protect Joe's back."

Catherine didn't argue. She gazed straight ahead and never looked back as they hurried toward the car that had just come to a halt a hundred yards from the grave site.

Kelsov stuck his head out of the window. "Hurry. We may be in trouble. Where's Quinn?"

"Right behind us." Catherine jumped into the backseat. "He won't be long. He had to — He won't be long."

Kelsov was cursing. "We can't wait. I'll give him two more minutes."

"You'll give him as long as it takes," Eve said. "We won't leave him. If you do, I'll personally hunt you down and castrate you."

The glance he gave her was not pleasant. "So much for your caring, gentle expert, Catherine."

"Joe has the skull, Kelsov," Catherine said. "What's wrong?" Her gaze was on the trees. "Someone's coming? I don't see any lights."

"They're either on foot or driving without lights, but they're here. I know these marshes." He nodded toward the southwest. "They're coming from that direction."

"How do you know?"

"The birds. You can always tell by the birds. Right before I reached the car, I heard them screeching and then the sound of their wings as they took off." His gaze was raking the trees. "The birds in this area haven't been panicked yet. When they are, we'll be in real trouble."

It made sense to Eve. She wasn't about to try to find any other more innocent reason for the disturbance in the swamp. Not tonight. She reached for the door handle. "I'll go get Joe."

"Wait." Catherine was gazing beyond her. "He's coming."

The next moment Joe was diving into the passenger seat. He threw Eve's forensic case on the floor. "Move! Something's wrong out there."

Kelsov gunned the car and it jumped forward. "The birds."

Joe nodded as he rolled down the window. "Southwest."

He would be on the same wavelength as Kelsov both in instinct and experience, Eve thought.

Joe went still. "No, not southwest anymore. Listen."

Screeching.

A flapping of wings.

Here.

Chapter 12

The first bullet hit the rear window thirty seconds later.

"Down!"

But Catherine had already pulled Eve to the floor and was reaching in her backpack for her gun. "Not on foot." She was looking over her shoulder at the tan Volvo racing after them. "How many in the car, Joe?"

"Six," Joe was taking aim. He fired. "Five."

Another bullet splintered the driver's mirrors and ricocheted into the roof of the car.

Catherine was rolling down the window. She tossed off a quick shot before ducking back down. "Four, Joe?"

"Four," he confirmed. He stiffened. "Move, Kelsov. I don't like this. I think they've got — Shit."

Eve's gaze flew to the rear window. "My God."

A small missile launcher was being aimed at their vehicle by the man in the rear seat of the Volvo.

"Out!" Joe yelled. "Pull over, Kelsov! Everyone out!"

Kelsov didn't question but skidded to a stop by the side of the road bordering the marsh. He was the first to jump into the muck.

Catherine jerked Eve out her door, and the next moment, she was floundering knee-deep in the mud.

"Joe!" Eve screamed. Where was he? She couldn't see him.

The car exploded into a fiery mass as the missile hit it.

"No!"

"Easy." Catherine was dragging her through the mud. "He jumped out the other side. He's okay."

"Are you sure?"

Catherine was glancing over her shoulder. "There he is across the road. He's aiming at — Oh, *yes*."

The Volvo's gas tank exploded as Joe's bullet hit it. The explosion ignited the missile launcher and the vehicle blew high in the air!

"Yes, your Joe is very much okay." Catherine's eyes were glittering with fierce admiration. "Great move. I couldn't have done better."

A tribute, warrior to warrior, Eve thought.

"Where's Kelsov?" Joe said as he jumped into the muck and waded toward them.

"Here." Kelsov called from some distance away. "I was just about to come and rescue all of you. But of course I had to make sure that I was safe first. That's the only intelligent way to proceed."

"You're nothing if not intelligent," Catherine said dryly as she started toward him. "It was lucky that Joe acted on instinct and not intelligence. It worked out better for all of us."

"You don't think that I'd have come back for you?"

"Actually, I do," Catherine said. "Unless Rakovac was standing between us. Then you'd go after him and let us take our chances."

"And you wouldn't?"

"Yes, I'd probably do the same thing."

"I don't think so," Eve said. "Hatred can only twist your character so far. I believe you have the same instincts as Joe and would act on them."

Catherine looked at Joe. "I'd like to think you're right, Eve. What do you think, Joe?"

He didn't answer her. "I think that we'd better get out of this marsh and find a car. Those explosions would have been heard for miles. We don't know that we're safe yet. Rakovac might have sent out a second team." He tucked the forensic case he was still carrying into Eve's backpack. "Kelsov, if we call Bravski, will he come and get us?"

"Maybe." He shook his head. "But we can't trust him not to talk about what he's doing. It's safer to get back to the village on our own. Then we can borrow his car to get back to where I dropped off the Mercedes and be on our way."

"Safer, not quicker," Eve said. "Six miles, if I remember correctly."

"You're not strong enough?" He smiled slyly. "And you were so full of threats of violence to my person when I only mentioned that we might have to leave Quinn. I'll have no trouble at all slogging my way through this marsh. I might even offer you a hand if you ask prettily."

"Knock it off, Kelsov." Joe took Eve's elbow and half led, half pulled her with him as he started out. "He's right; we shouldn't give away our position to anyone. We'll stay in the marsh for the first few miles to make sure no one else is going to be after us. Then we'll take to the road. It will make the going faster and easier." He glanced over his shoulder at Catherine. "Are you all right?"

"Of course." She smiled brilliantly at him.

"It takes a lot to take us down, doesn't it?"

He stared at her for a moment and then slowly nodded. "You're damn right it does."

He turned back to Eve and his arm tightened protectively around her. "And we'll get through this, too. Just keep moving . . ."

"Good Lord, you all look as if you survived a mudslide," Kelly said as she threw open the door. "What happened?"

Her description was probably accurate, Eve thought. She could see what Kelsov, Joe, and Catherine looked like, and she must be the same. She had caught a glimpse of herself in a mirror in Bravski's house where they had "borrowed" his car. Caked mud up to her waist, in her hair, tennis shoes muddy brown instead of white. The smell was almost as bad.

No, worse.

"We need baths," she said, as Natalie came to stand beside Kelsov. "I hope you have a large water heater."

She nodded, her gaze never leaving Kelsov. "You are well?"

"I will be when I get clean," Kelsov said.

"You will have the first bath," Natalie said.

"No, that wouldn't be polite. We have guests."

But Natalie didn't care about politeness

when it interfered with her caring for Kelsov, Eve thought. "We could draw straws," she suggested.

"Ladies first," Joe said. "I saw a creek about a mile from here. If you can give me soap, I'll make do there."

Catherine nodded eagerly. "Great idea. I'm used to roughing it. I'll go with you and —" She stopped suddenly. "No, I guess not. I'll have a hot bath. You go first, Eve. I'll wait for you." She turned to Kelsov. "And you're right, you're our host. You go down to the creek with Joe. I guarantee that it will feel better than trekking through that marsh."

"He will be cold," Natalie was frowning. "I do not think that —"

"He'll survive. Kelsov always survives."

Eve smiled. "And he's been telling me how strong and hardy he is. What's a little fresh springwater to a titan like him?" She moved toward the bathroom. "I'll hurry, Catherine."

"Take your time. Don't worry about me. I need to talk to Kelly anyway." She made a face as she sat down gingerly on one of the wooden kitchen chairs. "Though I'll have to scrub this chair as soon as I get up."

Eve didn't doubt it. They were all so filthy that she was reluctant to touch anything herself. Into that shower so that she could feel human again.

And the warm water did feel wonderful as it ran over her naked body. She worked the shampoo into her hair. Just stand here a moment and let the warmth seep into her muscles. She hated to be dirty.

But Catherine hadn't been too bothered about her foul condition. She had bounced back and that wonderful vitality had gone into high gear. She was like Joe in that reaction to adversity. The adrenaline began to flow, and they came alive. It had been a perfectly natural response when Catherine had been about to go down to the creek with Joe. Considering her assignments in the jungle, she probably had no qualms about bathing with the men she worked with. It was more unusual for her to have caught herself and quickly changed her mind.

Had she thought that Eve would resent that intimacy?

And would she?

She had a sudden visual picture of Catherine naked and beautiful, covered with drops of water.

Hell, yes. Eve wasn't perfect. She had the usual twinges of envy and possessiveness. She hoped that didn't translate to giving in to the green-eyed monster. She had no right. Joe had given far more to her than she ever had to him during these last years. The only thing she could give him in return was love and freedom.

Somehow, the fact she was telling herself that she had no right didn't seem to matter. The emotion was still there.

It had to matter. If Joe ever wanted to leave her, then she had to make it easy for him. He had lived with her obsession and endless hunt since the moment he had met her. He was entitled to walk away without having to look back at her. Whether it was alone or with another woman.

She had never thought of him with another woman until now.

Was it because Catherine was so much like him? Watching them together had been amazing. She and Joe were close, but Catherine was like his other self.

Stop it. She was borrowing trouble. She wasn't going to go around spying on them just because she had noticed that affinity. She trusted Joe, and Catherine was becoming closer to her than anyone but her Jane. She had an idea that Catherine's abrupt change of mind a few minutes ago was an indication that she was on guard to keep that closeness intact. Eve would not destroy either relationship because of doubts.

She began to wash the shampoo from her hair.

Enough of this soul-searching. What would be, would be. She could only do what she thought was right.

Loving Joe was right.

Helping Catherine find her son was right.

The rest would have to sort itself out as time went on.

"The Rakovac file," Catherine said to Kelly. "Have you found anything we can use?"

Kelly shook her head. "Not yet. Though I think I have a glimmer of a hope in finding him. Before he disappeared, he did establish his own pattern, but there's no regularity to it. Perhaps that will reveal itself the more I know about him. It may be numerical or it might have to do with his history. Everyone has a life pattern that they establish over the years. Rakovac wouldn't feel comfortable veering too far from his pattern. It would take some enormous upheaval to cause him to break his routine."

"Or he may be the exception to prove the rule."

She shook her head. "I don't think so."

"You don't know." Catherine's hands clenched into fists. "And even if we find Rakovac, will Luke be with him? And will it be in time?"

Kelly didn't answer. "You found the skeleton?"

Catherine nodded. "We brought the skull back. Eve said that the reconstruction won't be too difficult. The bullet didn't shatter the skull." Her lips twisted. "I was so weak I couldn't even look at the bullet hole. I kept seeing . . ." She stopped, thinking of that fragile skeleton lying on the mound of dirt. "I was ashamed. Eve was hurting, too, but she did her job."

Kelly reached out and touched Catherine's hand. "And you'll do yours when the time comes to help Luke. You saved me."

"It may be Luke's skull in that case in Eve's backpack. She said it was possible." She straightened and shook her head. "But he lied. I know it."

"He does lie," Natalie said from across the room. "But not all the time. Sometimes he makes the lies come true."

"Be quiet, Natalie," Kelly said. "She doesn't have to hear that."

Kelly was being protective, Catherine realized. She had come to a sorry pass when a fourteen-year-old felt she had to protect her. "Maybe I did. If it's the truth."

Natalie met her gaze. "It's the truth." She

turned away. "I'm making chicken soup for Kelsov. I'll make enough for all of you. He says I make good soup."

"I'm sure you do," Catherine said gently. "That stew you made the night we came was excellent."

"Your turn, Catherine." Eve came out of the bathroom dressed in a terry robe, her hair wrapped in a towel. "It felt wonderful. You'll enjoy it much more than the creek."

Was there a hint of hidden meaning in that last sentence? Catherine's gaze flew to Eve's face. No, Eve was smiling and met her eyes with nothing but friendliness. "That wouldn't take much." She got to her feet. "But Kelly and Natalie will be glad to get me out of here and in that shower. Natalie is ready to purify the room."

Natalie nodded gravely. "It may be necessary."

"I was joking," Catherine said. "Kelsov has to work on your sense of humor." She started toward the bathroom. "Remind me to talk —"

Her cell phone rang.

She stopped in midstride as she saw the ID.

She inhaled sharply. "Rakovac."

Eve went still, her eyes widening.

Catherine pressed the volume and answered. "What do you want, Rakovac?"

"Why, I just wanted to congratulate you, Catherine. You're proving to be a worthy opponent. Our little duel is turning out to be everything I hoped. Quinn and Kelsov must be extraordinary. Those three men I left to guard the grave were very competent."

"Not that competent. You had to send a carload of more scumbags after us when they didn't do their job."

"I really didn't want to have to do it, but that's the way the game is played. I didn't know they had a missile. That was a little more firepower than I expected. I must have come very close to losing you."

"Not that close. As you said, I have extraordinary friends."

"And you managed to tear the skull from that poor child's skeleton. Did that hurt you, Catherine?"

Her hand tightened on the phone. "A little."

"I knew it would. It almost makes losing those men worthwhile. I knew I would win either way. And Eve Duncan is going to do the reconstruction. Is she there with you now?"

"Yes."

"Tell her to do her usual fine job. I want

you to be able to recognize Luke with no problem. I imagine the period while you're waiting to know is going to be excruciating."

"He's not Luke."

"Of course he is. Look at the bone structure of his face. It's just like yours. Can't you see the resemblance?"

She was beginning to feel the panic rising. "Children change a lot in those first years."

"Duncan taught you that. How annoying. It modifies my efforts in increasing your pain. I'm going to remember that when I have her at my disposal." He paused. "I'll be thinking about you while Duncan is doing her wizardry. I'll be imagining every expression on your face, every bit of agony that you're feeling. Is it really your little Luke? Did the bullet hurt him before he died? I wish I could devote more time and concentration, but I've had to initiate the prologue to my farewell party, and it's requiring my attention."

"Prologue?"

"It was an opening foray worthy of what's to come. I was very pleased. But there are ends to tie up and congratulations to extract from doubting Thomases. It all takes time. But I'll be back on the phone with you as soon as possible. It adds a certain zest to realize how close you are to me. I can't tell you how I'm enjoying our being together at last. Remoteness does have its disadvantages." He hung up.

"Bastard." Catherine pressed the disconnect. "All he wanted to do was taunt me. No real threats. Except to you, Eve."

"It didn't bother me." She added thoughtfully, "He's looking at this as a supreme cat-and-mouse game. He wants this reconstruction to hurt you. He's going to enjoy every minute of it." Her lips tightened. "I've got to hurry it along so that I can cheat him of as much pleasure as possible."

"Unless it is my Luke."

"And you've got to try to block out what he said."

"I can't. He knows I can't." She moistened her lips. "But I'll try to keep busy so that he doesn't dominate my whole world." She shook her head. "What am I saying? He's dominated my world since the day he took my son." She stuffed her phone into her pocket. "When are you going to start to work?"

"Right after supper." She turned to Natalie. "I'll need a table set up by the window, clean damp cloths, and enough lanterns to cast a strong light on the reconstruction. Can you help me?"

Natalie nodded. "There's some old furniture in the barn in the back, and I think I saw a table."

Eve turned to Catherine. "And I don't want you hanging around watching me."

"It bothers you?"

"No, nothing bothers me when I'm absorbed. But it will bother you. At some points in the reconstruction, the skull looks like a voodoo doll or something from a horror film. You don't need to go through that. Go out and walk or help Kelly with her patterns."

"I don't need her," Kelly said. "She can't help me with —"

"Kelly, that's the first time I've noticed you acting fourteen instead of thirty," Eve said. "I'm sure it's healthy, but you picked the wrong time for it. I was trying for a diversion. Now keep Catherine busy and out of my way."

Kelly nodded. "But I can't let her —"

"It's okay, Kelly." Catherine headed for the shower. "I'm not interfering in your business. You don't have to be so protective of your blessed patterns."

"There's nothing blessed about Rakovac's patterns," Kelly said gravely. "I can already see hints of what he is just from reading this report. It's all cut-and-dried, with no comments from the people who were shadowing him. But every now and then, they put in a result of what he did the day before." She sat back down at the table and opened her computer. "And I'm beginning to get . . . anxious. His pattern is leading him . . . I don't know. Somewhere . . . dark."

"You can tell that by analyzing these patterns? Sounds like hocus-pocus to me."

"An astronomer studying black holes isn't into hocus-pocus, but the darkness is there."

"Whatever. By all means continue. I didn't like it when he was talking about his prologue. Prologue to what? I don't think it had anything to do with Luke."

"I don't either," Eve said as she moved toward the bedroom. "But I'm not going to dwell on it. I have to concentrate on that reconstruction."

Kelly nodded, her gaze on the computer screen. "But I know I'm right. He's heading somewhere . . . dark."

Venable phoned Catherine while they were having dinner that night. She put it on speaker.

"How close are you?" he asked curtly.

"You shouldn't have sent Kelly here," Catherine said. "You don't have a great deal of conscience, but I'd think a fourteen-year-old girl would be off-limits."

"No one is off-limits now. How close are you to finding Rakovac?" he asked curtly. "For God's sake, that's why I sent her. Is she helping?"

She had never heard Venable sound so tense. She could almost feel the vibrations crackle over the cell. "She's doing the best she can. It takes time."

"We don't have time." He drew a deep breath. "I think time's running out."

She could see Eve straighten in her chair across the table from her. Catherine knew how she felt. Venable's tension was contagious.

"What are you talking about?"

"Have you been watching the news?"

"No, we've been busy."

"Pull it up on your computer. And then get back to me."

"What am I supposed to be looking for?"

"Nine-eleven." He hung up.

She sat there for an instant, stunned. "Nine-eleven?"

"I'll do it." Kelly had jumped to her feet and grabbed her computer. She was quickly surfing the Internet for news. She didn't have to look long. It was the lead story. "Vantaro Airlines. Lima, Peru. Terrorist attack. A suicide bomber took over the cockpit and killed the pilot and forced the copilot to fly low into the heart of the city. He radioed the tower at the airport that he was doing this for the glory of Islam and the Red Darkness, a terrorist group based in Libya." She paused, reading the next page. "He set off his explosion when he was near the capitol building. The death count may have reached over twenty-two hundred people."

"Two thousand . . ." Eve said. "Peru's 9/11." She shook her head as if to clear it. She couldn't clear it. The horror was too overwhelming. "I remember our 9/11. Watching those planes dive into the two towers. I couldn't believe it. I couldn't imagine the evil that could spawn something like that."

"Neither could I," Joe said. "I went up to New York as a volunteer and helped dig out survivors . . . and bodies."

"Maybe it's not Peru's 9/11," Kelly said slowly. Her gaze was fixed on the wreckage of the plane in the news story. "Maybe not."

Catherine's gaze flew to her face. "What?"

"Prologue," Kelly said. "Rakovac said prologue."

Eve inhaled sharply. "My God. Call Venable, Catherine. Call him now."

Catherine was already dialing the number.

"What does that suicide bomber have to do with Rakovac?" she asked as soon as he picked up. "What actually happened in Lima?"

"It has everything to do with Rakovac. But we don't know all the details about that suicide bombing yet. We're still piecing the story together. We weren't expecting Lima."

"What do you know?"

"We know what the media tells you about the actual suicide bombing. The bomber was Manuel Camarez. He was an office-supply salesman and lived in southern Peru. No known affiliations to any Islamic group though he did spend a summer in Istanbul a few years ago. He could have been recruited at that time."

"Recruited? He had to be a fanatic if he blew himself up."

"Yes, and clever enough so that no one in his immediate circle even realized he was a prime candidate to do it."

"How did this happen? What happened to all the airport security?"

"It's only as strong as the weakest link."

"So he was able to just walk onto that plane with enough explosives to kill that many people?"

"The weakest link," Venable repeated. "In this case we're almost sure the link was Pedro Gonzalez, the gate agent who worked the flight."

"What did he do? Was he an Islamic recruit, too?"

"No, we think he was a victim and forced to cooperate with the terrorists."

"How?"

"He was seen giving the bomber a black briefcase before he got on the plane. There was a mention that security had sent it up to the gate."

"And that never happened?"

"Security didn't know anything about it. Gonzalez probably smuggled it into the gate area the day before."

"Wasn't he checked by security before he was hired?"

"He was checked and came out smelling like the proverbial rose. Patriotic, steady family man, religious, took care of his aged father. He was everything he should have been."

"You said he was a victim. What happened?"

"We don't have the details yet. We may never have them. We can only make suppositions. When we went to Gonzalez's home to question him, we found a slaughterhouse. His wife, son, two daughters, and his father had been shot and killed execution style in the upstairs bedrooms. Gonzalez himself was killed in the downstairs foyer as he came in the front door."

"You think his family was being held hostage to force Gonzalez to cooperate?"

"That's my guess. And then, after Gonzalez had done his job, they murdered everyone so that there would be no one to tell the tale." He paused. "And to make sure that there was no evidence that the bomber's story wasn't as factual as it should be."

"Hideous," Eve said shakily. "And you're saying the bomber lied when he gave credit to Red Darkness?"

"We can't prove it. The spokesman for that terrorist group is claiming it was their work, and the group has scattered and gone under cover."

"Then why don't you think it's their work?"

"It's too coincidental."

"Coincidental. What are you talking about?" Joe said. "Spit it out, Venable."

"We think that the bombing was done by a member of Warriors of Paradise, a group headed by Ali Dabala. The entire operation was too slick and obviously well funded. Red Darkness operates on a shoestring."

"Then why would they claim this atrocity when it meant they'd know every country in the world would make it hot for them?"

"Not every country. And they'd gain prestige among their own kind. Also they might have been given enough money to make it worth their while." He paused. "As I said, Ali Dabala is well funded. He has friends in very high and lucrative places in the Middle East. He obviously didn't want to draw attention to his group at this time." He paused. "Which scares the hell out of me."

"Why?" Joe asked.

"Rakovac's surveillance reported a confirmed visit from Ali Dabala several months ago," Kelly said. "And another possible meeting between them just before Rakovac went undercover."

"You've obviously been working, Kelly," Venable added harshly, "but not hard enough. We made a deal. Find me something, anything to nail down where the bastard is."

"You haven't given her time," Catherine said. "And what does Rakovac have to do with Ali Dabala?"

"We've been getting information for the past three years that the Warriors of Paradise have been planning a massive 9/11-type attack on the U.S. But Ali Dabala regarded that attack as clumsy and lacking in scope to show the world how weak and ineffectual the U.S. was against the power of Islam. He wanted an attack to stun the world. He had the suicide bombers who he could send to paradise and the money to fund the attack. The only thing he lacked was someone to set up the individual airport personnel and arrange for the explosives to be put in the hands of his men at the correct time." He added, "So he went to Rakovac and obviously made him a deal he couldn't refuse. He was to locate the vulnerable and the greedy and set up ways to override airport security."

"Like Gonzalez," Catherine said. "But why Peru?"

"A test? It would make sense. Too far away from the U.S. to arouse real panic. I can talk myself blue in the face and still not get Homeland Security to do more than raise the security code level."

"Prologue," Catherine said softly. "Rakovac said he was involved in a prologue and didn't have time to give me the concentration I deserved."

Venable muttered a curse. "And how long before they delve into the main selection?"

"You tell us," Joe said. "You obviously have informants. When and how many cities are going to be affected?"

"I don't know. I'm just getting dribbles of information, and some of that could be red herrings. Do you think I'd be relying on a fourteen-year-old kid if I could get reliable intelligence?"

"Thank you," Kelly said dryly.

"How many cities?" Joe persisted. "You have to have some idea."

He was silent a moment. "I've got a map with nineteen red flags on it."

"My God."

"It could be less. It probably is less. I told you, red herrings. But even if it's only half that number, it's a disaster."

"One city would be a disaster," Eve said. "Two thousand people in Lima . . ."

"New York, Washington, Chicago," Catherine said. "Those cities are prime targets. Where else?"

"You name it. L.A., Atlanta, Miami, St. Louis. Large population centers and areas that have patriotic or sentimental value to the American people. Strikes to the wallet and the emotions."

"Those sons of bitches," Joe said.

"Yes. And Rakovac is making it all possible. That's why we have to find him. He has to have all the information about the airport personnel who are going to help the terrorists. His people have to be on-site and ready to roll when Rakovac gives the orders. He has to have records, disks . . . something. You can't touch him until I have those records, Catherine."

Catherine was silent. "If he's dead, then he couldn't give any orders."

"And what if Ali Dabala knows the names and contacts Rakovac is using and tries to initiate the attack without Rakovac's go-ahead?"

"Listen to me." She drew a deep breath, her hand tightening on the phone. "When I find Rakovac, his first act is going to be to try to kill Luke in front of me. He'd consider that the ultimate revenge. I've got to find some way to save Luke and you're trying to take away one of the only ways I can do it. You want me to risk Luke to keep Rakovac alive until you get those records? How can I promise to —"

"Catherine, think. I know what you're going through. But this is —"

"You don't know what I'm going through," she said harshly. "You've never known. Now you're saying I should give up Luke on the chance that —" She drew a deep breath. "I can't talk to you any longer. I'm not thinking straight. All I can do is feel."

"It has to be done, Catherine," Venable

said quietly. "I have to have those records, and soon."

"We're not even close to finding Luke yet. We've just started."

"But there's a promise if Rakovac's gone to the trouble of luring you into his world. Act on that promise."

"You don't think we are? We're doing everything we can."

"And I'm not seeing any signs that you're doing much to help, Venable," Joe said. "Don't you have any idea where Rakovac could be?"

"I'm working on it. I'm heading for Moscow now so that I'll be on the spot," Venable said. "But I don't have your advantage, Catherine. He's waving Luke like a toreador does his cape at a bull. You might be able to get close enough to gore him."

"After we find those records," Joe said grimly. "Catherine's right, it's not a win-win situation."

"Those people in Lima didn't have a chance. If you want to see a no-win situation, take a look at the photos of the aftereffects of that explosion on your computer. It looks like —" Venable stopped. "It's hell. I don't want to have to see the same thing happen on our turf. I'll sacrifice Catherine's son and all the rest of you if I can stop that from happening. Now find that son of a bitch. If you tell me where he is, I'll send an army to get him. But you'd better be damn sure that you have those records before he can destroy them." He hung up.

The room was silent as Catherine pressed the disconnect.

"I won't give up Luke," she said shakily. "Venable may be ready to sacrifice all of us for the general good, but not my little boy. I can't do that."

"I know," Eve said. "Venable is desperate."

"Not my son," Catherine said. She gazed around the room at them. "I'm actually feeling guilty. I won't feel guilty, dammit. I *won't.*"

"Venable wasn't fair," Joe said. "But the choice isn't fair. I can see where he's at."

"Do you think I can't?" She shook her head. "The way this damn scenario is shaping up, I may be blamed for Armageddon. Well, let them blame me. I won't let my son be killed." Her voice dropped to a whisper. "But what about all those other children who will die if —"

"Enough of this." Eve got to her feet. "Stop torturing yourself, Catherine. This isn't only up to you. We're in this together. We have to figure a way to get the records from Rakovac and still keep Luke safe."

"All this worry about her son may be for nothing," Natalie said baldly, speaking for the first time. "What if that skull in that case is her Luke?"

Kelsov flinched. "Natalie, no one can say that you mince words."

"Why should I? It's what you're all thinking. You should kill Rakovac. That's all that's important."

"In this case, it's not all that's important." He turned to Catherine. "I apologize. Natalie is single-minded on the subject of Rakovac."

"Aren't we all," Joe said. "Particularly now." He turned to Eve. "I think we have to know very soon if Luke is going to be factor in this."

She pushed back her chair. "I'll start right away."

"Could we get DNA instead?" Kelly asked.

"Not enough time," Joe said. "It's going to have to be up to Eve." He glanced at Catherine. "If you'll trust her."

"Do you mean will I trust her not to put my son's face on that skull no matter what is there?" Her lips twisted. "Tell me, how do you like the idea of that much responsibility, Eve?"

"I hate it," Eve said. "But not enough to lie to you. If you think I will, then all of this is for nothing." She crossed her arms across her chest and stared Catherine in the eye. "Well?"

Catherine hesitated and then slowly nodded. "I trust you. You'll tell me the truth." Her jaw squared. "And I'm going to tell all of you the truth. You want to keep all that horror from happening? So do I. But it's up to you to save the world. I'm going to save my son. You make your choice, I make mine. They may not coincide. So you'd better watch out for me." She started clearing the table. "Let's get these dishes out of the way and leave Eve alone to get to work. Your worktable and your tools are over there by the window. Is there anything else I can do for you?"

"Keep everyone out of my space," Eve said. "And keep me supplied with coffee."

"And food," Joe said. "She tends to forget about it."

"I noticed that." Catherine carried a stack of dishes to the sink. "When she was doing the age progression. I'll see that she's stoked and primed."

"You make me sound like a machine," Eve said ruefully.

"You're no machine. You're too human,"

Catherine said. "Which I imagine is going to make this one of the most difficult jobs you've ever done."

"We'll get through it." Eve moved over to the worktable and began to set out her equipment. "Together."

"How long will it take?"

She shrugged. "At least a day and a half for the initial setup and depth measurements. After that, I never know for certain. The sculpting can go fast or slow. It depends on . . ." She made a face. "It's not like the age progressions. That's much more logical. The sculpting is more creative and tells the tale." She looked at Catherine. "It's during that part of the process that I could lie to you if I chose."

"But you won't choose," Catherine said. "And since you're going to take that long, I believe Kelly will be stuck with my help while she's working on the Rakovac report." She stared sternly at Kelly. "And no complaints."

Kelly smiled. "I'm not complaining."

"Joe?" Eve's gaze was narrowed on his face. "I saw your expression when you were talking to Venable. You're not going to sit around waiting for me to finish."

He shook his head. "Everything has changed. I can't let Rakovac cause a disaster of that scope. I'm a cop and it's my job to protect. You're safe here with Catherine and Kelsov and don't need me. I'm calling Venable back to see what I can do about finding Rakovac on my own. I'm going into Moscow to start pushing Venable." His lips tightened. "Though this time I don't believe he's going to take much pushing. He sounded scared shitless."

"Why should he be different?" Eve said. "Let me know as soon as you find out anything."

"If," Joe substituted as he headed for the bedroom. "The word is definitely 'if.' "

He was right, Catherine thought. She had thought there was uncertainty before, but now the prospects seemed infinitely worse. Darkness was all around them, and nothing was clear.

Except that the clock was ticking for Luke.

And for all those other thousands of innocent victims Rakovac was planning on destroying.

CHAPTER 13

"Food," Catherine said firmly. "You've skipped two meals, and I promised Joe I'd keep you fed."

" 'Stoked'," Eve said. "Isn't that the term you used?"

"Whatever. You've been working for a solid twelve hours without a break."

"I'm in a hurry. You'll agree there's a certain urgency to my getting this finished."

"You still need food. I have a ham sandwich and a salad for you. Just eat it, and I won't bother you again for another four or five hours. Okay?"

"Okay." Eve wiped her hands on her cleansing cloth and moved away from the worktable to the kitchen table across the room. She needed the break anyway. Her eyes were stinging from focusing on the precise measurements, and the back of her neck was starting to ache. "What would you do if I said no?"

"Nag." She sat down across from Eve. "The alternative is force-feeding, and I'm trying to avoid it. It tends to arouse massive resistance." She lifted her cup of coffee to her lips. "But you wouldn't let it go that far. You have the sense to know that you need fuel to keep on going."

"There you go again. 'Stoke.' 'Fuel.' " She picked up her sandwich. "But you're right, I'm sensible. Sometimes." Her gaze wandered back to the reconstruction on the table across the room. "I do tend to get involved."

"Yes, like the way you became involved with me. Venable warned you against it, didn't he?"

"You know he did. I even tried to listen. It didn't work out," Eve said. "But that wasn't the kind of involvement I was talking about."

"Your work," Catherine said. "That reconstruction that looks like —"

"A nightmare." It wasn't difficult for Eve to realize the impact her work on the skull had on Catherine. Right now she was at the stage when she'd just put in the depth markers that resembled dozens of swords sticking out of the skull. It looked as if the skull were being tortured. "I told you that I didn't want you to watch me working on it.

I was afraid it would hurt you."

"I tried not to do it. I couldn't help myself. There was a kind of morbid fascination."

"There's nothing morbid about what I'm doing," Eve said quietly. "I'm bringing him home. I don't care whose child he turns out to be. He'll have a face, an identity, and I hope eventually a name. Perhaps someone will remember him and think of him with love. That's all I care about."

Catherine nodded. "I know it is." She looked back at the reconstruction. "You always give your reconstructions a name." She paused, then forced herself to continue. "What did you call him?"

"Not Luke," Eve said. "Even if I hadn't wanted to hurt you, I would never call a reconstruction by the name of someone who is a possible. I'm always afraid it might influence the sculpting in the final stage. His name is Jeremy."

She could see the relief on Catherine's face. "That's a nice name." She studied the reconstruction more carefully. "I'm trying to be objective, but it's not easy. I've got this weird maternal feeling that you're torturing my child. Why those stick-pins?"

"Depth markers," Eve corrected. She finished her sandwich and leaned back in the chair. She wanted to get back to work, but she could spare a few moments to ease Catherine's disturbance. "What do you know about forensic sculpting?"

"Not much. I read up on the age progression because I knew I was going to ask you to do it." She grimaced. "But I never wanted to see you do this voodoo."

"It's not voodoo. There's a science to it up to a point, when instinct takes over."

"The stick-pins," Catherine prompted. "AKA depth markers. Why do you do that?"

"They're tissue-depth markers. They're made of ordinary erasers. I cut each marker to the proper measurement and glue it onto its proper point on the face. There are over twenty points of the skull for which there are known tissue depths. Facial tissue depth has been found to be fairly consistent in people of the same age, race, sex, and weight."

"How do they know?"

"There are anthropological charts that give a specific measurement for each point."

"What do you do then?"

"I take strips of plasticine and apply them between the markers, then build up to all of the tissue-depth points. Someone I know once called it a sort of connect-the-dots."

"Is it?"

"If you want to dumb it down. Only it's three-dimensional and a hell of a lot more complicated. It's necessary to concentrate on the scientific elements of building the face, like keeping true to the tissue-depth measurements as I fill in between the plasticine strips, considering where the facial muscles are located and how they affect the contours of the face. And then there's the nose, which is a real headache." She took a sip of her coffee. "But you don't want to go into this right now. I could dazzle you with measurements of the nasal spine and the midphiltrum tissue measurements and how I finally get down to the basic answers, but all I really want to do is make you comfortable with what I'm doing to Jeremy here. It's not voodoo, it's science." She smiled. "And instinct. After all the measurements and calculated judgments, it all ends with Jeremy and me one-on-one. In those hours, I'll try to let him tell me who he really is. I think perhaps he will. That's what this is all about. Do you understand now?"

Catherine nodded slowly.

"Good." Eve finished her coffee and got to her feet. "Because I have to get back to work. What have you been doing when you weren't trying to make me eat? Has Kelly come up with anything?"

"Nothing definitive. I've been combing through the reports too, but I can't see anything that will help us. Kelsov has been tapping all his contacts and no one knows anything. It's as if Rakovac has dropped off the edge of the world."

"We should be so lucky." Eve moved toward the worktable, where her reconstruction waited. "I talked to Joe on the phone this morning and he said Venable was working frantically to locate the bastard but time is running out."

"What about Homeland Security? Dammit, can't they just close down the airports?"

"Venable gave them all the information he has but you know they won't act without more proof. That's why that suicide bomber threw out that red herring about belonging to another terrorist group. Homeland Security is running around trying to pump everyone about members of Red Darkness."

"Typical. One of the CIA's major problems is getting other agencies to listen to them. There's so much bureaucracy and competitiveness that we often wonder who we're fighting. But we know why we're fighting, and that has to do." She took Eve's plate and carried it to the sink. "You need rest. Can't you take a nap?"

"I'll take a few hours right before the final

smoothing and sculpting. I have to be fresh before I begin that part."

"I'd think that would be a given." She didn't look at Eve as she rinsed the plate. "I'm trying not to bother you, but will you let me know as soon as you finish?"

"You know I will," Eve said absently as she adjusted one of the markers on the left cheek. Clear your head. Concentrate. She had to get this part done with absolute accuracy. Yes, time was important, but she couldn't let that influence her. "I know what it means to you. I think I'm almost done with . . ." She trailed off as she become lost once more in Jeremy's world.

She didn't hear Catherine as she left the room.

3:40 a.m.

It was time to begin.

Eve got off the couch and went into the bathroom and washed her face. She'd had two hours' sleep but spent the last two hours just lying there and forcing herself to relax. It was enough. She'd known that she was too charged to sleep for long. Adrenaline would get her through as it always did.

Are you ready for me, Jeremy?

She moved toward the worktable.

He was waiting for her.

She stood before him.

The blank face was without identity or life.

And I'm ready for you, Jeremy.

Come to me.

Whisper your secrets.

Tell me how to bring you home.

She started to work.

Sensitivity.

Care.

Delicacy.

Don't think.

Let the tips of fingers smooth, build, smooth again.

Help me, Jeremy.

The clay was cool, but her touch was warm, almost hot, as her fingers flew over the face.

Generic ears. She had no idea whether they had protruded or if the lobes were longer.

Nose? Another mystery.

You solve it, Jeremy.

It became shorter, slightly turned up.

Mouth?

Generic again. She had figured the width, but the shape was unknown. No expression. That could change everything, and it might affect the measurements.

Eyes?

Incredibly difficult. She had no measurements and practically no scientific indicators. Don't get frustrated. For heaven's sake, don't rush. Just study the shape and angle of the orbits. The size of eyeballs was all pretty much standard and grew very little from infancy. Study the angle of the orbits and the ridge above and decide whether Jeremy's eyes should protrude or be deep-set or fall somewhere in between.

All right, you've done it. Now leave the orbits. Don't put in the glass eyes yet. It always disturbed her concentration to see the reconstruction watching her as she worked.

No offense, Jeremy.

More smoothing along the line of the cheek.

Not quite right.

Fill in.

Smooth.

Mold.

Don't get carried away. You can't let go yet. Don't forget to check the measurements.

Nose width. Correct.

Projection. As accurate as she could make it.

Lip height. Correct. She'd brought the top lip down because it was usually thinner than the bottom. There's a major muscle under thc mouth, build up around the area.

Shape.

Mold.

Smooth.

Deepen the creasing around the nostrils.

Cheeks fuller.

Fill in.

Okay, now let go.

Let's come home, Jeremy.

Her fingers flew feverishly over the child's face. Forget the measurements. Forget the science.

Smooth.

Mold.

Fill in.

Come out, Jeremy.

Help me.

Who are you?

I don't want you to be lost any longer.

Smooth.

Mold.

We're almost done.

Smooth.

Mold.

Enough.

She drew a deep breath and pushed the hair back from her face. She was shaking, and her face was flushed as if she'd been racing.

She had been racing. It had been over three hours since she'd started the final phase, but the time had flown.

Don't look at his face. Not yet.

She opened her wooden eye case. Brown eyes. They were the most common. She carefully inserted the eyeballs into the cavities. "We're done, Jeremy. We did it together."

The brown eyes stared back at her from the reconstruction.

Jeremy or Luke?

Step back. Look at him.

No, don't look at him.

She turned on her heel and strode toward the bedroom. She threw open the door. "Catherine."

Catherine jerked awake. "What is it?"

"I promised you I'd tell you as soon as I finished."

She inhaled sharply. "Is it —"

"I don't know. I never see the reconstruction as a whole while I'm working on it. It's just a blur. I thought it was your right to see it first. Get the photo of Luke at age five."

Catherine was already out of bed and going through her duffel. Her voice was shaking. "I'm scared, Eve."

"So am I." Eve tossed Catherine her robe. "Let's go see if that fear is warranted. I hope it's not."

Catherine was clutching the photo as she walked slowly into the kitchen.

Eve followed her.

Jeremy or Luke?

Sadness or total heartbreak?

Catherine stopped in front of the reconstruction, her gaze focused on the face.

Sweet face. Round cheeks. Turned up nose. Slightly pouty lips.

Not Luke's face.

"Thank God." The tears were running down Catherine's cheeks. "It's not him." She was looking at the photo, then the face of the reconstruction. "I'm right, aren't I? I'm not just fooling myself? It's not Luke."

"It's not Luke." Eve was staring critically at the reconstruction. The child was heavier boned than the age progression she'd done of Luke at age five. The corners of the eyes had a slightly Slavic tilt. "No, he's still Jeremy until we find out who he is."

"But he's not Luke!" Catherine grabbed Eve and whirled her around in a circle. "Rakovac lied. Luke could still be alive. No, he *is* alive. I know it."

"Stop." Evc pushed her away. "I'm dizzy enough from lack of sleep. I don't need you making it any worse."

"I'm sorry." She was staring again at the

reconstruction. "And I'm sorry for that poor child. But I'm glad he's not my Luke."

"I gathered that." Eve smiled. "It's fairly obvious, Catherine."

Catherine's smile faded. "And I'm glad you didn't see fit to make him look like Luke. You could have done it, couldn't you? The stakes are high. Weren't you tempted?"

"I'd lie if I told you I wasn't. The situation is difficult, and knowing Luke is alive makes it even harder. But I found I couldn't do it. If anything happens because I made that choice, my guilt is as deep as yours." She shrugged. "Which means that I have to make sure what I did won't have any bearing on Rakovac's ability to put that catastrophe in motion. Otherwise, I'll have guilt crushing me for the rest of my life." She stared her in the eye. "We go after those records, Catherine. We'll find your son, but we make sure that those records are in our hands before you kill Rakovac."

She shook her head. "I'm grateful to you. But I can't promise."

"I'm not asking you to promise. I'm telling you how it's going to be." She took a step closer to the reconstruction. "Now go back to bed. I have to clean up here and put Jeremy in the case. You might start thinking about what we're going to do and say when Rakovac calls you. He's overdue. I thought we'd hear from him before this."

Catherine didn't move. "I want to promise you, Eve," she whispered.

"I know you do. There's no use talking about it. We've both already stated our intentions." Eve was gazing at Jeremy. "We have to find out his identity. It's not going to be easy. I don't even know if Russia has a lost-children program." She shook her head. "What am I thinking? Maybe it won't be that difficult. How did Rakovac know where to find a skeleton with which to taunt you? We should just probably follow the source."

"You think he killed this child?"

"Until I'm proven wrong." She began to pick up bits of clay that had fallen on the table. "Go on. Try to get some sleep. I'll go to bed myself after I unwind a little."

She heard the bedroom door close behind Catherine a moment later.

Sleep well, Catherine. I have an idea we'll need all the rest we can get in the days ahead.

If they even had days. She was overwhelmingly conscious of the giant shadow cast by Rakovac's horror looming over all of them. Her stomach was twisting as she kept remembering those planes diving into the Twin Towers.

Catherine wouldn't be able to hold her hand from killing Rakovac if it came to a choice. Would Eve? Sacrifice that sweet, innocent child so full life and joy?

Please God, don't let it come to that choice.

Her eyes stung with tears as she stared at the reconstruction of Jeremy. Another victim of Rakovac. He, too, had been full of life before Rakovac had entered his world.

"It's not fair, is it?" she murmured as she gently touched the cool clay of Jeremy's cheek. "We're all so concerned about Luke, wondering, worrying, happy that you're not him. It's not that you're not important. You have value, you are important. It's just that he has a chance to stay with us."

A chance.

If they could find and get him away from Rakovac before he killed him.

It wasn't even certain that Luke was still alive. That skeleton in the grave might have been a macabre twist to raise their hopes, then dash them later.

But she didn't believe that was true. Rakovac's revenge had been simmering too long for him to cheat himself out of being able to watch Catherine's final agony. No, Catherine's son was alive.

But where are you, Luke?

■ ■ ■ ■

The rat was staring at him, bright, black eyes fixed as he edged closer in the cell.

He was probably hungry, Luke thought. Rats came up from the basement and were often caught here. He didn't blame him. He was hungry, too. He wasn't afraid of the rat. Mikhal hadn't tied him this time, and he could fight the rat off if it got too bold. He'd try not to kill it. Hunger was a good reason to attack and kill.

Maybe the best reason.

"Luke, your time is up," Mikhal Czadas called out as he came down the corridor to the cell. "Now be a good lad and do what you're told."

Luke didn't answer.

"Don't be stubborn, Luke." Mikhal opened the cell door, and the rat scampered away. "You've been in here for two days. Do you think I like to punish you? But Rakovac is determined you do this kill. All you have to do is point the gun and pull the trigger. Then you walk away, and I give you a fine dinner and let you get back to your books."

"No."

Mikhal knelt beside him. "Do it," he coaxed. "It's not as if you haven't killed before. I put a gun in your hand when you were scarcely able to hold it. I've taken you on so many of my raids since you were eight. You fought for the great cause. Do you think when you fired that gun that you didn't kill? What's the difference? This is just easier. He's tied and can't try to kill you. You walk up to the man and press the trigger."

"There's a difference." He would not have known that difference if his books had not said that fighting in a war and the killing of the helpless were not the same. He was still confused about it, but he would believe his books. He believed nothing Rakovac said. Rakovac was the enemy. When he had been younger, he had never thought at all. He had just done as he was told. But that was before he had found the books. "Why does Rakovac want me to do it?"

"I believe he thinks it may upset your dear mother. As I've told you, all your pain is caused by her."

Luke had heard those words all his life too when he was growing up and at first he hadn't doubted them. It was only in the past few years that his hatred of Rakovac had cleared his head of those lies. It was Rakovac who wielded the whip. It was Rakovac who punished and tormented. Usually not personally; he relied on Mikhal to carry out his orders. Luke had lived with Mikhal Czadas as long as he could remember in this crumbling stone house on the lake.

He had gradually become vaguely aware that Mikhal took orders from Rakovac about his care in exchange for the weapons he supplied him. It was a rare occasion when Rakovac visited Savrin House, and it usually involved a beating and Rakovac showing him the picture of the woman he said was Luke's mother and telling him that she was responsible.

She was not responsible. She was not real to him. He had only a vague memory of her, but it was of kindness and warmth. But no one was responsible for this pain but Rakovac. When he'd finally gotten over the confusion and hurt, he'd realized that everything Rakovac or Mikhal told him was lies. Why should he believe the man who hurt him?

"Do it for me, Luke," Mikhal said. "Look at all I do for you. Are you not treated well? Except for these little rebellions when you cause me trouble, I'm very kind to you. I keep you fed and housed and supplied with all those books you love so much."

Books. It had been a magical day when he had been exploring and discovered the library, with the thousands of books that had belonged to Nikolai Savrin and his English wife, the former owners of the house. And when Mikhal had discovered how fascinated he was by them, they had become weapons. He had even had Luke taught to read both Russian and English so that the love would grow. Now the books were kept or withdrawn at Mikhal's whim . . . or Rakovac's order.

"Why should it matter to my mother if I kill this man or not?"

"Rakovac believes she has the foolish idea that your soul may be damaged in some way. It will hurt her. Don't worry your head about it. Just do as Rakovac says."

He was silent a moment. Was it worth enduring the beating that was bound to come? All it would take would be to pull the trigger.

Rakovac wanted it. It was worth the pain. "No."

Mikhal sat back on his heels. "The man's going to die anyway. Rakovac thinks Medvar cheated him. He only sent him here because he had this brilliant idea of how he could use him."

"No."

Mikhal sighed and got to his feet. "Then I'll have to do it myself." He started to turn away. "Though Rakovac will be angry with both of us."

He was leaving, Luke realized, stunned.

"You're not going to beat me?"

"It doesn't work anymore. The last few times I became very frustrated. I spoke to Rakovac about it, and he told me not to worry. That our time together was almost over anyway." He smiled maliciously over his shoulder. "So instead, I'll just burn all your books."

"No!"

"I've been thinking about doing it for a long time. They're beginning to be troublesome. At first, I found them useful in controlling you. It came as a surprise to me since I've never cared much for books. I couldn't see why they meant so much to you."

Because they took me away from this place, Luke thought in agony. Because when I was reading, you and Rakovac and what you did to me didn't matter anymore.

"But that time is past," Mikhal said. "I actually believe that's where you got the idea of running away from here." He tilted his head. "In fact, I'll let you watch. We'll make a bonfire beside the lake. Come along."

It was no use refusing. Mikhal had ways

to make sure he saw the burning. Luke got to his feet and stumbled toward the door.

"Unless you change your mind. Why make me do this? You know I'm right."

Luke shook his head. He had to fight them, he thought in agony. They weren't right. Everything they said and did were lies. Maybe the whole world was full of lies. There were stories in the books about truth and kindness and courage, but they might also not be true. How could he be sure? He only knew Mikhal and Rakovac and the few people he'd met when Mikhal had taken him away from Savrin House on the raids.

And he supposed he knew the woman, Catherine Ling, who Rakovac called his mother. But he only knew her face and Rakovac's ugly words and that faint memory.

"You're a fool, Luke," Mikhal said softly. He turned on his heel. "Come and see your precious books go up in flames."

Thirty minutes later, Luke stood on the bank of the lake and watched the black smoke curl up to the gray sky from the pile of books heaped on the shore. The wind was whipping sharply, stinging his cheeks and causing the fire to leap higher.

Don't cry, Luke told himself.

Mikhal was staring hungrily at his face,

waiting for him to break, for the tears to come.

He wouldn't cry.

He stared defiantly at Mikhal across the fire. If he looked at Mikhal instead of the burning books that had been his only friends, he could hold the tears back.

And he would never let him see how much it hurt.

"The skull wasn't Luke," Kelly repeated. "I'm so glad, Catherine."

"So was I. I wanted to fall down at Eve's feet this morning when she brought me in to see the reconstruction." Catherine poured a cup of coffee from the fresh pot that Natalie had just made. "But the problem still exists. I have to find him." She sat down at the table. "We can't just wait for him to call and hope that he'll let something slip or give us our chance."

Kelly nodded as she lifted her orange juice to her lips. "The surveillance report. I'm doing the best I can. You're reading it, too. You can see that there isn't anything that you can put your finger on."

"I thought you said there was always a pattern."

"The pattern is there, but it's hard to define." Kelly frowned thoughtfully. "But lately I've thought I've caught glimpses."

Catherine tensed. "What do you mean?"

"I've tried to fill in Rakovac's background, so that I could get a handle on him. In the past nine years he's been involved in all sorts of corruption. Bribing of officials in the Russian Parliament, drugs, vice, arms deals. His manipulation of the members of the parliament is what made him golden in the eyes of the U.S. Congress. He seems to have a magic touch where that kind of dealing is concerned. He used bribery, intimidation, even murder to get what he wanted from them."

"Which is why Ali Dabala hired him to set up his Armageddon project."

Kelly nodded. "He came highly qualified."

"But none of this is doing us any good," Catherine said impatiently. "I read the reports of the agents shadowing him and every meeting he's had with his so-called clients was purely business. They were all checked out, and none of them had anything to do with Luke. It's as if once he took my son, Luke no longer existed." Her hand tightened on her cup. "And that scares the hell out of me."

"He had to know he was being tailed," Kelly said. "The agents even mention that they had no problem keeping track of his movements. You tell me he's very clever. That means he didn't care whether Venable knew about those meetings or his activities with all those other criminal groups. Until he started meeting with Ali Dabala. One meeting, then we start to see more holes."

"Holes?"

"Periods when the agents appear to have lost contact with Rakovac. Sometimes for as much as forty-eight hours."

"You said more. You noticed other periods like that?"

"The first time I went through the report, I skimmed over them. The holes didn't appear with any regularity and some of them might have been periods that weren't at all suspicious. Times when Rakovac might just have stayed in his villa for twenty-four hours or more. But I was getting desperate and decided to go back in and examine them more carefully." She added, "They're definitely worth looking at and seeing if I can see any pattern. We have to assume that Rakovac knew and let himself be followed when it didn't matter to him. He had protection from Venable as long as he gave him what he wanted, and no matter what other dirtiness he became involved with, the CIA wasn't going to step in."

"Until they had information he might

have become involved with terrorists."

"That was too much for anyone to swallow. Rakovac conveniently disappeared." She took a sip of her orange juice. "But he left the holes for me. That may help."

"Then what are you doing just lolling here drinking orange juice? Get to work."

"I'm working. I'm thinking about the sequences and how I can tie it together with what I know about Rakovac." She took another drink. "But I don't know enough about him. I know the filth he became later in life, but I don't know how he started out. Most patterns start in childhood and stay in effect throughout life. What do you know about his early years?"

"Not much. He was born in the Republic of Georgia and involved in that short vicious conflict that involved South Ossetia and Russia. He was jumping from one side to the other all during the war. I wasn't interested in his early years. I was too busy trying to fight the hell he was creating all around him as an adult."

"I'll see if Venable can e-mail me more details. I do know that he was only a teenager when he was first fighting the Ossetians, and he was exceptionally brutal and ugly. He's had no permanent relationship with a woman. He prefers to have a variety of affairs with the kind of sadistic sex that he put Natalie through."

"Oh, I can believe that. He's mentioned in detail what he has in store for me."

Kelly nodded. "But I'd like to find out more about his childhood. Maybe Kelsov can help me. No one should know more about him. After all, they did fight together before Rakovac betrayed him to Moscow." She finished her orange juice and got to her feet. "I think I'll go and find him. I saw him going toward the barn with Natalie."

"You're wrong. There's one person who knows more about Rakovac than Kelsov."

"Natalie?" Kelly nodded soberly. "I tried to do a little probing, but she shut down right away. I may try again. Or ask Kelsov to question her." She opened the front door. "She seems willing to do anything for him."

"Wait. You think these holes are really important?"

"Don't you?"

"They could be. I'm hoping we're not grasping at straws."

"Sometimes grasping at straws can be productive. They're a consistent in a multi-changing landscape in Rakovac's life. I have to look for consistencies and what events and personalities they're associated with."

"And then?"

She smiled. "Then I may see a pattern that may help you find your son."

"I couldn't make him do it," Mikhal said when Rakovac answered the phone. "Luke's become very stubborn. He's beginning to defy me."

"The little viper is like his mother. He's just getting his teeth. You punished him?"

"In the most painful way possible for him. He'll regret not obeying you."

Rakovac was still disappointed. The idea to have Luke murder in cold blood had been pure inspiration. Though he had made sure that Luke was involved in Mikhal's most brutal raids, there was something much more horrifying about a deliberate murder. It would have been agony for Catherine to realize what her son had become.

"You told me that you were coming to get him," Czadas said. "When?"

"Is he becoming too much for you, Mikhal? After all, he's only a child."

"He's not too much. At times, it's been amusing . . . and profitable."

"And you're wondering if the profits will continue after I take Luke away from you." Boarding Luke with Mikhal had been expensive but safe. Mikhal was the last person that Venable would suspect Rakovac of using to hide Luke since Rakovac had betrayed Mikhal's precious cause to the Russians when he'd left the Republic of Georgia. Supplying Mikhal and his small group of freedom fighters with weapons periodically had been worth the price.

Besides, Mikhal had the streak of sadistic cruelty he had been looking for in a guardian for Luke. It would not have been safe for Rakovac to come often to Savrin House, but he had to be sure that Catherine's whelp had the proper upbringing.

He smiled at the term "proper." Not the word usually applied for the way Luke had been raised in the violence and blood of Mikhal's savage attacks on the South Ossetia villages protected by Russia. Rakovac had grown up in that war and knew how ugly it could be. He had wanted all the gentleness and humanity torn out of Luke and Mikhal had done his best. "It's a shame to break up a partnership that's worked so well. We may come to a new arrangement if you're cooperative in the next few days. There may be some difficulty that I have to overcome."

"You have only to ask." He paused. "I killed Medvar when the boy refused. He whimpered and cried like a puking baby.

Luke was braver. Our treatment has put some steel in his backbone."

Or maybe it was Catherine who had given him that courage, Rakovac thought sourly. Even as a much smaller child, he had noticed that Luke never backed down unless he was knocked down.

Mikhal was hesitating. "I wondered if you wanted me to rid you of the bother of eliminating the boy. It would be no trouble. That is your intention?"

Rakovac didn't answer directly. "You've been more than generous. I believe I can handle it from here. You may see me soon."

"With the guns?"

Mikhal's persistence was beginning to annoy him. "I'll think about it." He hung up.

It was not wise to break totally with Mikhal yet. He still might have to be a vital part of his final confrontation with Catherine.

Which was going to have to happen soon. The bombing in Lima had been a tremendous success and Ali Dabala was salivating with eagerness to turn loose his fanatic idiots on more desirable targets. Rakovac had barely been able to rein him in on the pretext that everything was not yet in place.

In fact, it was in place. It was Rakovac who wasn't ready. He hadn't completed his business with Catherine and Luke. He wanted to have his final revenge, then phone Ali Dabala on the way to the airport to board his flight for his island. He would give him all the details that he'd been keeping from him and fly off into the sunset.

But it was dangerous to wait any longer. He knew that Venable had an inkling of what was going on and he had been deliberately feeding him false information. The possibility that Venable might stumble onto something that would blow Ali Dabala's plans was not to be tolerated.

He gazed at Catherine's photo. He was going to miss looking at her beautiful witch's face. She had become part of his life.

"I believe I've given you enough time for your Eve to find out that skeleton isn't Luke," he murmured. "Did it make you happy? Yes, I'm sure it did. Relief from agony can be very heady. But I put you through torment while she was working on it, didn't I? I had some pleasant moments thinking of how you were being torn apart by my little deception." He glanced at the bulletin board. He'd cleaned it up and eliminated all but the positive targets. "I'd let you worry a bit longer, but it's not possible. Sadly, I'm having to deal with a few things that are interfering with our game. We're going to have to proceed with all due speed . . ."

Chapter 14

Eve called Joe at seven that evening. "I finished the reconstruction early this morning. I meant to call you earlier, but I went to bed and passed out."

"What a surprise. After only working the better part of two days without sleep. Well?"

"It's not Luke."

"Catherine must be over the moon."

"So am I." She paused. "We've got to find him quickly, Joe. If he's alive, he's not going to stay that way. And Catherine will go crazy if she actually sees him in danger. Hell, so would I." If she had been in the same position as Catherine when Bonnie had disappeared, she would have done anything to get her back. She knew exactly the torment Catherine was going through.

No, she didn't. She'd had no real hope that her Bonnie was safe. From the beginning, everyone had thought that Bonnie was a victim who would never return. Catherine still had the possibility of getting Luke back. "Is Venable just spinning his wheels trying to get Rakovac?"

"He can't locate him. But we're working on a way to get around that. Venable's been pulling strings and offering bribes to the NSA to get them to let him use their satellite to track the phone calls that Rakovac is making to Catherine. If they can latch onto his signal, they can trace the call. But the NSA is dragging their feet, and it's driving Venable crazy. They say that they can't focus their satellite beam indefinitely on Catherine's phone on the chance that he'll call. That satellite is used on thousands of other projects. They're telling us that if we can give them a small window of certainty, then they'll go for it."

"Are they crazy? Those other projects aren't as important as preventing Ali Dabala from attacking."

"We're running into the same problem as we did with Homeland Security. There's doubt that there will be an attack from Dabala since Red Darkness supposedly did the Lima bombing, and they're on the run. I want to knock their asses into —" He stopped. "Venable's still talking, but I don't think that it's going to do any good."

She could feel his frustration. "Why do

we have to go through the NSA? The CIA has their own satellites."

"Not as sophisticated as the NSA's. Even the military doesn't have one that's as powerful a tool for identifying and tracking. The NSA can get us the information within a few minutes. It would take any other satellite hours to process the information."

"That's kind of scary. I don't like the idea of a spy in the sky having that much power to be intrusive with private citizens."

"It's the world we live in. And, in this case, be grateful they have the technology."

"If they'll use it. Rakovac is bound to call Catherine soon. Can't they —"

"A small window of opportunity," he repeated. "We have to give them a time, and they won't give us more than fifteen minutes either way, then they're gone."

"Which means we're supposed to dictate to Rakovac when he's to call? How can we do that?"

"Work it out. We won't be able to catch Rakovac's next call, but set him up to call back for some reason."

"At the exact time that you want him to do it?" she said in despair. "Do you know how hard it will be for her to —" She broke off. Stop whining. If it was their only chance, then they'd find a way to do it.

"Catherine will only push him so far. She's walking a fine line."

"It has to be done, Eve."

"I said Catherine wouldn't push him. If I have to take over, I'll do it. But I'll tell her what's happening and see if I can persuade her to cooperate, if only on a minimal level." She hoped Catherine could be swayed. It was going to be difficult enough for them to fight Rakovac without having to battle Catherine. Rakovac regarded Catherine as the primary foe, and he might pay no attention to Eve. "See if you can make those idiots in the NSA get a little sense."

"I will." He added roughly, "Be careful how you handle this, Eve. Dammit, the last thing I want is for you to switch Rakovac's focus to you."

"It would be a lot easier if we could just snatch Luke from him and get him out of the equation."

"What about the progress on the surveillance reports?"

"Kelly says that she may have found something promising. But it sounds pretty tentative to me. Of course, all of this pattern business sounds a little far-fetched to me. I don't understand how it works."

Joe chuckled. "And your own work is absolutely clear and not at all far-fetched or hard to understand."

"That's different . . . to me." She suddenly grinned. "You're right, of course. We always doubt what we don't understand. Maybe Kelly is on the right track. I'll talk to her and see if she's come up with anything else."

"Get back to me as soon as you hear from Rakovac."

"I will." She paused. She didn't want to let him go yet, but she had to do it. He was busy. Now that the reconstruction was finished, she was feeling without purpose. That was very bad for her. Purpose guided her life.

But Joe made that life worth living.

"Eve?"

"Good-bye, Joe. Take care."

"I love you." He hung up.

And she loved him. She didn't want him in Moscow wheeling and dealing with all those agencies. She wanted him here with her.

It didn't matter what she wanted. They both had a job to do, and she should stop wishing for the moon.

She got to her feet and headed for the door to try to find Catherine.

I should be there with her, Joe thought, as he hung up the phone.

Yes, he thought she was safe, but who knew how the situation would change.

Everyone around Catherine was in danger. Rakovac had already threatened Eve.

Nine-eleven.

How the hell could he leave here until they had a fix on Rakovac?

Joe turned to Venable, who was sitting across the room, papers spread all over the desk in front of him. "Who directs that NSA satellite?"

"The man in charge of the program?"

"The man who pushes the buttons at the tech center."

"That's George Helder. Why?"

"I want to know everything about him." He paused. "And when we set up the phone trace, I want to be in charge."

"What? That's my job."

"I want to do it." He met Venable's eyes. "You want to save those thousands of people. I'm with you on that. But I have a hell of a lot more personal investment. Do you doubt that I'm the best man for the job?"

Venable studied him. "No."

"Then let me do it."

Venable shook his head. "You're not even government. They won't recognize that you have any authority. They wouldn't listen to you."

"They'll listen to me."

Venable smiled faintly. "They might at that. I'll give you a dossier on Helder's background. That's all I'll promise right now. And the question is moot until we have a call for the NSA to monitor. Has Catherine heard from him yet?"

"Not yet."

But it would happen soon and the tension was beginning to tighten within him.

Damn, he wanted to be with Eve now.

"An NSA satellite," Catherine repeated thoughtfully. "I remember that Venable's used it before, but most of the time it's more trouble than it's worth. Those assholes are so uptight about their precious schedule that it's a nightmare."

"We don't have any choice. Joe said he'd deal with it."

She smiled faintly. "I'd like to be around when he does. Joe against the establishment. It would be interesting."

"But it won't do a damn bit of good if you don't manage to find a way to manipulate Rakovac into calling you at a given time."

"So that you can find those records." Her

smile faded. "I knew that was coming."

"Look, I know you said that it was up to us to take care of finding a way to getting those files from Rakovac, that you wouldn't do anything to compromise rescuing Luke. But this is our opportunity to grab those records and still give you a chance to save Luke. Rakovac's probably not keeping Luke with him. He wouldn't take the chance. We might be able to infiltrate wherever he's hiding out and steal the plans for Dabala's raid without his knowing. Then we can follow him to where he's keeping Luke." She paused. "Or if Luke is with Rakovac, we don't have to rely on Kelly to find him. We can go in and rescue Luke, then get the records afterward."

"So simple. So easy." Catherine's lips twisted. "It won't be either simple or easy. No matter what the scenario. I can see a multitude of problems."

"I'm not trying to persuade you that there won't be problems. I'm just saying that we'll have a valid chance. We don't have that now. Help us, Catherine."

Catherine didn't answer for a long moment. "Do you think I don't want to help you?" she whispered. "I've been ripped apart by doubts ever since I heard about Lima. I've spent most of my adult life fighting to keep slugs like Rakovac from destroying all the good things in life. But this is Luke. Don't I have the right to let someone else step up to the plate, and just be Luke's mother?"

"I don't know anything about rights," Eve said. "Not in a situation like this. The good of the one against the good of the majority? Someone else can decide all that philosophical bullshit. I just want to keep Luke alive and give those other thousands of victims their shot at survival, too. This could be the way to do it, Catherine."

She looked away from Eve. "I know."

"Then help us."

"I'll think about it."

She was still holding back, not committing. "What's your main objection, Catherine?"

"What do you think? I'd be giving up control," she said tersely. "It's life or death for Luke. I don't want to put that power in anyone else's hands. People make mistakes. I'm the only one who cares enough. I'm the only one I trust."

It was difficult for Eve to question that argument. It was how she would feel under the same circumstances. "Then you'll have to make up your own mind. I just want to say that I do care. Joe cares. Whether that's enough to make you trust us to make Venable and the others toe the line will be your decision."

"Yes, it will," Catherine said. "I said that I'd think about it, Eve."

Eve had done all she could. She got to her feet. "Will you let me know when he phones you?"

Catherine nodded. "Nothing has changed. I told you that I'd always be open with you." She hesitated. "And I do trust you, Eve. You know what kind of life I've lived. I have trouble having faith in anyone. But the moment I met you, I realized that . . ." She was having trouble putting the words together. "I felt . . . comfortable. As if I'd come home. I wanted to stay there in that cottage and talk to you, have you tell me what you thought, how you felt. I wanted to be your . . . friend." She met Eve's eyes. "Are you my friend, Eve?"

Eve felt her throat tighten as she gazed at Catherine. So tough yet so vulnerable. "Yes, I'm your friend, Catherine."

Catherine smiled luminously. "I thought so. I'm glad, Eve." Her smile faded, then vanished. "But it doesn't make any difference. I still have to think about this."

Eve opened the door. "By all means."

"Eve."

"What?"

"Don't tell Kelsov about the satellite. I don't want him bugging me about it until I make a decision. Kelsov can be difficult. He doesn't care about Luke. Not really. All he cares about is killing Rakovac."

"I'm sure he cares about Luke," Eve said gently. "How could he help it? He's your friend."

She shook her head. "We get along, and we have a joint purpose." She added, "I told you, I have trouble with friendship. So does Kelsov. The closest he's come is Natalie."

Eve nodded. "He's very kind to her."

"She fills a need. She must make him feel like a god."

"She was ready to kill Joe when she thought he was hurting Kelsov," Eve said.

"He'd leave her in a heartbeat if he got his chance at Rakovac. I've had to rein him in for years to keep a balance that would keep Luke safe. He'd think that damn satellite was his way to get him at last."

"I won't mention it to him. You're the only one Joe wanted me to discuss it with."

"Thank you. I know it's tempting to let him add his pressure to yours."

She shook her head. "You'd probably balk and go the other way."

Catherine smiled. "You're beginning to

know me very well."

"I have my moments. It's getting easier to gauge your reactions. Do you suppose that's because I'm your friend?" The door shut behind her.

"What about these holes?" Eve asked an hour later as she sat down at the table across from where Kelly was sitting with her computer. "Yes, I know what Catherine told me, but have you pinned down when, why, and where?"

"You sound like a newspaper editor," Kelly said. "I wanted to be on the school newspaper at college, but all my professors said that I shouldn't waste my time. I didn't think it was a waste of time."

"Not if you wanted to do it." Eve wondered how many other fun activities Kelly had been kept from doing because of that extraordinary and unique brilliance. "You should have told them to go jump in the lake."

"It's hard to know what's right when everyone thinks you're wrong." She looked down at the yellow notepad on the table beside her. "I think the holes were the periods when Rakovac visited Luke. That was the only secret Rakovac wouldn't have wanted Venable to know about. I was looking for triggers to his behavior that might give me a clue. I made Catherine think back and try to tell me when Rakovac's phone calls occurred. But she couldn't remember everything or every time he called her."

"Of course not. For goodness' sake, it's been nine years. How could she possibly remember?"

"He didn't call her that frequently. Only several times a year. Just enough to twist the knife and keep her under his thumb." She made a face. "But there were some calls that she'll never forget. The ones in which he hurt her the most. She was able to remember where she was, what she was doing, and the approximate date. I was able to pull those periods out of the report and do a graph that indicated where he was approximately and who he was dealing with at that particular time."

"What good will that do? You said that probably none of these clients had anything to do with Luke."

"Probably. We don't know anything yet. I'm just trying to explore those black holes. I'm paying particular attention to the early days after he took Luke. He made more calls than usual to her during that period. He must have been enjoying himself." She shook her head. "What a terrible man he is, Eve."

"Yes. What next, Kelly? How do you connect the dots?"

Kelly smiled faintly. "Catherine said that was what you did with your reconstructions. It's strange that we work in the same way. I thought perhaps we might."

Eve nodded. "I keep telling Catherine it's science combined with instinct. What about you? Do you have hunches?"

"Everyone has hunches occasionally." She looked down at her pad. "I try not to let them get in the way. In this case, dealing with a personality and not a concept, I'm going to have to rely on Rakovac's background and personality to help me."

Eve leaned back in the chair and gazed at her. Kelly was really incredible. Eve kept forgetting how young the girl was. She had been talking to Kelly as if she were an adult and professional on her own level. Yet hunched over that computer, with her blond hair tied back in a ponytail, Kelly appeared even younger than her fourteen years. "Like a puzzle. But I don't know how realizing just how much of a bastard Rakovac can be is going to help you."

"That's not what I'm looking at. It's the way he reacts, his past pattern of behavior.

I've analyzed his behavior in the last nine years, then called Venable and had him send me his entire file. He's . . . remarkable."

"What do you mean?"

"He's totally self-serving and definitely has a God complex. But I was interested in the way he handled his business interests. He's totally without any sense of loyalty. When he was a child, his father brought him up as a rebel and later was killed in the war. You would think he would have some feelings for the cause, but it didn't happen. He betrayed Kelsov at the first opportunity to better himself. But after the betrayal, there's some information that he may have worked a few deals with the rebels once he'd established himself with the mafia in Moscow. You'd think he'd be afraid of getting his throat cut by the rebels after what he'd done. But he's totally fearless. Wherever the money was, wherever the power was, he was willing to take the chance to grasp it. Later, he did the same thing with the Pakistani government on a munitions deal. He jumped back and forth between Pakistan and India. There are several other instances where he went back and managed to use a client he'd treated shoddily in the past. I don't know whether he regards it as a challenge or if that God complex is so extreme that he just thinks that he can get away with anything he chooses to do. He uses everyone and manages to keep all his balls in the air." She looked up from her pad. "I think that may be what he's doing now. Taking Luke was a big risk, but he did it anyway. Now this deal with Ali Dabala is very important to him, but he's juggling his revenge against Catherine, and he's not willing to give it up. Very dangerous but in keeping with his past behavior."

"And how is all this analysis helping?"

"It shows me that he doesn't deviate from his pattern." She added, "And that we have to expect the unexpected about where Luke has been hidden away."

"Did you tell all this to Catherine?"

"Of course, I'd never keep anything from Catherine. She's why I'm here."

"But you made a deal with Venable."

"And I'll keep it. But it's Catherine who is important."

Yes, it was Catherine who was important to Kelly. The girl's single-minded devotion and stubbornness had led her down this strange path to this house in Russia. Well, how could she blame her? Not only had Catherine saved her life, but she seemed to have chosen her to fill her loneliness that was so apparent. "I believe we all realize that's your main priority."

Kelly nodded. "You're thinking that I'm some kind of nut because I've been following her around like a lost puppy. I know Luke's the only one who is important to Catherine right now. It doesn't matter. I'm not going to bother her."

"I don't think you're a nut," Eve said gently. "I think you're loyal and brave and trying to find something or someone." She reached out and squeezed Kelly's hand. "And I know that Catherine cares about you."

"Me, too." Kelly smiled. "And she'll like me even more after I find Luke for her." She looked back down at her computer. "Excuse me, Eve. I have to get back to work."

She was dismissed, Eve realized, amused. Politely but definitely. Again, she could see similarities between her own work habits and Kelly's. She hoped the girl did not become as obsessive about her work as Eve.

She had a chance of escaping that fate. Her own obsession had been triggered by Bonnie. She only prayed that Kelly's life would not be marred and twisted so badly that it would draw her into cocooning herself away from all the things a young girl had the right to experience.

"Then I'll leave you to it." She got to her feet. "You seem to be much busier than I am at present. I'll go twiddle my thumbs."

"The ultimate torture for you?" Kelly grinned. "It can't last long, Eve. Something's going to break."

She was afraid that was all too true. Yes, she was restless and wanted to be busier, but she was aware of Rakovac hovering, waiting, just over the horizon. This was the calm before the storm.

She just hoped that storm didn't sweep them all away.

Catherine got the call from Rakovac six hours later. She was alone with Eve in the living room and put it on the speakerphone.

"You've been very clever," he said when she picked up the call. "I thought it would take you a little longer to find that skeleton. Of course, I did leave you clues. But I was anticipating your running around frantically trying desperately to find your son. I was disappointed."

"Too bad. And that skeleton was not my son."

"You say that with complete conviction. I take it that Eve Duncan has completed her reconstruction. I thought I gave her enough time. She's a professional and can work very quickly under pressure. Were you tremendously relieved?"

"You know I was."

"My words concerning Luke's death may have been exaggerated, but your relief is only temporary, you know. He *will* die, Catherine."

"But he's not dead yet."

"Not yet."

She couldn't speak for a moment as the waves of relief struck her. It was the first time he had stated uncategorically that Luke was alive. "And he's well?"

"It depends on what you call well. I took care to make sure that he wouldn't resemble that cute little toddler that you knew and loved. He's a young savage. He's killed, you know."

"For God's sake, he's only eleven years old."

"I killed my first man on a raid when I was nine. As his guardian, I thought it fitting that he follow in my footsteps. So I set him on the proper path."

"You bastard."

"Now Catherine, you've been asking me questions about your Luke all these years. Yet when I oblige you, all I get is abuse."

He had been lying and playing cat and mouse with her emotions since the moment he had taken Luke. The only reason he was giving her all the painful details was that it didn't matter to him any longer. "No matter what you did to Luke, you couldn't change him."

He laughed. "How naïve you are. Life changes everyone, and I helped the process along. You'd be surprised what a corrupt little son of a bitch he's become. And I use that term with complete accuracy. You'd never be able to recognize any of the qualities you think Luke possessed. Are you sure that you even want to make the attempt to regain your little darling?"

"Why should I believe you? You've lied to me before. Maybe this is just another lie."

"I think in your heart you know that there's no reason for our little charade to go on. Luke is what I've made him. Not the child you created in your womb."

He was speaking with absolute certainty, and his words terrified her. "I'll never give up on him."

"That's what I hoped you'd say. I just thought I'd give you the opportunity to walk away from him and save your life and lives of your friends. Wasn't that kind of me?"

"I won't walk away. But the people who have helped me have nothing to do with this any longer. You don't have to go after them."

"But I do. I told you what would happen to them, and I always keep my word. You should know that by now, Catherine. Our involvement during these past years should have been ample proof. And I already have plans to have you watch their removal. Guilt and regret should add a spice to the occasion."

She shuddered. "So many deaths. The adults are bad enough, but the children . . . Did you kill that little boy whose skull Eve reconstructed?"

"Oh, yes, that's what gave me the idea of using the skeleton to lead you here. He was the youngest son of Karl Taskov, a Georgian guerilla that Russia paid me a handsome fee to hunt down and eliminate."

"One of your old comrades like Kelsov?"

"Yes, I had my new nest to feather after I went to Moscow. And I feathered it well."

"But why kill the son? You didn't get money for the murder of a child."

"He got in the way. I found Taskov on his farm with his wife and three children. I didn't want his wife to blab to the other members of the resistance that I was the one who was doing the executions. You can never tell when it may become profitable to go back to your roots."

He jumps back and forth. It's part of the pattern.

Kelly had hit the nail on the head with her analysis, she thought sickly. "You killed all of them?"

"It was the practical thing to do. I buried the bodies at different locations. I had to think for a moment to remember where I'd buried the little boy."

"Because he wasn't important."

"Exactly. You understand me so well. But your Luke is important. I kept very good track of him over the years."

She drew a shaky breath. "What's next, Rakovac? You're calling the shots."

"Yes, I am. Strange you should use that phrase. I called the shots figuratively with you and literally with your son. Did I tell you what a fine shot he is?"

"It doesn't matter how you've twisted him. He's still my Luke. Tell me where he is."

"Come and get him."

She drew a deep breath. "How? Where?"

"I assume you're still in Russia?"

"Of course. I wouldn't leave here without Luke. Not this time."

"So eager. Your determination amazes me. A mother's love . . ."

"It shouldn't surprise you. That's what

you've relied on all these years. How do I find Luke?"

"First, separate yourself from Duncan and Quinn. I want our meeting to be one-on-one as I've always intended it to be. I'll attend to them at a later date."

"What else?"

"No arguments?"

"They've tried to help me. Why should I want to pull them into a trap? If they're not with me, then they have a chance." She paused. "And I have to make sure Luke has a chance, too. Which means I have to have my chance. You can't have it all your own way. I'm not walking up to you and letting you line Luke and me against a wall for a firing squad."

"How could you believe I would have so little imagination? That would be no fun at all for me. I have to have my final game of cat and mouse before I bring the two of you together. Unfortunately, I have little time so the game must get under way with speed and dispatch."

"I've no objection." She could see Eve sitting straight and tense across the room, waiting.

Make up your mind, she told herself. Do it or don't do it. It was time to decide.

What the hell. She'd already decided. Take

charge. Don't be a victim. That would be the supreme mistake if she was going to have any chance at all. The telephone call. She had to set up the telephone call. "So I'll tell you what I'm going to do. I'll separate myself from Eve and Joe as you've told me to do. It won't be easy. They're both very protective. I'll slip away and go to the Danilovsky Market. It's a huge open-air market, and I can move around there in the crowd, and I'll be able to see you or any of the slimeballs you might send after me. At two P.M., you'll call me and tell me where I'm to go from there."

"You're being very demanding. I'm not sure I like that, Catherine."

"It's time I was demanding. What have I got to lose? You've had me under your thumb for years and enjoyed every minute of it. Right now I'm not afraid you're going to kill Luke if I don't bow down before you. You've already told me that you want your cat-and-mouse game to come to a glorious conclusion. You want cat and mouse? I'll give it to you. But it can't be all your own way. If I can grab Luke away and rid the earth of you at the same time, I'll do it. You should be happy. It will make your game all the more exciting."

He chuckled. "You're magnificent, Catherine. I admit I enjoyed making you subservient. It pleased my ego. But this may be still more stimulating."

"I'll be at the market. Call me at two."

"Don't be pushy. I'll be in touch." He hung up.

Catherine gazed at Eve as she hung up. "I could have blown it at the end. It was hard to strike a balance. I didn't even know if he'd let me get away with setting up the call at the market. I still don't know if he'll call or not." Her lips twisted. "Or if it will be at two P.M."

"You did the best you could," Eve said. "I wasn't sure until you did it that you'd actually set up that call."

"Neither did I." She shook her head in despair. "There are so many variables. Is he close enough so that Joe can get to his location quickly after the call is tapped? And how do we know he'll call from where he's staying so that we can get at those records? It's a mobile world."

"We need luck. But if Joe can't find his actual permanent location, then he can at least zero in on his cell phone and go after him from that angle."

"That's why I'm afraid," Catherine said grimly. "I know Venable. He wouldn't be able to resist sending someone to pick up

Rakovac to try to squeeze the information out of him. I can't let that happen. Rakovac will do anything to win. He'd arrange for Luke to be killed if he was caught or captured. I went along with this because I know it's right, but it's tearing me apart." Her lips firmed. "But Joe has to promise me that he won't let Venable get his hands on Rakovac. He can follow him if they get the chance, but he can't touch him until I have Luke."

Eve nodded slowly. "You must trust Joe a lot if you're willing to take that risk with Luke."

"I've never known anyone I'd trust more. Joe is . . . special." She met Eve's gaze. "You're very lucky, Eve." She got to her feet. "Now I have to get on the move. I have to change, get my automatic, then go get Kelsov and have him drive me into Moscow to the market. Rakovac is waiting." She glanced over her shoulder as she reached the door. "It's odd saying that. I've always been the one waiting for something to happen, Rakovac to relent, God to send a miracle . . . Anything to change the status quo. But now I can move, and Rakovac can wait."

"We can move," Eve said quietly. "I don't want you going to that market by yourself."

"I have to be by myself. He has to see that

I'm vulnerable."

"I don't like it. You may have told Rakovac you were jettisoning us, but we're still in this with you. You were a little too sincere on the phone with Rakovac. Don't try to make the lie true."

"I told you that I'd always be honest with you." Catherine was silent, staring at her for a long moment. "Thank you for everything, Eve. I meant every word I said to you. You're very special, too." She disappeared into the bedroom.

Dammit, that last sentence had been entirely too final, Eve thought as the front door closed behind Catherine five minutes later. Catherine wouldn't lie, but she wouldn't say the words Eve wanted to hear.

Eve quickly dialed Joe and filled him in on Catherine's conversation with Rakovac. "She wants your promise to keep Venable away from Rakovac until she gets Luke, Joe. She says that she's cooperating as much as she can, but she has to have your word."

Joe swore beneath his breath. "She doesn't ask much. If we don't get a residence location, Venable will be on Rakovac like a tiger the minute we get a cell fix."

"Catherine knows that." She paused. "She said to tell you that she trusts you."

"Which is the best thing she could do to tie my hands," he said sourly. "Catherine is nothing if not clever."

"She meant it, Joe."

He was silent a moment. "I know she did. I'd trust her, too." His breath expelled in a frustrated sigh. "Okay, I'll do it. Though God knows how. I may have to knock Venable out and then hog-tie him. We've just got to hope Rakovac is at a location where we can find his sources, and not on the move. It will be safer for all of us."

"Catherine isn't concerned about safety right now. Not for herself. But I think she may be trying to close us out."

"No," he said definitely. "That's not going to happen. We're not going to let Rakovac have her. She may like to work alone, but she'll have to learn new ways."

"Then you talk to her. You have more influence than I do with her. You two have a . . . connection."

"What?"

"Come on, Joe. It's there in the open for everyone to see. You're alike. It's as if you're two halves of a whole." She added quietly, "I'm not trying to make anything of it. I accept it. I like both of those halves, and I don't believe there's any threat to me."

"You're damn right there's not. And I

don't have a connection with anyone but you. You're all I want or need."

She felt a rush of warmth, mixed with relief. It was all very well to be adult and reasonable, but the way she felt about Joe had elements of passion and possessiveness that weren't at all reasonable. "That's good to know. But you should still be the one to convince Catherine."

"Stubborn. You're being a little too tolerant. I'd like it more if you were ready to claw her eyes out. It would please the primitive streak in me." He paused. "Unless you're trying to get rid of me?"

She should have known he might have that reaction. Their relationship in the past had had its moments of turbulence, but it had been relatively tranquil sailing recently. "You're the one who has a right to walk out of our relationship. I've given you nothing but frustration and grief since the moment you came into my life when I lost Bonnie."

He was silent a moment. "Hell, yes, I've been torn apart. I won't deny it. The good times balance it out."

"Sometimes."

"Sometimes. But you're not going to get away from me. I'll track you down."

He wouldn't have a hard time doing it. She cleared her throat and tried to keep her tone light. "At the moment, your job is to track down Catherine and Rakovac. You're sending someone to the Danilovsky Market in case she needs help?"

"Yes, but she'll kill me if they interfere unless she's at death's door. That will be their orders."

"Let me know if that satellite comes up aces. Catherine was worried that Rakovac may not keep to the time she set him."

"Which would be one big headache for me."

"But you can make it work?"

"I'll deal with it." He hung up.

Rakovac got up from his desk and strolled over to the window to look out at the garden. He was feeling the exultant blood surge through his body. The sun was shining brightly, and it was a good sign that all was going to go well.

Of course it would. Killing Catherine was the last piece in the scenario that he'd toyed with for the last nine years.

"Ali Dabala just phoned," Russo said behind him. "He wants to know why you've canceled Philadelphia. He said he wanted Philadelphia."

"He wants the whole world. Or at least the entire Christian world."

"He said that the city has historical significance for the Americans. He mentioned the Liberty Bell."

"Oh, for God's sake. Screw the Liberty Bell."

"He was very adamant. He wants Philadelphia. Why did you cancel it?"

"Because the baggage handler who was going to do the handoff on the explosives proved unstable. I had a report he was about to break. I couldn't get a safe substitute at this late date."

"Unstable. That's very dangerous," Russo said. "What if the man —"

"I took care of it. They won't find the baggage handler's body and the air strikes can go on as planned. I just eliminated Philadelphia from the agenda. Ali Dabala doesn't need Philadelphia. The operation is going to go off like clockwork. He has enough cities to make him a big man in Islam."

"Is that what I'm to tell him? He'll want to talk to you."

"I'm going to be busy today. Take the flack. That's what I pay you for."

"You're treating me like a servant." Russo was frowning. "I've been very loyal through the years. I've done you favors. I've given up a lot for you."

He stared at him in disbelief. The whining

son of a bitch. "And taken a lot in return. You'll get your payoff as soon as I get mine. Tell Dabala the rest of the cities are golden, and I'll give my teams in the target cities the go-ahead tomorrow on schedule." He turned to face him. "Our Catherine has decided to take charge of her fate. She said she's left the safe haven that Duncan and Quinn provided for her. I'm a bit skeptical, but we'll see if it turns out to be true. She's going to be at the Danilovsky Market this afternoon to show me that she's done as I asked and gotten rid of Duncan and Quinn. It's almost as if she was throwing down a challenge." He leaned back in his chair and smiled. "Why don't you have Borzoi take a few men to go and greet her? She's extremely competent. It will be amusing to see if they can do the job."

"You want her brought here?"

"I'll make that decision when I see if they're able to do it."

"You said she didn't have help."

"As far as I know. Again, we'll have to see."

He turned back to the window as Russo left the study. The excitement was growing higher. Tonight. All the years, all the hatred and fear. It was going to end tonight.

You're so close I can almost touch you, Catherine. How frantic you must be.

And desperate if she left the protection of her friends to expose herself in that market.

He liked the taste of her desperation. It had a bittersweet, coppery flavor.

Like blood.

Chapter 15

"Two o'clock, Helder," Joe said on the phone to the NSA satellite-control agent. "Don't be a second late. I don't know how long she's going to be able to hold him on the phone."

"It won't take us more than thirty seconds to zero in and make the trace," Helder said. "Our satellite is much more sophisticated than your law-enforcement methods. We've got everything developed down to a fine state of science."

And the men who handled the information gathering of those satellites had developed a fine state of arrogance, Joe thought in annoyance. He glanced down at the dossier on Helder that Venable had provided him. George Helder was in his thirties with slick black hair, triangular face, and dark eyes behind wire-rimmed glasses. He had a master's in Computer Science and had been with the NSA for ten years. He was in

Mensa, an ardent cyclist, and was a geek of the highest order.

Joe had no problem with any of those things. He did have issue with the arrogance. "I'm sure you've had opportunities the rest of us peasants weren't privy to. That's why we've come to you to help us out."

"I'm happy you appreciate how valuable we can be. We've got you on the schedule for two. We've tapped Ms. Ling's phone, and we'll be ready. Is there anything else? I'm very busy."

Yes, he wished the prick wasn't so damn egotistical. He'd dealt with too many bureaucrats not to recognize the signs in this NSA controller. "No, as long as we understand each other, and you're aware how important it is that you cooperate with us."

"Cooperate?" Helder said in disbelief. "We're doing you a favor, Mr. Quinn. Do you know how much of a favor that is? Corporations pay us millions for just a few minutes of our time. You'd be wise not to demand more than we choose to give you."

Don't pop his balloon, Joe told himself. Save the big guns if it became necessary later. "If there are any problems, call and let me know. I'll straighten them out."

And straighten him out.

It would be a pleasure.

1:50 p.m.
Danilovsky Market

The market was just as crowded and noisy as Catherine had hoped it would be. Located outside the Garden Ring and off the Tulskaya Metro Station, the Danilovsky was one of the most popular open-air markets in the city, and she'd used it before for a meeting place with her contacts. The crowded booths and vendors hawking their wares, the scent of fresh vegetables and exotic cheeses were all very familiar to her.

"This is stupid," Kelsov said roughly as he parked the car at the curb next to the market. "Anyone could sidle up to you in this crowd and slip a stiletto between your ribs. You need someone to watch your back. I'm going with you."

"You are not," Catherine said as she got out of the car. "You're out of this, Kelsov. The only reason I had you bring me here instead of driving myself was that I wanted to be sure that you still had a car at the house. I didn't want to leave Eve and Kelly without wheels."

"I'm out of this?" His voice was harsh. "No way, Catherine. We've worked together for years trying to find a way to kill that bastard. You're not going to shut me out."

"Killing Rakovac was always second on my agenda."

"Well, he's first on mine."

"I know," she said quietly. "And that's why you're not going with me. I've been fighting everyone to get my chance to save my son, and I won't have you ruining that chance."

He got out of the car. "You won't have any chance at all if you get your throat cut."

"He's not going to kill me. Not here. Whatever else he plans, it won't be murder. He's not through toying with me yet. He'll call me and tell me how to take the next step in his game plan." She checked her watch. "And I don't have time to argue with you. I've got to move around that market and make myself seen. It's 1:55. I get the call from Rakovac at two. I don't want anyone reporting to him that I didn't show up." She started toward the booths. "Take off, Kelsov. I don't want you seen. Get that car back to Eve and Kelly."

He didn't move.

She glanced back over her shoulder. "I mean it," she said softly. "If you blow this for me, you'll wish you'd never been born. You're always telling me how miserable that work camp in Siberia was, how they beat you and froze you and made you feel like half a man. I guarantee you'll think of it as a balmy day camp after I get through with you."

He believed her. He was aware of all her lethal capabilities though they had never been aimed at him. "Bitch."

She nodded. "I take it our relationship is at an end. I'm sorry, Kelsov. I hoped we might both get what we wanted. It just didn't work out. One more thing. You take good care of Eve and Kelly, or I'll track you down and amputate your nuts." She turned and disappeared into the crowd.

His hands clenched into fists. He wanted to strike out at her. Strangle her. She was getting close to Rakovac. He knew it.

Bitch. Bitch. Bitch.

Go after her?

No, she had meant what she said. He wouldn't put it past her to turn on him and give him a karate chop just to prove to any onlooker that he was not supporting her in any way.

Rage was searing through him. He was losing his chance at Rakovac.

And all because of that damn kid. He had known her son could screw things up for him, but he'd had to accept Luke if he wanted Catherine's expertise and dedication.

Okay, don't go after her.

Stay across the street in the vestibule of that butcher shop and watch and wait for her to surface.

He strode across the street, dodging the pushcarts.

The butcher shop's interior was as crowded as the rest of the market. He pressed against the far side of the vestibule to allow people to come and go.

He tried to smother his anger as he settled down to wait.

2:05 p.m.

"She hasn't gotten the call yet," Venable said. "Helder just contacted me and wants to know what's happening." He added sarcastically, "He tells me time's money, you know."

"He's only five minutes late so far," Joe said. "Helder wouldn't realize that people aren't robots you can program." But he was as tense as Venable. "I placed Cal Parkins in the market, and he said she arrived ten minutes ago. She's moving from booth to booth, and there's been no sign of aggressive action against her. He hasn't spotted anyone who appears suspicious."

"If he could spot them, Rakovac wouldn't use them," Venable said. He was staring at the clock. "Why the hell doesn't he call her?"

The butcher shop smelled of sawdust, herbs, fresh salmon, and the sour sweat of the people who were coming and going, Kelsov thought.

Not pleasant.

He wanted out of there.

Where the hell are you, Catherine?

He'd give her another five minutes, then go into the market after her. He'd talk fast, tell her that he'd go along with anything she wanted, persuade her that he'd had a change of heart.

It might work.

It was better than standing here being overwhelmed by this stink. Catherine should be —

"Excuse me." Another bulky man was trying to squeeze by him. He must have been three hundred pounds and was dressed in a red sweater, black pants, and a gray cap. "You should not be here. It's a fine day. Why are you huddled in the corner? Are you ill?"

Pretty close to it. And this monster of a man wasn't helping. Get rid of him. He inhaled and pressed even tighter back against the wall. "I'm sorry I'm in your way. Go on past me. I'm fine."

"Not ill?" The man asked again with concern.

"I told you, I'm not —"

Sharp pain . . . his wrist . . .

2:10 p.m.

No call.

Catherine stared blindly down at the odd purple carrot in the bin before her.

Dammit, why didn't he call? She had been afraid that she had pushed Rakovac too hard. With her luck, he might decide to call her in a half hour . . . or not at all.

"You buy?" The chunky woman at the carrot booth urged. "A special Azerbaijani carrot. Very rare — 150 rubles per kilo."

Catherine shook her head and moved on.

Her fifteen-minute window the NSA had given her was almost up. She knew those bastards. It would take a miracle to get them to extend that time.

Call, Rakovac, she prayed. Call now.

2:14 p.m.

"We're releasing the focus on the Ling phone in one minute," Helder said when Joe picked up the phone. "This is your official notification."

"Is it?" Joe said softly. "How kind of you to let us know."

"It's policy," Helder said. "We're not happy. This has been a complete waste of our time."

"I believe Venable has informed you that this may be a matter of Homeland Security."

"May," Helder repeated. "Do you know how often we get agencies telling us the same thing? We can't let every little threat cause us to disrupt our schedule."

"I'm sure an important unit like yours is swamped. We're very grateful."

"One minute," Helder repeated.

"You don't care that it's very likely a national emergency that might kill thousands of citizens?"

"You haven't given me proof. I gave you your window. That's it."

"No, it's not," Joe added a thread of steel to the softness of his voice. "You'll give us as long as it takes. And you'll ask permission to take your satellite anywhere else."

There was an astonished silence. "Screw you."

"Listen carefully, Helder. You like your job? Of course you do. It gives a stunning amount of power to a man whose life was destined to be humdrum. But it can be taken away from you in a heartbeat."

"By you?" Helder jeered. "You have no authority. I don't even know why Venable let you become involved. I have ten years' seniority and experience with the NSA."

"You also have an arrogance that the general public finds offensive in public servants. Particularly when it concerns their safety. I've recorded our conversations. I'm going to play it back to you." He turned the switch and played the recording. "As you can hear, you stated you cared nothing about aiding Homeland Security. Nor were you willing to stretch the time you allowed us even after it was stated that a public emergency existed. It didn't sound warm and caring, did it?"

Silence. "What do you intend to do with that?"

"Your boss, media . . . I haven't decided. It would be particularly damaging if there was really a national emergency. I think probably a vigilante posse might lynch you."

"It wouldn't matter. I'd apologize and say I was goaded."

"Why bother? The problem goes away the minute you agree to keep the satellite fixed on Catherine Ling's phone until I tell you it's no longer necessary."

Another silence. "I might consider it."

"You'll do it," Joe said. "Because I'll tell you why Venable thought I could deal with you. I don't care, Helder. Not about my job, or my superiors, or what anyone thinks of me. You're right, I don't have authority because it would just get in my way. That leaves me free to use blackmail or violence or anything necessary to stop that attack from happening. I don't play by the rules. If you decide having this disk aired won't bother you, I'll find another way to take you down." He paused, letting the words sink in. "Now, do we work together to get this done?"

Helder hesitated before saying jerkily, "The NSA is always willing to cooperate in any security endeavor."

"Then call me after you have the completed trace, even if you have to wait for another hour." He hung up.

Venable was gazing ruefully at him. "You realize you've put the CIA-NSA relationship in dire danger?"

"Then keep the disk on hand," he said indifferently. "Or call me, and I'll have another talk with Helder."

Venable's brows rose. "You really don't care."

"I care about Eve. I care about my daughter, Jane. I care about my country. None of the rest is worth worrying about." He checked his watch again. "It's 2:17 P.M. No call. Catherine is probably ready to explode . . ."

It was 2:25, Catherine saw in despair as she glanced at her watch.

Rakovac had done it again. It would be a miracle if that NSA satellite was still aimed at her.

And there were at least three men focusing their attention on her. She had been scanning the crowd as she moved from booth to booth and spotted Rakovac's men. One short, burly man in a yellow Windbreaker, a taller, thin man in an olive green sweatshirt, the third man had been a huge man in a gray cap and red sweater, but he had disappeared from view shortly after she had spotted him. It wasn't difficult to identify them as Rakovac's men when they were trying so hard not to look at her and to appear casual in a venue that was clearly not their cup of tea.

It was okay. Now that she knew with whom she had to contend, she could be on watch. They wouldn't move on her with this many witnesses. The crowds were proving as helpful to her as she had thought when she had set up the call for this marketplace.

Two twenty-six.

Blast it, at this rate, the market would close before she heard from —

Her cell phone rang.

She grabbed it and punched the button. "You took your time, Rakovac."

"I don't like orders. And I have all the time in the world. You, on the other hand, do not. Nor does Luke."

"I don't think you have all that much time. You keep telling me that you're being forced to bring our relationship to a close. Why?"

"That's none of your concern, Catherine. Though I may tell you before the end what splendors my life is going to hold. It will make your final moments all the more bitter."

"Cut to the chase. Where do you want me to go? I'm sure that your three goons have told you that neither Duncan nor Quinn are with me here at the market."

"You've spotted them? Of course you have."

"Short, burly man in a yellow Windbreaker, a tall, thin man, a giant who looked like a weight lifter."

"That would be Zeller, Sminoff, and the giant is Borzoi. Borzoi may look like he's got more muscle than brains, but actually he's the pick of the bunch. I thought you'd spot them. You're very experienced, and Borzoi's men aren't as subtle as I'd hope.

But they're good at the basics, so I tolerate them. Yes, Borzoi reported that Duncan and Quinn have left you to your own devices. So I think we can proceed. I want you to meet me at St. Basil's Cathedral in two hours, and we'll start the journey to your Luke."

"I'll meet you at St. Basil's, but I'm not getting in any car with you. I'll follow you in my own car."

He chuckled. "Incredible. You're still hopeful of being able to whisk him away from me."

"I'm still hopeful, period. What else have I got? But I know that hope will go straight down the tubes, and it will all be over the minute I get in any car with you."

"True. And I have no objection to stretching out the end a little longer. By all means, follow me." He paused. "As long as you can slip away from my men. They have orders to capture and bring you to me." He added with sly malice, "And, as you say, that will be the beginning of the end." He hung up.

She drew a deep breath and shoved the phone into her pocket. Had NSA managed to trace the call? Rakovac had called so late that it was doubtful that they'd hung around for it. She wanted to call Joe, but that would be a dead giveaway to the three goons, who were monitoring her every move.

Okay, get away from them. Leave the market. She'd call Joe as soon as she lost them. Then she'd have only two hours to find a place to rent a car and get to St. Basil's.

She started moving in and out of the crowds as she made her way toward the streets bordering the market. The man in the yellow Windbreaker was following, so was the one in the olive green sweatshirt. Zeller and Sminoff, Rakovac had called them. But where was the huge man, Borzoi, who she had spotted ten minutes ago, then lost in the crowd?

His absence made her uneasy. Wrong man? She didn't think she'd made a mistake about him being one of Rakovac's men, and Rakovac had recognized the description. Her every instinct had locked in on him as soon as she'd seen him.

But where was he now?

An enemy in view was much safer than one who had fallen from the radar.

Leave the market, let them follow her to a place where she could take them out. She moved quickly through the crowd, dodging between carts and booths.

Yes, they were following.

But she had to get a good distance ahead

of them and out of sight.

She was almost running by the time she reached the street bordering the market and started for the far corner.

The gray Mercedes still parked at the curb. Kelsov's car. No one in it. Dammit, she had told him to go back to the farmhouse.

She ran past the car and down the block. She remembered there was an area of flower shops around the corner. It was much quieter than the market itself and should suit her purpose.

She glanced over her shoulder. They were behind her, running, the man in the yellow Windbreaker Rakovac had called Zeller in the lead, Sminoff following a few yards behind.

She turned the corner. This street was virtually deserted. If there were customers, they must be inside the flower stores. She pressed against the wall beside a flower cart before a shop.

They should be here at the corner in seconds.

Take the first one as he made the turn.

It should startle the second one and give her a few seconds.

She'd need those seconds.

A flash of yellow Windbreaker, and Zeller

came around the corner.

She leaped forward and gave him a karate chop to the jugular. As he dropped, she sprang forward.

Sminoff had hesitated as she'd thought he would, but not long enough. He was reaching for his knife.

Her own knife stabbed deep into his hand, piercing it to the bone.

He screamed.

She lifted her knee between his legs, and he bent forward in agony. She struck him in the nose with the ball of her hand, breaking his bones and sending them into his brain.

She didn't wait for him to drop to the ground. It might be only a few minutes before someone came out of that flower shop, and she didn't want to have to answer questions.

She ran back onto the main street, then walked quickly toward the Tulskaya Metro Station.

Two thirty-five.

Why didn't Joe call her? Eve thought in frustration. He'd promised to get back to her as soon as possible after the NSA trace. Catherine was supposed to take the call at two.

Be patient. Sometimes things didn't go as

planned.

With Rakovac things seldom went as they wanted them to.

Two thirty-six.

"You keep looking at the clock." Kelly nodded. "You're worried about Catherine. So am I. You should have told me that she was leaving. It wasn't right for her to just run out on us. Is she supposed to call you?"

"No." Catherine had asked her not to tell Kelsov about the NSA trace, and Eve had opted to tell no one. Natalie was joined at the hip with Kelsov, and Kelly would immediately try to take over any operation and make it her own. That had been her modus operandi from the instant Eve had met her.

"You're not telling the truth." Natalie's gaze was fixed on Eve from across the room. "Why did Kelsov go with Catherine?"

"I told you that she needed a ride to the city. Don't worry. He won't be staying with her, Natalie." It was difficult to tell only half-truths and still make them comforting. She had never been good at deception. "I'm sure he'll be back in an hour or so."

"I don't want him with Catherine," Natalie said with sudden fierceness. "She doesn't care if he's hurt or not. All she cares about is finding her son."

"And all he cares about is killing Rakovac," Eve said quietly. "And that's all you care about, too, Natalie. So how can you blame Catherine?"

"That's not all I care about," Natalie said. "I don't know if anyone will ever kill Rakovac. Some people are so evil that they kill everything they touch, and no one can stop it." She was shivering, and she folded her arms over her chest to control it. "I want him dead. For a while I thought that was all I wanted. But that's not true. I want Kelsov to stay alive. That's more important. Catherine is going to get him killed."

"And I'm not worried about Kelsov, I'm worried about Catherine," Kelly said. "And I have something important to tell her. So tell me where I can —"

"Stop." Eve held up her hand to stem the flow. "I hope she'll contact us, but you know Catherine can be obstinate. She didn't want any of us to be hurt. I couldn't talk her out of going off on her own." At least that was the truth. "But the best thing that we can do is to keep working on finding Luke and maybe we can phone her and convince her to let us help."

"Bull." Kelly was frowning. "You're patting me on the head and telling me to go back to work. That's not the best thing. The best thing is for us to go after Catherine and try to keep her alive."

"I am telling you to go back to work," Eve said. "Because that's our only option to solve the problem."

Kelly suddenly smiled. "Then I may have it licked." She flipped down the lid of her computer and gestured to her yellow notepad. "Maybe. It's less grounded than I usually pull together, but I believe I've found it."

"Licked?" Eve was staring at her incredulously as she stiffened in the chair. "You've found your pattern?"

"I've found *a* pattern. Rakovac is complicated, but it was easier when I realized that he has no code or ethic he lives by. His loyalty is to no one, and that was the key." She tapped the yellow sheet. "So I built a history of the phone calls Catherine could remember and cross-referenced them to the meetings Rakovac arranged around that period."

Eve jumped up from her chair and was across the room in seconds. She gazed down at the yellow pad. "Show me."

Kelly tapped the first peak on the graph. "This is the first call from Rakovac to Catherine. He was still at his apartment in Moscow. It's not really important because he evidently hadn't arranged any permanent stash for Luke." She pointed to another peak. "This call was particularly cruel and came shortly afterward." She pointed to the name underneath it. "Surveillance showed an appointment with Mikhal Czadas on the day before the call at the town of Sergriev. Rakovac had an arms deal with him." She pointed at another peak. "The next meeting was with Ivan Rithski at Krasnos. Arms deal, again. The same day as the phone call." She pointed to another peak. "A year later. Rakovac met with James Nordell at Vichaga. Nordell was using him to bribe Russian politicians. A call to Catherine the next day." She tapped the other names on the peaks of the graph. "It's the same every time."

"What are you getting at, Kelly? These are all separate individuals. Are you saying they all had something to do with Luke's kidnapping?"

Kelly shook her head. "I've checked into every one of Rakovac's customers on these surveillance reports. I investigated them in depth. They were all powerhouses in their own right. Rakovac wouldn't have been able to manipulate them, he only used them." She paused. "Except one." She pointed to the second peak in the graph. "Mikhal Czadas, a man who was born in the Republic of Georgia and became caught up in all the ethnic madness and guerilla fighting there. He's a fighter who's been involved in a dying cause since he was a boy. He hated the Ossetians *and* the Russians. He never gave up. Therefore, he would always need money. I can see that he might be persuaded to hide Luke away. And he wouldn't be under suspicion. Rakovac had betrayed Czadas's cause and gone over to the Russians. It would be assumed that he and Rakovac would only have a guarded relationship." She shook her head. "But if you study Rakovac's pattern, that isn't necessarily true. He has no loyalty and will work with anyone if it benefits him. If he could use Czadas, he'd find a way to overcome any obstacle. He's a master manipulator."

"But he only met with him once?"

"As far as the surveillance report shows. It would have been too great a risk. That first visit to Czadas was probably to set up the situation. Rakovac wouldn't be stupid enough to show frequent visits to anyone. But he'd still want to keep in contact with Czadas and the boy. And he wouldn't be able to resist calling Catherine afterward to taunt her. That's part of his basic makeup."

"Oh, yes," Eve said bitterly. "That goes without saying. How would he do it?"

"All of these cities are where he met with his other clients." She pointed to Krasnos, Vichaga, and the other Russian cities down the line of the graph. Then she put Sergriev in the middle of them. "They're all within an hour-and-a-half drive to Sergriev. The meetings with all his clients on these particular days were at hotels, not their own offices, or on their own turf. Rakovac must have arranged them. He could conduct business, then slip away and go to meet with Mikhal Czadas at Sergriev." She looked at Eve. "Connect the dots, Eve."

Eve gave a low whistle. "Kelly, you may just be as brilliant as they say you are."

"Of course I am."

"Czadas," Eve repeated. "You think Luke's being held by Mikhal Czadas?"

"It's only an educated guess." Kelly's grin widened. "I'm lying. And being modest. That pattern is pretty clear. I'd bet that Rakovac arranged with Czadas to keep Luke."

"Rakovac boasted of making Luke kill." Eve was thinking, trying to put the pieces together. "If Czadas is still active in the Georgian resistance movement, that would mesh with what he said. There would be an opportunity."

"Call Catherine." Kelly closed her computer and set it on top of her yellow notepad. "Tell her to come back."

"I will." Eve dropped down in her chair and took out her phone. "But first I'll call Joe." She started to dial. "He may be able to find out more information before —"

"No," Natalie said. "Don't call him."

"Natalie, I know you're concerned about Kelsov, but this will only —"

"No," Natalie said sharply. "Hang up."

The girl looked desperate, Eve thought. Why couldn't she see that this might be a way to solve their problem? She had to convince her. She was getting Joe's voice mail anyway, so she hung up. "Look, Natalie, Czadas may be the answer. We can rescue the little boy, and Kelsov will get what he wants, too."

"It's too late for the little boy. Rakovac will never let him go." Natalie was moistening her lips as she reached into the cooktop drawer. "He told me so."

Eve straightened, her eyes widening. "Told you —"

Natalie was pointing a .38 caliber pistol at them.

Eve froze. "What are you doing, Natalie?" Eve asked quietly. "Put that gun down."

"You can't tell anyone about the boy. Rakovac wouldn't like it."

"It doesn't matter what he'd like. You're

confused. You told me you hate him, Natalie."

"Oh, I do," she whispered. "But that doesn't matter. He'll hurt me. He always hurts me. I tried to run away, but he found me and hurt me again. When Kelsov took me out of that . . . place, I knew he'd find me again." Her grasp was shaking on the gun. "And he did."

"Rakovac found you after Kelsov and Catherine freed you from that house?" Eve asked. "When?"

"Six months, seven . . . I don't know."

"I said, put that gun down, Natalie."

"I can't. You'll call Joe Quinn and tell him about Czadas and the boy. You can't do that. Rakovac told me if you got close, I had to stop you."

"Wait." Kelly was gazing at Natalie. "You're saying that Rakovac knew where Kelsov was staying all this time? He knew about this place?"

Natalie nodded.

"And he knew that Kelsov was trying to hunt him down? Why didn't he come after him and kill him?"

"Kelsov was helping Catherine. Rakovac knew that he only had to reach out to grab Catherine if she was with Kelsov. That was all he cared about. He knew she would come back. He thought it was funny that she thought she was safe here."

Eve could see how Rakovac would get a malicious pleasure from having that power to scoop up an unknowing Catherine at any time. It would be a part of his damn cat-and-mouse game with her. "But she wasn't safe from you, was she, Natalie? She helped Kelsov free you from that house. Didn't that mean anything to you?"

"I didn't want to hurt her," Natalie said. "I don't want to hurt anyone. But I have to do what Rakovac tells me. He was angry with me when I didn't tell him that you'd gone to the marsh. I was so afraid he would hurt Kelsov." She added eagerly, "But he says he won't bother Kelsov if I do everything else he wants."

"And you believe him?"

"I don't know. I guess I have to believe him."

"You don't want to do this, Natalie." Eve slowly stood up. If she could get close enough, she could dive for that gun. Though that might be just as dangerous as trying to get her to lay the weapon down. The woman was shaking as if she had a fever. No, not a woman, a child who had been so brutalized she might never emerge from that terrible cocoon where Rakovac had imprisoned her.

But Eve mustn't let pity sway her now. Natalie was dangerous to Kelly and to her. Perhaps to all of them. Thank God, she hadn't told Natalie or Kelsov about the possibility that the NSA phone trace might hold for them. Just move toward her and keep Natalie talking and her attention occupied. "What do you know about Czadas, Natalie?"

"Not much. Rakovac took me to his place once before I ran away from him. Savrin House. It's on a lake somewhere in the north. Czadas is like Rakovac. He likes to hurt people."

Eve took a step nearer. "Luke?"

She nodded jerkily. "And me. Rakovac gave me to him for a few nights. That's when I knew I had to run away. The boy helped me. He heard me screaming, and he hit Czadas on the head with a wine bottle. Then he showed me a way out through the back door that led out of the house. He took me to the woods, then left me to go back to the house."

She took another step. "Why didn't he go with you?"

"He said I had a chance, but they'd never stop looking for him. He'd tried it before. He had to wait until he could steal enough money from Czadas to help him hide from them." She moistened her lips. "He lied. I didn't have a chance. He shouldn't have told me to go. They found me four days later."

"Luke was trying to help you. And he was obviously running a risk to do it."

"But Rakovac found me." It was clearly the only thing on which she could focus. "And he hurt me again. Worse than before. The boy shouldn't have made me go."

"Made?" Kelly repeated. "You were old enough to make the choice. He couldn't have been more than nine then. And I'd say he had an amazing amount of guts."

"Kelly," Eve cautioned. Natalie was in an extremely emotional state, and they didn't need to throw her into more of a tailspin. Not with that .38 in her hand. "Was Luke punished for it?"

"I don't know. Rakovac took me away from there after he found me. He said he couldn't stay at Czadas's house for more than a couple days at any one time. I'd made him overstay his time." Her voice was a whimper. "I didn't care about the boy. Why should I? Rakovac kept hurting me. In all kinds of new ways he hadn't tried before. It might not have been so bad for me if the boy hadn't told me to run away."

She kept calling him "the boy" as if he

had no identity, Eve thought with annoyance. It reminded her of the killers who threw their victims into anonymous graves and walked away. Natalie might not be a murderer, but she had the same careless, selfish view as those predators. Eve was beginning to feel any pity she had felt begin to dissipate. But she mustn't show the anger she was feeling. She moved a step nearer. "How can you be sure Rakovac will keep his word? You want Kelsov to live. Wouldn't it be better to call and warn him that Rakovac knows where this place is?"

"It's too late. Rakovac called me right after Kelsov and Catherine left here. He said that it was time to wrap it up. I don't know what that means, but I don't think it's about me."

She was now only a few yards away. Eve started to take another step.

"Stop! Don't come any closer." Natalie was suddenly beside Kelly and pressing the muzzle of the gun to her temple. "I'll pull the trigger. I swear I will. I can't let you take the gun away from me."

Eve froze. If she didn't press the trigger intentionally, she might do it accidentally. "I'm not moving. Take the gun away from her head."

"No, I know what you were going to do. I

can't let you — Rakovac said he'd punish me if it didn't go well."

"If what didn't go well?"

"He wants you, too. You and Quinn, but I can't help it if Joe Quinn went away. It's not my fault. Maybe he won't — It's not my fault." Her head lifted swiftly. "I hear a car."

Eve heard it, too. "Maybe it's Kelsov. Put away the gun. You don't want him to —"

"It's not Kelsov. I know the sound of his car. I've heard him come home so many times." She gazed at Eve. "I'm sorry. It's not my fault."

"You said that before. I'm sympathetic to your problems, but you have to take responsibility at some point, Natalie."

"No, she doesn't." A brown-haired man with gray flecks in his carefully barbered hair had opened the front door and stood pointing a Magnum revolver at them. "Haven't you discovered that Natalie is just a puppet? She never had a great amount of brains even before Rakovac took her. To expect her to feel guilt or responsibility isn't reasonable."

"Who are you?"

He inclined his head. "Nicholas Russo. I'm Rakovac's assistant."

"He's my father," Natalie said dully.

Eve's eyes widened in shock. "What?"

"A state which has been fraught with both benefits and dangers," Russo said. "All the stupid bitch had to do was shut up and take it. She ran away. I'm lucky Rakovac didn't take his anger at her out on me."

"No, he took it out on her. And probably Catherine's son."

Russo's brows lifted. "I can see that your heart is bleeding. I should have expected as much from what I've heard about you from Rakovac." He motioned with his gun. "And I'm in no mood to listen to abuse. Come along. This has to be concluded tonight. Rakovac has taken far too many risks over this Catherine Ling business for my liking. If he goes down, I go down. If he hits the top of the heap, then I'm a billionaire."

"Where are you taking me?"

"Why, to see Luke Ling. Isn't that what this charade is all about?"

"It's no charade."

"It seems that to me, but then I'm standing on the outside."

"Shall I tie her up?" Natalie asked.

"What a helpful daughter you are. I wish you'd have been a little more helpful when you were with Rakovac. Yes, by all means. I have a man waiting in the car, but I don't want problems." He tossed her a rawhide cord and waited while she tied Eve's hands in front of her. He turned to Kelly. "And her, too."

"She has nothing to do with this," Eve said quickly. "Rakovac wouldn't want you to take her."

"She figured out that Luke is with Czadas," Natalie said.

Eve wanted to strangle her.

Russo nodded. "And she's a witness."

Kelly rose to her feet. "I want to go with you, Eve. If I stayed with that viper, I'd chop her head off."

"Then we'll oblige you." Russo stepped aside after Natalie finished tying Kelly's wrists. "Go straight to the car and get in the backseat. Try to run, and I'll shoot the girl first, then you, Duncan."

"I'm not running." It would do no good, and she wasn't about to risk getting Kelly killed. Besides, Russo was right. All of their efforts had been bent on finding Luke. Now they were being taken to the boy. It would be better to wait to attempt any escape until they were with him. "How far away is this place?"

"About four hours." He opened the rear door and gestured for them to get inside.

He hadn't lied, Eve realized. The man who

waited inside the car appeared rough and lethal.

"What's going to happen to me?" Natalie asked from the doorstep. "I did everything Rakovac said."

"This time."

"He promised me Kelsov would be coming back to me."

"He will be." Russo got into the driver's seat. "I've arranged an escort to take both of you out of the country. We can't have you left behind to be questioned. You'd break too easily. Now see if you can be quiet until he gets here."

She was still standing in the doorway as they drove down the road.

"She didn't even question you," Eve said incredulously. "You might have ways to keep her quiet, but what about Kelsov? There's no way that he won't keep after Rakovac."

"Oh, there is a way." He lifted his hand to wave at Natalie. "And I told you that my daughter isn't the sharpest tool in the shed. Now, be quiet. I want a peaceful trip to Savrin House."

Eve shivered as he turned on the player and a classical CD blared. She had thought that all she had heard about Rakovac was evil, but Russo might be his equal. Was it Rakovac's influence, or did they feed on each other?

"Eve." Kelly leaned closer to Eve, and said in an undertone, "We'll be okay, right?"

Was she offering comfort or asking for it? With Kelly it was difficult to know.

Eve's nodded. "We'll be okay."

CHAPTER 16

"Got it." Helder's voice was less than enthusiastic as Joe picked up the phone. "It's a house located in the small town of Navaltov outside Moscow."

"It took you long enough. Fifteen minutes. You were bragging that it would take you less than thirty seconds."

"I wanted to be absolutely accurate. After all, it's a matter of national security."

And he had been dragging his feet to get a little of his own back, Joe thought.

"What's the address?

"Twenty-five Zarnok."

"Who is in the house now?"

"You didn't ask me to get that information."

"I didn't have to ask you. It's routine with you. You probably know how many lights are lit and how many times a toilet has been flushed in the last two hours."

"Twice," Helder said. "But at different

parts of the house."

"How many people?"

"One. Female. Lower floor. Possibly domestic. Two males exited the house ten minutes ago and departed in separate vehicles." He paused. "But there's still one man in the area across the street and another one on the far terrace in back. Guards?"

"Locate the study or office in the house for us."

"It's on the first floor. Second room on the left as you enter the house."

"Helder, you're an asshole, but you know your stuff."

"Are you finished with me?"

"Probably. I'll call you if we need anything else."

Helder hung up.

"You heard." Joe turned to Venable, who was typing at top speed on the computer. "What have you got?"

"Give me a minute," Venable said. "I'm printing out a diagram of the house and assessing the security-system information."

"Between you and Helder, the private sector doesn't stand a chance of staying private, does it?" Joe said. "Big Brother is definitely watching."

"You should be grateful we are," Venable

said. "Because there are a hell of a lot of countries in the world who have their own Big Brother watching us. And they're definitely not doing it to protect us." He printed out the diagram, rattled orders to the four agents in the room, and whirled toward the door. "Let's get going."

They had almost reached the town of Navaltov when Joe's phone rang.

Catherine came on the line. "Did NSA get you the trace?"

"Yes, we've got a location at a house north of Moscow. We're on our way. We don't believe Rakovac is still on the premises. Where the hell have you been? I've been trying to reach you."

"I know. I had you on vibrate. I didn't want Rakovac's men to report that I was talking to someone on the phone right after I hung up with him. I had to wait until I got rid of them first. Rakovac had given orders that I be picked up and delivered to him."

"And are you safe now?"

"Maybe. I saw three of his men in the crowd. I put down two of them, but I lost the third man." She paused. "I'm on my way to meet with Rakovac. He's going to take me to my son."

"Where are you going to meet him? We'll

arrange a tail."

"No, you won't. You won't do a damn thing. Do you think Rakovac won't be expecting a double cross? Don't tell me that he wouldn't know because Venable will be pulling out some sophisticated razzle-dazzle. I know every trick the CIA has in its arsenal. Rakovac will be on the alert for any high-tech or plain old-fashioned gumshoe method available that would give me the slightest edge or break. If he sees any sign of any of that happening, he could make a call, and my son would be dead. I won't blow this, Joe."

He was silent a moment. "You'd rather take your shot at him alone?"

"I always knew that was how it was going to play out."

"Well, I didn't," Joe said roughly. "And I don't like it. I'm not going to let it happen."

"If things don't go your way, you're going to change the entire scenario? Not this time, Joe. I did what you all wanted and gave you your chance to stop that hideous disaster from taking place. It's up to you to go do it. But stay away from me. I'm going after my son."

He muttered a curse. "Catherine, this isn't smart. It isn't even —"

"I'm hanging up, Joe. I probably won't be

able to call you again." She paused. "Kelsov. Check on Kelsov. He was supposed to go back to the farm, but I saw his car still parked at the market. I hope to hell he didn't go after me."

"We'll send an agent to check out the car. Don't hang up, we need to —"

She had hung up.

Joe muttered a curse as he jammed his phone in his pocket.

"She's going after her son, and we're not invited?" Venable said. "Good luck to her."

"Is that all you can say?" Joe said. "She doesn't have a chance alone."

"Catherine always has a chance," Venable said. "When I recruited her in Hong Kong, she'd already been taught practically every deadly art under the sun by an old friend, Hu Chang. She's learned a hell of a lot more since then. She's been preparing for this for nine years. She might have been writhing on the hot coals Rakovac threw down for her, but she wouldn't ignore the possibility that she might end up in this situation. She might be able to pull it off."

"How?"

"It's not something she would confide in me. Unfortunately, I'm not on her need-to-know list." He glanced at Joe as he began to dial again. "Who are you calling?"

"I promised to call Eve when I heard from Catherine, and we found out where Rakovac was located. Though I'll be lucky if she doesn't want to meet us there. She was definitely not happy about not being able to be more hands-on in —"

She wasn't answering. The call went immediately to voice mail.

Not good.

"Problem?" Venable asked.

"I don't know. She's not answering."

"She's still at Kelsov's house in the country? Safe location?"

As safe as it could be in this hellish situation. "Yes."

"Then it could be the phone. Leave a message."

"No, I'll call her back."

Venable slowed the car. "Twenty-five Zarnok is a block up ahead. Should I send my people after those two guards, or do you want to do it?"

"You can do what you like with the man across the street and the woman on the lower floor. I'll take the man on the back terrace."

"Whatever." He smiled. "I thought you'd want action. Being cooped up in the office dealing with Helder wore on your nerves. You should come to work for me. I'd put you in the field, and you could utilize all that stored energy."

"I find ways to take care of it." He dialed Eve again. Still no answer. He could feel the tension growing within him. He wanted to take off and bolt to that blasted farm.

But he was clear on the other side of Moscow, and if there was a problem, then she might need someone on the spot now. "She's not answering. I don't like it," he told Venable. "Get one of your men out there to the farmhouse right away and check it out. Have him report back to us right away."

Venable reached for his phone.

It could be nothing, Joe thought. But he had a gut feeling it was definitely something.

Finish the job and get back to the farmhouse.

He jumped out of the car and moved down a cross street and around the block.

Large brick house. Open veranda.

A thin man in a navy blue jacket had his back to him, his gaze fixed on the French doors.

No guns. Knives or hands.

Hands.

Joe moved silently across the tile pavers toward the guard.

Finish the job.

■ ■ ■ ■

A car was coming up the drive toward the farmhouse.

Kelsov!

Natalie ran out of the house to meet him.

Not Kelsov.

The car was being driven by a huge man in a gray cap and red sweater.

She stopped, frowning.

He stuck his head out the window, and a wide smile creased his full face. "Mr. Russo sent me. My name is Borzoi. I'm to take care of you. You're going away."

"My father told me." Her hands clenched. "Not without Kelsov. Where is Kelsov?"

"He's gone on ahead of you." Borzoi got out of the car. "But Mr. Russo told me to make sure that you got away safely."

"I won't go anywhere without Kelsov. Where did you send him?"

"I'm not sure. They say you can never tell what will be your destination. Though I believe I know mine."

"You're confusing me." And he was making her uneasy. "I'm going to call my father and ask —"

"Don't do that. It would upset him. He said clean. You want to see where I sent

Kelsov?" He opened the rear door of the car.

Kelsov's body tumbled headfirst out into the dirt.

"No!"

His eyes were wide open and staring at her as she ran to him and fell to her knees.

Dead. He was dead.

She screamed.

"Hush." Borzoi was pointing a gun at her. "I was quick with him. I'll be quick with you."

"No, it wasn't supposed to be like this. I did what he wanted." Tears were running down her cheeks. "Don't do —"

"Shh." He pressed the trigger.

The bullet entered her heart.

Venable was cursing when Joe ran into the office from the veranda. He was sitting at the mahogany desk staring in frustration at the computer. "He wiped it clean. There's not a damn thing on it. I'd bet he figured we were onto him."

Joe was kneeling at the hearth. "Something was burned here recently. There are still embers glowing." He reached in and poked the embers. "Probably the paper trail." He picked up a slender piece of paper that had been untouched by the flames. "A map?"

"That's my bet," Venable said grimly. "And I'd guess one similar to one I have on my wall. Only with a hell of a lot more information."

"This was all done within the past few hours," Joe said. "He was literally burning his bridges." He glanced at the computer. "Can you get the information back?"

"Yes, there's no such thing as a total wipe-out if you have the right equipment for retrieval. It will just take time."

"How much time?"

"How the hell do I know?" He turned to the agent who was bundling up the computer. "How long, Ted?"

"Twenty-four hours maybe."

"Too long."

Joe agreed. Every word that Rakovac had spoken to Catherine indicated that they had entered the final stage of planning. "Get to work." He turned to Venable. "He wouldn't have destroyed everything until the actual go-ahead on the attack."

"Don't say that."

"No, I mean he has to have a small computer, a file, a thumb drive on him. Something that's portable for him to use or turn over to Dabala."

"If he hasn't sent him the file already." Venable shook his head. "And I don't think he has. He's still working at completing his revenge on Catherine. He wouldn't turn loose the wolves until he was on his way to a safe little haven to wait out all the turmoil till it blows over."

"Optimistic view. This attack will never blow over."

"They said that about the Nazi war criminals. They may still be hunted, but many of them had wonderfully comfortable lives until they were caught. Some of them have never been caught." He was frowning. "So I'll bet he's going to keep his charts and records to himself until he boards a plane."

"Why are we standing here trying to decide what he will or won't do?" Joe said impatiently. "We have to find the bastard." He started going through the desk. Scribbled notes, photos . . . He pulled out a framed photo of Catherine Ling. "This is a desk photo. I don't like the idea that he put it away in a drawer. Very final." He put the photo aside and checked a few of the notes. Nothing that he could make sense of. He took out the pile of photos. "It seems Rakovac likes to document his vices. I remember he said something about the miracle of photography when he e-mailed the picture of the skeleton."

Women. Adolescent girls. Even a photo of

a much younger Natalie. All involved in S and M acts that were graphic and hard to stare at for more than a moment. No young boys who could be Luke. He went through the pile again. No Luke.

Of course, he wouldn't want to risk anyone finding a photo of a boy he was keeping captive. But judging by the other photos he kept close to him, Joe couldn't believe that he wouldn't have a picture of the boy whose capture had been the supreme evidence of his triumph over Catherine.

Where would it . . .

He suddenly threw the photos down and picked up Catherine's picture again.

"What are you looking for?" Venable said.

"This one is framed. He had to have kept it on his desk where he could look at it." He was unscrewing the leather back of the frame. "What better place to keep a photo of her son? He'd enjoy the thought of keeping the picture close to her heart when she could never be near him and —" He stopped as he saw the five-by-seven photo turned facedown. He didn't want to turn it over. Not after seeing the other photos in that pile.

He flipped it over. Nothing obscene, he realized with relief. Just the photo of a nine- or ten-year-old boy in front of a large stone house. The boy was thin, dressed in worn gray pants and a black shirt. His hair was long and as dark as his shirt. A handsome boy, his slightly tilted dark eyes and high cheekbones definitely resembling Catherine's.

Venable gave a low whistle. "My God, that's Luke? He looks like he's ready to attack everyone and everything."

Joe had been so involved with checking out the resemblance to Catherine that he had not noticed the boy's expression. Venable was right: The boy's dark eyes seemed to burn, glaring out of the photo in defiance, his lips slightly parted, his white teeth bared.

"Well, I don't think Rakovac managed to break him," Joe said dryly. "Not if this is any indication."

"Maybe he didn't want to break him," Venable said. "Maybe he wanted to turn her baby boy into a demon not even a mother could love. This kid is nothing like that picture Catherine has been carrying around with her."

"Then she'll have to deal with Luke after we find him." He handed the photo to Venable. "We managed to find that skeleton after having experts go over the photo with a fine-tooth comb. This photo has more to work with than that grave. A large two-story house, stone, with turrets that look Victorian. And there's a lake or body of water in the background. Get your people to work on it and find that place." He reached for his phone and dialed Eve again. No answer. He turned on his heel. "Soon."

"Where are you going?"

"The farmhouse."

Venable followed him. "I sent Billings to check it out."

"I know you did. Why haven't you heard back from him?"

"It would take time to get from downtown Moscow to —"

But Joe was already gone.

Venable hurried after him.

Savrin House was a huge stone structure that appeared to be part two-story, part split-level due to the fact that it was balanced on the side of a craggy hill. Its Victorian turrets seemed more in keeping with English architecture than Russian. The peculiar structure towered over a clear blue lake that seemed to stretch endlessly into the horizon.

"Impressive, isn't it?" Russo asked as he pulled into the driveway. "It once belonged to Nikolai Savrin, a rich manufacturer who married an Englishwoman from London and brought her here. He built the house for her, and they lived here for forty years. Now, isn't that romantic? Czadas had an English mother who was killed in a massacre during the wars. When Rakovac decided to buy a house for him and Luke, Czadas insisted that he wanted this one." He shrugged. "Crazy. Who would guess Czadas would be sentimental about anything? But then Czadas isn't the most stable person. It's a wonder Rakovac has been able to control him all these years." He added mockingly, "At any rate, Luke is lucky to be able to live in such a fine place. I'm sure he'd be devastated to have to leave it."

It was impressive, Eve thought, but not in a good way. The terrain was all wild grasses and rocky ground. The house appeared very old, the windows long and narrow, the stones crumbling. "You say Mikhal Czadas still lives here?"

"Yes, when he's not moving around the countryside causing havoc. He has the same violent nature as Rakovac." He got out of the car. "Only Rakovac has managed to channel it to his benefit. Mikhal doesn't have his adaptability. He still occasionally raids the villages here in Russia that were settled by the Republic of Georgia's archenemies, the Ossetians. He'll be a revolutionary until the day he dies." He chuckled. "Which may be soon. He's only survived this long because of the steady flow of bribes Rakovac has been tossing to the local police to keep them from focusing their attention on him."

"Why?" Kelly was gazing up at the house. "Because of Luke?"

"Yes, it was all about the boy," Russo said. "So much expense and foolishness all to keep the boy away from his mother. I was very impatient with Rakovac. It interfered with business."

"What a pity," Eve said sarcastically. "It's even more of a pity that you didn't convince Rakovac to give that poor child back to his mother."

"Poor child?" Russo's brows lifted. "Little tiger, according to Rakovac. Come along; you need to meet him. Rakovac wants you all to be together. I'll have to ask Mikhal where —" He broke off as a big, bearded man came out of the house. "Mikhal, I've brought our guests. Eve Duncan and a young playmate for Luke. Kelly Winters I believe is her name. Where is Luke?"

"Rakovac called and told me to put him up in the cell. He's bringing Catherine Ling tonight." Mikhal frowned. "I don't see why we need to bother with these people. I'm willing to do Rakovac favors, but this may be too much."

"I wouldn't say that to him." Russo pushed Eve forward. "Go along with him. I'm sure you're eager to meet Luke and see if your age progression was true to him."

"Rakovac hasn't said that he'd continue with our arrangements after the boy is gone." Mikhal was still scowling. "Has he told you anything?"

"I wouldn't count on it. Though I could be wrong." He turned toward the car. "I'd discuss it in depth with you, but I'm on my way to St. Petersburg to board a flight. My part of this is over. Rakovac said he wouldn't need me again after I brought you the women."

"That's what he told me too." Mikhal reached into his jacket pocket and pulled out an automatic. "He's done with you." He shot Russo in the head.

Kelly made a whimpering sound as she instinctively moved closer to Eve.

"It's okay, Kelly." Eve's arm slid around her waist. It wasn't okay, but she didn't know what else to say. She was as shocked as Kelly. Russo might have been as evil as Rakovac, but she hadn't been expecting his murder. If Eve was this stunned, she could imagine what the young girl was feeling. "No, it's bad, but we have to hang in there."

Kelly nodded jerkily.

Mikhal had turned toward them and was gesturing with the weapon. "Come. I'll have one of my men take care of that garbage. Luke is waiting."

That sentence sounded faintly ominous, Eve thought. "Where are you taking us?"

"To the cell." He was urging them up the staircase. "Luke's second home. Actually, it's not really a cell. Savrin House had none of those convenient advantages. It's just a bedroom that we converted for that purpose. Rakovac insisted he be isolated on occasion as punishment. Sometimes I think Luke likes it better than his room. He certainly makes me lock him up there enough."

"A cell?" Eve said distastefully. "A child in a cell?"

"But this child is like no other. Rakovac made sure of that." Mikhal laughed. "And I admit I helped enormously." His smile faded. "Though now it seems I'm to receive no gratitude for past favors." He glanced over his shoulder at the front door. "Not even for ridding him of that carrion. Though I might have done it anyway. Whenever he came here with Rakovac, I could see he thought himself above us." He stopped before a thick wood door and took a key out of his pocket. "Oh, I almost forgot." He took out a camera phone and snapped a picture. "Rakovac is very fond of photos. Come. I have no more time for you." He unlocked the door, untied their wrists, and pushed them both over the threshold into the half darkness. "Luke," he called. "You have visitors. Treat them well. They may be your last." He slammed the door shut behind them, and Eve heard the key turn in the lock.

No sound from the dimness of the room.

Eve waited an instant for her eyes to become accustomed to the lack of light before she looked around the small room. A small table with two metal kitchen chairs, an old leather chest pushed against the wall, wood floors. Late-afternoon sunlight trickled through the bars of the one high window directly across from them.

But the room was empty.

No, there was a small, dark shape huddled in the corner.

Luke?

Eve hesitated. Dear God, was the child hurt?

Or dead.

"Are you Luke?" Kelly had brushed past

her and had fallen to her knees beside the boy. "I'm Kelly. Are you okay? Do you speak English?"

The boy didn't reply.

"Answer me," Kelly said shakily. "This is terrible enough without you —"

"I speak English." The boy sat up straighter against the wall. His words had the slightest trace of a Russian accent. "And I don't have to talk to you if I don't want to do it. I don't know you."

"How do you speak English?" Kelly asked curiously. "You were only two when —"

"Kelly, it's not uncommon for children to learn their birth language by age two and retain it afterward," Eve said. "And Russo said Czadas had an attachment to everything English. He probably didn't try to erase that part of Luke's former life. Now stop questioning him. We need to tell him who we are and why we're here." She came over and stood in the stream of light so that he could clearly see her. "I'm Eve Duncan, and this is Kelly Winters. Your mother has been searching for you, and we came with her to find you."

He didn't speak.

Well, what had she been expecting? She had no idea what he thought about Catherine. The memory of her might have been so faint as to be almost nonexistent. "She loves you very much, Luke. She's going to try to come here and get you even though it may be very dangerous."

No reply.

"We have to find a way to get you out of here. Then there would be no reason for her to run that risk. Will you do as I say if I can figure a way to —"

"I *won't* do as you say," He leaned suddenly forward into the stream of light. Eve smothered a gasp. Luke, the Luke of her age progressions, but so much more . . . and less. The same beautiful bone structure as his mother's, olive skin, and wide-set dark eyes. But his face was thinner, harder, and his eyes were glittering with defiance and knowledge far beyond his years. He was probably the most beautiful boy Eve had ever seen, but the joyousness that had touched her heart in that photo was no longer there.

"Is this some trick?" Luke asked. "Why would he let you come here to me? Why should I trust you? Why should I trust her? All my life they've been telling me what a whore and a beast she is. Sometimes I believe them. Why should I —"

"Shut up!" Kelly was kneeling facing him, her eyes blazing into his. "You don't talk about Catherine like that. I guess I'm supposed to feel sorry for you, but I don't. Everyone is trying to help you. So be quiet and let us do it. Catherine loves you and deserves better. Don't you call her names."

Darkness and light. The two beautiful young people were kneeling facing each other, and Eve found herself mesmerized by the sight of them. Kelly, so fair-haired and fragile appearing, Luke dark and hard as a diamond. Both glaring at each other, caught in a storm of emotion.

Then Luke's expression changed, anger ebbing, replaced with curiosity. "You like her."

"Of course I like her. She saved my life. And she wants to save yours. Don't you realize that these people will kill you? Did they brainwash you or something? You're in a cell, for goodness' sake. Are you stupid?"

"I'm not stupid," Luke said fiercely. "And I don't know anything about this brainwashing, but I think that's an insult, too. Do it again, and I'll knock you into that wall."

"You and who —"

"Kelly." Eve stepped forward. "Catherine wouldn't want you to defend her in this way."

"No, she wouldn't defend herself at all. She'd feel sorry for him and think she's to blame for what that monster Rakovac and Mikhal Czadas did to him." Her voice was shaking. "She's not to blame. They hurt her as much as they did you. And now she's going to let him bring her here, and he'll try to kill her because of you. Now you tell us how to stop it."

"Kelly, what are you asking?" Eve said. "He's a kid and a prisoner just as we are. There's no way you can expect him to —"

"Yes, I can," Kelly interrupted. "It's a part of his pattern. He survives. Do you think he would have lasted this long if he didn't have that drive? I've been thinking about him since we began to get hints from Rakovac that he was still alive. He's Catherine's son, and that would count a lot toward making him like her. He'd have her strength and endurance. And he learns from his mistakes. Two years ago, he knew enough about this place to help Natalie escape. And he was smart enough to know that he couldn't go with her unless he had enough money to keep himself hidden from them. Luke thinks and waits and takes whatever is done to him." She looked him in the eye. "But you don't give up, do you? You never give up."

He didn't answer.

"Did they punish you for helping Natalie?"

"Yes."

"Badly?"

"Yes."

"But then you waited and started planning again."

"Yes."

Kelly looked at Eve. "So don't tell me about this poor defenseless kid. His pattern is as strong as Catherine's. If he wants to do it, he can help us."

"Could you help us get out of here?" Eve asked Luke.

He nodded.

"Will you? Do you want to do it?"

He gazed at her without answering. Then he said slowly, "I don't know. You come in here and tell me things that are confusing me. I don't like to be confused. I don't know if I can trust you."

"And I don't know how to make you trust us," Eve said. "But it's important that you do. Can't you see that you have to trust someone?"

"No."

Of course he didn't, Eve thought. He hadn't been able to trust anyone but himself for his entire life after he'd been taken from Catherine.

"We can help each other," Kelly said. "We're not like Natalie. You felt sorry for her. You don't have to feel sorry for us."

"I didn't feel sorry for her. They were just hurting her, and she was like me. I couldn't leave yet, but I could take her away from them." His lips thinned. "I want to take everything away from them."

"Good. I wouldn't mind being taken away from them," Kelly said dryly. "Can we start with that thought?"

"Why? You're not like me, and I don't feel sorry for you." He leaned back against the wall and was once again lost in the dimness. "But I may need to use you to help me get away. I was able to steal some money from Mikhal, but I don't think it's enough. I don't know much about what things cost. But I don't think I can wait any longer. I think he's coming to the end."

"End?"

"Rakovac will kill me," Luke said simply. "He's always told me that it was coming. I just never knew when."

Eve shivered as she thought of a child living forever under that constant chilling threat. Kelly must be right. Luke was indeed a survivor. "Then if you think that we can help you, by all means use us."

"If I can trust you."

"Well, you can't fool around trying to decide," Kelly said impatiently. "Make up your mind."

"What can we do to help, Luke?" Eve said. "She's right, we don't know how much time we have. Rakovac may be on the way. What do you need from us?"

Silence. "You're . . . strangers," Luke said. "I don't really know who you are or where you came from. I don't know you."

"Then we'll tell you anything you want to know." Eve leaned back against the wall. "But it goes both ways. There are things we want to know about you, too. Will you answer questions?"

"Maybe."

"That's not fair, Luke," Kelly said.

"Maybe," he repeated. "Take it or leave it."

Kelly settled back on her heels. "You're going to learn that you can't get away with that kind of —" She stopped. "Go ahead. Ask your questions."

Luke hesitated, obviously thinking about it.

Let Kelly handle it, Eve thought. She was neither diplomatic nor particularly sympathetic. It was Catherine to whom she gave her sympathy and loyalty. But she was young and smart, and Eve could see that she was reaching Luke on his level.

"Well, what do you want to know?" Kelly

demanded. "Anything."

"Stop pushing me." He thought again. "One thing. That word . . . What is . . . brainwashing?"

The first thing that Joe saw when he arrived at the farmhouse was the blood.

A huge smear of red on the stones in front of the doorstep.

Fresh blood.

Shit.

Eve.

He drew his gun, jumped out of the car, and moved to the left of the door that had been left a little ajar.

He kicked it open and dove into the room and to one side of the door.

No shots.

Darkness.

Silence.

His heart was beating hard, fast. God, he was scared.

"Eve."

No answer from the darkness.

There was something liquid and sticky running against his wrist that was braced against the floor.

Blood?

Eve?

He had to know. He carefully reached up

to the light switch on the wall beside the door. He hit it, then rolled sidewise behind the couch.

No shots.

The room was empty.

Except for the woman huddled beside the front door, covered in blood.

He was kneeling beside her in an instant.

Not Eve. Natalie.

And a few feet away, the body of Kelsov.

That didn't mean that there weren't more bodies in the bedrooms. Eve and Kelly Winters were still not accounted for.

He was on his feet and moving.

"Quinn," Venable was behind him in the doorway. "Don't go —"

He ignored him.

No bodies in either bedroom.

Nor in the bathroom.

"What the hell happened here?" Venable asked.

"How do I know?" Joe was looking around the room. "No sign of a struggle here. Natalie and Kelsov were killed outside and dragged into the house. Where's your agent who was supposed to have been here?"

"He's not answering his phone." Venable paused. "We haven't found him yet."

Not a good sign.

Dammit, he should have been here. "I

should never have left her alone."

"She wasn't alone. You thought she was safe."

Wrong.

"She might be okay, Quinn."

"And she might not." Get a grip. Stop being negative. Think. He went back into the bedroom. Eve's suitcase and belongings were still in the room.

Including her gun.

He didn't recognize any of Kelly Winters's belongings, but her duffel was still here.

Joe ran out to the barn.

No one there either.

Venable lifted his brows inquiringly as Joe came back into the living room.

"If they left here, it was in the clothes they were wearing. They took nothing with them." His gaze raked the room. "Kelly didn't even take her computer. It's still there on the kitchen table."

"Then maybe we'd better go and talk to the neighbors and see if they've seen anyone —"

The computer.

He strode over to the table and opened the program Kelly had been working on. Rakovac's surveillance report. Catherine's phone calls from Rakovac.

Patterns.

Dates. Names. Notations. Nothing that he could figure out.

A yellow notepad was beneath the computer.

Kelly's scribbling all over the top sheet. A graph with Catherine's name on the top of each peak and below it another name.

Czadas.

He tensed. "Holy shit."

Venable was at his side. "You found something?"

"Yes, and I think Kelly found something." His index finger ran over the graph, outlining the peaks. "Dates. Catherine's name. Other names. Then city names." He punched his finger down. "Then this at the end of the graph."

Czadas. Yes!

Joe tore off the sheet of paper and thrust it at Venable.

"Czadas. What do you know about him?"

Venable's brow furrowed as he tried to remember. "Georgian revolutionary. Been on the scene for years. Takes every opportunity to strike out at the Ossetians and Russia. Nasty character, but not important enough to deserve special attention."

"He might have been important enough to deserve Catherine's attention. See how fast you can find out more about him.

Where does he live?"
"I don't remember."
Joe remembered the name scribbled on top of the graph. "Sergriev?"
"Maybe."
"Find out." He headed for the door. "Get us a helicopter. I want to be there in a hurry."
"You think Eve was taken there?"
"I hope she was," Joe said. "It's the only logical answer. I'd like to think that she went there on her own, but that would be too good to be true. Kelly thought she'd found out where Luke was being kept. Rakovac threatened Eve several times on the calls to Catherine. If he was going to put an end to his cat-and-mouse game, then he might want to include Eve on his agenda." It was all supposition, but it was all he had, and the alternative was making him panic.
He got into the car. "Just find out where Czadas lives." He had a sudden memory of the photo of Luke in Rakovac's study. "And if the place is on a lake."

St. Basil's Cathedral was just ahead.
Catherine's hands tightened on the wheel of the rental car as she saw the splendid onion-shaped towers of the cathedral come into view.

Rakovac could be there. If not, then one of his men who would take her to him. Take her to Luke.

After all the years of torture and waiting, it was going to happen.

Was she ready? There was no doubt that she would be searched thoroughly. Would they find it?

Stop having second thoughts. She had made both her decision and her plans over a year ago. If it didn't work, if Luke died, then she'd have to make another decision, and that would be easier.

She drew close to the curb a half block from the cathedral.

Get out. Let them see you.

She stood by the car for only a few minutes before she got the call.

"Right on time," Rakovac said.

"Where are you?"

"Not anywhere near you. Get back in your car. In a few minutes a black Volkswagen will come around the corner driven by a black man wearing a blue muffler. Follow him. As soon as we determine that you're not being followed, he'll bring you to me."

"I'm not being followed. I wouldn't take that chance."

"I hope that's true, because the situation has changed. You have much more to lose now." He hung up.

She was frowning as she got back into the car. How could she have more to lose than her son? Bluff? She didn't know, but her tension was increasing by the second as the Volkswagen came around the corner.

Twenty minutes later Rakovac called once again. "Very good. You haven't wasted our time. That would have been regrettable."

"I've been driving in and out of every street in this city. When are you going to surface?"

"You sound a bit upset. Nerves, Catherine?"

"Where are you?"

"You're being led to me right now. I've decided that you should leave your car and let me take you to Luke."

"No, I told you that I wouldn't do that. I'll follow you."

"Your desperate bid to have a little control of your destiny? I don't want you to have any control, Catherine. I want you totally subservient to my every whim."

"Screw you."

"You have no choice. I'm tired of being indulgent with you." His voice hardened. "I'm sending you a photo that may interest you. I'll call you back after you have time to access it."

Luke? She had a chilling memory of the last photo of the skeleton he had sent to her. Had he done something to Luke?

She accessed the photo.

"Shit!"

Kelly and Eve, hands tied, standing in front of a huge oak door.

"No!"

It couldn't be worse.

Calm down. Yes, it could. Rakovac had taken them prisoner, not killed them.

Yet.

Her phone rang.

"Why?" she asked Rakovac when she picked up. "They have nothing to do with what's between us."

"They annoyed me. I told you that anyone who helped you wouldn't be safe," Rakovac said. "And I knew Eve Duncan would want to compare her likeness of Luke to the real thing. Wasn't it kind of me to give her the opportunity?"

"Let them go."

"Too late. But you can stretch out their lives for a little while longer if you do as I say. I'm parked on the edge of the road about two miles from where you are. You'll stop, abandon your car, and get in the passenger seat of mine. If you show any resistance, I'll give the order to kill one of your friends. The young girl, I think. She's of lesser importance. If you continue, Eve Duncan will take her turn. Isn't it better to relinquish control to me and let them have a few more precious hours of life?"

"Bastard."

"One minute, Catherine. Then I'll hang up and give the order to kill the girl."

He would do it. Nothing would please him more than to put her through that hell.

She would have to give in. The slim chance she'd had of getting Luke and her out of this situation alive had just become even slimmer. The fragile scenario she'd concocted was becoming dangerously complicated.

Dangerous? No matter which way she turned, it could be lethal. This was just one more obstacle to overcome.

"Catherine."

"You win," she said through set teeth. "Don't hurt them."

"I'll always win. You had one victory, and the rest of the prizes were mine. I'll be standing beside my car waiting for you. You do remember what I look like?"

Satan.

"How could I forget?" She could see the car on the side of the road.

Rakovac was standing by the passenger

door. His thick black hair was blowing in the breeze, and the expression on his heavy, flushed face was eager, hungry.

Well, she was hungry, too.

She pulled over behind his car and got out of the driver's seat.

"Beautiful," he murmured. "I'd forgotten how exquisite you are, Catherine. I had a photo of you back in my office, but the reality far surpasses it." He held out his hand. "Come here, I want to touch you. Do you know how often I've thought about you in all kinds of positions and ways?"

She was standing next to him now. "I imagine the most frequent was of me dead."

"That was one of my favorites." His fingers delicately brushed her forearm. "But there were others . . . more sexual."

She forced herself to stand stiff and unmoving beneath his touch. She felt sick. She wanted to reach out and strangle him, break his bones, spit in his face.

Not the time. Take it. Endure.

"You hate this, don't you?" he said softly. "And I'm not even hurting you yet. Do you know how exciting I find it to hurt a woman with sex? It's male domination brought to the highest peak. With you, it will be the ultimate pleasure."

"Take me to see my son."

"Oh, I will. That will all be a part of it." He stepped back and opened the passenger door for her. "Step into my world, Catherine. I guarantee it's going to be an experience you never forget."

His hand was still on her elbow as she bent to get into the car. "Let me go."

"I will. Just one more thing . . ."

Then she saw the tiny hypodermic needle emerge from the palm of his hand on her arm and plunge deep.

"No!"

Swirling heat.

Darkness.

CHAPTER 17

Venable received the information Joe had asked him to request about Czadas twenty minutes after they'd left the farmhouse.

"I've got it." Venable had to shout to compete against the noise of the helicopter rotors as they strode across the tarmac toward the aircraft. He shoved his phone into his pocket. "Mikhal Czadas. Still active in the resistance movement, but more discreetly these days. He purchased the family home of a rich businessman, Nikolai Savrin, some years ago. It's out in the middle of the back of beyond, which must be convenient for his less-than-legal activities. Some question of how he came by the funds to buy it."

"How many years ago?"

"Nine."

"Curious coincidence. What do you want to bet that those funds came from Rakovac to ensure that Luke was kept in the most out-of-the-way place possible." He boarded the helicopter. "What else?"

"Not much," Venable said grimly. "Except there are rumors that Czadas has an illegitimate son who he took on several raids over the last few years. The boy was very quiet. Czadas didn't allow him to talk to strangers."

"And everyone was a stranger."

"Exactly." Venable buckled his seat belt. "It's shaping up to be an interesting evening. They transmitted a photo of Savrin House. It's located on a lake. I'll show you the photo after we get in the air. According to the last report we have, Czadas has a few men patrolling the area, but very few at the house itself. He's reputedly too full of bravado and a king-size ego to believe anyone can invade his space successfully."

"We'll have to see if he's right. How do we get to the house after we land?"

"I'll have a car and men waiting at the closest airport to Savrin House, which is in the town of Sergriev. We'll go there and see what we can find out." He added somberly, "And damn carefully."

He was a strange boy, Eve thought as she studied Luke's intent face while he listened to Kelly. He had fired questions at her for the last twenty minutes, some of them random, some of them searingly personal. All the while the flitting expressions on his face had been a mixture of curiosity, distrust, and a kind of insatiable thirst. There were so many things he didn't know about people and the world around him. How could he, kept in this remote house and only allowed limited access to the outside world?

Yet melded with that strangely spotty ignorance was an overlay of wariness and cynicism that could have belonged to a man in his thirties. It was evident Luke had never had a childhood. He'd mentioned being cared for by a village woman as a tiny child but had been immediately turned over to Czadas when he'd left babyhood. She wanted to feel sorry for him, but it would be like pitying a wild animal. He was so much on the defensive that she doubted he would ever allow anyone close enough to pity him.

Or to love him.

"Why are you looking at me like that?" Luke's gaze had suddenly narrowed on her face. Those intense dark eyes were probing, weighing, judging. "What are you thinking?"

"I was thinking that Catherine is going to have a very hard time with you."

He shrugged. "I don't care about her.

She's not here. You're the ones I have to worry about."

She suddenly realized something about him. "You live totally in the present, don't you?"

He stared at her in bewilderment. "What else is there?"

No, his past, except for a dim memory of his mother, was a nightmare fight for survival, his future, uncertain and lacking in hope.

"A great deal." But this was not the time to try to explain that to him. She had listened intently to the exchange between Luke and Kelly. Kelly had not only answered questions; she had asked them. Luke had not replied to all of them, but Eve had heard enough to start to piece together the enigma that was Catherine's son.

The violence, the beatings, the cruelty that extended far beyond the physical.

The loneliness.

Even when Czadas had taken him out into the world, he had not permitted him to socialize with anyone. It was a wonder he had not withdrawn entirely within himself.

But then there had been the library of books. They had probably been his salvation. Feeding that quick, agile mind and giving him refuge.

"You're looking at me again. I don't like it." He was frowning. "Is it because you've got that funny kind of job Kelly was talking about?"

"You think she's seeing you as a skeleton?" Kelly scoffed. "Don't be dumb. Eve wouldn't waste her time on you."

"According to what you said, she's already wasted a lot of time on me," Luke said. "So I'm not the one who's dumb."

"I was wondering if you think you knew enough about us by now," Eve interceded quickly. These two young people, who were ordinarily mature far beyond their years, were striking sparks off each other and reacting in a way that was out of character. Hell, maybe that was healthy. It was just getting in the way right now. She glanced at the stream of light that was now pale and fading. "The sun is going down. Czadas said Rakovac was coming tonight. He didn't say what time."

Luke gazed at her without speaking.

"Do something," Kelly said. "We're both here because of you. Now get us out of here." She paused. "If you can do it. I don't know whether to believe you or not. Maybe you're just full of bull."

He gazed at her without expression. "You're trying to make me show you that I can do it."

"Yes."

"It wouldn't be smart of me to do what you want just to prove I can."

Kelly threw up her hands. "Oh, for goodness' sake, then just do whatever you want."

"I will." Luke suddenly rose to his feet. "But not because I want to help you. I just won't let them kill me." He was moving toward the chest across the room. "But I guess you can come along."

"Thank you," Eve said dryly. "Kelly was only guessing that you might know a way out of here. Is it —"

"It wasn't a guess," Kelly corrected. "It was a natural progression of his pattern."

Eve ignored her. "You said you could do it, Luke. You led Natalie out of the house. But I can't imagine that route wouldn't have been sealed after they discovered how she had gotten out."

"They didn't 'discover', she told them. She told them everything." He nodded. "And they put double locks on that door."

And Luke had been brutally punished because she had told them he had been involved. It was no wonder he didn't trust strangers.

"Chateau d'If." He opened the lid and fumbled at the bottom of the chest. He drew out a wooden panel that had obviously been the floor of the chest.

"Chateau d'If?" Kelly repeated, bewildered.

He glanced at her impatiently. "*The Count of Monte Cristo.* Only he had it harder. These floors are wood, not stone. And I was able to cut them with the metal leg of that chair at the table over there. I bent the leg once, but Mikhal didn't notice. No one thought I'd try to get away when I didn't go with that Natalie woman."

"*Count of Monte Cristo.*" Then Kelly's frown cleared. "A book. Alexandre Dumas."

Kelly was of the generation of Harry Potter, and it wasn't surprising she hadn't made an instant connection, Eve thought. "Chateau d'If was a prison, and the hero took years to dig his way out to freedom, Kelly."

"Is that where you got the idea, Luke?" Kelly asked.

"It worked for him," Luke said as he climbed into the chest. "Or it would have if the other prisoner hadn't died, and he found a better —" He broke off. "I'll go first. This floor is above the basement. It's a ten-foot drop. Hold on by your arms, then jump. It's a dirt basement, and there's a high window that leads outside. I've piled lots of boxes so that I could get up and down without anyone hearing me."

"Where does the window lead?" Eve asked.

"A stretch of grass at the back of the house that leads down to the lake. Mikhal keeps a rowboat three miles down the bank."

"Guards?"

"They aren't usually at the back. There's one at the front and another at the side by the garage. One of them usually goes down to the bank and patrols the lakefront once or twice a night."

"You've evidently studied the situation," Eve said. "Just like the Count of Monte Cristo."

"But he managed to gather lots of money together," Luke said. "I didn't do so good." He was gazing at Eve critically. "Kelly will fit. But you're kind of big. Oh, you're skinny enough, but I'm not sure you'll fit through this hole."

"Then make it bigger," Kelly said curtly.

"You go on." Luke got out of the chest. "And don't knock over the boxes."

"I'll wait for Eve."

"Stop arguing, Kelly," Eve said quietly. "Get out of here. I'll be right behind you."

Kelly hesitated, then stepped into the

chest and levered herself through the hole. The next instant, Eve heard a soft thud as Kelly hit the dirt floor of the basement.

"You go on, too, Luke," Eve said. "There's not much time. I'll find a way to make that opening big enough for me."

He was gazing at her with a strange expression on his face. "You're not afraid, are you? If you stay here, you could die."

"No, I'm not afraid."

"I am. I'm afraid of dying."

"Then you'd better hurry and get out of here."

He slowly turned toward the chest. Then suddenly he whirled. He was across the room and turning over the chair. In a minute he had pried the leg off the chair and ran back across the room.

"Luke."

"Shut up." He was prying up the boards around the hole in the floor until there was a wide jagged opening. He threw the metal leg aside. "Go on. Hurry."

Eve nodded. "Right." A moment later, she was hanging by her hands, then dropping to the basement floor.

"Where is he?" Kelly whispered.

"Following. It seems Luke has the instincts of a gentleman. Odd, isn't it?" Odd and encouraging. For a moment she had thought the boy would leave her to her own devices. Considering his background, she couldn't have expected anything else.

Luke dropped down beside them. "Come on. The window."

He was climbing on a box and gently prying the window open, then he was hoisting himself up and wriggling through the opening.

Eve followed Kelly as she went after the boy.

It was dark now, and Eve hadn't been able to see what lay beyond the glass. Not that she would have been able to anyway. As she climbed through the window, she found the outside of the glass was smeared with mud so that no one could look into the basement.

Luke's work?

Probably. She was finding the boy amazingly inventive and detail-oriented.

Like Catherine.

What was happening to Catherine now?

Pain!

"Wake up!"

Catherine's head jerked sidewise as another slap rocked her.

"Come on. You pretend to be so strong. A little sedative shouldn't have put you under for this long."

Rakovac . . .

Another slap.

She opened her eyes. Rakovac's face loomed above her. He was smiling.

Bastard.

"She's appears to be a little fuzzy, Czadas." Rakovac was talking to a man standing beside him. A big man, muscular, bearded . . .

She was lying on a couch in a spacious room with high ceilings. "Where am I?"

"Now that's a trite question. Can't you be original?" He slapped her again. "I'm becoming bored. It's time to move things forward." He gave a sly glance at Czadas. "Though the search wasn't boring, was it, Czadas? I told you that she was a fine piece of flesh."

"You were right," Czadas grinned. "Thank you for sharing."

Search?

She became suddenly aware that both her blouse and black slacks were unbuttoned, and her bra was lying on the floor beside the couch. Her gaze flew to Rakovac's face.

"You might be a bit sore," he said. "Our search was very thorough." He smiled. "But with such a competent and lethal CIA agent, we had to make sure that you had no weapons to trouble us."

She was already feeling sore, tender. Don't feel dirty. Don't think of their hands on her, in her. It would be a victory for them if she let it bother her. She was just glad she hadn't been awake through it. Rakovac had made a mistake giving her too much of the sedative. He would have been much happier seeing how she hated going through that search.

"Besides your gun, we found this." Rakovac picked up a dagger from the end table. "Pretty little toy. It was in a holster in your bra underneath your armpit. Were you going to sting me with it, Catherine?"

"I was considering it."

He threw back his head and laughed. "Oh, I imagine you were."

"Where am I?" she asked again.

"Savrin House," Czadas said. "Isn't it a fine place? Rakovac made a present of it for doing him a special favor. I thought it was a great bargain." He chuckled. "Though that favor ended up lasting nine years. So who got the best of it?"

"You had no problem with taking care of the boy," Rakovac said.

"Not in the beginning. He was very docile and eager to please. But then he changed. I haven't had it entirely easy during these past years." He paused. "You should keep that in mind. You owe me."

"I paid you," Rakovac said. "And you took care of those changes with a whip."

"Only because that was your wish." He looked at Catherine. "I would have been a wonderful father to the boy if Rakovac hadn't urged me in another direction. I have a tender soul."

"You . . . hurt him."

"Of course he did," Rakovac said. "And enjoyed every minute of it. I told you that Luke was not having an easy time of it." He added softly, "And every time the whip fell, I showed him your photo and told him that all his pain came from you."

"It did come from me. I should have found a way to kill you before you took him from me."

"Oh, you must tell him that. It will be confirmation of all my teachings." He smiled. "And when I kill him, I'll tell him the same thing. Only I won't have to show him a photo. I can have him look at the real thing as I pull the trigger."

Panic was tearing at her. Don't let him see it. She had to keep a clear head and work out a scenario that would save as many as possible. "Where are Kelly and Eve? Are they still alive?"

"Would I deprive myself of the pleasure of watching you as I rid myself of them? Mikhal, here, took them to the room where we keep the boy when I want him available to me. Well, it's more of a cell, really."

Catherine's heart skipped a beat. "Available?"

"You think I might have sexually abused him? I considered it, but I would have had to force myself. I've no liking for little boys." He smiled. "I prefer women like you, Catherine. Breaking a strong woman is utterly delicious."

"Like you did Natalie Ladvar?"

"She wasn't strong, just young and pretty. It was enough at the time." He glanced at Czadas. "Wasn't it, Mikhal?"

"She was more trouble than she was worth." Czadas scowled. "Weak."

"Then you wouldn't be interested in Eve or Kelly," Catherine said quickly. "Neither of them is —"

"You're trying to protect them," Rakovac interrupted. "It's not necessary. I don't have time for anyone but you, Catherine. Shall I tell you how it's going to go? I'll take you up to Luke's cell and let you meet your son. Then I'll have Czadas kill Eve Duncan and the girl."

"No."

"Yes, but I'll save the boy for myself. I'll kill Luke before your eyes. I'll press the muzzle of the gun to his temple and blow his brains out."

The muscles of her stomach clenched. "What can I do to change your mind?" she asked shakily. "Tell me. I'll do anything."

"Yes, you will. Anything and everything." He reached out and cupped her breast in his palm. "I'll take you on the floor where your son lies dead. I'll use you like a whore in a house I know in Istanbul where they know the art of making a woman beg to be put out of her misery. I'll show you pain as you've never known it."

"Then do it. You'll enjoy that, won't you? Just don't kill my son. Don't kill Eve or Kelly."

He frowned. "Are you still being the sacrificing mother? That's not all I want from you. Think of yourself. I'm becoming annoyed." His hand closed on her breast with bruising force. His eyes narrowed on her face, devouring every sign of pain. "Yes, that's better." He released her breast and jerked her to her feet. "Come along, it's time we started. I have a plane to catch in a few hours. I want this to be a long and satisfying night." He was dragging her toward the short flight of stairs. "Come and meet Luke."

She braced herself. It was coming. Think. How to set it up? Lord, it was going to be difficult. The prospect had been bad enough when she had thought there would only be Luke to rescue. Now she had to consider Eve and Kelly.

Czadas was following Rakovac and Catherine up the steps. It didn't surprise her. From the short time since she'd regained consciousness, he had seemed a true soul mate to that bastard Rakovac. Okay, she had Czadas and Rakovac to take care of. But she hadn't seen any sign of guards within the house. After she disposed of Rakovac, she'd have only Czadas to deal with until they got outside.

But how to get Luke to go with her? If he'd been taught to think of her as the devil, wouldn't he panic? Worry about that later. One disaster at a time.

No, don't think disaster. It had to go well. She had to save Luke.

Czadas had stepped in front of them and was unlocking the oak door. "Luke," he called jovially as he stepped inside. "I've brought Rakovac. He wants to have a party. You remember Rakovac's parties. First, he sent you visitors, and now he's brought a special guest. You'll recognize her at —" He stopped, stiffening, as his gaze raked the darkness. "Luke?" He reached out to the wall and turned on the light.

The room was empty!

"What the hell!" Rakovac pushed her through the doorway. "Where are they, Czadas? Is this some kind of trick? Are you holding me up for more money?"

"They were here," Czadas said quickly. "Son of a bitch, I wouldn't try to double-cross you, Rakovac."

Rakovac's face was flushed with anger. "Then where are —" His gaze went to the open trunk and the chair lying on the floor with one metal leg missing. "Is he hiding?" He strode over to the trunk. "Get that kid —" He stopped as he stared down into the chest. He started to swear. "You told me that the kid wasn't trying to run away any longer. That you'd taught him a lesson."

"I did." Czadas was beside him, looking down into the gaping hole that pierced both the chest and the floor beneath it. "It will be all right, Rakovac. I promise."

Catherine couldn't believe it. Something had happened. Luke was free. They were all free. Thank you, God. Oh, thank you, God.

"Where does that hole lead?" Rakovac asked.

"Only the basement," Czadas answered.

"And is there a window in the basement?"

"Yes."

Rakovac spoke clearly, slowly, each word enunciated with precision. "Then don't you think you'd better get down there and see if you can find out if they managed to get outside?"

"Right away." Czadas had turned and was hurrying toward the door. "Even if they're on the grounds, it won't be a problem. I'll have the guards scour the area and call in additional help from the village. We'll find them."

"Quickly." Rakovac met Czadas's eyes. "No excuses. I've planned this ending for years. I won't have it ruined by your clumsiness."

"Thirty minutes." Czadas moistened his lips. "Forty minutes tops." He hurried from the room.

"He's a fool." Rakovac whirled on Catherine. "But he knows better than to spoil this for me. He'll have your son back in no time."

"I hope you're wrong." How had it happened? Had Eve and Kelly helped her son to escape? It didn't matter. Now wasn't the time to analyze the miracle. Just accept it and try to build on it. "Maybe it was meant to be."

"It was meant to be that I kill him and you, too, bitch," Rakovac said. "And don't hope. It won't do you any good. Nothing is going to happen except exactly what I described to you. It's just been postponed a short time."

"If one thing is changed, maybe others will change, too," Catherine said. "Chain reaction."

"That sounds a little too optimistic." He pulled out his gun and pointed it at her. "Don't try anything, bitch."

A bullet whistled by Eve's ear as they reached the bank of the lake.

"Run!" Luke called back to her. "They must have found out that we're gone." He sprinted ahead of them.

Kelly was not far behind.

Eve cast a glance over her shoulder as she tore after them.

Men with flashlights, running.

Luke was looking at them, too. "The big man is Mikhal. He's going to be —"

Another bullet.

Closer.

"Run!" Luke shouted. "Faster. What's wrong with you?"

What was wrong? She wanted to shake him. "I'm not eleven years old. Go on. I'll keep up."

Luke muttered something and slowed. "There's another guard up ahead. You go hide in the trees while I lead him away."

"No, we stay together." Eve quickened her pace. "Where is this boat?"

"A mile. Maybe a little more."

And the men behind them were gaining.

Don't panic.

Run . . .

"It's Eve!" Joe jumped out of the car, his gaze on the three fleeing figures on the bank. He took off down the rocky embankment. Savrin House was towering on a hill in the distance, but he let Venable go after Rakovac. Joe didn't know what circumstances had permitted Eve to escape, but he was going to take full advantage of them.

Three men in pursuit. One tall, heavyset man in the lead, two others following close behind.

He ran parallel to Eve and the others, keeping pace, waiting.

Gunshots. The large man was firing.

Take him out.

He fell to his knees and aimed carefully. A little bit in front of the man to take in consideration his impetus.

One . . . Two . . .

The big man stumbled, arched, then fell to the ground.

The two other men stopped, confused.

Take out the leader, and you often took out the team.

Just to be sure, he aimed again and took out the man closest to him. The other man stopped, then took a few steps back, turned, and started running back toward the house.

Joe jumped to his feet and started after Eve.

"Behind you!" A boy's voice.

Joe whirled, lifted his weapon to fire at the other guard, who had come out of nowhere.

The guard was lifting his gun.

But he toppled forward as he was tackled from behind.

Joe was on the guard in an instant and broke his neck with one twist. He whirled on the man who had tackled the guard, ready for anything.

"No, Joe!" Eve was running toward him. "It's Luke. Don't hurt him."

Not a man, a boy. But a boy with dark eyes blazing in his taut face, his body crouched and ready to spring.

Eve ran in front of the boy. "It's okay, Luke. This is Joe Quinn. He's here to help us."

Luke didn't move, his gaze fixed warily on

Joe. "He did help. He shot Mikhal. Did you kill him?"

"I don't know," Joe said. "The big man?"

Luke didn't answer. He was on his feet and running back toward the two fallen men.

"Mikhal Czadas," Eve told Joe as she followed him.

Luke was standing over the body of Mikhal Czadas when Joe, Eve, and Kelly caught up with him.

Luke prodded Czadas with his foot, staring down at him. "He's dead. He looks surprised." His smile was savage. "I wish he'd seen it coming."

The boy was fierce, Joe thought. Well, who could blame him? He had grown up in a den of voracious wolves. "We can't have everything." He turned to Eve. "Did you see Rakovac?"

She shook her head. "But Czadas told us earlier that he was supposed to be coming. He might be here."

He waved at Venable, who had pulled the car alongside them on the road above. "Then by all means, let's go see if he is."

Catherine stared at Rakovac's gun pointed at her heart. It was now or never. Czadas was chasing after Luke and wouldn't be a problem. Luke, Eve, and Kelly were not on the scene to worry about. She had only to contend with Rakovac.

He was enough.

"I didn't mean that I thought I had a chance to get out of this alive," she said. "But what about my son and the others? I thought perhaps I could persuade you that they could live." She stared at him, not hiding the fear that was always with her. Let him see her desperation. It could be a weapon to help her get close to him.

Rakovac shook his head. "Wrong."

"You want me." She moistened her lips. "Oh, I know it's all twisted in your mind. But you do want me. Why not do it now? Let me convince you that you'd be better off keeping me as a toy than killing my son right now. You could always do that later. Let him live until you get tired of me."

He was silent, his expression arrested. "Interesting." She had reached him, tapped into the perversity that was an essential element of his character. "I wasn't expecting this, Catherine."

"Why not? You know that I'll do anything to save my son. Maybe if I delay it long enough, it will be like Scheherazade telling her tales every night. It won't happen."

"You wouldn't live past the first night,

Scheherazade."

"Yes, I would. You said I was strong. I *am* strong." She stared him in the eye. "You liked your hands on me when you were searching. I could make you like everything about me. You mentioned that house in Istanbul. I grew up on the streets of Hong Kong. Do you think there's anything I don't know about the ways to please a man? You want to hurt me? I can endure and bring you to heights you've never reached."

"And try to kill me after you've done it."

"You're a strong man. Keep me from doing it." She could see that he was fascinated by the idea. Why not? She was offering him the kind of submissive sex that he adored. Clinch it. Show him.

She reached up and took down her dark hair and shook it about her shoulders. She took off her shirt and dropped it on the floor.

"Before they find Luke, let me show you," she whispered. "You won't be sorry."

"You'll take anything I do to you?"

"And beg you for more." She started toward him. Hold his eyes. She knew about seduction. Draw him. Arouse him. Make him look at her eyes and her naked breasts. Glow, shimmer with sexuality. He might be a monster, but he was a man. "Will you let

me try to please you enough to save Luke?"
"It won't work. I'll break you."
"I'm not afraid. I know I've got a chance to change your mind." She was standing in front of him so close the muzzle of his gun was pressed against her bare stomach. "And you want to do it." She could see the pulse leap in his temple. "Do what you want, Rakovac. Anything you want."
"Whore." His cheeks were flushed and his lips full and slightly parted. "Oh, I'll do what I want. You'll scream for me, Catherine." His hand closed on her breast. "And it might as well start here and now."
Ignore the pain. Watch the gun in his left hand. He might have a second to respond.
"How do you like that?" His teeth sank into the lobe of her ear and brought blood.
Good. Perfect. His movement had brought her mouth to press against his neck.
Her tongue ran quickly over the back of her front teeth.
"You're not answering, bitch." He was panting, gnawing at her like an animal. "Tell me: how much of this you can stand for your son?"
She had the cap off the tooth. She opened her mouth, and her teeth sank deep into his neck!
He jerked away from her. "What are —"

His hand lashed out at her.

She had to get the cap back over that tooth quickly. Done.

Now it would take three seconds.

The gun. She blocked it as he started to raise the weapon.

Three seconds.

He only made it to two seconds.

Rakovac's eyes glazed over, the gun dropped from his nerveless hand. He was staring at her in horror.

"Is the pain starting?" She was panting as she took another step back and gazed up at him with glittering ferocity. "Hu Chang promised me that it would be excruciating. He said, 'Don't worry, my friend, it won't be as long as you would like, but for him, it will seem forever. A fitting prelude to the hell where you're sending him.' "

Rakovac was looking at her in bewilderment. He tried to speak, "Hu . . . Chang . . ."

"As I said, an old friend from my days in Hong Kong. He made his living concocting very lethal poisons and undetectable delivery systems for them. I did a favor for him once. When I went to him four years ago and told him I needed his help, he was happy to oblige."

Rakovac suddenly moaned and staggered back.

"Ah, now it's hitting. It's mamba venom mixed with one of Hu Chang's more painful additives. At first, he didn't want to use it. I told him to replace one of my canine teeth with a hypodermic containing the poison, then cap it. He was worried that the cap might break and loose the poison into my system." Her smile was tiger bright. "But we worked it out."

He was trying to stagger toward her throat.

She took a step back. "I knew that you'd be searching every orifice if you ever got your hands on me, and it had to be a part of the tooth and completely hidden. I had to promise to come back to him and let him replace it with something a little more stable right after I'd used it."

His face was growing red, livid. He was starting at her with hatred . . . and fear. "Hurts . . . hurts . . . stop . . . it."

"Did you stop?" she asked through set teeth. "Did you stop the taunts and the torture? You took my son, and you hurt him. I don't even know all the ways that you hurt him yet. When I find out, I'll probably want you to live for a hundred years so that I can keep you writhing with agony."

He was panting, his eyes bulging from his

swollen face. "Stop . . . it."

"The venom attacks the respiratory system, Hu Chang's additive adds heat to the mix. He promised you'd feel as if your lungs and every nerve in your body were on fire. Is that how it feels, Rakovac?"

He groaned, his hands reaching for her throat.

She took another step back. "Yes, I can see it does. Do you feel helpless? That's how you like your victims to feel. I wanted you to feel helpless."

He was sinking to his knees. Tears were running down his cheeks from eyes that were almost bulging from his face. "Please . . ."

"Please what? Please forgive you for taking and hurting my son? Please stop punishing you for doing it? No way on earth, you bastard."

He was reaching blindly for the weapon he'd dropped to the floor.

She put her foot on the gun. "In five minutes, it will be over. But those minutes will seem like a millennium. Hu Chang promised. I could have made it quicker, it would have been safer for me. But I had to have at least this much time." She bent down and looked into his eyes. "You've lost everything. I'm going to ruin all your fine plans. I'm going to take back everything you stole from us. I'm going to make my son's life so good that he'll never even remember what you did to him." He understood, she could see that realization through the twisted agony in his face. "So suffer, Rakovac. Suffer . . ."

CHAPTER 18

Catherine was still standing over Rakovac's body when Eve ran into the room.

Eve stopped short, her gaze flying from the dead man on the floor to Catherine. She looked . . . barbaric. Half-naked, her long hair lying half-over her breasts, a trace of blood on her lips. No, more like pictures she'd seen of the ancient goddesses in battle.

"Catherine . . . ?"

"He's dead," Catherine said regretfully. "I wanted it to last longer." She shook her head as if to clear it. She picked up the gun on the floor and turned to Eve. "I was coming after you. Are you hurt?"

"No." She picked up Catherine's shirt, which was lying on the floor, and crossed the room. "We're all fine. Czadas is dead, too. Joe and Venable are right behind me. Joe was cursing a blue streak when I ran up here ahead of him." She shrugged. "I made Venable give me a gun. I had to make sure you were safe."

"Joe? How did he — Later." She lifted her hand to her head. "I can't seem to think right now." She slipped into the shirt Eve was holding for her. "My son is alive?"

"Yes, Luke is alive. Kelly says he's a survivor. He's with her now."

"Then it's over, isn't it?"

"It's over." Eve buttoned Catherine's shirt. She couldn't blame Catherine for being dazed. She had obviously gone through hell in the past hours, but no more than the hell she had endured for the last nine years. "Or it's the beginning. It depends on how you look at it."

"Yes, that's a good way to look at it. That's what I told Rakovac." She looked down at Rakovac's face, still twisted with agony. "He ruined the last nine years for Luke and me. I can't let him take anything else from us. He'd win. I can't let him win."

Eve gave her a quick, hard hug. "Not you. That's not going to happen."

"I didn't want this to happen to you and Kelly. I thought I was going to keep him away from you."

"It didn't happen. You couldn't know. Don't think about it right now."

"How is she?" Joe stood in the doorway.

"Good enough." Eve nodded at Rakovac.

"He's dead."

Venable pushed Joe aside and strode into the room. "I checked the car out front. There was a computer, but I didn't see —" He was searching Rakovac's pockets. He pulled out a keychain. "Thumb drive! This has got to be it. I'll go to the study and check it out on his computer." He jumped to his feet and ran out of the room and down the stairs.

"You didn't find what you needed at Rakovac's house?" Catherine asked.

"It was purged. Venable says we can get it eventually, but we need it now." Joe crossed to look down at Rakovac. "You got him. How?"

She smiled faintly. "I struck him with my fangs. Mamba venom."

"A fitting end. I thought you'd have made preparations. You wouldn't have just gone in without a plan." His glance shifted to her face. He reached out and took both her hands in his and looked into her eyes. "Did it feel good, Catherine?"

"Oh, yes."

"Then forget about the bastard." He squeezed her hands and turned away. "I've got to go down and check with Venable on that thumb drive. Eve, why don't you take her down to see her son?"

"I was planning on it," Eve said. "As soon as I get the blood off her. Neither of you appear to have noticed it."

"From what I saw of Luke out there, he wouldn't have noticed either," Joe said as he left the room.

"Luke . . ." Catherine said. "I didn't think I'd feel like this. I'm scared, Eve. All the things I meant to say to him have flown out of my head."

"They were probably the wrong things anyway. You can't comprehend what Luke has become."

Her eyes widened in alarm. "What's wrong? Why do you say that?"

"Calm down. I didn't mean anything is wrong." She caught her lower lip between her teeth. Catherine had been looking forward to this reunion for nine years. How to warn her, without dashing that hope? "You'll have to decide that for yourself. I didn't have enough time with him to judge. Luke is going to be difficult. You may have a long way to go. There's no way around that." She paused, feeling her way. "But he's like you, Catherine. That's a very good start."

She smiled shakily. "Then heaven help him. I was always so glad that my baby wasn't like me."

"But he's no longer a baby, and he has many of your qualities."

"You're being so gentle," Catherine said. "That's scaring me even more."

"Then it's time I shut up and took you down to see him." She took Catherine's hand. "Come on. He's with Kelly, and she's not always patient with him. I don't want him walking out on her."

"They don't get along?"

"I didn't say that. They may be good for each other. They're just . . . young."

Catherine pulled her hand away from Eve's as they reached the stairs. "You don't have to treat me like a child. I'll be fine." She started down the steps, her gaze searching the foyer below. "Where is —" Her breath left her as she saw Luke standing beside Kelly by the door. "Oh, my God," she whispered. "He *is* beautiful, isn't he, Eve? Just like that progression you did."

"Yes, I did a good job. But I only did the computer rendering; you're responsible for the actual creation." She watched Catherine go slowly down the steps. She was so vulnerable right now. Please don't let him hurt her.

As if he felt her gaze on him, Luke suddenly looked up with that wary instinct that seemed such a part of him.

He tensed as he saw Catherine on the stairs.

His expression closed, became even more shuttered.

"Catherine!" Kelly pushed past him and ran up the steps to her. "I've been scared to death. Are you okay?"

Catherine gave Kelly a hug, her gaze still on Luke over the girl's head. "I'm fine."

Kelly stepped back and gazed at her a moment. "Come on, I'll go down with you." She slipped her arm protectively around Catherine's waist and started back down the stairs. She said softly, "He's not so bad. You just have to take him down when he gets too full of himself."

"I'll remember that." Catherine hadn't taken her gaze from Luke's dark eyes staring up at her.

She was now face-to-face with him.

But Kelly was suddenly standing between them. "You listen to me, Luke," she said fiercely. "This is Catherine, this is your mother. She's wonderful, and you don't deserve her. But you've got her, and you'd better not hurt her."

Then she whirled away and ran back up to where Eve was standing on the stairs.

Luke didn't answer Kelly. He hadn't taken his eyes off Catherine.

"Hello, Luke, I've waited a long time," Catherine said awkwardly. "Now that you're here, I don't know the right things to say. Maybe there aren't any right things. I've tried so hard to get you back." She paused. It was so difficult. She wanted desperately to take him in her arms and tell him all the hurt and loneliness was over. But she had to move with such heartbreaking slowness. "I love you. If you give me a chance, I'll try to give you a good life. Those are the only things that are important, I think. What do you think?"

He didn't answer.

"Talk to me, Luke. Are there any questions you'd like to ask me?"

"Yes." He asked baldly, "Did you tell Rakovac to hurt me?"

"No!" Her eyes closed for an instant before they opened to reveal them shimmering with unshed tears. "As God is my witness, Luke."

"I didn't think so. He lies. I don't believe anything he says."

"You won't ever have to worry about him again, Luke."

His gaze flew to the staircase leading to the upper floor. "He's dead?"

"Yes."

"You did it?"

"Oh, yes."

"Good." The ferocity was back in his expression. "I'm glad. I was going to do it if I had to."

She flinched. "No. Don't say that. You shouldn't have to do anything like that to protect yourself. I'll protect you from now on."

He stared at her skeptically.

"You don't believe me? I love you, Luke."

"Why should I believe you? I don't know you. I don't love you. I don't love anyone."

She drew a deep breath. "You're right. Trust has to be earned. Will you give me a chance to earn it? You have a choice now."

"I do?" he asked warily.

"Did you think I was going to force you?" she asked. "You can come with me and see if you like it. Everything is going to be strange for you for a while. I think we can work through it together. Or, if you don't want to give me my chance, then I'll find a place for you where you'll be happy. That's all I want. For you to be happy." She smiled unsteadily. "What makes you happy, Luke?"

He hesitated, then said slowly, "Books. Mikhal burned them."

"Then we'll get you more. As many as you like. I'll make sure you have an entire library of your own."

Another silence. "Where? Where would I have to go?"

"We could decide that between us. I used to live in Boston, but I haven't really had a home since I lost you."

"I've read about Boston in one of my books. They had some kind of crazy tea party there."

"Yes, they did. You used to live there, too, when you were a little boy."

Another silence. "Would we go there right away?"

"I have to go somewhere else first. I promised a friend, Hu Chang, I'd go to Hong Kong and have a dental procedure done. He seemed to think it was urgent. But after that, we'll go wherever you want to go."

"Hong Kong." He tasted the words. "It sounds . . . funny."

"It's not a funny place. Oh, I guess it could be. But where I grew up, it wasn't. I was on my own."

"Like me."

She nodded. "Like you. Will you —" She stopped. "I want to push you because I want you to come so badly. But you've been pushed enough since you left me. I won't do that to you." She impulsively took a step forward, reaching a hand out to touch him.

She saw his face tense, become even more shuttered. Her hand fell to her side. She whispered, "It's so hard, Luke."

He gazed at her. "I don't know you," he said again.

"I don't know you anymore either. Sometimes getting to know someone can be an adventure, like reading a wonderful book. It could be like that for us."

"A book? Maybe." He paused, thinking. "If I don't go with you, I can just walk out of here? You wouldn't stop me?"

"I don't want to let you go. Please. I'd rather you let me find somewhere safe for —"

"You wouldn't stop me?"

She swallowed, then said, "I won't stop you." She added, "But I can't lie to you. I'll have to find a way to watch over you even if you leave me. I've just found you. I can't let anything happen to you."

"Nothing can happen to me now that Mikhal and Rakovac are gone."

"Czadas and Rakovac were monsters, but there are other monsters out there. I could help you to recognize them." She held up her hands helplessly. "You see, I can't stop trying to persuade you. Will you think long and hard about coming with me, Luke?"

He stared at her for another moment.

"Yes." He turned on his heel and headed for the door. "I don't want to be here anymore right now. You're confusing me."

Catherine stared after him as the door closed. "I was clumsy. Did I drive him away, Eve?"

"You weren't clumsy," Eve said as she came down the stairs. "You were honest and had more restraint than I would have had. You can't blame him for being confused. His whole world has changed in a few hours. And I don't believe that he's going to run away from here right now."

"I'll see that he doesn't." Kelly moved past them and headed after Luke. "He won't run away from me. I annoy him, but I'm no threat."

"Be careful, Kelly," Catherine said. "We have to give him space."

Kelly snorted. "You're both treating him as if he's made of glass. Luke is probably stronger than all of us."

"I hope that she's right," Catherine said, as the door shut behind Kelly. "I pray that she's right."

"She's right." Eve hesitated. "If Luke decides not to go with you, he can come to me, Catherine."

"Thank you." Catherine's lips twisted. "You're always offering to take in my strays,

Eve. At least Kelly is civilized. I don't know what kind of problems you'd have with Luke."

"But you'd accept them in a heartbeat."

"Oh, yes."

"So would I." Eve smiled luminously. "He's alive. This one, we managed to bring home alive, Catherine. Do you know how wonderful that is? What difference does it make that we're having a little trouble getting him to decide where that home is going to be?"

Catherine took her hand and smiled back at her. "No difference at all. What am I thinking?"

"We'll work it out," Eve said. "But now we need to go and see if that thumb drive is giving Venable and Joe the information they need."

When they walked into the study, it was clear that the thumb drive had been the key they'd hoped it would be.

Venable was on the phone barking out orders. Joe was printing out from the computer. Another one of Venable's men was on another phone, with a list in front of him.

Eve asked the question anyway. "You got it?"

Joe nodded. "It was to start tomorrow at

six P.M. Eastern Standard Time. A simultaneous attack that would make sure that at least ten of the targeted thirteen cities would be affected."

"Ten?" Eve was stunned. "So many? How is that possible?"

"Precise planning. They wanted to strike a massive blow, and it's been in the works for a long time." Joe's lips twisted. "And Rakovac no doubt had been invaluable to Dabala's cause."

"Bastard," Catherine murmured.

"One who we're all grateful is no longer walking the earth," Joe said. "You did well, Catherine."

"It was my pleasure." Catherine's gaze was on Venable. "You don't have much time. It's close to nine P.M. here. That means it's already one P.M. in the U.S. That only gives us five hours. Give me something to do to help. There have to be phone calls to make. Agents to whip into shape."

"We had to pull the FBI into it. We have no authority within any of those cities. I called the director, and he gave us permission to call the FBI field agent in every targeted city with the name of the airline employee who was going to facilitate the boarding of the explosives. They'll keep the explosive handoff from happening," Venable said. "We're hoping that we can keep our movements quiet from Dabala so that we can pick up the suicide bombers at flight time."

"I'm calling my own FBI contacts," Joe said. "Those FBI agents may have other contacts for you to call for them. Venable is delegating as much as possible, but I'd rather trust it to you." He handed her a list. "Get to work."

Eve held out her hand. "Give me one, too. I'll leave Catherine to whip everyone into shape. I'll just make sure that they know why it's being done so she can go on to the next one."

"Right." Joe handed her the list and went back to the printer.

They didn't finish the phone calls till close to midnight. Even then, Venable was still on the phone with Homeland Security when Eve, Joe, and Catherine walked out of the house to get some fresh air.

The air was not only fresh, it was chilly.

The coolness felt good to Eve. She took a deep breath. "I think we got to everyone. Lord, I hope no one slipped through the cracks."

"We had the identity of the cities. Their airports will be on alert, too. It's all we can do," Joe said. "And if there's a leak, maybe it will scare off Dabala from trying to ram through an attack."

"Maybe," Eve repeated.

"Probably," Joe substituted. "It's been a lucky night. I don't think that luck's going to go sour on us now. We'll know pretty soon."

"Where are Kelly and Luke?" Eve's gaze was wandering around the grounds. "I haven't seen them since Kelly stopped by the study about midnight. She said Luke didn't want to come back inside, and she'd stay out here with him."

"I don't blame him for not wanting to go back into that house. It was a prison," Catherine said. "Hell, I'd probably camp out in a tent if I were him."

"Not surprising," Joe said. "I recall you camped out at our place in one. He evidently shares your —" He stopped, his gaze on the hill leading down to the lake. "There's Kelly coming back. I don't see Luke."

"I'll go meet her." Catherine was already gone, halfway down the hill before she finished speaking. Kelly was trudging slowly along the rocky bank, and Catherine reached her in less than a minute. "Where's Luke? Is he —"

"He's cool." Kelly held up her hand to

stem the flow. "Actually, he's probably cold. He decided to go skinny-dipping. Though he didn't recognize the term for it. I told him to go ahead. I wasn't about to follow him into that lake."

"Will he be all right? I don't even know if he can swim."

"He can swim. Like a fish." Kelly hesitated. "I saw his back, Catherine. He has scars. He didn't even try to hide them. It was as if he assumed everybody had them."

"Oh, shit." Catherine could feel the tears sting her eyes. She wished Rakovac was still alive, so that she could kill him again.

"Don't feel sorry for him," Kelly said. "I'm not sure if he'd know how to handle it. I don't think he'd know what it was all about, and it would make him uneasy. He's a strange kid, Catherine."

"No wonder you two are getting along," Catherine said. "You're not the usual run-of-the-mill kid yourself, Kelly."

"No, I'm weird." Kelly smiled. "But I'm coming to terms with it." She looked out at the lake. "He looks like he's coming back in. Why don't you go down and be there when he gets out? You don't need my help with him any longer. I only wanted to come to meet you to tell you about Luke's back. I didn't want you to burst into tears and embarrass both of you." She glanced back at Catherine. "Don't do it."

"I'll keep that in mind."

"Good, I'm going to the house and see if I can find something hot to drink." Kelly started up the hill. "I spent the last year in Colombia, and I'm feeling this chill. I'll see you when you come back."

"Yes." She called after her, "Thank you, Kelly."

"Sure." Kelly waved but kept on walking and didn't look back.

Catherine stood staring after her for a moment. So small and delicate and yet full of strength. Who would have known when she'd first seen Kelly huddled in that tent in Munoz's camp how close they would become in such a short time.

She turned and looked out at the lake. The moonlight was streaking it with silver, and she could see Luke's head bobbing as he swam back toward the bank. He appeared very small from this distance.

He was not small, but he was only a child.

Her child.

Be my child, Luke. If only for a little while, be my child.

She was sitting on a knoll overlooking the lake, her arms linked loosely about her knees, when Luke climbed onto the bank.

He gazed at her without speaking, then started to dress.

Don't look at his back. Kelly was right, she wouldn't be able to keep control if she did.

His clothes were clinging to his wet body, and she wanted to hold him close to ward off the cold.

She didn't move. He would not accept that intimacy from her.

And he didn't seem to feel the cold. Another sign of the toughness that he'd had to develop to survive. That hurt her, too.

"Did the water feel good?"

He nodded.

"Who taught you to swim?"

"Mikhal threw me in the lake when I was little. I was scared, but he kept throwing me in until I learned how to keep from drowning. Later, I found some stuff in one of the books that helped."

His books, again.

He stood looking at her for a moment, then sat down beside her. "Where's Kelly?"

"She was chilly. She went to the house. She said since she'd spent so much time in South America that she felt the cold."

"She told me that her father was killed there." He was looking out at the lake. "She said that's where you saved her life. She's angry with me for not feeling about you the way she does."

"Kelly is very protective. I've tried to talk her out of it, but she thinks she owes me something."

He frowned. "I've never felt like that toward anyone."

How could he? No one had ever tried to protect Luke from anything. He'd had to protect himself from them. Now he was entering a new world, where everything was different. "Don't worry about it."

He ignored her words. "I was thinking that maybe I owe you something, too."

"Because I'm your mother?"

He shook his head. "Because you killed Rakovac."

Short, brutal, devoid of sentiment. It was what she had to expect from Luke from now on. It was hard to realize that, when she had held that image of a sunny two-year-old in her heart all these years. "You don't owe me anything for getting rid of Rakovac. I did it because I couldn't do anything else, Luke."

"But it was because of me." He seemed to be trying to work it out. "Kelly said you risked your life for me."

"Purely selfish. I couldn't go on unless I

found you and tried to make things right."

He was silent. "I don't understand."

"You will someday."

"If I went with you to this Hong Kong, would that be paying you back?"

She wanted to tell him yes. It was her chance to grab at the brass ring of opportunity. She couldn't do it. "No, don't come for that reason. Only come if it's what you want, if you think it's worth giving us a chance together."

He was gazing at her with those huge black eyes that held so many shades of emotion; ferocity, curiosity, wariness. It was like looking in a mirror of herself as a child.

No joy. The joyous wonder that had been such a part of him had vanished.

Please God, let her find a way of bringing that joy to the surface again.

"When are you leaving?" he asked.

"In a few hours. I'm going to hop a ride on the helicopter Venable arranged to take him back to Moscow. Then I'll take a plane to Hong Kong. Have you ever ridden on a helicopter?"

"No, I've seen them. Mikhal always took me in a truck whenever we left here. He always had weapons and didn't want to be noticed."

"I can see why." She paused. "Eve asked

me to let you come to her. If you don't want to be with me, will you go to her?"

"Maybe."

She got to her feet. "It would please me very much if you would. I know you don't care what a stranger thinks, but I just want you to know." She forced a smile. "Now why don't we go and find a change of clothes for you. You may not be cold, but I'm shivering just looking at you."

He nodded absently. "I'll change." He didn't move. "Soon."

He wasn't going with her back to the house. Perhaps he'd had enough of her. She didn't know what he was thinking or how he'd react to anything, she thought in frustration. "Then I'll say good-bye to you later." She started up the hill. The long grasses were stirring in the wind. "I'll see you at the house, Luke."

He nodded but didn't answer.

Kelly had left them alone together so that they could come to some kind of understanding. It hadn't happened. He still found her beyond his comprehension. She was reaching desperately for a way to peel away those layers of mental scar tissue from those terrible years, but it wasn't going to happen in an hour or even a day.

She could see Eve standing by the front

door, and she suddenly remembered what she had said.

He's alive. We've brought him home. What difference does it make that he's having trouble deciding where that home is?

She had forgotten that in those moments with Luke when she had been trying desperately to reach him.

Her pace quickened, and she waved at Eve.

He was alive. She had to be patient. Time and work, and she'd find a way to bring back the joy.

"We've got them!" Joe came striding out of the study into the living room. "No incidents. Though we were only able to pick up half of the suicide bombers. Homeland Security panicked and closed down all airports for three hours."

"I approve of that kind of panic," Eve said. "And they picked up the airline employees involved?"

Joe nodded. "It was a delicate operation. Some of them had been bribed, but others had been forced by a hostage situation like the one in Lima." He lifted his head, listening. "I hear the helicopter. Is Catherine ready to go?"

"No." Her gaze went to Catherine, who

was standing, looking out the window across the room. "But she will. I told her we'd keep Luke for a while. Is that okay?"

"You'd still do it if I said it wasn't." Joe smiled. "No problem. It will be good having another male around the place. I'm constantly surrounded by women."

"Luke isn't your average 'male.' Sometimes he looks at me as if I were from another planet."

"That's probably how he feels. About all of us."

"Venable says it's time to leave, Catherine." Kelly had come into the room. "The helicopter is landing."

"I'm coming." Catherine turned and moved across the room to Eve and Joe. "You won't forget? You'll let me know how he's doing?"

"Every few days." She took Catherine in her arms and gave her a hug. "And I'll let him know what he's missing."

"No, don't cram me down his throat. He wouldn't understand." She turned to Joe and reached up to kiss his cheek. "Take care of her, Joe. And take care of my son." She stepped back, and said to Kelly, "How would you like to go to Hong Kong?"

Kelly's eyes widened. "You'll take me with you?"

"How can I do anything else? There's no telling where you'll turn up if I don't keep my eye on you."

She frowned. "Duty, Catherine?"

Catherine shook her head. "It was never duty. I just wanted to do what was best for you. I still do." She smiled. "But now I'm being selfish. I figure that maybe I'm what's best for you." She paused. "So I'm willing to battle your mother and your professors and everyone else. Maybe we can work something out together, Kelly?"

"Yes!" Kelly's face was flushed with color. "You won't be sorry, Catherine."

"I know I won't." She turned back to Eve. "I haven't forgotten my promise. I owe you more than words can say. I'll pay you back, Eve."

"Catherine, we found your son. That's payment enough."

She shook her head. "I'll pay you back." She gave her a final hug and strode out of the room. Kelly hurried after her.

They had already boarded the helicopter when Eve and Joe walked out to join them.

"Let's move." Venable hopped into the helicopter. "I've got a ream of paperwork waiting for me in Moscow. Besides meeting with the reps from Homeland Security."

"Wait!" Kelly was looking toward the

house. "Just a minute."

Luke was walking toward the helicopter. He stopped a few feet away from the aircraft. The wind from the rotors was blowing his dark hair about his face and his clothes against his thin, muscular body.

"You came to say good-bye?" Catherine asked. "I'm so glad, Luke."

He shook his head. "I've never been to Hong Kong."

She tensed. "I know. You said it sounded funny."

"It does. And I've never ridden in a helicopter."

"What are you saying, Luke?"

"I thought . . . I might go with you. If it's all right?"

Catherine's expression lit with a luminous smile. "Oh, yes. Yes, yes, yes. It's very much all right. Get on board."

"Take my seat, Luke." Kelly unbuckled her seat belt and jumped out of the helicopter. "I've decided not to go."

Catherine pulled her gaze away from Luke. "Of course you're going. There's another seat in back for him."

"No, I've decided I want to stay with Eve for a while." She smiled. "I'll see you when you get back to Atlanta. Good-bye, Catherine." She turned to Luke. "Get going, Luke.

You're keeping everyone waiting."

"You're the one who can't make up your mind." He jumped on board, and Catherine helped him fasten his belt. His gaze was suddenly searching Kelly's face. "Or can you?" He was still staring at her intently as the helicopter lifted off the ground.

Kelly waved and stepped back. Her smile faded as the aircraft disappeared over the trees.

"You want to go," Eve said. "Anyone could see it. Why didn't you, Kelly?"

"Do you mind me staying with you?"

"Of course not." She repeated, "Why, Kelly?"

"It's not my time," she said simply. "It belongs to Catherine and Luke. I'd get in the way."

"Catherine would never say that. She cares about you."

"No, she'd never say it. But I'd interfere with their pattern. Right now, it could go either way. I want to give Catherine the chance to concentrate on Luke so that it will go her way." She smiled at Joe. "Eve told me once that you taught her karate so that she could take care of herself. I think that would be a very useful thing to study while we're waiting for Catherine to come back. Would you teach me, Joe?"

Joe's brows rose. "Karate? It's certainly different from your usual academic pursuits."

"I want it to be different. Oh, I'm smart enough, but it didn't help me when I was with Daddy in that camp. Maybe if I'd known more about defending myself, the pattern wouldn't have gone in that direction. I don't want to ever feel that helpless again. Will you help me?"

"I imagine I could teach you a few moves." He smiled. "There are patterns to karate, too. Some of them can be very intricate."

Kelly took Eve's hand and looked back in the direction where the helicopter had disappeared. "Yes, some patterns can be terribly complicated. You just have to try your best and hope."

Eve's grasp tightened on Kelly's. She said gently, "And have a few good friends to help you work through them. Let's go home, Kelly."

"It's your home, Eve," Kelly said. "I'm like Luke. I don't really have a home."

"Yet," Eve said. "It will come, Kelly." She led her toward the house. "You just have to find your way there. . . ."

EPILOGUE

Lake Cottage
Atlanta, Georgia
Three Weeks Later

"Catherine's coming. She's at the airport and should be here in about twenty minutes." Eve hung up the phone and turned to Joe. "It's about time. Kelly is getting restless."

"She's been content enough here," Joe said. "And we've been keeping her busy."

"Venable's been keeping her busy," Eve corrected. "Trying to work out a pattern to track Ali Dabala and his group down." She went to the window and gazed down at Kelly, strolling by the lake. "But she's only been marking time waiting for Catherine."

"Is Catherine bringing Luke?"

Eve nodded. "Though she said she'd been trying to give him space for the last couple weeks. They only stayed in Hong Kong for five days. Luke found it interesting, but she thought it was too frenetic an adjustment for him. She rented a place outside Louisville, Kentucky, with a library that would rival the one at Biltmore House. He dove in and hadn't surfaced except for meals until she told him that she wanted him to come here."

"And how is his adjustment?"

"Slow. She's taking baby steps, letting him call the shots." She paused. "She gave him a book on psychology and psychiatric sessions. She asked him if he'd like to talk to someone. He looked at her as if she were crazy."

Joe made a face. "You can't blame him. I'd probably react the same way."

"But you don't have nine years of emotional and physical mistreatment to handle. He needs to talk it out to someone."

"And he won't talk to Catherine?"

"She won't push him. She said that he could have a deep-seated resentment for all she knows. He's begun to talk to her about things that are happening here and now. That's enough for her." She added, "I noticed that he appears only to live in the present. It may be a long time before he does anything else."

"Living in the present isn't all that bad," Joe said quietly as he moved to stand behind her at the window.

He meant that she found it impossible not to live in a past that contained the taking of her Bonnie. He had always told her it might destroy her, and maybe he was right. What she feared most was that it would destroy him.

She turned and buried her face in his shoulder. "No, it could be pretty wonderful."

His arms went around her. "You're tense as a board," he said roughly. "I should have kept my mouth shut. Sometimes things just come out."

"Because they're always with you."

"It will end. It has to end."

When she brought her Bonnie home. When she found Bonnie's killer. Right now, that seemed a distant dream.

It would change when she got back on the hunt. Then there was hope. Then there was purpose.

And then there was the chance of losing Joe because of that eternal obsession.

She kissed him. "It will end, Joe." Her arms tightened around him. "I love you," she whispered.

"Do you want me to tell you I love you, too?" He kissed her back, hard, with a passion that took her breath away. "That's never going to go away. Not until the day I die. And maybe afterward. That's not the issue." He let her go and turned to the door. "I think I'll go down to the lake and tell Kelly Catherine is coming. Maybe we'll have a barbecue this evening."

He was gone.

She stood watching as he ran down the porch steps to where Kelly was standing. So strong, so confident . . . Dammit, so good. He deserved more than she was giving, more than she asked of him. That bittersweet moment had come out of nowhere, and its thorns were still tearing at her.

She should be used to those moments now. They came less often now, but they were still there waiting to emerge from the shadows.

So many shadows . . .

But she didn't want to think of shadows today. The sun was shining brightly, and even now Catherine was driving up the road toward the cottage.

Eve opened the door and went out onto the porch.

Catherine looked wonderful, she thought, as the woman got out of the car. Sleek and gorgeous, and that terrible tension was gone from her demeanor. She turned to Luke and smiled and said something. So much love, it glowed from her expression.

And Luke smiled back! Just a little smile, but it was definitely a smile.

Eve wanted to cheer.

"I told him that he had to put away his book, or you'd throw him in the lake, Joe," Catherine said, as she came toward Kelly and Joe. "And he told me that was okay, he liked the water."

"I was just in a good part." But Luke stuffed the paperback into the back pocket of his jeans. "Hello, Kelly. Mr. Quinn."

"Joe," Joe said. "And if you really want a swim, there are some trunks that might fit you at the cottage. Though I agree skinny-dipping is more fun. You're looking better than the last time I saw you."

He did look better, Eve thought. He had put on weight, and his jeans and shirt fit smoothly over that thin, wiry frame. He still appeared alert and guarded, but perhaps that wariness had lessened a little?

Luke was ignoring that last comment. "I'd like to go swimming."

"Go and see Eve first, Luke," Kelly said. "Stop thinking about yourself. You're her guest. Do it."

Eve smothered a laugh. Kelly was starting with him as she had left off. Blunt, honest, no holds barred.

"Don't tell me what to do." He looked up at Eve, standing on the porch. "I wanted to see her."

"I'm flattered." She was still chuckling as she watched Kelly and Luke walk up the stairs. "Since you didn't bother to say good-bye."

"I didn't think I needed to do it. That didn't change anything." He was standing before her. "Sometimes I don't know things. Catherine is trying to teach me, and I learn a lot from the books, but I make mistakes." He stared her in the eye, and said gravely, "Hello, Eve, I'm glad to see you."

"Stiff as a board," Kelly said.

"Sincere," Eve said. "Leave him alone, Kelly." To Luke, she said, "I'm very happy to see you, too. Now go down the hall to the linen closet in the bathroom and see if you can find a swimsuit that will fit you." He started to go into the house, then stopped as he saw Kelly's computer and notebook lying on the porch swing. He went over to the swing and looked down at the notepad. "Patterns? Catherine told me about what you do. It's interesting."

"Like a book?" Kelly smiled. "But it applies to everyday life, too. It's real, Luke."

"Is it?"

"Yes, everything that happens to us causes

a pattern to form, turns us into what we're going to be, what we're going to do."

He continued to look down at the notebook. "You're saying that what happened to me with Rakovac could cause me to keep doing what he —" He violently shook his head. "No, I *hate* him. That would mean he's still here. He's gone. You're crazy. I won't believe you."

"He's still in your mind," Kelly said. "Believe what you please. He's part of your pattern."

"Kelly," Eve said warningly.

"They don't want me to disturb you," Kelly said. "Eve and Catherine want you treated with kid gloves. You don't want that, do you, Luke? And I don't want that for Catherine. I can't stand the thought of her having to tiptoe around you."

"What are you saying?"

"I'm saying if you want to get rid of Rakovac and all that baggage forever, you have to trace the pattern from the beginning. From the time you were taken from Catherine. You have to do what I do, look at what happened, then see where it takes you next." She held his gaze. "I'll help you chart it, Luke. I'm really good at patterns."

He stared at her for a moment, then whirled and went into the house.

Eve shook her head. "Why, Kelly?"

"Because it's my time now." She shifted her glance from the door to Eve's face. "Because I like Luke and I love Catherine and I can help them mend. I told you once that I was trying to find a reason, something worthwhile, in this so-called wonderful gift I have."

"You found Luke. What's more valuable than that?"

"Maybe to help them find each other?" Kelly shrugged. "I don't know. I can look at all Luke's scars without it hurting me too much. Catherine couldn't do that. I can be the buffer. When you chart a pattern, you have to delve deep, learn everything about what's causing it. Sound familiar? Sort of like what goes on when you go to a psychiatrist for therapy? Only I'm no psychiatrist, I can only help Luke help himself. It may be enough. It could be that's the reason Catherine and I came together in the beginning. I just think it's my time, and this is what I should do."

Eve reached out and gently touched the curve of Kelly's cheek. "It's part of your pattern?"

"Yes." She smiled unsteadily. "And you've been a big part of it, too. I . . . care about you, Eve. I hope I haven't been in the way too much."

"Listen," Eve said. "You've never been in the way. You enriched us." She kissed her on the cheek. "And your damn pattern had better be intertwining with ours from now on." She took her hand and pulled her toward the stairs. "Come on. We need to go see Catherine. You've spent enough time harassing her son."

"He'd better get used to it. He gets enough tender loving care from the rest of you. He doesn't really understand it. Having to argue and fight with me will be good for him." She followed Eve down the steps. "I guarantee it."

"He's been very quiet, Eve." Catherine's gaze was on Luke, who had just finishing eating his barbecued steak and was sitting beneath a tree beside the lake. Joe motioned to him from the barbecue pit, and Luke jumped up and went to help. "He hasn't spoken to Kelly all afternoon."

"Are you blaming Kelly?"

"For Pete's sake, no. Kelly did what she thought was right. And I am overprotective. I can't bear the thought of losing Luke again." She made a face. "And you can't even call Kelly's attitude tough love. She's just doing what Kelly does."

"You're still going to take her with you?"

Catherine gazed at her in astonishment. "Of course I am. I meant what I said to her. Do you think because she and Luke are having differences that I'd change my mind? I love them both. They can work it out for themselves. She told you that she'd be the buffer, but that may end up being my job." She looked out at the lake, now bathed in a golden twilight sheen. "It's getting dark. Kelly!" she called to the girl who was sitting at a picnic table a few yards from the barbecue pit. As usual, Kelly was working on her computer, with notebooks scattered around her. "How can you see? Come up here where you can turn on the lights."

"Just a minute," Kelly called, her eyes on the computer screen. "I think I've found —"

"Eve wants you to come." Luke was suddenly beside Kelly. "You're her guest. Do it."

Eve stiffened. Almost the exact words Kelly had spoken to Luke. What was happening?

Kelly looked at Luke. "You're right." She closed down her computer. "I'm coming, Eve." She started to gather her notebooks.

"I'll help you." Luke was stacking the notebooks in a neat pile. He picked them up and started for the porch.

"Wait for me." Kelly grabbed the computer and ran to keep up with him. "What is this?"

"I'm interested." He looked straight ahead. "Venable thinks this pattern stuff can help catch Rakovac's partner? I want to see how you do it. I'll watch you while you're working."

"I don't like to be watched."

"I'll watch you." He paused as they reached the porch. "You said you had to start at the beginning with me. Is that what you're doing with Dabala?"

"Yes." She added quietly, "Watch me. You'll see. That's the way it has to be. The beginning, Luke."

For an instant, pain flickered over his face. Then it was gone. "I'll watch you. I may . . . As I said, it will be . . . interesting."

They disappeared into the house.

"Bless Kelly," Catherine said huskily. "I think she's going to pull it off. I can't tell you how desperately I wanted to clean all that poison stored up inside out of him." She reached up and wiped her eyes. "Another victory, Eve. It may take a long time, but we're going to bring him back to the boy he was."

"He's already on his way." Eve leaned

back in the swing. "I'm so glad you brought him so that I could see for myself. How long are you going to stay with us?"

"We're leaving tonight." She glanced at the door through which Kelly and Luke had disappeared. "Probably late tonight now. I want Kelly to have her chance at luring Luke into her web."

"She'll do it. The process is fascinating, and she knows exactly what she's doing," Eve said. "But why not leave in the morning?"

"We'll discuss it later." She got to her feet and went to the porch rail. "We've done nothing but talk about Luke and Kelly and all my problems. I don't want to inconvenience you any more than I have to. You've done enough for me, Eve." She paused, her gaze on Joe, standing below them at the barbecue pit. "Let's talk about you and Joe. Is everything all right between you?"

"Why do you ask?"

"I just thought I caught some vibes from him today." Her gaze was still on Joe. "You're very lucky, you know. He's pretty fantastic."

"Yes, he is." She added, "And I know you think he's special. You've told me."

"Yes, I've always been honest with you. I always will be." She turned to face her. "I'm no threat to you, Eve."

"You could be, if you wanted to be. You're an incredibly magnetic woman, Catherine." She gazed steadily at her. "But in the end, the threat would come only from Joe. He's the only one who can hurt me."

"I'd never hurt you." Catherine's voice was passionate. "I've never had a friend like you before. At first, I was only concerned about what you could do for me, but that changed. You changed my life. I felt . . . close to you."

"And I feel close to you." Eve smiled. "So stop agonizing about it, Catherine."

"I don't want to hurt you."

Eve's smile faded. "Are we still talking about Joe?"

"No. Yes. I guess in a way we are."

"Speak up. It's not like you to be inarticulate."

Catherine turned back to look down at Joe. "Did you finish the reconstruction on Cindy?"

"Of course, she was done a week after I came home. It wasn't that difficult." She smiled. "Not after I had a little help from my friends doing the initial prep work."

"Was she a pretty little girl?"

"Yes."

"Like your Bonnie?"

A tiny disturbance rippled through Eve. "She didn't look at all like Bonnie. Why are we talking about Bonnie, Catherine?"

"Because I think Joe is jealous of your obsession with Bonnie. Not of your daughter. Just of your feelings for her. He'd have to be a saint not to feel a little put in the shade by the way you feel. Isn't that true?"

She didn't speak for a moment. "Yes. But friend or not, I don't want to discuss this with you, Catherine."

"I have to discuss it with you. Do you think I want to do it? I was even thinking of walking away and forgetting about it. But I can't do that, Eve."

Eve frowned. "What are you talking about?"

"You and Joe have a giant problem, and I don't want to make it any bigger."

"How could you do that?"

"Easily." Her lips twisted. "I'm good at what I do. I'm an expert. I just set my mind to it and cause the sky to fall."

Eve slowly rose from the swing and went to stand beside Catherine. "Talk to me."

Catherine looked away from her again. "I told you I'd pay you back, remember. I was so grateful, I wanted to give you what you wanted most in the world."

"And I told you to forget it."

"That's not in my makeup." She was silent. "What you want most in the world is to bring your Bonnie home. To do that, you have to find her killer. When I came home from Hong Kong, I had lots of time to concentrate on thinking about your problem. Luke didn't want anything but his books. I tried to look at the crime from an objective and fresh point of view. Then I started to dig. I used every contact and information-gathering unit I had at my disposal and at Venable's disposal. We even tapped the NSA."

Eve could feel her chest tightening. Don't hope. The search had gone on too long for Catherine to just step in and perform a miracle. "Joe was FBI at the time Bonnie was taken. We didn't exactly stop at local law enforcement."

"But all the information wasn't available then."

"I know that. My friend Montalvo has recently given me a list of three new suspects. Two didn't pan out, but I still have the third one to investigate. Paul Black. Is that the name you ran across?"

"His name popped up."

Her gaze narrowed on Catherine's face. "But?"

"I was more interested in someone else."

"Who?"

"He had opportunity. He might have had motive." She was speaking quickly, tersely. "In this type of crime, there's ample precedent for this kind of perpetrator."

"Dammit. Why are you being so evasive?"

"Joe. I can see you're having to walk very carefully where he's concerned. He's very emotional about your obsession with Bonnie. He's nuts about you." Her hands tightened on the porch rail. "And he doesn't need to come face-to-face with this to tear him apart. Hell, it might tear you both apart."

"Catherine."

"Okay." She drew a deep breath. "Joe has been thinking about you as being totally his own since the moment you met. It's been the saving grace when he had to come to terms with your obsession with Bonnie. It would disturb the hell out of him to lose that security."

"There's no way he would lose it."

"No? You're very cool, very controlled, but it wasn't like that always. There was a time when you lost your head and spun out of control over a man."

Eve was beginning to see where Catherine was going. No, it couldn't be. It was impossible. "Catherine, who killed my Bonnie?"

"I didn't say I was certain."

She was shaking. "Tell me. Tell me the name."

"You want a name?" Catherine drew a deep breath. "The name you didn't even see fit to put on the birth certificate, Eve," she said gently. "Bonnie's father, John Gallo."

ABOUT THE AUTHOR

Iris Johansen is the *New York Times* bestselling author of *Eight Days to Live, Blood Game, Deadlock, Quicksand, Pandora's Daughter, Dark Summer,* and more. She lives near Atlanta, Georgia.

We hope you have enjoyed this Large Print book. Other Thorndike, Wheeler, Kennebec, and Chivers Press Large Print books are available at your library or directly from the publishers.

For information about current and upcoming titles, please call or write, without obligation, to:

Publisher
Thorndike Press
295 Kennedy Memorial Drive
Waterville, ME 04901
Tel. (800) 223-1244

or visit our Web site at:

http://gale.cengage.com/thorndike

OR

Chivers Large Print
published by BBC Audiobooks Ltd
St James House, The Square
Lower Bristol Road
Bath BA2 3SB
England
Tel. +44(0) 800 136919
email: bbcaudiobooks@bbc.co.uk
www.bbcaudiobooks.co.uk

All our Large Print titles are designed for easy reading, and all our books are made to last.